William Burroughs was born in St Louis, Missouri, in 1914. The son of a successful businessman, Burroughs studied English literature at Harvard in the 1930s. A drop-out thereafter, he lived in Mexico, Tangier and the UK, and for many years was a heroin addict. He began writing in the 1930s but had little success until the early 1950s when he wrote two confessional books, *Junky* (1953) and *Queer* (written in the 1950s but not published until 1985).

Although largely unpublished for many years, Burroughs was immensely influential among the Beat writers of the 1950s – notably Jack Kerouac and Allen Ginsberg – and already had an underground reputation before the appearance of his first important book, *Naked Lunch*. First published by Olympia Press (the original publishers of Henry Miller) in France in 1959, it aroused great controversy on publication and was not available in the US until 1962 and in the UK until 1964.

Burroughs's other works include *The Soft Machine* (1961), *The Ticket that Exploded* (1962), *Nova Express* (1964), *Cities of the Red Night* (1981) and *The Place of Dead Roads* (1984). In 1983 he was elected a Member of the American Academy and Institute of Arts and Letters.

William Burroughs died in 1997.

Also by William Burroughs

Junky
Queer
The Soft Machine
The Ticket that Exploded
Dead Fingers Talk
Nova Express
The Wild Boys
Exterminator!
Port of Saints
Cities of the Red Night
The Place of Dead Roads
Interzone

WILLIAM BURROUGHS

Naked Lunch

THE RESTORED TEXT

edited by JAMES GRAUERHOLZ
and BARRY MILES

With an introduction by J. G. BALLARD

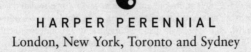

HARPER PERENNIAL
London, New York, Toronto and Sydney

Harper Perennial
An imprint of HarperCollins*Publishers*
77-85 Fulham Palace Road, Hammersmith
London W6 8JB

www.harperperennial.co.uk

This Harper Perennial Modern Classics *Naked Lunch: The Restored Text*
edition published in 2005
6

First published in the USA and Canada as
Naked Lunch: The Restored Text by Grove Press, 2003

Previously published as *Naked Lunch* in paperback by
Flamingo 1993 (reprinted twelve times) and by Paladin 1986

First published by Olympia Press, Paris 1959
First published in Great Britain by John Calder Ltd 1964

A catalogue record for this book is available from the British Libraiy

ISBN 978 0 00 787897 0

Set in Bodoni

Printed and bound in Great Britain by Clays Ltd, St Ives pic

Introduction by J. G. Ballard

Naked Lunch is a banquet you will never forget. This extraordinary novel is a comic apocalypse, a roller-coaster ride through hell, a safari to the strangest people of the strangest planet, ourselves. It is said of literary masterpieces that their genius is stamped into every line, and this is nowhere so true as it is of *Naked Lunch*. From its opening words we are aware that a unique world – comic, paranoid, visionary, delirious – is being revealed to us. Bizarre and nightmarish scenes flash by, like glimpses of some exotic and decadent city. Only later do we realise that this strange city is the one we all inhabit in our waking lives.

At first sight *Naked Lunch* is dominated by two closely linked themes, drugs and homosexuality, about which Burroughs is unsparingly frank. The landscape of subway dawns and cheap hotels, the numbing wait for the next fix, and the melancholy quest for an ever-elusive sexual happiness together describe the world through which Burroughs moved in the 1950s, in New York, Mexico and Tangier. Drugs are the ultimate merchandise, Burroughs has written, and he sees addiction as part of the global conspiracy by the presiding powers of our world – the media conglomerates, the vast political and commercial bureaucracies, and a profit-driven medical science – which are determined to reduce us to the total dependency of addicts, while teasing us with the mirage of transgressive sex.

Burroughs chooses to explode this conspiracy by inviting us all to lunch, and his menu is a novel that I believe to be the most important and original work of fiction by an American writer since the Second World War. *Naked Lunch* is both the addict's fix, the rush of pure sensation through the brain, and also the stark and unsentimental truth about ourselves, our self-delusions and deceits, served with a dressing of the spiciest humour. Here you will find a host of hilarious characters, led by the egregious Dr Benway, the most corrupt and charming physician in twentieth-century literature.

After the anaemic fare of most contemporary fiction, sit back and gorge yourself on this feast of a novel.

CONTENTS

NAKED
LUNCH

I can feel the heat closing in, feel them out there making their moves, setting up their devil doll stool pigeons, crooning over my spoon and dropper I throw away at Washington Square Station, vault a turnstile and two flights down the iron stairs, catch an uptown A train ... Young, good looking, crew cut, Ivy League, advertising exec type fruit holds the door back for me. I am evidently his idea of a character. You know the type: comes on with bartenders and cab drivers, talking about right hooks and the Dodgers, calls the counterman in Nedick's by his first name. A real asshole. And right on time this narcotics dick in a white trench coat (imagine tailing somebody in a white trench coat. Trying to pass as a fag I guess) hit the platform. I can hear the way he would say it holding my outfit in his left hand, right hand on his piece: "I think you dropped something, fella."

But the subway is moving.

"So long flatfoot!" I yell, giving the fruit his B production. I look into the fruit's eyes, take in the white teeth, the Florida tan, the two hundred dollar sharkskin suit, the button-down Brooks Brothers shirt and carrying *The News* as a prop. "Only thing I read is Little Abner."

A square wants to come on hip ... Talks about "pod," and smoke it now and then, and keeps some around to offer the fast Hollywood types.

"Thanks, kid," I say, "I can see you're one of our own." His face lights up like a pinball machine, with stupid, pink affect.

"Grassed on me he did," I said morosely. (Note: Grass is English thief slang for inform.) I drew closer and laid my dirty junky fingers on his sharkskin sleeve. "And us blood brothers in the same dirty needle. I can tell you in confidence he is due for a hot shot." (Note: This is a cap of poison junk sold to addict for liquidation purposes. Often given to informers. Usually the hot shot is strychnine since it tastes and looks like junk.)

"Ever see a hot shot hit, kid? I saw the Gimp catch one in Philly. We rigged his room with a one-way whorehouse mirror and charged a sawski to watch it. He never got the needle out of his arm. They don't if the shot is right. That's the way they find them, dropper full of clotted blood hanging out of a blue arm. The look in his eyes when it hit—Kid, it was tasty . . .

"Recollect when I am traveling with the Vigilante, best Shake Man in the industry. Out in Chi . . . We is working the fags in Lincoln Park. So one night the Vigilante turns up for work in cowboy boots and a black vest with a hunka tin on it and a lariat slung over his shoulder.

"So I say: 'What's with you? You wig already?'

"He just looks at me and says: 'Fill your hand stranger' and hauls out an old rusty six shooter and I take off across Lincoln Park, bullets cutting all around me. And he hangs three fags before the fuzz nail him. I mean the Vigilante earned his moniker . . .

"Ever notice how many expressions carry over from queers to con men? Like 'raise,' letting someone know you are in the same line?

"'Get her!'

"'Get the Paregoric Kid giving that mark the build up!'

"'Eager Beaver wooing him much too fast.'

"The Shoe Store Kid (he got that moniker shaking down fetishists in shoe stores) say: 'Give it to a mark with K.Y. and he will come back moaning for more.' And when the Kid spots a mark he begin to breathe heavy. His face swells and his lips turn purple like an Eskimo in heat. Then slow, slow he comes on the mark, feeling for him, palpating him with fingers of rotten ectoplasm.

"The Rube has a sincere little boy look, burns through him like blue neon. That one stepped right off a *Saturday Evening Post* cover with a string of bullheads, and preserved himself in junk. His marks never beef and the Bunko people are really carrying a needle for the Rube. One day Little Boy Blue starts to slip, and what crawls out would make an ambulance attendant puke. The Rube flips in the end, running through empty automats and subway stations, screaming: 'Come back, kid!! Come back!!' and follows his boy right into the East River, down through condoms and orange peels, mosaic of floating newspapers, down into the silent black ooze with gangsters in concrete, and pistols pounded flat to avoid the probing finger of prurient ballistic experts."

And the fruit is thinking: "What a character!! Wait till I tell the boys in Clark's about this one." He's a character collector, would stand still for Joe Gould's seagull act. So I put it on him for a sawski and make a meet to sell him some "pod" as he calls it, thinking, "I'll catnip the jerk." (Note: Catnip smells like marijuana when it burns. Frequently passed on the incautious or uninstructed.)

"Well," I said, tapping my arm, "duty calls. As one judge said to another: 'Be just and if you can't be just, be arbitrary.'"

I cut into the Automat and there is Bill Gains huddled in someone else's overcoat looking like a 1910 banker with paresis, and Old Bart, shabby and inconspicuous, dunking pound cake with his dirty fingers, shiny over the dirt.

I had some uptown customers Bill took care of, and Bart knew a few old relics from hop smoking times, spectral janitors, grey as ashes, phantom porters sweeping out dusty halls with a slow old man's hand, coughing and spitting in the junk-sick dawn, retired asthmatic fences in theatrical hotels, Pantopon Rose the old madam from Peoria, stoical Chinese waiters never show sickness. Bart sought them out with his old junky walk, patient and cautious and slow, dropped into their bloodless hands a few hours of warmth.

I made the round with him once for kicks. You know how old people lose all shame about eating, and it makes you puke to watch them? Old junkies are the same about junk. They gibber and squeal at the sight of it. The spit hangs off their chin, and their stomach rumbles and all their guts grind in peristalsis while they cook up, dissolving the body's decent skin, you expect any moment a great blob of protoplasm will flop right out and surround the junk. Really disgust you to see it.

"Well, my boys will be like that one day," I thought philosophically. "Isn't life peculiar?"

So back downtown by the Sheridan Square Station in case the dick is lurking in a broom closet.

Like I say it couldn't last. I knew they were out there powwowing and making their evil fuzz magic, putting dolls of me in Leavenworth. "No use sticking needles in that one, Mike."

I hear they got Chapin with a doll. This old eunuch dick just sat in the precinct basement hanging a doll of him day and night, year in year out. And when Chapin hanged in Connecticut, they find this old creep with his neck broken.

"He fell downstairs," they say. You know the old cop bullshit.

Junk is surrounded by magic and taboos, curses and amulets. I could find my Mexico City connection by radar. "Not this street, the next, right . . . now left. Now right again," and there he is, toothless old woman face and canceled eyes.

I know this one pusher walks around humming a tune and everybody he passes takes it up. He is so grey and spectral and anonymous they don't see him and think it is their own mind humming the tune. So the customers come in on "Smiles," or "I'm in the Mood for Love," or "They Say We're Too Young to

Go Steady," or whatever the song is for that day. Sometimes you can see maybe fifty ratty-looking junkies squealing sick, running along behind a boy with a harmonica, and there is The Man on a cane seat throwing bread to the swans, a fat drag queen walking his Afghan hound through the East Fifties, an old wino pissing against an El post, a radical Jewish student giving out leaflets in Washington Square, a tree surgeon, an exterminator, an advertising fruit in Nedick's where he calls the counterman by his first name. The world network of junkies, tuned on a cord of rancid jissom, tying up in furnished rooms, shivering in the junk-sick morning. (Old Pete men suck the black smoke in the Chink laundry back room and Melancholy Baby dies from an overdose of time or cold turkey withdrawal of breath.) In Yemen, Paris, New Orleans, Mexico City and Istanbul—shivering under the air hammers and the steam shovels, shrieked junky curses at one another neither of us heard, and The Man leaned out of a passing steam roller and I copped in a bucket of tar. (Note: Istanbul is being torn down and rebuilt, especially shabby junk quarters. Istanbul has more heroin junkies than NYC.) The living and the dead, in sickness or on the nod, hooked or kicked or hooked again, come in on the junk beam and the Connection is eating Chop Suey on Dolores Street, Mexico, D.F., dunking pound cake in the Automat, chased up Exchange Place by a baying pack of People. (Note: People is New Orleans slang for narcotic fuzz.)

The old Chinaman dips river water into a rusty tin can, washes down a yen pox hard and black as a cinder. (Note: Yen pox is the ash of smoked opium.)

Well, the fuzz has my spoon and dropper, and I know they are coming in on my frequency led by this blind pigeon known as Willy the Disk. Willy has a round, disk mouth lined with sensitive, erectile black hairs. He is blind from shooting in the eyeball, his nose and palate eaten away sniffing H, his body a mass of scar tissue hard and dry as wood. He can only eat the shit now with that mouth, sometimes sways out on a long tube of ecto-plasm, feeling for the silent frequency of junk. He follows my trail all over the city into rooms I move out already, and the fuzz walks in on some newlyweds from Sioux Falls.

"All right, Lee!! Come out from behind that strap-on! We know you," and pull the man's prick off straightaway.

Now Willy is getting hot and you can hear him always out there in darkness (he only functions at night) whimpering, and feel the terrible urgency of that blind, seeking mouth. When they move in for the bust, Willy goes all out of control, and his mouth eats a hole right through the door. If the cops weren't there to restrain him with a stock probe, he would suck the juice right out of every junky he ran down.

I knew, and everybody else knew they had the Disk on me. And if my kid customers ever hit the stand: "He force me to commit all kinda awful sex acts in return for junk" I could kiss the street goodbye.

So we stock up on H, buy a secondhand Studebaker, and start west.

*the
vigilante*

The Vigilante copped out as a schizo possession case:

"I was standing outside myself trying to stop those hangings with ghost fingers ... I am a ghost wanting what every ghost wants—a body—after the Long Time moving through odorless alleys of space where no life is, only the colorless no smell of death ... Nobody can breathe and smell it through pink convolutions of gristle laced with crystal snot, time shit and black blood filters of flesh."

He stood there in elongated court room shadow, his face torn like a broken film by lusts and hungers of larval organs stirring in the tentative ectoplasmic flesh of junk kick (ten days on ice at time of the First Hearing), flesh that fades at the first silent touch of junk.

I saw it happen. Ten pounds lost in ten minutes standing with the syringe in one hand holding his pants up with the other, his abdicated flesh burning in a cold yellow halo, there in the New York hotel room . . . night table litter of candy boxes, cigarette butts cascading out of three ashtrays, mosaic of sleepless nights and sudden food needs of the kicking addict nursing his baby flesh . . .

The Vigilante is prosecuted in Federal Court under a lynch bill and winds up in a Federal Nut House specially designed for the containment of ghosts: precise, prosaic impact of objects . . . washstand . . . door . . . toilet . . . bars . . . there they are . . . this is it . . . all lines cut . . . nothing beyond . . . Dead End . . . And the Dead End in every face . . .

The physical changes were slow at first, then jumped forward in black klunks, falling through his slack tissue, washing away the human lines . . . In his place of total darkness mouth and eyes are one organ that leaps forward to snap with transparent teeth . . . but no organ is constant as regards either function or position . . . sex organs sprout anywhere . . . rectums open, defecate and close . . . the entire organism changes color and consistency in split-second adjustments . . .

the
rube

The Rube is a social liability with his attacks as he calls them. The Mark Inside was coming up on him and that's a rumble nobody can cool; outside Philly he jumps out to con a prowl car and the fuzz takes one look at his face and bust all of us.

Seventy-two hours and five sick junkies in the cell with us. Now not wishing to break out my stash in front of these hungry coolies, it takes maneuvering and laying of gold on the turnkey before we are in a separate cell.

Provident junkies, known as squirrels, keep stashes against a bust. Every time I take a shot I let a few drops fall into my vest pocket, the lining is stiff with stuff. I had a plastic dropper in my shoe and a safety pin stuck in my belt. You know how this pin and dropper routine is put down: "She seized a safety pin caked with blood and rust, gouged a great hole in her leg which seemed to hang open like an obscene, festering mouth waiting for unspeakable congress with the dropper which she now plunged out of sight into the gaping wound. But her hideous galvanized need (hunger of insects in dry places) has broken the dropper off deep in the flesh of her ravaged thigh (looking rather like a poster on soil erosion). But what does she care? She does not even bother to remove the splintered glass, looking down at her bloody haunch with the cold blank eyes of a meat trader. What does she care for the atom bomb, the bedbugs, the cancer rent, Friendly Finance waiting to repossess her delinquent flesh . . . Sweet dreams, Pantopon Rose."

The real scene you pinch up some leg flesh and make a quick stab hole with a pin. Then fit the dropper *over, not in* the hole and feed the solution slow and careful so it doesn't squirt out the sides . . . When I grabbed the Rube's thigh the flesh came up like wax and stayed there, and a slow drop of pus oozed out the hole. And I never touched a living body cold as the Rube there in Philly . . .

I decided to lop him off if it meant a smother party. (This is a rural English custom designed to eliminate aged and bedfast dependents. A family so afflicted throws a "smother party" where the guests pile mattresses on the old liability, climb up on top of the mattresses and lush themselves out.) The Rube is a drag on the industry and should be "led out" into the skid rows of the world. (This is an African practice. Official known as the "Leader Out" has the function of taking old characters out into the jungle and leaving them there.)

The Rube's attacks become an habitual condition. Cops, door-men, dogs, secretaries snarl at his approach. The blond God has fallen to untouchable vileness. Con men don't change, they break, shatter—explosions of matter in cold interstellar space, drift away in cosmic dust, leave the empty body behind. Hustlers of the world, there is one Mark you cannot beat: The Mark Inside . . .

I left the Rube standing on a corner, red brick slums to the sky, under a steady rain of soot. "Going to hit this croaker I know. Right back with that good pure drugstore M . . . No, you wait here—don't want him to rumble you." No matter how long, Rube, wait for me right on that corner. Goodbye, Rube, goodbye kid . . . Where do they go when they walk out and leave the body behind?

Chicago: invisible hierarchy of decorticated wops, smell of atrophied gangsters, earthbound ghost hits you at North and Halsted, Cicero, Lincoln Park, panhandler of dreams, past invading the present, rancid magic of slot machines and roadhouses.

Into the Interior: a vast subdivision, antennae of television to the meaningless sky. In lifeproof houses they hover over the young, sop up a little of what they shut out. Only the young bring anything in, and they are not young very long. (Through the bars of East St. Louis lies the dead frontier, riverboat days.) Illinois and Missouri, miasma of mound-building peoples, groveling worship of the Food Source, cruel and ugly festivals, dead-end horror of the Centipede God reaches from Moundville to the lunar deserts of coastal Peru.

America is not a young land: it is old and dirty and evil before the settlers, before the Indians. The evil is there waiting.

And always cops: smooth college-trained state cops, practiced, apologetic patter, electronic eyes weigh your car and luggage, clothes and face; snarling big city dicks, soft-spoken country sheriffs with something black and menacing in old eyes color of a faded grey flannel shirt . . .

And always car trouble: in St. Louis traded the 1942 Studebaker in (it has a built-in engineering flaw like the Rube) on an old Packard limousine heated up and barely made Kansas City, and bought a Ford turned out to be an oil burner, packed it in on a Jeep we push too hard (they are no good for highway driving)— and burn something out inside, rattling around, went back to the old Ford V-8. Can't beat that engine for getting there, oil burner or no.

And the U.S. drag closes around us like no other drag in the world, worse than the Andes, high mountain towns, cold wind down from postcard mountains, thin air like death in the throat, river towns of Ecuador, malaria grey as junk under black Stetson, muzzle loading shotguns, vultures pecking through the mud streets—and what hits you when you get off the Malmö Ferry (no juice tax on the ferry) in Sweden knocks all that cheap, tax free juice right out of you and brings you all the way down: averted eyes and the cemetery in the middle of town (every town in Sweden seems to be built around a cemetery), and nothing to do in the afternoon, not a bar not a movie and I blasted my last stick of Tangier tea and I said, "K.E. let's get right back on that ferry."

But there is no drag like U.S. drag. You can't see it, you don't know where it comes from. Take one of those cocktail lounges at the end of a subdivision street—every block of houses has its own bar and drugstore and market and liquor store. You walk in and it hits you. But where does it come from? Not the bartender, not the customers, nor the cream-colored plastic rounding the bar stools, nor the dim neon. Not even the TV.

And our habits build up with the drag, like cocaine will build you up staying ahead of the C bring-down. And the junk was running low. So there we are in this no-horse town strictly from cough syrup. And vomited up the syrup and drove on and on, cold spring wind whistling through that old heap around our shivering, sick sweating bodies and the cold you always come down with when the junk runs out of you ... On through the peeled landscape, dead armadillos in the road and vultures over the swamp and cypress stumps. Motels with beaverboard walls, gas heater, thin pink blankets.

Itinerant short con and carny hype men have burned down the croakers of Texas ...

And no one in his right mind would hit a Louisiana croaker. State Junk Law.

Came at last to Houston where I know a druggist. I haven't been there in five years but he looks up and makes me with one quick look and just nods and says: "Wait over at the counter ..."

So I sit down and drink a cup of coffee and after a while he comes and sits beside me and says, "What do you want?"

"A quart of PG and a hundred nembies."

He nods. "Come back in half an hour."

So when I come back he hands me a package and says, "That's fifteen dollars ... Be careful."

Shooting PG is a terrible hassle, you have to burn out the alcohol first, then freeze out the camphor and draw this brown liquid off with a dropper—have to shoot it in the vein or you get an abscess, and usually end up with an abscess no matter where you shoot it. Best deal is to drink it with goof balls ... So we pour it in a Pernod bottle and start for New Orleans past iridescent lakes and orange gas flares, and swamps and garbage heaps, alligators crawling around in broken bottles and tin cans, neon arabesques of motels, marooned pimps scream obscenities at passing cars from islands of rubbish ...

New Orleans is a dead museum. We walk around Exchange Place breathing PG and find The Man right away. It's a small place and the fuzz always knows who is pushing so he figures what the hell does it matter and sells to anybody. We stock up on H and backtrack for Mexico.

Back through Lake Charles and the dead slot-machine country, south end of Texas, nigger-killing sheriffs look us over and check the car papers. Something falls off you when you cross the border into Mexico, and suddenly the landscape hits you straight with nothing between you and it, desert and mountains and vultures; little wheeling specks and others so close you can hear wings cut the air (a dry husking sound), and when they spot something they pour out of the blue sky, that shattering bloody blue sky of Mexico, down in a black funnel ... Drove all night, came at dawn to a warm misty place, barking dogs and the sound of running water.

"Thomas and Charlie," I said.

"What?"

"That's the name of this town. Sea level. We climb straight up from here ten thousand feet." I took a fix and went to sleep in the back seat. She was a good driver. You can tell as soon as someone touches the wheel.

Mexico City where Lupita sits like an Aztec Earth Goddess doling out her little papers of lousy shit.

"Selling is more of a habit than using," Lupita says. Non-using pushers have a contact habit, and that's one you can't kick.

Agents get it too. Take Bradley the Buyer. Best narcotics agent in the industry. Anyone would make him for junk. (Note: Make in the sense of dig or size up.) I mean he can walk up to a pusher and score direct. He is so anonymous, grey and spectral the pusher don't remember him afterwards. So he twists one after the other ...

Well the Buyer comes to look more and more like a junky. He can't drink. He can't get it up. His teeth fall out. (Like pregnant women lose their teeth feeding the stranger, junkies lose their yellow fangs feeding the monkey.) He is all the time sucking on a candy bar. Baby Ruths he digs special. "It really disgust you to see the Buyer sucking on them candy bars so nasty," a cop says.

The Buyer takes on an ominous grey-green color. Fact is his body is making its own junk or equivalent. The Buyer has a steady connection. A Man Within, you might say. Or so he thinks. "I'll just set in my room," he says. "Fuck 'em all. Squares on both sides. I am the only complete man in the industry."

But a yen comes on him like a great black wind through the bones. So the Buyer hunts up a young junky and gives him a paper to make it.

"Oh all right," the boy says. "So what you want to make?"

"I just want to rub up against you and get fixed."

"Ugh . . . Well all right . . . But why cancha just get physical like a human?"

Later the boy is sitting in a Waldorf with two colleagues dunking pound cake. "Most distasteful thing I ever stand still for," he says. "Some way he make himself all soft like a blob of jelly and surround me so nasty. Then he gets wet all over like with green slime. So I guess he come to some kinda awful climax . . . I come near wigging with that green stuff all over me, and he stink like a old rotten cantaloupe."

"Well it's still an easy score."

The boy sighed resignedly. "Yes, I guess you can get used to anything. I've got a meet with him again tomorrow."

The Buyer's habit keeps getting heavier. He needs a recharge every half hour. Sometimes he cruises the precincts and bribes the turnkey to let him in with a cell of junkies. It gets to where no amount of contact will fix him. At this point he receives a summons from the District Supervisor:

"Bradley, your conduct has given rise to rumors—and I hope for your sake they are no more than that—so unspeakably distasteful that . . . I mean, Caesar's wife . . . hrump . . . that is, the Department must be above suspicion . . . certainly above such suspicions as you have seemingly aroused. You are lowering the entire tone of the industry. We are prepared to accept your immediate resignation."

The Buyer throws himself on the ground and crawls over to the D.S. "No, Boss Man, no . . . The Department is my very lifeline."

He kisses the D.S.'s hand thrusting the fingers into his mouth (the D.S. must feel his toothless gums) complaining he has lost his teeth "inna thervith." "Please Boss Man. I'll wipe your ass, I'll wash out your dirty condoms, I'll polish your shoes with the oil on my nose . . ."

"Really, this is most distasteful! Have you no pride? I must tell you I feel a distinct revulsion. I mean there is something, well, rotten about you, and you smell like a compost heap." He puts a scented handkerchief in front of his face. "I must ask you to leave this office at once."

"I'll do anything, boss, *anything*." His ravaged green face splits in a horrible smile. "I'm still young, boss, and I'm pretty strong when I get my blood up."

The D.S. retches into his handkerchief and points to the door with a limp hand. The Buyer stands up looking at the D.S. dreamily. His body begins to dip like a dowser's wand. He flows forward . . .

"No! No!" screams the D.S.

"*Schlup . . . schlup schlup.*"

An hour later they find the Buyer on the nod in the D.S.'s chair. The D.S. has disappeared without a trace.

The Judge: "Everything indicates that you have, in some unspeakable manner uh . . . assimilated the District Supervisor. Unfortunately there is no proof. I would recommend that you be confined or more accurately contained in some institution, but I know of no place suitable for a man of your caliber. I must reluctantly order your release."

"That one should stand in an aquarium," says the arresting officer.

The Buyer spreads terror throughout the industry. Junkies and agents disappear. Like a vampire bat he gives off a narcotic effluvium, a dank green mist that anesthetizes his victims and renders them helpless in his enveloping presence. And once he has scored he holes up for several days like a gorged boa constrictor. Finally he is caught in the act of digesting the Narcotics Commissioner and destroyed with a flame thrower—the court of inquiry ruling that such means were justified in that the Buyer had lost his human citizenship and was, in consequence, a creature without species and a menace to the narcotics industry on all levels.

In Mexico the gimmick is to find a local junky with a government script whereby they are allowed a certain quantity every month. Our Man was Old Ike who had spent most of his life in the States.

We are getting some C on Rx at this time. Shoot it in the mainline, son. You can smell it going in, clean and cold in your nose and throat then a rush of pure pleasure right through the brain lighting up those C connections. Your head shatters in white explosions. Ten minutes later you want another shot . . . you will walk across town for another shot. But if you can't score for C you eat, sleep and forget about it.

This is a yen of the brain alone, a need without feeling and without body, earthbound ghost need, rancid ectoplasm swept out by an old junky coughing and spitting in the sick morning.

One morning you wake up and take a speed ball, and feel bugs under your skin. 1890 cops with black mustaches block the doors and lean in through the windows snarling their lips back from blue and gold embossed badges. Junkies march through the room singing the Moslem Funeral Song, bear the body of Bill Gains, stigmata of his needle wounds glow with a soft blue flame. Purposeful schizophrenic detectives sniff at your chamber pot.

It's the coke horrors . . . Sit back and play it cool and shoot in plenty of that GI M.

Day of the Dead: I got the chucks and ate my little Willy's sugar skull. He cried and I had to go out for another. Walked past the cocktail lounge where they blasted the Jai Alai bookie.

In Cuernavaca or was it Taxco? Jane meets a pimp trombone player and disappears in a cloud of tea smoke. The pimp is one of these vibration and dietary artists—which is a means he degrades the female sex by, forcing his chicks to swallow all this shit. He was continually enlarging his theories . . . he would quiz a chick and threaten to walk out if she hadn't memorized every nuance of his latest assault on logic and the human image.

"Now, baby. I got it here to give. But if you won't receive it there's just nothing I can do."

He was a ritual tea smoker and very puritanical about junk the way some teaheads are. He claimed tea put him in touch with supra blue gravitational fields. He had ideas on every subject: what kind of underwear was healthy, when to drink water, and how to wipe your ass. He had a shiny red face and great spreading smooth nose, little red eyes that lit up when he looked at a chick and went out when he looked at anything else. His shoulders were very broad and suggested deformity. He acted as if other men did not exist, conveying his restaurant and store orders to male personnel through a female intermediary. And no Man ever invaded his blighted, secret place.

So he is putting down junk and coming on with tea. I take three drags, Jane looked at him and her flesh crystallized. I leaped up screaming "I got the fear!" and ran out of the house. Drank a beer in a little restaurant—mosaic bar and soccer scores and bull-fight posters—and waited for the bus to town.

A year later in Tangier I heard she was dead.

benway

So I am assigned to engage the services of Doctor Benway for Islam Inc.

Dr. Benway had been called in as advisor to the Freeland Republic, a place given over to free love and continual bathing. The citizens are well adjusted, cooperative, honest, tolerant and above all clean. But the invoking of Benway indicates all is not well behind that hygienic façade: Benway is a manipulator and coordinator of symbol systems, an expert on all phases of inter-rogation, brainwashing and control. I have not seen Benway since his precipitate departure from Annexia, where his assignment had been T.D.—Total Demoralization. Benway's first act was to abol-ish concentration camps, mass arrest and, except under certain limited and special circumstances, the use of torture.

"I deplore brutality," he said. "It's not efficient. On the other hand, prolonged mistreatment, short of physical violence, gives rise, when skillfully applied, to anxiety and a feeling of special guilt. A few rules or rather guiding principles are to be borne in mind. The subject must not realize that the mistreatment is a deliberate attack of an anti-human enemy on his personal iden-tity. He must be made to feel that he deserves *any* treatment he receives because there is something (never specified) horribly wrong with him. The naked need of the control addicts must be decently covered by an arbitrary and intricate bureaucracy so that the subject cannot contact his enemy direct."

Every citizen of Annexia was required to apply for and carry on his person at all times a whole portfolio of documents. Citizens were subject to be stopped in the street at any time; and the Examiner, who might be in plain clothes, in various uniforms, often in a bathing suit or pyjamas, sometimes stark naked except for a badge pinned to his left nipple, after checking each paper, would stamp it. On subsequent inspection the citizen was required to show the properly entered stamps of the last inspection. The Examiner, when he stopped a large group, would only examine and stamp the cards of a few. The others were then subject to arrest because their cards were not properly stamped. Arrest meant "provisional detention"; that is, the prisoner would be released if and when his Affidavit of Explanation, properly signed and stamped, was approved by the Assistant Arbiter of Explanations. Since this official hardly ever came to his office, and the Affidavit of Explanation had to be presented in person, the explainers spent weeks and months waiting around in unheated offices with no chairs and no toilet facilities.

Documents issued in vanishing ink faded into old pawn tickets. New documents were constantly required. The citizens rushed from one bureau to another in a frenzied attempt to meet impossible deadlines.

All benches were removed from the city, all fountains turned off, all flowers and trees destroyed. Huge electric buzzers on the top of every apartment house (everyone lived in apartments) rang the quarter hour. Often the vibrations would throw people out of bed. Searchlights played over the town all night (no one was permitted to use shades, curtains, shutters or blinds).

No one ever looked at anyone else because of the strict law against importuning, with or without verbal approach, anyone for any purpose, sexual or otherwise. All cafés and bars were closed. Liquor could only be obtained with a special permit, and the liquor so obtained could not be sold or given or in any way transferred to anyone else, and the presence of anyone else in the room was considered prima facie evidence of conspiracy to transfer liquor.

No one was permitted to bolt his door, and the police had pass keys to every room in the city. Accompanied by a mentalist they rush into someone's quarters and start "looking for it."

The mentalist guides them to whatever the man wishes to hide: a tube of Vaseline, an enema, a handkerchief with come on it, a weapon, unlicensed alcohol. And they always submitted the suspect to the most humiliating search of his naked person on which they make sneering and derogatory comments. Many a latent homosexual was carried out in a straitjacket when they planted Vaseline in his ass. Or they pounce on any object. A pen wiper or a shoe tree.

"And what is this supposed to be for?"

"It's a pen wiper."

"A pen wiper, he says."

"I've heard everything now."

"I guess this is all we need. Come on, you."

After a few months of this the citizens cowered in corners like neurotic cats.

Of course the Annexia police processed suspected agents, saboteurs and political deviants on an assembly line basis. As regards the interrogation of suspects, Benway has this to say:

"While in general I avoid the use of torture—torture locates the opponent and mobilizes resistance—the threat of torture is useful to induce in the subject the appropriate feeling of helplessness and gratitude to the interrogator for withholding it. And torture can be employed to advantage as a penalty when the subject is far enough along with the treatment to accept punishment as deserved. To this end I devised several forms of disciplinary procedure. One was known as the Switchboard. Electric drills that can be turned on at any time are clamped against the subject's teeth; and he is instructed to operate an arbitrary switchboard, to put certain connections in certain sockets in response to bells and lights. Every time he makes a mistake the drills are turned on for twenty seconds. The signals are gradually speeded up beyond his reaction time. Half an hour on the Switchboard and the subject breaks down like an overloaded thinking machine.

"The study of thinking machines teaches us more about the brain than we can learn by introspective methods. Western man is externalizing himself in the form of gadgets.

"Ever pop coke in the mainline? It hits you right in the brain, activating connections of pure pleasure. The pleasure of morphine is in the viscera. You listen down into yourself after a shot. But C is electricity through the brain, and the C yen is of the brain alone, a need without body and without feeling. The C-charged brain is a berserk pinball machine, flashing blue and pink lights in electric orgasm. C pleasure could be felt by a thinking machine, the first stirrings of hideous insect life. The craving for C lasts only a few hours, as long as the C channels are stimulated. Of course the effect of C could be produced by an electric current activating the C channels . . .

"So after a bit the channels wear out like veins, and the addict has to find new ones. A vein will come back in time, and by adroit vein rotation a junky can piece out the odds if he don't become an oil burner. But brain cells don't come back once they're gone, and when the addict runs out of brain cells he is in a terrible fucking position.

"Squatting on old bones and excrement and rusty iron, in a white blaze of heat, a panorama of naked idiots stretches to the horizon. Complete silence—their speech centers are destroyed—except for the crackle of sparks and the popping of singed flesh as they apply electrodes up and down the spine. White smoke of burning flesh hangs in the motionless air. A group of children have tied an idiot to a post with barbed wire and built a fire between his legs and stand watching with bestial curiosity as the flames lick his thighs. His flesh jerks in the fire with insect agony.

"I digress as usual. Pending more precise knowledge of brain electronics, drugs remain an essential tool of the interrogator in his assault on the subject's personal identity. The barbiturates are, of course, virtually useless. That is, anyone who can be broken down by such means would succumb to the puerile methods used in an American precinct. Scopolamine is often effective in dissolving resistance, but it impairs the memory: an agent might be prepared to reveal his secrets but quite unable to remember them, or cover story and secret life info might be inextricably garbled. Mescaline, harmine, LSD6, bufotenine, muscarine successful in many cases. Bulbocapnine induces a state approximating schizophrenic catatonia . . . instances of automatic obedience have been observed. Bulbocapnine is a back-brain depressant probably putting out of action the centers of motion in the hypothalamus. Other drugs that have produced experimental schizophrenia—mescaline, harmine, LSD6—are back-brain stimulants. In schizophrenia the back brain is alternately stimulated and depressed. Catatonia is often followed by a period of excitement and motor activity during which the nut rushes through the wards giving everyone a bad time. Deteriorated schizos sometimes refuse to move at all and spend their lives in bed. A disturbance of the regulatory function of the hypothalamus is indicated as the 'cause' (causal thinking never yields accurate description of metabolic process—limitations of existing language) of schizophrenia. Alternate doses of LSD6 and bulbocapnine—the bulbocapnine potentiated with curare—give the highest yield of automatic obedience.

"There are other procedures. The subject can be reduced to deep depression by administering large doses of Benzedrine for several days. Psychosis can be induced by continual large doses of cocaine or Demerol or by the abrupt withdrawal of barbiturates after prolonged administration. He can be addicted by dihydro-oxy-heroin and subjected to withdrawal (this compound should be five times as addicting as heroin, and the withdrawal proportionately severe).

"There are various 'psychological methods,' compulsory psycho-analysis, for example. The subject is requested to free-associate for one hour every day (in cases where time is not of the essence). 'Now, now. Let's not be negative, boy. Poppa call nasty man. Take baby walkabout Switchboard.'

"The case of a female agent who forgot her real identity and merged with her cover story—she is still a *fricteuse* in Annexia—put me onto another gimmick. An agent is trained to deny his agent identity by asserting his cover story. So why not use psychic jiujitsu and go along with him? Suggest that his cover story is his identity and that he has no other. His agent identity becomes unconscious, that is, out of his control; and you can dig it with drugs and hypnosis. You can make a square heterosex citizen queer with this angle . . . that is, reinforce and second his rejection of normally latent homosexual trends—at the same time depriving him of cunt and subjecting him to homosexual stimulation. Then drugs, hypnosis, and—" Benway flipped a limp wrist.

"Many subjects are vulnerable to sexual humiliation. Nakedness, stimulation with aphrodisiacs, constant supervision to embarrass subject and prevent relief of masturbation (erections during sleep automatically turn on an enormous vibrating electric buzzer that throws the subject out of bed into cold water, thus reducing the incidence of wet dreams to a minimum). Kicks to hypnotize a priest and tell him he is about to consummate a hypostatic union with the Lamb—then steer a randy old sheep up his ass. After that the Interrogator can gain complete hypnotic control—the subject will come at his whistle, shit on the floor if he but say Open Sesame.

"Needless to say, the sex humiliation angle is contraindicated for overt homosexuals. (I mean let's keep our eye on the ball here and remember the old party line . . . never know who's listening in.) I recall this one kid, I condition to shit at sight of me. Then I wash his ass and screw him. It was real tasty. And he was a lovely fellah too. And sometimes a subject will burst into boyish tears because he can't keep from ejaculate when you screw him.

"Well, as you can plainly see, the possibilities are endless like meandering paths in a great big beautiful garden. I was just scratching that lovely surface when I am purged by Party Poops . . . Well, 'son cosas de la vida.'"

I reach Freeland, which is clean and dull my God. Benway is directing the R.C., Reconditioning Center. I drop around, and "What happened to so and so?" sets in like: "Sidi Idriss 'The Nark' Smithers crooned to the Senders for a longevity serum. No fool like an old queen." "Lester Stroganoff Smuunn—'El Hassein'—turned himself into a Latah trying to perfect A.O.P., Automatic Obedience Processing. A martyr to the industry . . ." (Latah is a condition occurring in Southeast Asia. Otherwise sane, Latahs compulsively imitate every motion once their attention is attracted by snapping the fingers or calling sharply. A form of compulsive involuntary hypnosis. They sometimes injure themselves trying to imitate the motions of several people at once.)

"Stop me if you've heard this atomic secret . . ."

Benway's face retains its form in the flash bulb of urgency, subject at any moment to unspeakable cleavage or metamorphosis. It flickers like a picture moving in and out of focus.

"Come on," says Benway, "and I'll show you around the R.C."

We are walking down a long white hall. Benway's voice drifts into my consciousness from no particular place . . . a disembodied voice that is sometimes loud and clear, sometimes barely audible, like music down a windy street.

"Isolated groups like natives of the Bismarck Archipelago. No overt homosexuality among them. God damned matriarchy. All matriarchies anti-homosexual, conformist and prosaic. Find yourself in a matriarchy walk don't run to the nearest frontier. If you run, some frustrate latent queer cop will likely shoot you. So somebody wants to establish a beach head of homogeneity in a shambles of potentials like West Europe and U.S.A.? Another fucking matriarchy, Margaret Mead notwithstanding . . .

"Spot of bother there. Scalpel fight with a colleague in the operating room. And my baboon assistant leaped on the patient and tore him to pieces. Baboons always attack the weakest party in an altercation. Quite right too. We must never forget our glorious simian heritage. Doc Brubeck was party inna second part. A retired abortionist and junk pusher (he was a veterinarian actually) recalled to service during the manpower shortage. Well, Doc had been in the hospital kitchen all morning goosing the nurses and tanking up on coal gas and Klim—and just before the operation he sneaked a double shot of nutmeg to nerve himself up."

(In England and especially in Edinburgh the citizens bubble coal gas through Klim—a horrible form of powdered milk tasting like rancid chalk—and pick up on the results. They hock everything to pay the gas bill, and when the man comes around to shut it off for the nonpayment, you can hear their screams for miles. When a citizen is sick from needing it he says "I got the klinks" or "That old stove climbing up my back.")

(Nutmeg. I quote from the author's article on narcotic drugs in the *British Journal of Addiction* (see Appendix): "Convicts and sailors sometimes have recourse to nutmeg. About a tablespoon is swallowed with water. Result vaguely similar to marijuana with side effects of headache and nausea. . . . There are a number of narcotics of the nutmeg family in use among the Indians of South America. They are usually administered by sniffing a dried powder of the plant. The medicine men take these noxious substances and go into convulsive states. Their twitchings and mutterings are thought to have prophetic significance.")

"I had a *yagé* hangover, me, and in no condition to take any of Brubeck's shit. First thing he comes on with I should start the incision from the back instead of the front, muttering some garbled nonsense about being sure to cut out the gall bladder it would fuck up the meat. Thought he was on the farm cleaning a chicken. I told him to go put his head back in the oven, whereupon he had the effrontery to push my hand, severing the patient's femoral artery. Blood spurted up and blinded the anesthetist, who ran out through the halls screaming. Brubeck tried to knee me in the groin, and I managed to hamstring him with my scalpel. He crawled about the floor stabbing at my feet and legs. Violet, that's my baboon assistant—only woman I ever cared a damn about—really wigged. I climbed up on the table and poise myself to jump on Brubeck with both feet and stomp him when the cops rushed in.

"Well, this rumble in the operating room, 'this unspeakable occurrence' as the Super called it, you might say was the blow off. The wolf pack was closing for the kill. A crucifixion, that's the only word for it. Of course I'd made a few *Dummheit*s here and there. Who hasn't? There was the time me and the anesthetist drank up all the ether and the patient came up on us, and I was accused of cutting the cocaine with Saniflush. Violet did it actually. Had to protect her of course . . .

"So the wind-up is we are all drummed out of the industry. Not that Violet was a *bona fide* croaker, neither was Brubeck for that matter, and even my own certificate was called in question. But Violet knew more medicine than the Mayo Clinic. She had an extraordinary intuition and a high sense of duty.

"So there I was, flat on my ass with no certificate. Should I turn to another trade? No. Doctoring was in my blood. I managed to keep up my habits performing cut-rate abortions in subway toilets. I even descended to hustling pregnant women in the public streets. It was positively unethical. Then I met a great guy, Placenta Juan the After Birth Tycoon. Made his in slunks during the war."

(Slunks are underage calves trailing afterbirths and bacteria, generally in an unsanitary and unfit condition. A calf may not be sold as food until it reaches a minimum age of six weeks. Prior to that time it is classified as a slunk. Slunk trafficking is subject to a heavy penalty.)

"Well, Juanito controlled a fleet of cargo boats he register under the Abyssinian flag to avoid bothersome restrictions. He gives me a job as ship's doctor on the S.S. *Filariasis*, as filthy a craft as ever sailed the seas. Operating with one hand, beating the rats offa my patient with the other and bedbugs and scorpions rain down from the ceiling.

"So somebody wants homogeneity at this juncture. Can do but it costs. Bored with the whole project, me . . . Here we are . . . Drag Alley."

Benway traces a pattern in the air with his hand and a door swings open. We step through and the door closes. A long ward gleaming with stainless steel, white tile floors, glass brick walls. Beds along one wall. No one smokes, no one reads, no one talks.

"Come and take a close look," says Benway. "You won't embarrass anybody."

I walk over and stand in front of a man who is sitting on his bed. I look at the man's eyes. Nobody, nothing looks back.

"INDs," says Benway, "Irreversible Neural Damage. Overliberated, you might say . . . a drag on the industry."

I pass a hand in front of the man's eyes.

"Yes," says Benway, "they still have reflexes. Watch this." Benway takes a chocolate bar from his pocket, removes the wrapper and holds it in front of the man's nose. The man sniffs. His jaws begin to work. He makes snatching motions with his hands. Saliva drips from his mouth and hangs off his chin in long streamers. His stomach rumbles. His whole body writhes in peristalsis. Benway steps back and holds up the chocolate. The man drops to his knees, throws back his head and barks. Benway tosses the chocolate. The man snaps at it, misses, scrambles around on the floor making slobbering noises. He crawls under the bed, finds the chocolate and crams it into his mouth with both hands.

"Jesus! These INDs got no class to them."

Benway calls over the attendant who is sitting at one end of the ward reading a book of J. M. Barrie's plays.

"Get these fucking INDs outa here. It's a bring down already. Bad for the tourist business."

"What should I do with them?"

"How in the fuck should I know? I'm a scientist. A *pure* scientist. Just get them outa here. I don't hafta look at them is all. They constitute an albatross."

"But what? Where?"

"Proper channels. Buzz the District Coordinator or whatever he calls himself . . . new title every week. Doubt if he exists."

Doctor Benway pauses at the door and looks back at the INDs. "Our failures," he says. "Well, it's all in the day's work."

"Do they ever come back?"

"They don't come back, won't come back, once they're gone," Benway sings softly. "Now this ward has some innarest."

The patients stand in groups talking and spitting on the floor. Junk hangs in the air like a grey haze.

"A heart-warming sight," says Benway, "those junkies standing around waiting for the Man. Six months ago they were all schizophrenic. Some of them hadn't been out of bed for years. Now look at them. In all the course of my practices, I have never seen a schizophrenic junky, and junkies are mostly of the schizo physical type. Want to cure anybody of anything, find out who doesn't have it. So who don't got it? Junkies don't got it. Oh, incidentally, there's an area in Bolivia with no psychosis. Right sane folk in them hills. Like to get in there, me, before it is loused up by literacy, advertising, TV and drive-ins. Make a study strictly from metabolism: diet, use of drugs and alcohol, sex, etc. Who cares what they think? Same nonsense everybody thinks, I daresay.

"And why don't junkies got schizophrenia? Don't know yet. A schizophrenic can ignore hunger and starve to death if he isn't fed. No one can ignore heroin withdrawal. The fact of addiction imposes contact.

"But that's only one angle. Mescaline, LSD6, deteriorated adrenaline, harmine can produce an approximate schizophrenia. The best stuff is extracted from the blood of schizos; so schizophrenia is likely a drug psychosis. They got a metabolic connection, a Man Within you might say."

(Interested readers are referred to Appendix.)

"In the terminal stage of schizophrenia the back brain is permanently depressed, and the front brain is almost without content since the front brain is only active in response to back-brain stimulation.

"Morphine calls forth the antidote of back-brain stimulation similar to schizo substance. (Note similarity between withdrawal syndrome and intoxication with *yagé* or LSD6.) Eventual result of junk use—especially true of heroin addiction where large doses are available to the addict—is permanent back-brain depression and a state much like terminal schizophrenia: complete lack of affect, autism, virtual absence of cerebral event. The addict can spend eight hours looking at a wall. He is conscious of his surroundings, but they have no emotional connotation and in consequence no interest. Remembering a period of heavy addiction is like playing back a tape recording of events experienced by the front brain alone. Flat statements of external events. 'I went to the store and bought some brown sugar. I came home and ate half the box. I took a three grain shot,' etc. Complete absence of nostalgia in these memories. However, as soon as junk intake falls below par, the withdrawal substance floods the body.

"If all pleasure is relief from tension, junk affords relief from the whole life process, in disconnecting the hypothalamus, which is the center of psychic energy and libido.

"Some of my learned colleagues (nameless assholes) have suggested that junk derives its euphoric effect from direct stimulation of the orgasm center. It seems more probable that junk suspends the whole cycle of tension, discharge and rest. The orgasm has no function in the junky. Boredom, which always indicates an undischarged tension, never troubles the addict. He can look at his shoe for eight hours. He is only roused to action when the hourglass of junk runs out."

At the far end of the ward an attendant throws up an iron shutter and lets out a hog call. The junkies rush up grunting and squealing.

"Wise guy," says Benway. "No respect for human dignity. Now I'll show you the mild deviant and criminal ward. Yes, a criminal is a mild deviant here. He doesn't deny the Freeland contract. He merely seeks to circumvent some of the clauses. Reprehensible but not too serious. Down this hall . . . We'll skip wards 23, 86, 57 and 97 . . . and the laboratory."

"Are homosexuals classed as deviants?"

"No. Remember the Bismarck Archipelago. No overt homosexuality. A *functioning* police state needs no police. Homosexuality does not occur to anyone as conceivable behavior . . . Homosexuality is a *political* crime in a matriarchy. No society tolerates overt rejection of its basic tenets. We aren't a matriarchy here, *Insh'allah*. You know the experiment with rats where they are subject to this electric shock and dropped in cold water if they so much as move at a female. So they all become fruit rats and that's the way it is with the etiology. And shall such a rat squeak out, 'I'm queah and I luuuuuuuuuve it' or 'Who cut yours off, you two-holed freak?,' 'twere a square rat so to squeak. During my rather brief experience as a psychoanalyst—spot of bother with the Society—one patient ran amok in Grand Central with a flame thrower, two committed suicide and one died on the couch like a jungle rat (jungle rats are subject to die if confronted suddenly with a hopeless situation). So his relations beef and I tell them, 'It's all in the day's work. Get this stiff outa here. It's a bring down for my live patients'—I noticed that all my homosexual patients manifested strong unconscious heterosex trends and all my hetero patients unconscious homosexual trends. Makes the brain reel, don't it?"

"And what do you conclude from that?"

"Conclude? Nothing whatever. Just a passing observation."

We are eating lunch in Benway's office when he gets a call. "What's that? . . . Monstrous! Fantastic! Carry on and stand by."

He puts down the phone. "I am prepared to accept immediate assignment with Islam Incorporated. It seems the electronic brain went berserk playing six-dimensional chess with the Technician and released every subject in the R.C. Leave us adjourn to the roof. Operation Helicopter is indicated."

From the roof of the R.C. we survey a scene of unparalleled horror. INDs stand around in front of the café tables, long streamers of saliva hanging off their chins, stomachs noisily churning, others ejaculate at the sight of women. Latahs imitate the passers-by with monkey-like obscenity. Junkies have looted the drugstores and fix on every street corner . . . Catatonics decorate the parks . . . Agitated schizophrenics rush through the streets with mangled, inhuman cries. A group of P.R.s—Partially Reconditioned—have surrounded some homosexual tourists with horrible knowing smiles showing the Nordic skull beneath in double exposure.

"What do you want?" snaps one of the queens.

"We want to *understand* you."

A contingent of howling simopaths swing from chandeliers, balconies and trees, shitting and pissing on passers-by. (A simopath—the technical name for this disorder escapes me—is a citizen convinced he is an ape or other simian. It is a disorder peculiar to the army, and discharge cures it.) Amoks trot along cutting off heads, faces sweet and remote with a dreamy half smile . . . Citizens with incipient Bang-utot clutch their penises and call on the tourists for help . . . Arab rioters yip and howl, castrating, disemboweling, throw burning gasoline . . . Dancing boys striptease with intestines, women stick severed genitals in their cunts, grind, bump and flick it at the man of their choice . . . Religious fanatics harangue the crowd from helicopters and rain stone tablets on their heads, inscribed with meaningless messages . . . Leopard Men tear people to pieces with iron claws, coughing and grunting . . . Kwakiutl Cannibal Society initiates bite off noses and ears . . .

A coprophage calls for a plate, shits on it and eats the shit, exclaiming, "Mmmm, that's my rich substance."

A battalion of rampant bores prowls the streets and hotel lobbies in search of victims. An intellectual avant-gardist—"Of course the only writing worth considering now is to be found in scientific reports and periodicals"—has given someone a bulbocapnine injection and is preparing to read him a bulletin on "the use of neo-hemoglobin in the control of multiple degenerative granuloma." (Of course, the reports are all gibberish he has concocted and printed up.)

His opening words: "You look to me like a man of intelligence." (Always ominous words, my boy . . . When you hear them stay not on the order of your going but go at once.)

An English colonial, assisted by five police boys, has detained a subject in the club bar: "I say, do you know Mozambique?" and he launches into the endless saga of his malaria. "So the doctor said to me, 'I can only advise you to leave the area. Otherwise I shall bury you.' This croaker does a little undertaking on the side. Piecing out the odds you might say, and throwing himself a spot of business now and then." So after the third pink gin when he gets to know you, he shifts to dysentery. "Most extraordinary discharge. More or less of a white yellow color like rancid jissom and stringy you know."

An explorer in sun helmet has brought down a citizen with blow gun and curare dart. He administers artificial respiration with one foot. (Curare kills by paralyzing the lungs. It has no other toxic effect, is not, strictly speaking, a poison. If artificial respiration is administered the subject will not die. Curare is eliminated with great rapidity by the kidneys.) "That was the year of the rinderpest when everything died, even the hyenas . . . So there I was completely out of K.Y. in the headwaters of the Baboonsasshole. When it came through by air drop my gratitude was indescribable . . . As a matter of fact, and I have never told this before to a living soul—elusive blighters"—his voice echoes through a vast empty hotel lobby in 1890 style, red plush, rubber plants, gilt and statues—"I was the only white man ever initiated into the infamous Agouti Society, witnessed and participated in their unspeakable rites."

(The Agouti Society has turned out for a Chimu Fiesta. [The Chimu of ancient Peru were much given to sodomy and occasionally staged bloody battles with clubs, running up several hundred casualties in the course of an afternoon.] The youths, sneering and goosing each other with clubs, troop out to the field. Now the battle begins.

Gentle reader, the ugliness of that spectacle buggers description. Who can be a cringing pissing coward, yet vicious as a purple-assed mandrill, alternating these deplorable conditions like vaudeville skits? Who can shit on a fallen adversary who, dying, eats the shit and screams with joy? Who can hang a weak passive and catch his sperm in mouth like a vicious dog? Gentle reader, I fain would spare you this, but my pen hath its will like the Ancient Mariner. Oh Christ what a scene is this! Can tongue or pen accommodate these scandals? A beastly young hooligan has gouged out the eye of his confrère and fuck him in the brain. "This brain atrophy already, and dry as grandmother's cunt."

He turns into Rock and Roll hoodlum. "I screw the old gash— like a crossword puzzle what relation to me is the outcome if it outcome? My father already or not yet? I can't screw you, Jack, you is about to become my father, and better 'twere to cut your throat and screw my mother playing it straight than fuck my father or vice versa mutatis mutandis as the case may be, and cut my mother's throat, that sainted gash, though it be the best way I know to stem her word hoard and freeze her asset. I mean when a fellow be caught short in the switches and don't know is he to offer up his ass to 'great big daddy' or commit a torso job on the old lady. Give me two cunts and a prick of steel and keep your dirty finger out of my sugar bum what you think I am a purple-assed reception already fugitive from Gibraltar? Male and female castrated he them. Who can't distinguish between the sexes? I'll cut your throat you white mother fucker. Come out in the open like my grandchild and meet thy unborn mother in dubious battle. Confusion hath fuck his masterpiece. I have cut the janitor's throat quite by mistake of identity, he being such a horrible fuck like the old man. And in the coal bin all cocks are alike."

So leave us return to the stricken field. One youth hath penetrate his comrade, whilst another youth does amputate the proudest part of that cock's quivering beneficiary so that the visiting member projects to fill the vacuum nature abhors and ejaculate into the Black Lagoon where impatient piranha snap up the child not yet born nor—in view of certain well established facts—at all likely.)

Another bore carries around a suitcase full of trophies and medals, cups and ribbons: "Now this I won for the Most Ingenious Sex Device Contest in Yokohama. (Hold him, he's desperate.) The Emperor gave it to me himself and there were tears in his eyes, and the runners-up all castrated theirselves with hara-kiri knives. And I won this ribbon in a Degradation Contest at the Teheran meeting of Junkies Anonymous."

"Shot up my wife's M.S. and her down with a kidney stone big as the Hope Diamond. So I give her half a Veganin and tell her,

'You can't expect too much relief . . . Shut up awready. I wanta enjoy my medications.'

"Stole an opium suppository out of my grandmother's ass."

The hypochondriac lassoes the passer-by and administers a straitjacket and starts talking about his rotting septum: "An awful purulent discharge is subject to flow out . . . just wait till you see it."

He does a striptease to operation scars, guiding the reluctant fingers of a victim. "Feel that suppurated swelling in my groin where I got the lymphogranulomas . . . And now I want you to palpate my internal hemorrhoids."

(The reference is to lymphogranuloma, "climactic buboes." A viral venereal disease indigenous to Ethiopia. "Not for nothing are we known as feelthy Ethiopians," sneers an Ethiopian mercenary as he sodomizes Pharaoh, venomous as the King's cobra. Ancient Egyptian papyrus talk all the time about them feelthy Ethiopians.

So it started in Addis Ababa like the Jersey Bounce, but these are modern times, One World. Now the climactic buboes swell up in Shanghai and Esmeraldas, New Orleans and Helsinki, Seattle and Capetown. But the heart turns home and the disease shows a distinct predilection for Negroes, is in fact the white haired boy of white supremacists. But the Mau Mau voodoo men are said to be cooking up a real dilly of a VD for the white folks. Not that Caucasians are immune: five British sailors contracted the disease in Zanzibar. And in Dead Coon County, Arkansas ["Blackest Dirt, Whitest People in the U.S.A.—Nigger, Don't Let The Sun Set On You Here"] the County Coroner come down with the buboes fore and aft. A vigilante committee of neighbors apologetically burned him to death in the Court House privy when his interesting condition came to light.

"Now, Clem, just think of yourself as a cow with the aftosa."

"Or a poltroon with the fowl pest."

"Don't crowd too close, boys. His intestines is subject to explode in the fire."

The disease in short arm hath a gimmick for going places unlike certain unfortunate viruses who are fated to languish unconsummate in the guts of a tick or a jungle mosquito, or the saliva of a dying jackal slobbering silver under the desert moon. And after an initial lesion at the point of infection the disease passes to the lymph glands of the groin, which swell and burst in suppurating fissures, drain for days, months, years, a purulent stringy discharge streaked with blood and putrid lymph. Elephantiasis of the genitals is a frequent complication, and cases of gangrene have been recorded where the amputation *in medio* of the patient from the waist down was indicated but hardly worth while. Women usually suffer secondary infection of the anus. Males who resign themselves up for passive intercourse to infected partners, like weak and soon to be purple-assed baboons, may also nourish a little stranger. Initial proctitis and the inevitable purulent discharge—which may pass unnoticed in the shuffle—is followed by stricture of the rectum requiring intervention of an apple corer or its surgical equivalent, lest the unfortunate patient be reduced to fart and shit in his teeth giving rise to stubborn cases of halitosis and unpopularity with all sexes, ages and conditions of *homo sapiens*. In fact a blind bugger was deserted by his seeing eye police dog—copper at heart. Until quite recently there was no satisfactory treatment. "Treatment is symptomatic"—which means in the trade there is none. Now many cases yield to intensive therapy with Aureomycin, Terramycin and some of the newer molds. However a certain appreciable percentage remain refractory as mountain gorillas . . . So, boys, when those hot licks play over your balls and prick and dart up your ass like an invisible blue blow torch of orgones, in the words of T. J. Watson, *Think.*

Stop panting and start palpating . . . and if you palpate a bubo draw yourself back in and say in a cold nasal whine: "You think I am innarested to contact your horrible old condition? I am not innarested at all.")

Rock and Roll adolescent hoodlums storm the streets of all nations. They rush into the Louvre and throw acid in the Mona Lisa's face. They open zoos, insane asylums, prisons, burst water mains with air hammers, chop the floor out of passenger plane lavatories, shoot out lighthouses, file elevator cables to one thin wire, turn sewers into the water supply, throw sharks and sting rays, electric eels and candiru into swimming pools (the candiru is a small eel-like fish or worm about one-quarter inch through and two inches long patronizing certain rivers of ill repute in the Greater Amazon Basin, will dart up your prick or your asshole or a woman's cunt *faute de mieux,* and hold himself there by sharp spines with precisely what motives is not known since no one has stepped forward to observe the candiru's life-cycle *in situ*), in nautical costumes ram the *Queen Mary* full speed into New York Harbor, play chicken with passenger planes and buses, rush into hospitals in white coats carrying saws and axes and scalpels three feet long, throw paralytics out of iron lungs (mimic their suffocations flopping about on the floor and rolling their eyes up), administer injections with bicycle pumps, disconnect artificial kidneys, saw a woman in half with a two-man surgical saw, they drive herds of squealing pigs into the Ka'bah, they shit on the floor of the United Nations and wipe their ass with treaties, pacts, alliances.

By plane, car, horse, camel, elephant, tractor, bicycle and steam roller, on foot, skis, sled, crutch and pogo-stick the tourists storm the frontiers, demanding with inflexible authority asylum from the "unspeakable conditions obtaining in Freeland," the Chamber of Commerce striving in vain to stem the debacle: "Please to be restful. It is only a few crazies who have from the crazy place outbroken."

joselito

And Joselito who wrote bad, class-conscious poetry began to cough. The German doctor made a brief examination, touching Joselito's ribs with long, delicate fingers. The doctor was also a concert violinist, a mathematician, a chess master, and a Doctor of International Jurisprudence with license to practice in the lavatories of the Hague. The doctor flicked a hard, distant glance across Joselito's brown chest. He looked at Carl and smiled—one educated man to another smile—and raised his eyebrow, saying without words:

"Alzo for the so stupid peasant we must avoid use of the word is it not? Otherwise he shit himself with fear. Koch and spit they are *both* nasty words I think?"

He said aloud: "It is a *catarro de los pulmones.*"

Carl talked to the doctor outside under the narrow arcade with rain bouncing up from the street against his pant legs, thinking how many people he tell it to, and the stairs, porches, lawns, driveways, corridors and streets of the world there in the doctor's eyes . . . stuffy German alcoves, butterfly trays to the ceiling, silent portentous smell of uremia seeping under the door, suburban lawns to sound of the water sprinkler, in calm jungle night under silent wings of the Anopheles mosquito. (Note: This is not a figure. Anopheles mosquitoes *are* silent.) Thickly carpeted, discreet nursing home in Kensington: stiff brocade chair and a cup of tea, the Swedish modern living room with water hyacinths in a yellow bowl—outside the china blue Northern sky and drifting clouds, under bad watercolors of the dying medical student.

"A schnapps I think Frau Underschnitt."

The doctor was talking into a phone with a chess board in front of him. "Quite a severe lesion I think . . . of course without to see the fluoroscope." He picks up the knight and then replaces it thoughtfully. "Yes . . . Both lungs . . . quite definitely." He replaces the receiver and turns to Carl. "I have observed these people show amazingly quick wound recovery, with low incidence of infection. It is always the lungs here ... pneumonia and, of course, Old Faithful." The doctor grabs Carl's cock, leaping into the air with a coarse peasant guffaw. His European smile ignores the misbehavior of a child or an animal. He goes on smoothly in his eerily unaccented, disembodied English. "Our Old Faithful Bacillus Koch." The doctor clicks his heels and bows his head. "Otherwise they would multiply their stupid peasant assholes into the sea, is it not?" He shrieks, thrusting his face into Carl's. Carl retreats sideways with the grey wall of rain behind him.

"Isn't there some place where he can be treated?"

"I think there is some sort of *sanitarium*," he drags out the word with ambiguous obscenity, "up at the District Capital. I will write for you the address."

"Chemical therapy?"

His voice falls flat and heavy in the damp air.

"Who can say. They are all stupid peasants, and the worst of all peasants are the so-called educated. These people should not only be prevented from learning to read, but from learning to talk as well. No need to prevent them from thinking; nature has done that.

"Here is the *address*," the doctor whispered without moving his lips.

He dropped a pill of paper into Carl's hand. His dirty fingers, shiny over the dirt, rested on Carl's sleeve.

"There is the matter of my fee."

Carl slipped him a wadded bank note ... and the doctor faded into the grey twilight, seedy and furtive as an old junky.

Carl saw Joselito in a big clean room full of light, with private bath and concrete balcony. And nothing to talk about there in the cold empty room, water hyacinths growing in a yellow bowl and the china blue sky and drifting clouds, fear flickering in and out of his eyes. When he smiled the fear flew away in little pieces of light, lurked enigmatically in the high cool corners of the room. And what could I say feeling death around me, and the little broken images that come before sleep, there in the mind?

"They will send me to the new sanitarium tomorrow. Come and visit me. I will be there alone."

He coughed and took a codeineeta.

"Doctor I understand, that is I have been given to understand, I have read and heard—not a medical man myself—don't pretend to be—that the concept of sanitarium treatment has been more or less supplanted, or at least very definitely supplemented, by chemical therapy. Is this accurate in your opinion? What I mean to say is, Doctor, please tell me in all sincerity, as one human being to another, what is your opinion of chemical versus sanitarium therapy? Are you a *partisan?*"

The doctor's liver sick Indian face was blank as a dealer's.

"Completely modern, as you can see," he gestures toward the room with the purple fingers of bad circulation. "Bath . . . water . . . flowers. The lot." He finished in Cockney English with a triumphant smirk. "I will write for you a letter."

"This letter? For the sanitarium?"

The doctor was speaking from a land of black rocks and great, iridescent brown lagoons. "The furniture . . . modern and comfortable. You *find* it so of course?"

Carl could not see the sanitarium owing to a false front of green stucco topped by an intricate neon sign dead and sinister against the sky, waiting for darkness. The sanitarium was evidently built on a great limestone promontory, over which flowering trees and vine tendrils broke in waves. The smell of flowers was heavy in the air.

The commandant sat at a long wooden trestle under a vine trellis. He was doing absolutely nothing. He took the letter that

Carl handed him and whispered through it, reading his lips with the left hand. He stuck the letter on a spike over a toilet. He began transcribing from a ledger full of numbers. He wrote on and on.

Broken images exploded softly in Carl's head, and he was moving out of himself in a silent swoop. Clear and sharp from a great distance he saw himself sitting in a lunchroom. Overdose of H. His old lady shaking him and holding hot coffee under his nose.

Outside an old junky in Santa Claus suit selling Christmas seals. "Fight tuberculosis, folks," he whispers in his disembodied, junky voice. Salvation Army choir of sincere, homosexual football coaches sings: "In the Sweet Bye and Bye."

Carl drifted back into his body, an earthbound junk ghost.

"I could bribe him, of course."

The commandant taps the table with one finger and hums "Coming Through the Rye." Far away, then urgently near like a foghorn a split second before the grinding crash.

Carl pulled a note half out of his trouser pocket ... The commandant was standing by a vast panel of lockers and deposit boxes. He looked at Carl, sick animal eyes gone out, dying inside, hopeless fear reflecting the face of death. In the smell of flowers a note half out of his pocket, the weakness hit Carl, shutting off his breath, stopping his blood. He was in a great cone spinning down to a black point.

"Chemical therapy?" The scream shot out of his flesh through empty locker rooms and barracks, musty resort hotels, and spectral, coughing corridors of T.B. sanitariums, the muttering, hawking, grey dishwater smell of flophouses and Old Men's Homes, great, dusty customs sheds and warehouses, through broken porticoes and smeared arabesques, iron urinals worn paper thin by the urine of a million fairies, deserted weed-grown privies with a musty smell of shit turning back to the soil, erect wooden phallus on the grave of dying peoples plaintive as leaves in the wind, across the great brown river where whole trees float with green snakes in the branches and sad-eyed lemurs watch the shore out over a vast plain (vulture wings husk in the dry air). The way is strewn with broken condoms and empty H caps and K.Y. tubes squeezed dry as bone meal in the summer sun.

"My furniture." The commandant's face burned like metal in the flash bulb of urgency. His eyes went out. A whiff of ozone drifted through the room. The "novia" muttered over her candles and altars in one corner.

"It is all Trak . . . modern, excellent . . ." he is nodding idiotically and drooling. A yellow cat pulls at Carl's pant leg and runs onto a concrete balcony. Clouds drift by.

"I could get back my deposit. Start me a little business someplace." He nods and smiles like a mechanical toy.

"Joselito!!!" Boys look up from street ball games, bull rings and bicycle races as the name whistles by and slowly fades away.

"Joselito! . . . Paco! . . . Pepe! . . . Enrique! . . ." The plaintive boy cries drift in on the warm night. The Trak sign stirs like a nocturnal beast, and bursts into blue flame.

the
black
meat

"We friends, yes?"

The shoe shine boy put on his hustling smile and looked up into the Sailor's dead, cold, undersea eyes, eyes without a trace of warmth or lust or hate or any feeling the boy had ever experienced in himself or seen in another, at once cold and intense, impersonal and predatory.

The Sailor leaned forward and put a finger on the boy's inner arm at the elbow. He spoke in his dead, junky whisper.

"With veins like that, Kid, I'd have myself a time."

He laughed, black insect laughter that seemed to serve some obscure function of orientation like a bat's squeak. The Sailor laughed three times. He stopped laughing and hung there motionless listening down into himself. He had picked up the silent frequency of junk. His face smoothed out like yellow wax over the high cheekbones. He waited half a cigarette. The Sailor knew how to wait. But his eyes burned in a hideous dry hunger. He turned his face of controlled emergency in a slow half pivot to case the man who had just come in. "Fats" Terminal sat there sweeping the café with blank, periscope eyes. When his eyes passed the Sailor he nodded minutely. Only the peeled nerves of junk sickness would have registered a movement.

. The Sailor handed the boy a coin. He drifted over to Fats' table with his floating walk and sat down. They sat a long time in silence. The café was built into one side of a stone ramp at the bottom of a high white canyon of masonry. Faces of The City poured through silent as fish, stained with vile addictions and insect lusts. The lighted café was a diving bell, cable broken, settling into black depths.

The Sailor was polishing his nails on the lapels of his glen plaid suit. He whistled a little tune through his shiny, yellow teeth.

When he moved an effluvium of mold drifted out of his clothes, a musty smell of deserted locker rooms. He studied his nails with phosphorescent intensity.

"Good thing here, Fats. I can deliver twenty. Need an advance of course."

"On spec?"

"So I don't have the twenty eggs in my pocket. I tell you it's jellied consommé. One little whoops and a push." The Sailor looked at his nails as if he were studying a chart. "You know I always deliver."

"Make it thirty. And a ten tube advance. This time tomorrow."

"Need a tube now, Fats."

"Take a walk, you'll get one."

The Sailor drifted down into the Plaza. A street boy was shoving a newspaper in the Sailor's face to cover his hand on the Sailor's pen. The Sailor walked on. He pulled the pen out and broke it like a nut in his thick, fibrous, pink fingers. He pulled out a lead tube. He cut one end of the tube with a little curved knife. A black mist poured out and hung in the air like boiling fur. The Sailor's face dissolved. His mouth undulated forward on a long tube and sucked in the black fuzz, vibrating in supersonic peristalsis, disappeared in a silent, pink explosion. His face came back into focus unbearably sharp and clear, burning yellow brand of junk searing the grey haunch of a million screaming junkies.

"This will last a month," he decided, consulting an invisible mirror.

All streets of the City slope down between deepening canyons to a vast, kidney-shaped plaza full of darkness. Walls of street and plaza are perforated by dwelling cubicles and cafés, some a few feet deep, others extending out of sight in a network of rooms and corridors.

At all levels criss-cross of bridges, cat walks, cable cars. Catatonic youths dressed as women in gowns of burlap and rotten rags, faces heavily and crudely painted in bright colors over a stratum of beatings, arabesques of broken, suppurating scars to the pearly bone, push against the passer-by in silent clinging insistence.

Traffickers in the Black Meat, flesh of the giant aquatic black centipede—sometimes attaining a length of six feet—found in a lane of black rocks and iridescent, brown lagoons, exhibit paralyzed crustaceans in camouflaged pockets of the Plaza visible only to the Meat Eaters.

Followers of obsolete unthinkable trades, doodling in Etruscan, addicts of drugs not yet synthesized, black marketeers of World War III, excisors of telepathic sensitivity, osteopaths of the spirit, investigators of infractions denounced by bland paranoid chess players, servers of fragmentary warrants taken down in hebephrenic shorthand charging unspeakable mutilations of the spirit, officials of unconstituted police states, brokers of exquisite dreams and nostalgias tested on the sensitized cells of junk sickness and bartered for raw materials of the will, drinkers of the Heavy Fluid sealed in translucent amber of dreams.

The Meet Café occupies one side of the Plaza, a maze of kitchens, restaurants, sleeping cubicles, perilous iron balconies and basements opening into the underground baths.

On stools covered in white satin sit naked Mugwumps sucking translucent, colored syrups through alabaster straws. Mugwumps have no liver and nourish themselves exclusively on sweets. Thin, purple-blue lips cover a razor-sharp beak of black bone with which they frequently tear each other to shreds in fights over clients. These creatures secrete an addicting fluid from their erect penises which prolongs life by slowing metabolism. (In fact all longevity agents have proved addicting in exact ratio to their effectiveness in prolonging life.) Addicts of Mugwump fluid are known as Reptiles. A number of these flow over chairs with their flexible bones and black-pink flesh. A fan of green cartilage covered with hollow, erectile hairs through which the Reptiles absorb the fluid sprouts from behind each ear. The fans, which move from time to time touched by invisible currents, serve also some form of communication known only to Reptiles.

During the biennial Panics when the raw, peeled Dream Police storm the City the Mugwumps take refuge in the deepest crevices of the wall, sealing themselves in clay cubicles, and remain for weeks in biostasis. In those days of grey terror the Reptiles dart about faster and faster, scream past each other at supersonic speed, their flexible skulls flapping in black winds of insect agony.

The Dream Police disintegrate in globs of rotten ectoplasm swept away by an old junky, coughing and spitting in the sick morning. The Mugwump Man comes with alabaster jars of fluid and the Reptiles get smoothed out.

The air is once again still and clear as glycerine.

The Sailor spotted his Reptile. He drifted over and ordered a green syrup. The Reptile had a little, round disk mouth of brown gristle, expressionless green eyes almost covered by a thin membrane of eyelid. The Sailor waited an hour before the creature picked up his presence.

"Any eggs for Fats?" he asked, his words stirring through the Reptile's fan hairs.

It took two hours for the Reptile to raise three pink transparent fingers covered with black fuzz.

Several Meat Eaters lay in vomit, too weak to move. (The Black Meat is like a tainted cheese, overpoweringly delicious and nauseating so that the eaters eat and vomit and eat again until they fall exhausted.)

A painted youth slithered in and seized one of the great black claws sending the sweet, sick smell curling through the café.

hospital

Ho-Hum Dept.: Willy The Agent taking the cure in Hassan's Hospital . . . Hassan's Hospital adjoining cemetery . . . Cremations in the patio . . . Professional mourners solicit relatives in the waiting room and corridors . . .

Disintoxication Notes.

Paranoia of early withdrawal . . . Everything looks blue . . . Flesh dead, doughy, toneless.

Withdrawal Nightmares.

A mirror-lined café. Empty . . . Waiting for something . . . A man appears in a side door . . . A slight, short Arab dressed in a brown djellaba with grey beard and grey face . . . There is a pitcher of boiling acid in my hand . . . Seized by a convulsion of urgency, I throw it in his face . . .

Everyone looks like a drug addict . . .

Take a little walk in the hospital patio . . . In my absence some-one has used my scissors, they are stained with some sticky, red brown gick . . . No doubt that little bitch of a *criada* trimming her rag.

Horrible-looking Europeans clutter up the stairs, intercept the nurse when I need my medicine, empty piss into the basin when I am washing, occupy the toilet for hours on end—probably fishing for a finger stall of diamonds they have stashed up their asshole . . .

In fact the whole clan of Europeans has moved in next to me . . . The old mother is having an operation, and her daughter move right in to see the old gash receive proper service. Strange visitors, presumably relatives . . . One of them wears as glasses those gadgets jewelers screw into their eyes to examine stones . . . Probably a diamond-cutter on the skids . . . The man who loused up the Throckmorton Diamond and was drummed out of the industry . . . All these jewelers standing around the Diamond in their frock coats, waiting on The Man. An error of one thousandth of an inch ruins the rock complete and they have to import this character special from Amsterdam to do the job . . . So he reels in dead drunk with a huge air hammer and pounds the diamond to dust . . .

I don't check these citizens . . . Dope peddlers from Aleppo? . . . Slunk traffickers from Buenos Aires? Illegal diamond buyers from Johannesburg? . . . Slave traders from Somaliland? Collaborators at the very least . . .

Continual dreams of junk: I am looking for a poppy field . . . Moonshiners in black Stetsons direct me to a Near East café . . . One of the waiters is a connection for Yugoslav opium . . .

Buy a packet of heroin from a Malay Lesbian in white belted trenchcoat . . . I cop the paper in Tibetan section of a museum. She keeps trying to steal it back . . . I am looking for a place to fix . . .

The critical point of withdrawal is not the early phase of acute sickness, but the final step free from the medium of junk ... There is a nightmare interlude of cellular panic, life suspended between two ways of being ... At this point the longing for junk concentrates in a last, all-out yen, and seems to gain a dream power: circumstances put junk in your way ... You meet an old-time Schmecker, a larcenous hospital attendant, a writing croaker ...

A guard in a uniform of human skin, black buck jacket with carious yellow teeth buttons, an elastic pullover shirt in burnished Indian copper, adolescent Nordic sun-tanned slacks, sandals from callused foot soles of young Malayan farmer, an ash-brown scarf knotted and tucked in the shirt. (Ash-brown is a color like grey *under* brown skin. You sometimes find it in mixed Negro and white stock; the mixture did not come off and the colors separated out like oil on water ...)

The Guard is a sharp dresser, since he has nothing to do and saves all his pay to buy fine clothes and changes three times a day in front of an enormous magnifying mirror. He has a Latin-handsome smooth face with a pencil line mustache, small black eyes, blank and greedy, undreaming insect eyes.

When I get to the frontier the Guard rushes out of his *casita*, a mirror in a wooden frame slung round his neck. He is trying to get the mirror off his neck ... This has never happened before, that anyone reached the frontier. The Guard has injured his larynx taking off the mirror frame ... He has lost his voice ... He opens his mouth, you can see the tongue jumping around inside. The smooth blank young face and the open mouth with the tongue moving inside are incredibly hideous. The Guard holds up his hand. His whole body jerks in convulsive negation. I go over and unhook the chain across the road. It falls with a clank of metal on stone. I walk through. The Guard stands there in the mist looking after me.

Then he hooks the chain up again, goes back into the *casita* and starts plucking at his mustache.

They just bring so-called lunch . . . A hard-boiled egg with the shell off revealing an object like I never seen it before . . . A very small egg of a yellow-brown color . . . Perhaps laid by the duck-billed platypus. The orange contained a huge worm and very little else . . . He really got there firstest with the mostest . . . In Egypt is a worm gets into your kidneys and grows to an enormous size. Ultimately the kidney is just a thin shell around the worm. Intrepid gourmets esteem the flesh of The Worm above all other delicacies. It is said to be unspeakably toothsome . . . An Interzone coroner known as Autopsy Ahmed made a fortune trafficking The Worm.

The French school is opposite my window and I dig the boys with my eight-power field glasses . . . So close I could reach out and touch them . . . They wear shorts . . . I can see the goose pimples on their legs in the cold spring morning . . . I project myself out through the glasses and across the street, a ghost in the morning sunlight, torn with disembodied lust.

Met Marv in front of the Sargasso with two Arab kids and he said:

"Want to watch these two kids screw each other?"

"Of course. How much?"

"I think they will perform for fifty cents. Hungry, you know."

"That's the way I like to see them."

Makes me feel sorta like a dirty old man but, "*Son cosas de la vida,*" as Sobera de la Flor said when the fuzz upbraids him for blasting this cunt and taking the dead body to the Bar O Motel and fucking it . . .

"She play hard to get already," he say . . . "I don't hafta take that sound." (Sobera de la Flor was a Mexican criminal convicted of several rather pointless murders.)

* * *

The lavatory has been locked for three hours solid . . . I think
they are using it for an operating room . . .

NURSE: "I can't find her pulse, doctor."

DR. BENWAY: "Maybe she got it up her snatch in a finger stall."

NURSE: "Adrenalin, doctor?"

DR. BENWAY: "The night porter shot it all up for kicks." He
looks around and picks up one of those rubber vacuum cups at
the end of a stick they use to unstop toilets . . . He advances on
the patient . . . "Make an incision, Doctor Limpf," he says to his
appalled assistant . . . "I'm going to massage the heart."

Doctor Limpf shrugs and begins the incision. Doctor Benway
washes the suction cup by swishing it around in the toilet bowl . . .

NURSE: "Shouldn't it be sterilized, doctor?"

DR. BENWAY: "Very likely but there's no time." He sits on the
suction cup like a cane seat watching his assistant make the incision . . . "You young squirts couldn't lance a pimple without an
electric vibrating scalpel with automatic drain and suture . . . Soon
we'll be operating by remote control on patients we never see . . .
We'll be nothing but button pushers. All the skill is going out of
surgery . . . All the know-how and make-do . . . Did I ever tell you
about the time I performed an appendectomy with a rusty sar-
dine can? And once I was caught short without instrument one
and removed a uterine tumor with my teeth. That was in the Upper
Effendi, and besides . . ."

DR. LIMPF: "The incision is ready, doctor."

Dr. Benway forces the cup into the incision and works it up
and down. Blood spurts all over the doctors, the nurse and the
wall . . . The cup makes a horrible sucking sound.

NURSE: "I think she's gone, doctor."

DR. BENWAY: "Well, it's all in the day's work." He walks across
the room to a medicine cabinet . . . "Some fucking drug addict

has cut my cocaine with Saniflush! Nurse! Send the boy out to fill this Rx on the double!"

Doctor Benway is operating in an auditorium filled with students: "Now, boys, you won't see this operation performed very often and there's a reason for that . . . You see it has absolutely no medical value. No one knows what the purpose of it originally was or if it had a purpose at all. Personally I think it was a pure artistic creation from the beginning. Just as a bull fighter with his skill and knowledge extricates himself from danger he has himself invoked, so in this operation the surgeon deliberately endangers his patient, and then, with incredible speed and celerity, rescues him from death at the last possible split second . . .

"Did any of you ever see Doctor Tetrazzini perform? I say perform advisedly because his operations were performances. He would start by throwing a scalpel across the room into the patient and then make his entrance like a ballet dancer. His speed was incredible: 'I don't give them time to die,' he would say. Tumors put him in a frenzy of rage. 'Fucking undisciplined cells!' he would snarl, advancing on the tumor like a knife-fighter."

A young man leaps down into the operating theater and, whipping out a scalpel, advances on the patient.

DR. BENWAY: "An *espontáneo*! Stop him before he guts my patient!"

(*Espontáneo* is a bull-fighting term for a member of the audience who leaps down into the ring, pulls out a concealed cape and attempts a few passes with the bull before he is dragged out of the ring.)

The orderlies scuffle with the *espontáneo*, who is finally ejected from the hall. The anesthetist takes advantage of the confusion to pry a large gold filling from the patient's mouth . . .

I am passing room 10 they moved me out of yesterday . . . Maternity case I assume . . . Bedpans full of blood and Kotex and nameless female substances, enough to pollute a continent . . . If someone comes to visit me in my old room he will think I gave birth to a monster and the State Department is trying to hush it up . . .

Music from *I Am an American* . . . An elderly man in the striped pants and cutaway of a diplomat stands on a platform draped with the American flag. A decayed, corseted tenor—bursting out of a Daniel Boone costume—is singing "The Star-Spangled Banner," accompanied by a full orchestra. He sings with a slight lisp . . .

THE DIPLOMAT (reading from a great scroll of ticker tape that keeps growing and tangling around his feet): "And we categorically deny that any male citizen of the United States of America . . ."

TENOR: "Oh thay can you thee . . ." His voice breaks and shoots up to a high falsetto.

In the control room the Technician mixes a bicarbonate of soda and belches into his hand: "God damned tenor's a brown artist!" he mutters sourly. "Mike! rumph," the shout ends in a belch. "Cut that swish fart off the air and give him his purple slip. He's through as of right now . . . Put in that sex-changed Liz athlete . . . She's a full-time tenor at least . . . *Costume?* How in the fuck should I know? I'm no dress designer swish from the costume department! *What's that?* The entire costume department occluded as a security risk? What am I, an octopus? Let's see . . . How about an Indian routine? Pocahontas or Hiawatha? . . . No, that's not right. Some citizen cracks wise about giving it back to the Indians . . . A Civil War uniform, the coat North and the pants South like it show they got together again? She can come on like Buffalo Bill or Paul Revere or that citizen wouldn't give up the shit, I mean the ship, or a GI or a Doughboy or the Unknown Soldier . . . That's the best deal . . . Cover her with a monument, that way nobody has to look at her . . ."

The Lesbian, concealed in a papier-mâché Arc de Triomphe, fills her great lungs and looses a tremendous bellow.

"Oh say do that Star-Spangled Banner yet wave . . ."

A great rent rips the Arc de Triomphe from top to bottom. The Diplomat puts a hand to his forehead . . .

THE DIPLOMAT: "That any male citizen of the United States has given birth in Interzone or at any other place . . ."

"O'er the land of the FREEEEEEEEEEE . . ."

The Diplomat's mouth is moving but no one can hear him. The Technician clasps his hands over his ears: "Mother of God!" he screams. His plate begins to vibrate like a Jew's harp, suddenly flies out of his mouth . . . He snaps at it irritably, misses and covers his mouth with one hand.

The Arc de Triomphe falls with a ripping, splintering crash, reveals the Lesbian standing on a pedestal clad only in a leopard-skin jockstrap with enormous falsie basket . . . She stands there smiling stupidly and flexing her huge muscles . . . The Technician is crawling around on the control room floor looking for his plate and shouting unintelligible orders: "Thess thupper thonic!! Thut ur oth thu thair!"

THE DIPLOMAT (wiping sweat from his brow): "To any creature of any type or description . . ."

"And the home of the brave."

The Diplomat's face is grey. He staggers, trips in the scroll, sags against the rail, blood pouring from eyes, nose and mouth, dying of cerebral hemorrhage.

THE DIPLOMAT (barely audible): "The Department denies . . . un-American . . . It's been destroyed . . . I mean it never was . . . Categor . . ." *Dies.*

In the Control Room instrument panels are blowing out . . . Great streamers of electricity crackle through the room . . . The Technician, naked, his body burned black, staggers about like a figure in *Götterdämmerung*, screaming: "Thubber thonic!! Oth thu thair!!!" A final blast reduces the Technician to a cinder.

"Gave proof through the night
That our flag was still there . . ."

Habit Notes.

Shooting Eukodol every two hours. I have a place where I can slip my needle right into a vein, it stays open like a red festering mouth, swollen and obscene, gathers a slow drop of blood and pus after the shot . . .

Eukodol is a chemical variation of codeine—dihydro-oxy-codeine.

This stuff comes on more like C than M . . . When you shoot coke in the mainline there is a rush of pure pleasure to the head . . . Ten minutes later you want another shot . . . The pleasure of morphine is in the viscera . . . You listen down into yourself after a shot . . . But intravenous C is electricity through the brain, activating cocaine pleasure connections . . . There is no withdrawal syndrome with C. It is a need of the brain alone—a need without body and without feeling. Earthbound ghost need. The craving for C lasts only a few hours as long as the C channels are stimulated. Then you forget it. Eukodol is like a combination of junk and C. Trust the Germans to concoct some really evil shit. Eukodol like morphine is six times stronger than codeine. Heroin six times stronger than morphine. Dihydro-oxy-heroin should be six times stronger than heroin. Quite possible to develop a drug so habit-forming that one shot would cause lifelong addiction.

Habit Notes continued.

Picking up needle I reach spontaneously for the tie-up cord with my left hand. This I take as a sign I can hit the one useable vein in my left arm. (The movements of tying up are such that you normally tie up the arm with which you reach for the cord.) The needle slides in easily on the edge of a callus. I feel around.

Suddenly a thin column of blood shoots up into the syringe, for a moment sharp and solid as a red cord.

The body knows what veins you can hit and conveys this knowledge in the spontaneous movements you make preparing to take a shot ... Sometimes the needle points like a dowser's wand. Sometimes I must wait for the message. But when it comes I always hit blood.

A red orchid bloomed at the bottom of the dropper. He hesitated for a full second, then pressed the bulb, watching the liquid rush into the vein as if sucked by the silent thirst of his blood. There was an iridescent, thin coat of blood left in the dropper, and the white paper collar was soaked through with blood like a bandage. He reached over and filled the dropper with water. As he squirted the water out, the shot hit him in the stomach, a soft sweet blow.

Look down at my filthy trousers, haven't been changed in months ... The days glide by strung on a syringe with a long thread of blood ... I am forgetting sex and all sharp pleasures of the body—a grey, junk-bound ghost. The Spanish boys call me *El Hombre Invisible*—the Invisible Man ...

Twenty pushups every morning. Use of junk removes fat, leaves muscle more or less intact. The addict seems to need less tissue ... Would it be possible to isolate the fat-removing molecule of junk?

More and more static at the drugstore, mutterings of control like a telephone off the hook ... Spent all day until 6 P.M. to score for two boxes of Eukodol ...

Running out of veins and out of money.

Keep going on the nod. Last night I woke up with someone squeezing my hand. It was my other hand ... Fall asleep reading and the words take on code significance ... Obsessed with codes ... Man contracts a series of diseases which spell out a code message ...

Take a shot in front of D.L. Probing for a vein in my dirty bare foot ... Junkies have no shame ... They are impervious to the repugnance of others. It is doubtful if shame can exist in the absence of sexual libido ... The junky's shame disappears with his nonsexual sociability which is also dependent on libido ... The addict regards his body impersonally as an instrument to absorb the medium in which he lives, evaluates his tissue with the cold hands of a horse trader. "No use trying to hit there." Dead fish eyes flick over a ravaged vein.

Using a new type sleeping pill called Soneryl ... You don't feel sleepy ... You shift to sleep without transition, fall abruptly into the middle of a dream ... I have been years in a prison camp suffering from malnutrition ...

The President is a junky but can't take it direct because of his position. So he gets fixed through me ... From time to time we make contact, and I recharge him. These contacts look to the casual observer like homosexual practices, but the actual excitement is not primarily sexual, and the climax is the separation when the recharge is completed. The erect penises are brought into contact—at least we used that method in the beginning, but contact points wear out like veins. Now I sometimes have to slip my penis under his left eyelid. Of course I can always fix him with an Osmosis Recharge, which corresponds to a skin shot, but that is admitting defeat. An O.R. will put the President in a bad mood for weeks, and might well precipitate an atomic shambles. And the President pays a high price for the Oblique Habit. He has sacrificed all control, and is dependent as an unborn child. The Oblique Addict suffers a whole spectrum of subjective horror, silent protoplasmic frenzy, hideous agony of the bones. Tensions build up, pure energy without emotional content finally tears through the body throwing him about like a man in contact with high tension wires. If his charge connection is cut off cold, the Oblique Addict falls into such violent electric convulsions that his bones shake loose, and he dies with the skeleton straining to climb out of his unendurable flesh and run in a straight line to the nearest cemetery.

The relation between an O.A. (Oblique Addict) and his R.C. (Recharge Connection) is so intense that they can only endure each other's company for brief and infrequent intervals—I mean aside from recharge meets, when all personal contact is eclipsed by the recharge process.

Reading the paper ... Something about a triple murder in the rue de la Merde, Paris: "An adjusting of scores." ... I keep slipping away ... "The police have identified the author ... Pepe El Culito ... The Little Ass Hole, an affectionate diminutive." Does it really say that? ... I try to focus the words ... they separate in meaningless mosaic ...

lazarus
go
home

Fumbling through faded tape at the pick up frontier, a languid grey area of hiatus miasmic with yawns and gaping goof holes, Lee found out that the young junky standing there in his room at 10 A.M. was back from two months skin diving in Corsica and off the junk ...

Here to show off his new body, Lee decided with a shudder of morning junk sickness. He knew that he was seeing—ah yes *Miguel* thank you—three months back sitting in the Metropole nodded out over a stale yellow éclair that would poison a cat two hours later, decided that the effort involved in seeing Miguel at all at 10 A.M.

was enough without the intolerable chore of correcting an error ("what is this a fucking farm?") which would also entail current picture of Miguel in much used areas like some great, inconvenient beast of an object on top in the suitcase.

"You look marvelous," Lee said, wiping away the more obvious signs of distaste with a sloppy, casual napkin, seeing the grey ooze of junk in Miguel's face, studying patterns of shabbiness as if man and clothes had moved for years through back alleys of time with never a space station to tidy up . . .

Besides by the time I could correct the error . . . Lazarus go home . . . Pay The Man and go home . . . What I want to see your old borrowed meat for?

"Well it's great to see you off . . . Do yourself a favor." Miguel was swimming around the room spearing fish with his hand . . .

"When you're down there you never think about horse."

"You're better off like this," said Lee, dreamily caressing a needle scar on the back of Miguel's hand, following the whorls and patterns of smooth purple flesh in a slow twisting movement . . .

Miguel scratched the back of his hand . . . He looked out the window . . . His body moved in little, galvanized jerks as junk channels lit up . . . Lee sat there waiting. "One snort never put anybody back on, kid."

"I know what I'm doing."

They always know.

Miguel took the nail file.

Lee closed his eyes: *It's too tiresome.*

"Uh thanks that was great." Miguel's pants fell to his ankles. He stood there in a misshapen overcoat of flesh that turned from brown to green and then colorless in the morning light, fell off in globs onto the floor.

Lee's eyes moved in the substance of his face . . . a little, cold, grey flick . . . "Clean it up," he said. "Enough dirt in here now."

"Oh uh sure." Miguel fumbled with a dustpan.

Lee put the packet of heroin away.

Lee lived in a permanent third-day kick, with, of course, certain uh essential intermissions to refuel the fires that burned through his yellow-pink-brown gelatinous substance and kept off the hovering flesh. In the beginning his flesh was simply soft, so soft that he was cut to the bone by dust particles, air currents and brushing overcoats while direct contact with doors and chairs seemed to occasion no discomfort. No wound healed in his soft, tentative flesh . . . Long white tendrils of fungus curled round the naked bones. Mold odors of atrophied testicles quilted his body in a fuzzy grey fog . . .

During his first severe infection the boiling thermometer flashed a quicksilver bullet into the nurse's brain and she fell dead with a mangled scream. The doctor took one look and slammed steel shutters of survival. He ordered the burning bed and its occupant immediately evicted from the hospital premises.

"Guess he can make his own penicillin!" snarled the doctor.

But the infection burned the mold out . . . Lee lived now in varying degrees of transparency . . . While not exactly invisible he was at least difficult to see. His presence attracted no special notice . . . People covered him with a project or dismissed him as a reflection, shadow: "Some kinda light trick or neon advertisement."

Now Lee felt the first seismic tremors of Old Faithful the Cold Burn. He pushed Miguel's spirit into the hall with a kind, firm tendril.

"Jesus!" said Miguel. "I gotta go!" He rushed out.

Pink fires of histamine spurted from Lee's glowing core and covered his raw periphery. (The room was fireproof, the walls of iron blistered and spotted with moon craters.) He took a large fix and falsified his schedule.

He decided to visit a colleague, NG Joe, who got hooked during a Bang-utot attack in Honolulu.

(Note: Bang-utot, literally, "attempting to get up and groaning ..." Death occurring in the course of a nightmare ... The condition occurs in males of Southeast Asiatic extraction ... In Manila about twelve cases of death by Bang-utot are recorded each year.

Victims often know that they are going to die, express the fear that their penis will enter the body and kill them. Sometimes they cling to the penis in a state of shrieking hysteria calling on others for help lest the penis escape and pierce the body. Erections, such as normally occur in sleep, are considered especially dangerous and liable to bring a fatal attack ... One man devised a Rube Goldberg contraption to prevent erection during sleep. But he died of Bang-utot.

Careful autopsies of Bang-utot victims have revealed no organic reason for death. There are often signs of strangulation [caused by what?]; sometimes slight hemorrhages of pancreas and lungs—not sufficient to cause death and also of unknown origin. It has occurred to the author that the cause of death is a misplacement of sexual energy resulting in a *lung erection* with consequent strangulation ... One man who recovered said that "a little man" was sitting on his chest and strangling him.

[See article by Nils Larsen M.D., "The Men with the Deadly Dream," in the *Saturday Evening Post*, December 3, 1955. Also article by Erle Stanley Gardner for *True* magazine.])

NG lived in constant fear of erection so his habit jumped and jumped. (Note: It is a well known tiresome fact, it is a notoriously dull and long winded fact, that anyone who gets hooked because of any disability whatever will be presented, during the periods of shortage or deprivation [such a thing as too much fun you know], with an outrageously padded, geometrically progressing, proliferating account.)

An electrode attached to one testicle glowed briefly and NG woke up in the smell of burning flesh and reached for a loaded syringe. He rolled into a foetal position and slid the needle into his spine. He pulled the needle out with a little sigh of pleasure, and realized that Lee was in the room. A long slug undulated out of Lee's right eye and wrote on the wall in iridescent ooze: "The Sailor is in the City buying up TIME."

I am waiting in front of a drugstore for it to open at nine o'clock. Two Arab boys roll cans of garbage up to a high heavy wood door in a whitewashed wall. Dust in front of the door streaked with urine. One of the boys bent over, rolling the heavy cans, pants tight over his lean young ass. He looks at me with the neutral, calm glance of an animal. I wake with a shock like the boy is real and I have missed a meet I had with him for this afternoon.

"We expect additional equalizations," says the Inspector in an interview with Your Reporter. "Otherwise will occur," the Inspector lifts one leg in a typical Nordic gesture, "the bends is it not? But perhaps we can provide the suitable chamber of decompression."

The Inspector opens his fly and begins looking for crabs, applying ointment from a little clay pot. Clearly the interview is at an end. "You're not going?" he exclaims. "Well, as one judge said to the other, 'Be just and if you can't be just be arbitrary.' Regret cannot observe customary obscenities." He holds up his right hand covered with a foul-smelling yellow ointment.

One's Reporter rushes forward and clasps the soiled hand in both of his. "It's been a pleasure, Inspector, an unspeakable pleasure," he says peeling off his gloves, rolling them into a ball and tossing them into the wastebasket. "Expense account," he smiles.

hassan's
rumpus
room

Gilt and red plush. Rococo bar backed by pink shell. The air is cloyed with a sweet evil substance like decayed honey. Men and women in evening dress sip pousse-cafés through alabaster tubes. A Near East Mugwump sits naked on a bar stool covered in pink silk. He licks warm honey from a crystal goblet with a long black tongue. His genitals are perfectly formed—circumcised cock, black shiny pubic hairs. His lips are thin and purple-blue like the lips of a penis, his eyes blank with insect calm. The Mugwump has no liver, maintaining himself exclusively on sweets. The Mugwump pushes a slender blond youth to a couch and strips him expertly.

"Stand up and turn around," he orders in telepathic pictographs. He ties the boy's hands behind him with a red silk cord. "Tonight we make it all the way."

"No, no!" screams the boy.

"Yes. Yes."

Cocks ejaculate in silent "yes." The Mugwump parts silk curtains, reveals a teak wood gallows against lighted screen of red flint. Gallows is on a dais of Aztec mosaics.

The boy crumples to his knees with a long "OOOOOOOOH," shitting and pissing in terror. He feels the shit warm between his thighs. A great wave of hot blood swells his lips and throat. His body contracts into a foetal position and sperm spurts hot into his face. The Mugwump dips hot perfumed water from alabaster bowl, pensively washes the boy's ass and cock, drying him with a soft blue towel. A warm wind plays over the boy's body and the hairs float free. The Mugwump puts a hand under the boy's chest and pulls him to his feet. Holding him by both pinioned elbows, propels him up the steps and under the noose. He stands in front of the boy holding the noose in both hands.

The boy looks into Mugwump eyes blank as obsidian mirrors, pools of black blood, glory holes in a toilet wall closing on the Last Erection.

An old garbage collector, face fine and yellow as Chinese ivory, blows The Blast on his dented brass horn, wakes the Spanish pimp with a hard-on. Whore staggers out through dust and shit and litter of dead kittens, carrying bales of aborted foetuses, broken condoms, bloody Kotex, shit wrapped in bright color comics.

A vast still harbor of iridescent water. Deserted gas well flares on the smoky horizon. Stink of oil and sewage. Sick sharks swim through the black water, belch sulphur from rotting livers, ignore a bloody, broken Icarus.

Naked Mr. America, burning frantic with self bone love, screams out: "My asshole confounds the Louvre! I fart ambrosia and shit pure gold turds! My cock spurts soft diamonds in the morning sunlight!" He plummets from the eyeless lighthouse, kissing and jacking off in face of the black mirror, glides obliquely down with cryptic condoms and mosaic of a thousand newspapers through a drowned city of red brick to settle in black mud with tin cans and beer bottles, gangsters in concrete, pistols pounded flat and meaningless to avoid short-arm inspection of prurient ballistic experts. He waits the slow striptease of erosion with fossil loins.

The Mugwump slips the noose over the boy's head and tightens the knot caressingly behind the left ear. The boy's penis is retracted, his balls tight. He looks straight ahead breathing deeply. The Mugwump sidles around the boy goosing him and caressing his genitals in hieroglyphs of mockery. He moves in behind the boy with a series of bumps and shoves his cock up the boy's ass. He stands there moving in circular gyrations.

The guests shush each other, nudge and giggle.

Suddenly the Mugwump pushes the boy forward into space, free of his cock. He steadies the boy with hands on the hip bones, reaches up with his stylized hieroglyph hands and snaps the boy's neck. A shudder passes through the boy's body. His penis rises in three great surges pulling his pelvis up, ejaculates immediately.

Green sparks explode behind his eyes. A sweet toothache pain shoots through his neck, down the spine to the groin, contracting the body in spasms of delight. His whole body squeezes out through his cock. A final spasm throws a great spurt of sperm across the red screen like a shooting star.

The boy falls with soft gutty suction through a maze of penny arcades and dirty pictures. A sharp turd shoots clean out his ass. Farts shake his slender body. Skyrockets burst in green clusters across a great river. He hears the faint put-put of a motor boat in jungle twilight . . . Under silent wings of the Anopheles mosquito.

The Mugwump pulls the boy back onto his cock. The boy squirms, impaled like a speared fish. The Mugwump swings on the boy's back, his body contracting in fluid waves. Blood flows down the boy's chin from his mouth, half-open, sweet and sulky in death. The Mugwump falls with a fluid, sated plop.

Windowless cubicle with blue walls. Dirty pink curtain cover the door. Red bugs crawl on the wall, cluster in corners. Naked boy in the middle of the room twang a two-string oud, trace an arabesque on the floor. Another boy lean back on the bed smoking keif and blow smoke over his erect cock. They play game with tarot cards on the bed to see who fuck who. Cheat. Fight. Roll on the floor snarling and spitting like young animals. The loser sit on the floor chin on knees, licks a broken tooth. The winner curls up on the bed pretending to sleep. Whenever the other boy come near kick at him. Ali seize him by one ankle, tuck the ankle under his arm pit, lock his arm around the calf. The boy kick desperately at Ali's face. Other ankle pinioned. Ali tilt the boy back on his shoulders. The boy's cock extends along his stomach, float free pulsing. Ali put his hands behind the boy's knees, push his legs over his head. Spit on his cock. The other sighs deeply as Ali slides his cock in. The mouths grind together smearing blood. Sharp musty odor of penetrated rectum. Nimun drive in like a wedge, force jissom out the other cock in long hot spurts. (The author has observed that Arab cocks tend to be wide and wedge shaped.)

Satyr and naked Greek lad in aqualungs trace a ballet of pursuit in a monster vase of transparent alabaster. The Satyr catches the boy from in front and whirls him around. They move in fish jerks. The boy releases a silver stream of bubbles from his mouth. White sperm ejaculates into the green water and floats lazily around the twisting bodies.

Negro gently lifts exquisite Chinese boy into a hammock. He pushes the boy's legs up over his head and straddles the hammock. He slides his cock up the boy's slender tight ass. He rocks the hammock gently back and forth. The boy screams, a weird high wail of unendurable delight.

A Javanese dancer in ornate teak swivel chair, set in a socket of limestone buttocks, pulls an American boy—red hair, bright green eyes—down onto his cock with ritual motions. The boy sits impaled facing the dancer who propels himself in circular gyrations, lending fluid substance to the chair. "Wheeeeeeeeee!" screams the boy as his sperm spurts up over the dancer's lean brown chest. One gob hits the corner of the dancer's mouth. The boy pushes it in with his finger and laughs: "Man, that's what I call suction!"

Two Arab women with bestial faces have pulled the shorts off a little blond French boy. They are screwing him with red rubber cocks. The boy snarls, bites, kicks, collapses in tears as his cock rises and ejaculates.

Hassan's face swells, tumescent with blood. His lips turn purple. He strips off his suit of banknotes and throws it into an open vault that closes soundless.

"Freedom Hall here, folks!" he screams in his phony Texas accent. Ten-gallon hat and cowboy boots still on, he dances the Liquefactionist Jig, ending with a grotesque cancan to the tune of "She Started a Heat Wave."

"*Let it be! And no holes barred!!!*"

Couples attached to baroque harnesses with artificial wings copulate in the air, screaming like magpies.

Aerialists ejaculate each other in space with one sure touch.

Equilibrists suck each other off deftly, balanced on perilous poles and chairs tilted over the void. A warm wind brings the smell of rivers and jungle from misty depths.

Boys by the hundred plummet through the roof, quivering and kicking at the end of ropes. The boys hang at different levels, some near the ceiling and others a few inches off the floor. Exquisite Balinese and Malays, Mexican Indians with fierce innocent faces and bright red gums. Negroes (teeth, fingers, toe nails and pubic hair gilded), Japanese boys smooth and white as china, Titian-haired Venetian lads, Americans with blond or black curls falling across the forehead (the guests tenderly shove it back), sulky blond Polacks with animal brown eyes, Arab and Spanish street boys, Austrian boys pink and delicate with a faint shadow of blond pubic hair, sneering German youths with bright blue eyes scream "Heil Hitler!" as the trap falls under them. Sollubis shit and whimper.

Mr. Rich-and-Vulgar chews his Havana lewd and nasty, sprawled on a Florida beach surrounded by simpering blond catamites:

"This citizen have a Latah he import from Indo-China. He figures to hang the Latah and send a Xmas TV short to his friends. So he fix up two ropes—one gimmicked to stretch, the other the real McCoy. But that Latah gets up in feud-state and puts on his Santa Claus suit and make with the switcheroo. Come the dawning. The citizen puts one rope on and the Latah, going along the way Latahs will, puts on the other. When the traps are down the citizen hangs for real and the Latah stand with the carny-rubber stretch rope. Well, the Latah imitate every twitch and spasm. Come three times.

"Smart young Latah keep his eye on the ball. I got him working in one of my plants as an expeditor."

Aztec priests strip blue feather robe from the Naked Youth. They bend him back over a limestone altar, fit a crystal skull over his head, securing the two hemispheres back and front with crystal screws. A waterfall pours over the skull snapping the boy's neck. He ejaculates in a rainbow against the rising sun.

Sharp protein odor of semen fills the air. The guests run hands over twitching boys, suck their cocks, hang on their backs like vampires.

Naked lifeguards carry in iron lungs full of paralyzed youths.

Blind boys grope out of huge pies, deteriorated schizophrenics pop from a rubber cunt, boys with horrible skin diseases rise from a black pond (sluggish fish nibble yellow turds on the surface).

A man with white tie and dress shirt, naked from the waist down except for black garters, talks to the Queen Bee in elegant tones. (Queen Bees are old women who surround themselves with fairies to form a "swarm." It is a sinister Mexican practice.)

"But where is the *statuary*?" He talks out of one side of his face, the other is twisted by the Torture of a Million Mirrors. He masturbates wildly. The Queen Bee continues the conversation, notices nothing.

Couches, chairs, the whole floor begins to vibrate, shaking the guests to blurred grey ghosts shrieking in cock-bound agony.

Two boys jacking off under railroad bridge. The train shakes through their bodies, ejaculates them, fades with distant whistle. Frogs croak. The boys wash semen off lean brown stomachs.

Train compartment: two sick young junkies on their way to Lexington tear their pants down in convulsions of lust. One of them soaps his cock and works it up the other's ass with a corkscrew motion. "Jeeeeeeeeeeeeeesus!" Both ejaculate at once standing up. They move away from each other and pull up their pants.

"Old croaker in Marshall writes for tincture and sweet oil."

"The piles of an aged mother shriek out raw and bleeding for the Black Shit . . . Doc, suppose it was your mother, rimmed by resident leeches, squirming around so nasty . . . De-active that pelvis, Mom, you disgust me already."

"Let's stop over and make him for an Rx."

The train tears on through the smoky, neon-lighted June night.

Pictures of men and women, boys and girls, animals, fish, birds, the copulating rhythm of the universe flows through the room, a great blue tide of life. Vibrating, soundless hum of deep forest—sudden quiet of cities when the junky cops. A moment of stillness and wonder. Even the Commuter buzzes clogged lines of cholesterol for contact.

Hassan shrieks out: "This is your doing, A.J.! You poopa my party!"

A.J. looks at him, face remote as limestone: "Uppa your ass, you liquefying gook."

A horde of lust-mad American women rush in. Dripping cunts, from farm and dude ranch, factory, brothel, country club, penthouse and suburb, motel and yacht and cocktail bar, strip off riding clothes, ski togs, evening dresses, Levis, tea gowns, print dresses, slacks, bathing suits and kimonos. They scream and yip and howl, leap on the guests like bitch dogs in heat with rabies. They claw at the hanged boys shrieking: "You fairy! You bastard! Fuck me! Fuck me! Fuck me!" The guests flee screaming, dodge among the hanged boys, overturn iron lungs.

A.J.: "Call out my Sweitzers, God damn it! Guard me from these she-foxes!"

Mr. Hyslop, A.J.'s secretary, looks up from his comic book: "The Sweitzers liquefy already."

(Liquefaction involves protein cleavage and reduction to liquid which is absorbed into someone else's protoplasmic being. Hassan, a notorious liquefactionist, is probably the beneficiary in this case.)

A.J.: "Gold-bricking cocksuckers! Where's a man without his Sweitzers? Our backs are to the wall, gentlemen. Our very cocks at stake. Stand by to resist boarders, Mr. Hyslop, and issue short arms to the men."

A.J. whips out a cutlass and begins decapitating the American Girls. He sings lustily:

> *Fifteen men on a dead man's chest*
> *Yo Ho Ho and a bottle of rum.*
> *Drink and the devil had done for the rest*
> *Yo Ho Ho and a bottle of rum.*

Mr. Hyslop, bored and resigned: "Oh Gawd! He's at it again." He waves the Jolly Roger listlessly.

A.J., surrounded and fighting against overwhelming odds, throws back his head and makes with the hog call. Immediately a thousand rutting Eskimos pour in grunting and squealing, faces tumescent, eyes hot and red, lips purple, fall on the American women.

(Eskimos have a rutting season when the tribes meet in short summer to disport themselves in orgies. Their faces swell and lips turn purple.)

A House Dick with cigar two feet long sticks his head in through the wall: "Have you got a menagerie in here?"

Hassan wrings his hands: "A shambles! A filthy shambles! By Allah I never see anything so downright nasty!"

He whirls on A.J. who is sitting on a sea chest, parrot on shoulder, patch over one eye, drinking rum from a tankard. He scans the horizon with a huge brass telescope.

HASSAN: "You cheap Factualist bitch! Go and never darken my rumpus room again!"

campus
of interzone
university

Donkeys, camels, llamas, rickshaws, carts of merchandise pushed by straining boys, eyes protruding like strangled tongues—throbbing red with animal hate. Herds of sheep and goats and long-horned cattle pass between the students and the lecture platform. The students sit around on rusty park benches, limestone blocks, outhouse seats, packing crates, oil drums, stumps, dusty leather hassocks, moldy gym mats. They wear Levis—djellabas—hose and doublet . . . drink corn from mason jars, coffee from tin cans, smoke gage (marijuana) in cigarettes made of wrapping paper and lottery tickets . . . shoot junk with a safety pin and dropper, study racing forms, comic books, Mayan codices . . .

The Professor arrives on a bicycle carrying a string of bullheads. He mounts the platform holding his back (crane swings a bellowing cow over his head).

PROF: "Fucked by the Sultan's Army last night. I have dislocate the back in the service of my resident queen . . . Can't evict that old gash. Need a licensed brain electrician disconnect her synapse by synapse and a surgical bailiff put her guts out on the sidewalk. When Ma move in on a boy bag and baggage he play Hell dispossess that Gold Star Boarder . . ."

He looks at the bullheads, humming tunes from the 1920s. "The nostalgia fit is on me boys and will out willy silly . . . boys walk down the carny midway eating pink spun sugar . . . goose each other at the peep show . . . jack off in the Ferris wheel . . . throw sperm at the moon rising red and smoky over the foundries across the river. A Nigra hangs from a cottonwood in front of The Old Court House . . . whimpering women catch his sperm in vaginal teeth . . .

"(Husband looks at the little changeling with narrow eyes the color of a faded grey flannel shirt . . . 'Doc, I suspect it to be a Nigra.'

The Doctor shrugs: 'It's the Old Army Game, son."

Pea under the shell . . . Now you see it now you don't . . .')

"And Doc Parker in the back room in his drugstore shooting horse heroin three grains a jolt—'Tonic,' he mutters. 'It's always spring.'

"'Hands' Benson, Town Pervert, has took up a *querencia* in the school privy (*querencia* is bullfight term . . . The bull will find a spot in the ring he likes and stay there and the bullfighter has to go in and meet the bull on his bull terms or coax him out—one or the other). Sheriff A.Q. 'Flat' Larsen say 'Some way we gotta lure him outa that *querencia*.' . . . And Old Ma Lottie sleep ten years with a dead daughter and home cured too, wakes shivering in the East Texas dawn . . . vultures out over the black swamp water and cypress stumps . . .

"And now gentlemen—I trust there are no transvestites present—he he—and you are all gentlemen by Act of Congress it being only remain to establish you *male humans*, positively no Transitionals in either direction will be allowed in this decent hall. Gentlemen, present short arms. Now you have all been briefed on the importance of keeping your weapons well lubricated and ready for any action flank or rear guard."

STUDENTS: "Hear! Hear!" They wearily unbutton their flies. One of them brandishes a huge erection.

PROF: "And now, gentlemen, where was I? Oh yes, Ma Lottie . . . She wake shivering in the gentle pink dawn, pink as the candles on a little girl's birthday cake, pink as spun sugar, pink as a seashell, pink as a cock pulsing in a red fucking light . . . Ma Lottie . . . hurumph . . . if this prolixity be not cut short will succumb to the infirmities of age and join her daughter in formaldehyde.

"'The Rime of the Ancient Mariner,' by Coleridge the poet . . . I should like to call your attention to the symbolism of the Ancient Mariner *himself*."

STUDENTS: "*Himself* the man says."

"Thereby call attention to his own unappetizing person."

"That wasn't a nice thing to do, Teach."

A hundred juvenile delinquents, switchblades clicking like teeth, move at him.

PROF: "Oh landsakes!" He tries desperately to disguise himself as an old woman with high black shoes and umbrella ... "If it wasn't for my lumbago can't rightly bend over I'd turn to them offering my Sugar Bum the way baboons do it ... If a weaker baboon be attacked by a stronger baboon the weaker baboon will either (a) present his hrump fanny I believe is the word, gentlemen, heh heh for passive intercourse *or* (b) if he is a different type baboon more extrovert and well-adjusted, lead an attack on an even weaker baboon if he can find one."

Dilapidated Diseuse in 1920 clothes like she sleep in them ever since undulates across dreary neon-lighted Chicago street ... dead weight of the Dear Dead Days hanging in the air like an earthbound ghost.

DISEUSE (canned heat tenor): "Find the weakest baboon."

Frontier saloon: Fag Baboon dressed in little girl blue dress sings in resigned voice to tune of "Alice Blue Gown": "I'm the weakest baboon of them all."

A freight train separates the Prof from the juveniles ... When the train passes they have fat stomachs and responsible jobs ...

STUDENTS: "We want Lottie!"

PROF: "That was in another country, gentlemen ... As I was saying before I was so rudely interrupted by one of my multiple personalities ... troublesome little beasts ... consider the Ancient Mariner without curare, lasso, bulbocapnine or straitjacket, albeit able to capture and hold a live audience ... What is his hrump gimmick? He he he he ... He does not, like so-called artists at this time, stop just *anybody* thereby inflicting unsent-for boredom and working random hardship ... He stops those who cannot choose but hear owing to already existing relation between The Mariner (however ancient) and the uh Wedding Guest ...

"What the Mariner actually says is not important ... He may be rambling, irrelevant, even crude and rampant senile. But something happens to the Wedding Guest like happens in psychoanalysis when it happens if it happens. If I may be permitted a slight digression . . . an analyst of my acquaintance does all the talking—patients listen patiently or not . . . He reminisces . . . tells dirty jokes (old ones) . . . achieves counterpoints of idiocy undreamed of by The County Clerk. He is illustrating at some length that nothing can ever be accomplished on the verbal level . . . He arrived at this method through observing that The Listener—The Analyst—was not reading the mind of the patient . . . The patient—The Talker—was reading *his* mind . . . That is, the patient has ESP awareness of the analyst's dreams and schemes whereas the analyst contacts the patient strictly from front brain . . . Many agents use this approach—they are notoriously long-winded bores and bad listeners . . .

"Gentlemen I will slop a pearl: *You can find out more about someone by talking than by listening.*"

Pigs rush up and the Prof pours buckets of pearls into a trough . . .

"I am not worthy to eat his feet," says the fattest hog of them all.

"Clay anyhoo."

a.j.'s
annual
party

A.J. turns to the guests. "Cunts, pricks, fence straddlers, tonight I give you—that internationally known impresario of blue movies and short-wave TV, the one, the only, The Great Slashtubitch!"

He points to a red velvet curtain sixty feet high. Lightning rends the curtain from top to bottom. The Great Slashtubitch stands revealed. His face is immense, immobile like a Chimu funeral urn. He wears full evening dress, blue cape and blue monocle. Huge grey eyes with tiny black pupils that seem to spit needles. (Only the Coordinate Factualist can meet his gaze.) When he is angered the charge of it will blow his monocle across the room. Many an ill-starred actor has felt the icy blast of Slashtubitch's displeasure: "Get out of my studio, you cheap four-flushing ham! Did you think to pass a counterfeit orgasm on me! THE GREAT SLASHTUBITCH! I could tell if you come by regard the beeg toe. Idiot! Mindless scum!! Insolent baggage!!! Go peddle thy ass and know that it takes sincerity and art, and devotion, to work for Slashtubitch. Not shoddy trickery, dubbed gasps, rubber turds and vials of milk concealed in the ear and shots of yohimbine sneaked in the wings."

(Yohimbine, derived from the bark of a tree growing in Central Africa, is the safest and most efficient aphrodisiac. It operates by dilating the blood vessels on the surface of the skin, particularly in the genital area.)

Slashtubitch ejects his monocle. It sails out of sight, returns like a boomerang into his eye. He pirouettes and disappears in a blue mist, cold as liquid air . . . Fadeout . . .

On Screen. Red-haired, green-eyed boy, white skin with a few freckles . . . kissing a thin brunette girl in slacks. Clothes and hairdo suggest existentialist bars of all the world cities. They are seated on low bed covered in white silk. The girl opens his pants with gentle fingers and pulls out his cock which is small and very hard. A drop of lubricant gleams at its tip like a pearl. She caresses the crown gently: "Strip, Johnny." He takes off his clothes with swift sure movements and stands naked before her, his cock pulsing. She makes a motion for him to turn around and he pirouettes across the floor parodying a model, hand on hip. She takes off her shirt. Her breasts are high and small with erect nipples. She slips off her underpants. Her pubic hairs are black and shiny. He sits down beside her and reaches for her breast. She stops his hands.

"Darling, I want to rim you," she whispers.

"No. Not now."

"Please, I want to."

"Well, all right. I'll go wash my ass."

"No, I'll wash it."

"Aw shucks now, it ain't dirty."

"Yes it is. Come on now, Johnny boy."

She leads him into the bathroom. "All right, get down." He gets down on his knees and leans forward, with his chin on the bath mat. "Allah," he says. He looks back and grins at her. She washes his ass with soap and hot water sticking her finger up it.

"Does that hurt?"

"Noooooooooo."

"Come along, baby." She leads the way into the bedroom. He lies down on his back and throws his legs back over his head, clasping elbows behind his knees. She kneels down and caresses the backs of his thighs, his balls, running her fingers down the perineal divide. She pushes his cheeks apart, leans down and begins licking the anus, moving her head in a slow circle. She pushes at the sides of the asshole, licking deeper and deeper. He closes his eyes and squirms. She licks up the perineal divide. His small, tight balls . . . A great pearl stands out on the tip of his circumcised cock. Her mouth closes over the crown. She sucks rhythmically up and down, pausing on the up stroke and moving her head around in a circle. Her hand plays gently with his balls, slides down and middle finger up his ass. As she sucks down toward the root of his cock she tickles his prostate mockingly. He grins and farts. She is sucking his cock now in a frenzy. His body begins to contract, pulling up toward his chin. Each time the contraction is longer.

"Wheeeeeeee!" the boy yells, every muscle tense, his whole body straining to empty through his cock. She drinks his jissom which fills her mouth in great hot spurts. He lets his feet flop back onto the bed. He arches his back and yawns.

Mary is strapping on a rubber penis: "Steely Dan III from Yokohama," she says, caressing the shaft. Milk spurts across the room.

"Be sure that milk is pasteurized. Don't go giving me some kinda awful cow disease like anthrax or glanders or aftosa . . ."

"When I was a transvestite Liz in Chi used to work as an exterminator. Make advances to pretty boys for the thrill of being beaten as a man. Later I catch this one kid, overpower him with supersonic judo I learned from an old Lesbian Zen monk. I tie him up, strip off his clothes with a razor and fuck him with Steely Dan I. He is so relieved I don't castrate him literal he come all over my bedbug spray."

"What happen to Steely Dan I?"

"He was torn in two by a bull dyke. Most terrific vaginal grip I ever experienced. She could cave in a lead pipe. It was one of her parlor tricks."

"And Steely Dan II?"

"Chewed to bits by a famished candiru in the Upper Baboons-asshole. And don't say 'Wheeeeeeee!' this time."

"Why not? It's real boyish."

"Barefoot boy, check thy bullheads with the madam."

He looks at the ceiling, hands behind his head, cock pulsing. "So what shall I do? Can't shit with that dingus up me. I wonder is it possible to laugh and come at the same time? I recall, during the war, at the Jockey Club in Cairo, me and my asshole buddy, Lu, both gentlemen by Act of Congress . . . nothing else could have done such a thing to either of us . . . So we got laughing so hard we piss all over ourselves and the waiter say: 'You bloody hash-heads, get out of here!' I mean, if I can laugh the piss out of me I should be able to laugh out jissom. So tell me something real funny when I start coming. You can tell by certain premonitory quiverings of the prostate gland . . ."

She puts on a record, metallic cocaine bebop. She greases the dingus, shoves the boy's legs over his head and works it up his ass with a series of corkscrew movements of her fluid hips. She moves in a slow circle, revolving on the axis of the shaft. She rubs her hard nipples across his chest. She kisses him on neck and chin and eyes. He runs his hands down her back to her buttocks, pulling her into his ass. She revolves faster, faster. His body jerks and writhes in convulsive spasms. "Hurry up, please," she says. "The milk is getting cold." He does not hear. She presses her mouth against his. Their faces run together. His sperm hits her breast with light, hot licks.

Mark is standing in the doorway. He wears a turtleneck black sweater. Cold, handsome, narcissistic face. Green eyes and black hair. He looks at Johnny with a slight sneer, his head on one side, hands in his jacket pockets, a graceful hoodlum ballet. He jerks his head and Johnny walks ahead of him into the bedroom.

Mary follows. "All right, boys," she says, sitting down naked on a pink silk dais overlooking the bed. "Get with it!"

Mark begins to undress with fluid movements, hip-rolls, squirms out of his turtleneck sweater revealing his beautiful white torso in a mocking belly dance. Johnny deadpan, face frozen, breath quick, lips dry, removing his clothes and dropping them on the floor. Mark lets his shorts fall on one foot. He kicks like a chorus-girl, sending the shorts across the room. Now he stands naked, his cock stiff, straining up and out. He runs slow eyes over Johnny's body. He smiles and licks his lips,

Mark drops on one knee, pulling Johnny across his back by one arm. He stands up and throws him six feet onto the bed. Johnny lands on his back and bounces. Mark jumps up and grabs Johnny's ankles, throwing his legs over his head. Mark's lips are drawn back in a tight snarl. "All right, Johnny boy." He contracts his body, slow and steady as an oiled machine, pushing his cock up Johnny's ass. Johnny gives a great sigh, squirming in ecstasy.

Mark hitches his hands behind Johnny's shoulders, pulling him down onto his cock which is buried to the hilt in Johnny's ass. Great whistles through his teeth. Johnny screams like a bird. Mark is rubbing his face against Johnny's, snarl gone, face innocent and boyish as his whole liquid being spurts into Johnny's quivering body.

A train roars through him whistle blowing ... boat whistle, foghorn, sky rockets burst over oily lagoons ... penny arcades open into a maze of dirty pictures ... ceremonial cannon boom in the harbor ... a scream shoots down a white hospital corridor ... out along a wide dusty street between palm trees, whistles out across the desert like a bullet (vulture wings husk in the dry air), a thousand boys come at once in outhouses, bleak public school toilets, attics, basements, treehouses, Ferris wheels, deserted houses, limestone caves, rowboats, garages, barns, rubbly windy city outskirts behind mud walls (smell of dried excrement) ... black dust blowing over lean copper bodies ... ragged pants dropped to cracked bleeding bare feet ... (place where vultures fight over fish heads) ... by jungle lagoons, vicious fish snap at white sperm floating on black water, sand flies bite the copper ass, howler monkeys like wind in the trees (a land of great brown rivers where whole trees float, bright colored snakes in the branches, pensive lemurs watch the shore with sad eyes), a red plane traces arabesques in blue substance of sky, a rattlesnake strikes, a cobra rears, spreads, spits white venom, pearl and opal chips fall in a slow silent rain through air clear as glycerine.

Time jumps like a broken typewriter, the boys are old men, young hips quivering and twitching in boy-spasms go slack and flabby, draped over an outhouse seat, a park bench, a stone wall in Spanish sunlight, a sagging furnished room bed (outside red brick slum in clear winter sunlight) ... twitching and shivering in dirty underwear, probing for a vein in the junk-sick morning, in an Arab café muttering and slobbering—the Arabs whisper

"Medjoub" and edge away—(a Medjoub is a special sort of religious Moslem lunatic . . . often epileptic among other disorders).

"The Moslems must have blood and jissom . . . See, see where Christ's blood streams in the spermament," howls the Medjoub . . . He stands up screaming and black blood spurts solid from his last erection, a pale white statue standing there, as if he had stepped whole across the Great Fence, climbed it innocent and calm as a boy climbs the fence to fish in the forbidden pond— in a few seconds he catches a huge catfish—The Old Man will rush out of a little black hut cursing, with a pitchfork, and the boy runs laughing across the Missouri field—he finds a beautiful pink arrowhead and snatches it up as he runs with a flowing swoop of young bone and muscle—(his bones blend into the field, he lies dead by the wooden fence a shotgun by his side, blood on frozen red clay seeps into the winter stubble of Georgia) . . . The catfish billows out behind him . . . He comes to the fence and throws the catfish over into blood-streaked grass . . . the fish lies squirming and squawking—vaults the fence. He snatches up the catfish and disappears up a flint-studded red clay road between oaks and persimmons dropping red-brown leaves in a windy fall sunset, green and dripping in summer dawn, black against a clear winter day . . . the Old Man screams curses after him . . . his teeth fly from his mouth and whistle over the boy's head, he strains forward, his neck-cords tight as steel hoops, black blood spurts in one solid piece over the fence and he falls a fleshless mummy by the fever grass. Thorns grow through his ribs, the windows break in his hut, dusty glass-slivers in black putty—rats run over the floor and boys jack off in the dark musty bedroom on summer afternoons and eat the berries that grow from his body and bones, mouths smeared with purple-red juices . . .

The old junky has found a vein . . . blood blossoms in the dropper like a Chinese flower . . . he pushes home the heroin and the boy who jacked off fifty years ago shines immaculate through the ravaged flesh, filling the outhouse with the sweet nutty smell of young male lust . . .

How many years threaded on a needle of blood? Hands slack on lap he sits looking out at the winter dawn with the cancelled eyes of junk.

The old queer squirms on a limestone bench in Chapultepec Park as Indian adolescents walk by, arms around each other's necks and ribs, straining his dying flesh to occupy young buttocks and thighs, tight balls and spurting cocks.

Mark and Johnny sit facing each other in a vibrating chair, Johnny impaled on Mark's cock.

"All set, Johnny?"

"Turn it on."

Mark flips the switch and the chair vibrates . . . Mark tilts his head looking up at Johnny, his face remote, eyes cool and mocking on Johnny's face . . . Johnny screams and whimpers . . . His face disintegrates as if melted from within . . . Johnny screams like a mandrake, blacks out as his sperm spurts, slumps against Mark's body an angel on the nod. Mark pats Johnny's shoulder absently . . .

Room like gymnasium . . . The floor is foam rubber, covered in white silk . . . One wall is glass . . . The rising sun fills the room with pink light. Johnny is led in, hands tied, between Mary and Mark. Johnny sees the gallows and sags with a great "Ohhhhhhhhhhh!" his chin pulling down towards his cock, his legs bending at the knees. Sperm spurts, arching almost vertical in front of his face. Mark and Mary are suddenly impatient and hot . . . They push Johnny forward onto the gallows platform covered with moldy jock-straps and sweat shirts. Mark is adjusting the noose.

"Well, here you go." Mark starts to push Johnny off the platform.

MARY: "No, let me." She locks her hands behind Johnny's buttocks, puts her forehead against him, smiling into his eyes she moves back, pulling him off the platform into space . . . His face swells with blood . . . Mark reaches up with one lithe movement and snaps Johnny's neck . . . sound like a stick broken in wet towels. A shudder runs down Johnny's body . . . one foot flutters like a trapped bird . . . Mark has draped himself over a swing and mimics Johnny's twitches, closes his eyes and sticks his tongue out . . . Johnny's cock springs up and Mary guides it up her cunt, writhing against him in a fluid belly dance, groaning and shrieking with delight . . . sweat pours down her body, hair hangs over her face in wet strands. "Cut him down, Mark," she screams. Mark reaches over with a snap knife and cuts the rope, catching Johnny as he falls, easing him onto his back with Mary still impaled and writhing . . . She bites away Johnny's lips and nose and sucks out his eyes with a pop . . . She tears off great hunks of cheek . . . Now she lunches on his prick . . . Mark walks over to her and she looks up from Johnny's half-eaten genitals, her face covered with blood, eyes phosphorescent . . . Mark puts his foot on her shoulder and kicks her over on her back . . . He leaps on her, fucking her insanely . . . they roll from one end of the room to the other, pinwheel end-over-end and leap high in the air like great hooked fish.

"Let me hang you, Mark . . . Let me hang you . . . Please, Mark, let me hang you!"

"Sure baby." He pulls her brutally to her feet and pins her hands behind her.

"No, Mark!! No! No! No," she screams, shitting and pissing in terror as he drags her to the platform. He leaves her tied on the platform in a pile of old used condoms while he adjusts the rope across the room . . . and comes back carrying the noose on a silver tray. He jerks her to her feet and tightens the noose. He sticks his cock up her and waltzes around the platform and off into space swinging in a great arc . . . "Wheeeeee!" he screams, turning into Johnny. Her neck snaps. A great fluid wave undulates through her body.

Johnny drops to the floor and stands poised and alert like a young animal. He leaps about the room. With a scream of longing that shatters the glass wall he leaps out into space. Masturbating end-over-end, three thousand feet down, his sperm floating beside him, he screams all the way against the shattering blue of sky, the rising sun burning over his body like gasoline, down past great oaks and persimmons, swamp cypress and mahogany, to shatter in liquid relief in a ruined square paved with limestone. Weeds and vines grow between the stones, and rusty iron bolts three feet thick penetrate the white stone, stain it shit-brown of rust.

Johnny dowses Mary with gasoline from an obscene Chimu jar of white jade . . . He anoints his own body . . . They embrace, fall to the floor and roll under a great magnifying glass set in the roof . . . burst into flame with a cry that shatters the glass wall, roll into space, fucking and screaming through the air, burst in blood and flames and soot on brown rocks under a desert sun.

Johnny leaps about the room in agony. With a scream that shatters the glass wall he stands spread-eagle to the rising sun, blood spurting out his cock . . . a white marble god, he plummets through epileptic explosions into the old Medjoub writhe in shit and rubbish by a mud wall under a sun that scars and grabs the flesh into goose pimples . . . He is a boy sleeping against the mosque wall, ejaculates wet dreaming into a thousand cunts pink and smooth as sea-shells, feeling the delight of prickly pubic hairs slide up his cock.

Johnny and Mary in hotel room (music of "East St. Louis Toodle-oo"). Warm spring wind blows faded pink curtains in through open window . . . Frogs croak in vacant lots where corn grows and

boys catch little green garter snakes under broken limestone ste-
lae stained with shit and threaded with rusty barbed wire ...
  (*Neon*—chlorophyll green, purple, orange—flashes on and off.)
  Johnny extracts a candiru from Mary's cunt with his calipers
... He drops it into a bottle of mescal where it turns into a
maguey worm ... He gives her a douche of jungle bone-softener,
her vaginal teeth flow out mixed with blood and cysts ... Her
cunt shines fresh and sweet as spring grass ... Johnny licks
Mary's cunt, slow at first, with rising excitement parts the lips
and licks inside feeling the prickle of pubic hairs on his tumescent tongue ... Arms thrown back, breasts pointing straight up,
Mary lies transfixed with neon nails ... Johnny moves up her
body, his cock with a shining round opal of lubricant at the open
slit, slides through her pubic hairs and enters her cunt to the
hilt, drawn in by a suction of hungry flesh ... His face swells
with blood, green lights burst behind his eyes and he falls with
a scenic railway through screaming girls ...

  Damp hairs on the back of his balls dry to grass in the warm
spring wind. High jungle valley, vines creep in the window. Johnny's
cock swells, great rank buds burst out. A long tuber root creeps
from Mary's cunt, feels for the earth. The bodies disintegrate in
green explosions. The hut falls in ruins of broken stone. The boy
is a limestone statue, a plant sprouting from his cock, lips parted
in the half-smile of a junky on the nod.

* * *

The Beagle has stashed the heroin in a lottery ticket.
  One more shot—tomorrow the cure.
  The way is long. Hard-ons and bring-downs are frequent.
  It was a long time over the stony *reg* to the oasis of date palms
where Arab boys shit in the well and Rock and Roll across the sands
of muscle beach eating hot-dogs and spitting out gold teeth in
nuggets.

Toothless and strictly from the long hunger, ribs you could wash your filthy overalls on, that corrugate, they quaver down from the outrigger in Easter Island and stalk ashore on legs stiff and brittle as stilts ... they nod in club windows ... fallen into the fat of lack-need to sell a slim body.

The date palms have died of meet lack, the well filled with dried shit and mosaic of a thousand newspapers: "Russia denies ... The Home Secretary views with pathic alarm ..."

The trap was sprung at 12:02. At 12:30 the doctor went out to eat oysters, returned at 2:00 to clap the hanged man jovially on the back. "What? Aren't you dead yet? Guess I'll have to pull your leg. Haw haw! Can't let you choke at this rate—I'd get a warning from the President. And what a disgrace if the dead wagon cart you out alive. My balls would drop off with the shame of it and I apprenticed myself to an experienced ox. One two three pull."

The sail plane falls silent as erection, silent as greased glass broken by the young thief with old-woman hands and cancelled eyes of junk ... In a noiseless explosion he penetrates the broken house, stepping over the greased crystals, a clock ticks loud in the kitchen, hot air ruffles his hair, his head disintegrates in a heavy duck load ... The Old Man flips out a red shell and pirouettes around his shotgun. "Aw, shucks, fellers; tweren't nothing ... Fish in the barrel ... Money in the bank ... round-heeled boy, one greased shot brain goose and he flop in an obscene position ... Can you hear me from where you are, boy?

"I was young myself once and heard the siren call of easy money and women and tight boy-ass and land's sake don't get my blood up I am subject to tell a tale make your cock stand up and yip for the pink pearly way of young cunt or the lovely brown mucus-covered palpitating tune of the young boy-ass play your cock like a recorder ... and when you hit the prostate pearl sharp diamonds gather in the golden lad balls inexorable as a kidney stone ... Sorry I had to kill you ... The old grey mare ain't what she used to be . . . Can't run down an audience . . . got to *bring* down that house on the wing, run or sit . . . Like an old lion took bad with cavities he need that Amident toothpaste keep a feller biting fresh at all times . . . Them old lions shit sure turn boy-eater . . . And who can blame them, boys being so sweet so cold so fair in St. James Infirmary?? Now, son, don't you get rigor mortis on me. Show respect for the aging prick . . . You may be a tedious old fuck yourself some day . . . Oh, uh; I guess not . . . You have, like Housman's barefoot shameless catamite The Congealed Shropshire Ingenue set your fleet foot on the silo of change . . . But you can't kill those Shropshire boys . . . been hanged so often he resist it like a gonococcus half castrate with penicillin rallies to a hideous strength and multiplies geometric . . . So leave us cast a vote for decent acquittal and put an end to those beastly exhibitions for which the sheriff levy a pound of flesh."

SHERIFF: "I'll lower his pants for a pound, folks. Step right up. A serious and scientific exhibit concerning the locality of the Life Center. This character has nine inches, ladies and gentlemen, measure them yourself inside. Only one pound, one queer three dollar bill to see a young boy come three times at least—I never demean myself to process a eunuch—*completely against his will.* When his neck snaps sharp, this character will shit-sure come to rhythmic attention and spurt it out all over you."

The boy stands on the trap shifting his weight from one leg to the other: "Gawd! What a boy hasta put up with in this business. Sure as shit some horrible old character get physical."

Trap falls, rope sings like wind in wire, neck snaps loud and clear as a Chinese gong.

The boy cuts himself down with a switchblade, chases a screaming fag down the midway. The faggot dives through the glass of a penny arcade peep-show and rims a grinning Negro . . .

Fade Out.

(Mary, Johnny and Mark take a bow with the ropes around their necks. They are not as young as they appear in the Blue Movies ... They look tired and petulant.)

Meeting of International Conference of Technological Psychiatry

Doctor "Fingers" Schafer, the Lobotomy Kid, rises and turns on the Conferents the cold blue blast of his gaze:

"Gentlemen, the human nervous system can be reduced to a compact and abbreviated spinal column. The brain, front, middle and rear must follow the adenoid, the wisdom tooth, the appendix ... I give you my Master Work: *The Complete All American Deanxietized Man* ..."

Blast of trumpets: The Man is carried in naked by two Negro Bearers who drop him on the platform with bestial, sneering brutality ... The Man wriggles ... His flesh turns to viscid, transparent jelly that drifts away in green mist, unveiling a monster black centipede. Waves of unknown stench fill the room, searing the lungs, grabbing the stomach ...

Schafer wrings his hands sobbing: "Clarence!! How can you do this to me?? Ingrates!! Every one of them ingrates!!"

The Conferents start back muttering in dismay:

"I'm afraid Schafer has gone a bit too far ..."

"I sounded a word of warning ..."

"Brilliant chap Schafer ... but ..."

"Man will do anything for publicity ..."

"Gentlemen, this unspeakable and in every sense illegitimate child of Doctor Schafer's perverted brain must not see the light ... Our duty to the human race is clear ..."

"Man he done seen the light," said one of the Negro Bearers.

"We must stomp out the Un-American crittah," says a fat, frog-faced Southern doctor who has been drinking corn out of a mason jar. He advances drunkenly, then halts, appalled by the formidable size and menacing aspect of the centipede ...

"Fetch gasoline!" he bellows. "We gotta burn the son of a bitch like an uppity Nigra!"

"I'm not sticking my neck out, me," says a cool hip young doctor high on LSD25 ... "Why a smart D.A. could ..."

Fadeout.

"Order in the Court!"

D.A.: "Gentlemen of the jury, these 'learned gentlemen' claim that the innocent human creature they have so wantonly slain suddenly turned himself into a huge black centipede and it was 'their duty to the human race' to destroy this monster before it could, by any means at its disposal, perpetrate its kind ...

"Are we to gulp down this tissue of horse shit? Are we to take these glib lies like a greased and nameless asshole? Where *is* this wondrous centipede?

"'We have destroyed it,' they say smugly ... And I would like to remind you, Gentlemen and Hermaphrodites of the Jury, that this Great Beast"—he points to Doctor Schafer—"has, on several previous occasions, appeared in this court charged with the unspeakable crime of brain rape ... In plain English"—he pounds the rail of the jury box, his voice rises to a scream—"in plain English, Gentlemen, *forcible lobotomy* ..."

The Jury gasps ... One dies of a heart attack ... Three fall to the floor writhing in orgasms of prurience ...

The D.A. points dramatically: "He it is—he and no other—who has reduced whole provinces of our fair land to a state bordering on the far side of idiocy ... He it is who has filled great warehouses with row on row, tier on tier of helpless creatures who must have their every want attended ... 'The Drones' he calls them with a cynical leer of pure educated evil . . . Gentlemen, I say to you that the wanton murder of Clarence Cowie must not go unavenged! This foul crime shrieks like a wounded faggot for justice at least!"

The centipede is rushing about in agitation.

"Man, that mother fucker's hungry," screams one of the Bearers. "I'm getting out of here, me."

A wave of electric horror sweeps through the Conferents . . . They storm the exits screaming and clawing . . .

the market

Panorama of the City of Interzone. Opening bars of "East St. Louis Toodle-oo" . . . at times loud and clear then faint and intermittent like music down a windy street . . . The Composite City where all human potentials are spread out in a vast silent market.

Minarets, palms, mountains, jungle . . . A sluggish river jumping with vicious fish, vast weed-grown parks where boys lie in the grass, play cryptic games. Not a locked door in the City. Anyone comes into your room at any time. The Chief of Police is a Chinese who picks his teeth and listens to denunciations presented by a lunatic. Every now and then the Chinese takes the toothpick out of his mouth and looks at the end of it. Hipsters with smooth copper-colored faces lounge in doorways twisting shrunk heads on gold chains, their faces blank with an insect's unseeing calm.

Behind them, through open doors, tables and booths and bars and kitchens and baths, copulating couples on rows of brass beds, crisscross of a thousand hammocks, junkies tying up for a shot, opium smokers, hashish smokers, people eating talking bathing, back into a haze of smoke and steam.

Gaming tables where the games are played for incredible stakes. From time to time a player leaps up with a despairing cry, having lost his youth to an old man or become Latah to his opponent. But there are higher stakes than youth or Latah, games where only two players in the world know what the stakes are.

All houses in the City are joined. Houses of sod—high mountain Mongols blink in smoky doorways—houses of bamboo and teak, houses of adobe, stone and red brick, South Pacific and Maori houses, houses in trees and river boats, wood houses one hundred feet long sheltering entire tribes, houses of boxes and corrugated iron where old men sit in rotten rags cooking down canned heat, great rusty iron racks rising two hundred feet in the air from swamps and rubbish with perilous partitions built on multi-leveled platforms, and hammocks swinging over the void.

Expeditions leave for unknown places with unknown purposes. Strangers arrive on rafts of old packing crates tied together with rotten rope, they stagger in out of the jungle their eyes swollen shut from insect bites, they come down the mountain trails on cracked bleeding feet through the dusty windy outskirts of the city, where people defecate in rows along adobe walls and vultures fight over fish heads. They drop down into parks in patched parachutes . . . They are escorted by a drunken cop to register in a vast public lavatory. The data taken down is put on pegs to be used as toilet paper.

Cooking smells of all countries hang over the City, a haze of opium, hashish, the resinous red smoke of *yagé*, smell of the jungle and salt water and the rotting river and dried excrement and sweat and genitals.

High mountain flutes, jazz and bebop, one-stringed Mongol instruments, gypsy xylophones, African drums, Arab bagpipes . . .

The City is visited by epidemics of violence, and the untended dead are eaten by vultures in the streets. Albinos blink in the sun.

Boys sit in trees, languidly masturbate. People eaten by unknown diseases watch the passerby with evil, knowing eyes.

In the City Market is the Meet Café. Followers of obsolete, unthinkable trades doodling in Etruscan, addicts of drugs not yet synthesized, pushers of souped-up harmine, junk reduced to pure habit offering precarious vegetable serenity, liquids to induce Latah, Tithonian longevity serums, black marketeers of World War III, excisors of telepathic sensitivity, osteopaths of the spirit, investigators of infractions denounced by bland paranoid chess players, servers of fragmentary warrants taken down in hebephrenic shorthand charging unspeakable mutilations of the spirit, bureaucrats of spectral departments, officials of unconstituted police states, a Lesbian dwarf who has perfected operation Bang-utot, the lung erection that strangles a sleeping enemy, sellers of orgone tanks and relaxing machines, brokers of exquisite dreams and memories tested on the sensitized cells of junk sickness and bartered for raw materials of the will, doctors skilled in the treatment of diseases dormant in the black dust of ruined cities, gathering virulence in the white blood of eyeless worms feeling slowly to the surface and the human host, maladies of the ocean floor and the stratosphere, maladies of the laboratory and atomic war . . . A place where the unknown past and the emergent future meet in a vibrating soundless hum . . . Larval entities waiting for a Live One . . .

(Section describing The City and the Meet Café written in state of *yagé* intoxication . . . *yagé*, *ayahuasca*, *pilde*, *nateema* are Indian names for *Banisteriopsis caapi*, a fast-growing vine indigenous to the Amazon region. See discussion of *yagé* in Appendix.)

Notes from yagé *state:*

Images fall slow and silent like snow . . . Serenity . . . All defenses fall . . . everything is free to enter or to go out . . . Fear is simply impossible . . . A beautiful blue substance flows into me

... I see an archaic grinning face like South Pacific mask ... The face is blue purple splotched with gold ...

The room takes on aspect of Near East whorehouse with blue walls and red tasseled lamps ... I feel myself turning into a Negress, the black color silently invading my flesh ... Convulsions of lust ... My legs take on a well-rounded Polynesian substance ... Everything stirs with a writhing furtive life ... The room is Near East, Negro, South Pacific, in some familiar place I cannot locate ... *Yagé* is space-time travel ... The room seems to shake and vibrate with motion ... The blood and substance of many races, Negro, Polynesian, Mountain Mongol, Desert Nomad, Polyglot Near East, Indian, races as yet unconceived and unborn, passes through the body ... Migrations, incredible journeys through deserts and jungles and mountains (stasis and death in closed mountain valley where plants grow out of genitals, vast crustaceans hatch inside and break the shell of body) across the Pacific in an outrigger canoe to Easter Island, ...

(It occurs to me that preliminary *yagé* nausea is motion sickness of transport to *yagé* state ...)

All medicine men use it in their practice to foretell the future, locate lost or stolen objects, to diagnose and treat illness, to name the perpetrator of a crime.

Since the Indian (straitjacket for Herr Boas—trade joke—nothing so maddens an anthropologist as Primitive Man, referring to them contemptuously as "our naked cousins") does not regard any death as accidental, and they are unacquainted with their own self-destructive trends or perhaps feeling that these trends above all are subject to the manipulation of alien and hostile wills, any death is murder. The medicine man takes *yagé* and the identity of the murderer is revealed to him. As you may imagine, the deliberations of the medicine man during one of these jungle inquests give rise to certain feelings of uneasiness among his constituents.

"Let's hope Old Xiuptutol don't wig and name one of the boys."

"Take a curare and relax. We got the fix in . . ."

"But if he *wig*? Picking up on that *nateema* all the time he don't touch the ground in twenty years . . . I tell you, Boss, nobody can hit the stuff like that . . . It cooks the brains . . ."

"So we declare him incompetent . . ."

So Xiuptutol reels out of the jungle and says the boys in the Lower Tzpino territory done it, which surprises no one . . . Take it from an old *brujo*, dearie, they don't like surprises . . .

A funeral passes through the Market. Black coffin—Arabic inscriptions in filigreed silver—carried by four pallbearers. Procession of mourners singing the funeral song . . . Clem and Jody fall in beside them carrying a coffin, the corpse of a hog bursts out of it . . . The hog is dressed in a djellaba, a keif pipe juts from its mouth, one hoof holds a packet of feelthy pictures, a *mezuzzoth* hangs about its neck . . . Inscribed on the coffin: "This was the noblest Arab of them all." They sing hideous parody of the funeral song in false Arabic.

Jody can do a fake Chinese spiel that'll just kill you—like an hysterical ventriloquist's dummy. In fact, he precipitated an anti-foreign riot in Shanghai that claimed 3,000 casualties.

"Stand up, Gertie, and show respect for the local gooks."

"I suppose one *should*."

"My dear, I'm working on the most marvelous invention . . . a boy who disappears as soon as you come, leaving a smell of burning leaves and a sound effect of distant train whistles."

"Ever make sex in no gravity? Your jissom just floats out in the air like lovely ectoplasm, and female guests are subject to immaculate or at least indirect conception . . . Reminds me of an old friend of mine, one of the handsomest men I have ever known and one of the maddest and absolutely ruined by wealth. He used to go about with a water pistol shooting jissom up career women at parties. Won all his paternity suits hands down. Never use his own jissom you understand."

Fadeout . . .

"Order in the Court!"

ATTORNEY FOR A.J.: "Conclusive tests have established that my client has no uh personal connection with the uh little accident of the charming plaintiff . . . Perhaps she is preparing to emulate the Virgin Mary and conceive immaculately, naming my client as a hurumph ghostly pander . . . I am reminded of a case in fifteenth-century Holland where a young woman accused an elderly and respectable sorcerer of conjuring up a succubus who then had uh carnal knowledge of the young person in question with the under the circumstances regrettable result of pregnancy. So the sorcerer was indicted as an accomplice and rampant voyeur before during and after the fact. However, gentlemen of the jury, we no longer credit such uh legends; and a young woman attributing her uh interesting condition to the attentions of a succubus would be accounted, in these enlightened days, a romanticist or in plain English a God damned liar hehe hehe heh . . ."

And now The Prophet's Hour:

"Millions died in the mud flats. Only one blast free to lungs.

"'Eye Eye, Captain,' he said, squirting his eyes out on the deck . . . And who would put on the chains tonight? It is indicate to observe some caution in the upwind approach, the downwind having failed to turn up anything worth a rusty load . . . Señoritas are the wear this season in Hell, and I am tired with the long climb to a pulsing Vesuvius of alien pricks."

Need Orient Express out of here to no hide place(r) mines are frequent in the area . . . Every day dig a little it takes up the time . . .

Jack off phantoms whisper hot into the bone ear . . .

Shoot your way to freedom.

"*Christ?*" sneers the vicious, fruity old Saint applying pancake from an alabaster bowl . . . "That cheap ham! You think I'd demean myself to commit a miracle? . . . That one should have stood in carny . . .

"'Step right up, Marquesses and Marks, and bring the little Marks too. Good for young and old, man and beast . . . The one and only legit *Son of Man* will cure a young boy's clap with one hand—by contact alone, folks—create marijuana with the other, whilst walking on water and squirting wine out his ass . . . Now keep your distance, folks, you is subject to be irradiated by the sheer charge of this character.'

"And I knew him when, dearie . . . I recall we was doing an Impersonation Act—very high class too—in Sodom, and that is one cheap town . . . Strictly from hunger . . . Well, this citizen, this fucking Philistine wandered in from Podunk Baal or some place, called me a fuckin fruit right on the floor. And I said to him: 'Three thousand years in show business and I always keep my nose clean. Besides I don't hafta take any shit off any uncircumcised cocksucker' . . . Later he come to my dressing room and made an apology . . . Turns out he is a big physician. And he was a lovely fellah, too . . .

"*Buddha?* A notorious metabolic junky . . . Makes his own you dig. In India, where they got no sense of time, The Man is often a month late . . . 'Now let me see, is that the second or the third monsoon? I got like a meet in Ketchupore about more or less.'

"And all them junkies sitting around in the lotus posture spitting on the ground and waiting on The Man.

"So Buddha says: 'I don't hafta take this sound. I'll by God metabolize my own junk.'

"'Man, you can't do that. The Revenooers will swarm all over you.'

"'Over me they won't swarm. I gotta gimmick, see? I'm a fuckin Holy Man as of right now.'

"'Jeez, boss, what an angle.'

"'Now some citizens really wig when they make with the New Religion. These frantic individuals do not know how to come on. No class to them ... Besides, they is subject to be lynched like who wants somebody hanging around being better'n other folks? "What you trying to do, Jack, give people a bad time? ..." So we gotta play it cool, you dig, cool ... We got a take it or leave it proposition here, folks. We don't shove anything up your soul, unlike certain cheap characters who shall be nameless and are nowhere. Clear the cave for action. I'm gonna metabolize a speed ball and make with the Fire Sermon.'

"*Mohammed?* Are you kidding? He was dreamed up by the Mecca Chamber of Commerce. An Egyptian ad man on the skids from the sauce write the continuity.

"'I'll have one more, Gus. Then, by Allah, I will go home and receive a Sura ... Wait'll the morning edition hits the *souks*. I am blasting Amalgamated Images wide open.'

"The bartender looks up from his racing form. 'Yeah. And theirs will be a painful doom.'

"'Oh ... uh ... quite. Now, Gus, I'll write you a check.'

"'You are only being the most notorious paper hanger in Greater Mecca. I am not a wall, Mr. Mohammed.'

"'Well, Gus, I got like two types publicity, favorable and otherwise. You want some otherwise already? I am subject to receive a Sura concerning bartenders who extendeth not credit to those in a needy way.'

"'And theirs will be a painful doom. Sold Arabia.' He vaults over the bar. 'I'm not taking any more, Ahmed. Pick up thy Suras and walk. In fact, I'll help you. And *stay out*.'

"'I'll fix your wagon good, you unbelieving cocksucker. I'll close you up tight and dry as a junky's asshole. I'll by Allah dry up the Peninsula.'

"'It's a continent already ...'

"Leave what Confucius say stand with Little Audrey and the shaggy dogs. Lao-Tze? They scratch him already . . . And enough of these gooey saints with a look of pathic dismay as if they getting fucked up the ass and try not to pay it any mind. And why should we let some old brokendown ham tell us what wisdom is? 'Three thousand years in show business and I always keep my nose clean . . .'

"First, every Fact is incarcerate along with the male hustlers and those who desecrate the gods of commerce by playing ball in the streets, and some old white-haired fuck staggers out to give us the benefits of his ripe idiocy. Are we never to be free of this grey-beard loon lurking on every mountain top in Tibet, subject to drag himself out of a hut in the Amazon, waylay one in the Bowery? 'I've been expecting you, my son,' and he make with a silo full of corn. 'Life is a school where every pupil must learn a different lesson. And now I will unlock my Word Hoard . . . '

"'I do fear it much.'

"'Nay, nothing shall stem the rising tide.'

"'I can't stem him, boys. *Sauve qui peut.*'

"'I tell you when I leave the Wise Man I don't even feel like a human. He converting my live orgones into dead bullshit.'

"So I got an exclusive why don't I make with the live word? The word cannot be expressed direct . . . It can perhaps be indicated by mosaic of juxtaposition like articles abandoned in a hotel drawer, defined by negatives and absence . . .

"Think I'll have my stomach tucked . . . I may be old, but I'm still desirable."

(The Stomach Tuck is surgical intervention to remove stomach fat at the same time making a tuck in the abdominal wall, thus creating a flesh corset, which is, however, subject to break and spurt your horrible old guts across the floor . . . The slim and shapely F.C. models are, of course, the most dangerous. In fact, some extreme models are known as O.N.S.—One Night Stands—in the industry.

Doctor "Doodles" Rindfest states bluntly: "Bed is the most dangerous place for an F.C. man."

The F.C. theme song is "Believe Me If All These Endearing Young Charms." An F.C. partner is indeed subject to "fleet from your arms like fairy gifts fading away.")

In a white museum room full of sunlight pink nudes sixty feet high. Vast adolescent muttering.

Silver guard rail . . . chasm a thousand feet down into the glittering sunlight. Little green plots of cabbage and lettuce. Brown youths with adzes spied by the old queen across a sewage canal.

"Oh dear, I wonder if they fertilize with human excrement . . . Maybe they'll do it right now."

He flips out mother of pearl opera glasses—Aztec mosaic in the sun.

Long line of Greek lads march up with alabaster bowls of shit, empty into the limestone marl hole.

Dusty poplars shake across the red brick Plaza de Toros in the afternoon wind.

Wooden cubicles around a hot spring . . . rubble of ruined walls in a grove of cottonwoods . . . the benches worn smooth as metal by a million masturbating boys.

Greek lads white as marble fuck dog style on the portico of a great golden temple . . . naked Mugwump twangs a lute.

Walking down by the tracks in his red sweater met Sammy the Dock Keeper's son with two Mexicans.

"Hey, Skinny," he said, "want to get screwed?"

"Well . . . . . . Yeah."

On a ruined straw mattress the Mexican pulled him up on all fours—Negro boy dance around them beating out the strokes . . . sun through a knot hole pink spot lights his cock.

A waste of raw pink shame to the pastel blue horizon where vast iron mesas crash into the shattered sky,

"It's all right." The God screams through you three thousand year rusty load . . .

Hail of crystal skulls shattered the greenhouse to slivers in the winter moon . . .

The American woman has left a whiff of poison behind in the dank St. Louis garden party.

Pool covered with green slime in a ruined French garden. Huge pathic frog rises slowly from the water on a mud platform playing the clavichord.

A Sollubi rushes into the bar and starts polishing The Saint's shoes with the oil on his nose . . . The Saint kicks him petulantly in the mouth. The Sollubi screams, whirls around and shits on The Saint's pants. Then he dashes into the street. A pimp looks after him speculatively . . .

The Saint calls the manager: "Jesus, Al, what kinda creep joint you running here? My brand new fishskin *dégagées* . . ."

"I'm sorry, Saint. He slipped by me."

(The Sollubi are an untouchable caste in Arabia noted for their abject vileness. De luxe cafés are equipped with Sollubi who rim the guests while they eat—holes in the seating benches being provided for this purpose. Citizens who want to be utterly humiliated and degraded—so many people do, nowadays, hoping to jump the gun—offer themselves up for passive homosexual intercourse to an encampment of Sollubis . . . Nothing like it, they tell me . . . In fact, the Sollubi are subject to become wealthy and arrogant and lose their native vileness. What is origin of untouchable? Perhaps a fallen priest caste. In fact, untouchables perform a priestly function in taking on themselves all human vileness.)

A.J. strolls through the Market in black cape with a vulture perched on one shoulder. He stands by a table of agents.

"This you gotta hear. Boy in Los Angeles fifteen year old. Father decide it is time the boy have his first piece of ass. Boy is lying on the lawn reading comic books, father go out and say: 'Son, here's twenty dollars; I want you to go to a good whore and get a piece of ass off her.'

"So they drive to this plush jump joint, and the father say, 'All right, son. You're on your own. So ring the bell and when the woman come give her the twenty dollars and tell her you want a piece of ass.'

"'Solid, Pop.'

"So about fifteen minutes later the boy comes out:

"'Well, son, did you get a piece of ass?'

"'Yeah. This gash comes to the door, and I say I want a piece of ass and lay the double sawski on her. We go up to her trap, and she remove the dry goods. So I switch my blade and cut a big hunk off her ass, she raise a beef like I am reduce to pull off one shoe and beat her brains out. Then I hump her for kicks.'"

Only the laughing bones remain, flesh over the hills and far away with the dawn wind and a train whistle. We are not unaware of the problem, and the needs of our constituents are never out of our mind being their place of residence and who can break a ninety-nine year synapses lease?

Another installment in the adventures of Clem Snide the Private Ass Hole: "So I walk in the joint, and this female hustler sit at the bar, and I think, 'Oh God you're *poule de luxe* already.' I mean it's like I see the gash before. So I don't pay her no mind at first, then I dig she is rubbing her legs together and working her feet up behind her head shoves it down to give herself a douche job with a gadget sticks out of her nose the way a body can't help but notice."

Iris—half Chinese and half Negro—addicted to dihydro-oxy-heroin—takes a shot every fifteen minutes to which end she leaves droppers and needles sticking out all over her. The needles rust in her dry flesh, which, here and there, has grown completely over a joint to form a smooth green brown wen. On the table in front of her is a samovar of tea and a twenty-pound hamper of brown sugar. No one has ever seen her eat anything else. It is only just before a shot that she hears what anyone says or talks herself. Then she makes some flat, factual statement relative to her own person.

"My asshole is occluding."

"My cunt got terrible green juices."

Iris is one of Benway's projects. "The human body can run on sugar alone, God damn it . . . I am aware that certain of my learned colleagues, who are attempting to belittle my genius work, claim that I put vitamins and proteins into Iris's sugar clandestinely . . . I challenge these nameless assholes to crawl up out of their latrines and run a spot analysis on Iris's sugar and her tea. Iris is a wholesome American cunt. I deny categorically that she nourishes herself on semen. And let me take this opportunity to state that I am a reputable scientist, not a charlatan, a lunatic, or a pretended worker of miracles . . . I never claimed that Iris could subsist exclusive on photosynthesis . . . I did not say she could breathe in carbon dioxide and give off oxygen—I confess I have been tempted to experiment being of course restrained by my medical ethics . . . In short, the vile slanders of my creeping opponents will inevitably fall back onto them and come to roost like a homing stool pigeon."

*ordinary
men
and
women*

Luncheon of Nationalist Party on balcony overlooking the Market. Cigars, scotch, polite belches . . . The Party Leader strides about in a djellaba smoking a cigar and drinking scotch. He wears expensive English shoes, loud socks, garters, muscular hairy legs—overall effect of successful gangster in drag.

P.L. (pointing dramatically): "Look out there. What do you see?"

LIEUTENANT: "Huh? Why, I see the Market."

P.L.: "No you don't. You see men and women. *Ordinary* men and women going about their ordinary everyday tasks. Leading their ordinary lives. That's what we need . . ."

A street boy climbs over the balcony rail.

LIEUTENANT: "No, we do not want to buy any used condoms! Cut!"

P.L.: "Wait! . . . Come in, my boy. Sit down . . . Have a cigar . . . Have a drink." He paces around the boy like an aroused tom cat.

P.L.: "What do you think about the French?"

"Huh?"

P.L.: "The French. The Colonial bastards who is sucking your live corpuscles."

"Look mister. It cost two hundred francs to suck my corpuscule. Haven't lowered my rates since the year of the rinderpest when all the tourists died, even the Scandinavians."

P.L.: "You see? This is pure uncut boy in the street."

LIEUTENANT: "You sure can pick 'em, boss."

"M.I. never misses."

P.L.: "Now look, kid, let's put it this way. The French have dispossessed you of your birthright."

"You mean like Friendly Finance? . . . They got this toothless Egyptian eunuch does the job. They figure he arouse less antagonism, you dig, he always take down his pants to show you his condition. 'Now I'm just a poor old eunuch trying to keep up my habit. Lady, I'd like to give you an extension on that artificial kidney, I got a job to do is all . . . Disconnect her, boys.'

"He shows his gums in a feeble snarl . . . 'Not for nothing am I known as Nellie the Repossessor.'

"So they disconnect my own mother, the sainted old gash, and she swell up and turn black and the whole *souk* stink of piss and the neighbors beef to the Board of Health and my father say: 'It's the will of Allah. She won't piss any more of my loot down the drain.'

"Sick people disgust me already. When some citizen start telling me about his cancer of the prostate or his rotting septum make with that purulent discharge I tell him: 'You think I am innarested to hear about your horrible old condition? I am not innarested at all.'"

P.L.: "All *right*. Cut . . . You hate the French, don't you?"

"Mister, I hate everybody. Doctor Benway says it's metabolic, I got this condition of the blood . . . Arabs and Americans got it special . . . Doctor Benway is concocting this serum."

P.L.: "Benway is an infiltrating Western Agent."

LT. 1: "A rampant French Jew . . ."

LT. 2: "A hog-balled, black-assed Communist Jew Nigger."

P.L.: "Shut up, you fool!"

LT. 2: "Sorry, Chief. I am after being stationed in Pigeon Hole."

P.L.: "Don't go near Benway." (Aside: "I wonder if this will go down. You never know how primitive they are . . .") "Confidentially he's a black magician."

LT. 1: "He's got this resident *djinn*."

"Uhuh . . . Well I got a date with a high-type American client. A real classy fellah."

P.L.: "Don't you know it's shameful to peddle your ass to the alien unbelieving pricks?"

"Well that's a point of view. Have fun."

P.L.: "Likewise."

Exit boy.

P.L.: "They're hopeless I tell you. Hopeless."

LT. 1: "What's with this serum?"

P.L.: "I don't know, but it sounds ominous. We better put a telepathic direction finder on Benway. The man's not to be trusted. Might do almost anything . . . Turn a massacre into a sex orgy . . .

LT. 1: "Or a joke."

P.L.: "Precisely. Arty type . . . No principles . . ."

AMERICAN HOUSEWIFE: (opening a box of Lux): "Why don't it have an electric eye the box flip open when it see me and hand itself to the Automat Handy Man he should put it inna water already . . . The Handy Man is outa control since Thursday, he been getting physical with me and I didn't put it in his combination at all . . . And the Garbage Disposal Unit snapping at me, and the nasty old Mixmaster keep trying to get up under my dress . . . I got the most awful cold, and my intestines is all constipated . . . I'm gonna put it in the Handy Man's combination he should administer me a high colonic awready."

SALESMAN (he is something between an aggressive Latah and a timid Sender): "Recollect when I am traveling with K.E., hottest idea man in the gadget industry.

"'Think of it!' he snaps. 'A cream separator in your own kitchen!'

"'K.E., my brain reels at the thought.'

"'It's five, maybe ten, yes, maybe twenty years away . . . But it's coming.'

"'I'll wait, K.E. No matter how long it is, I'll wait. When the priority numbers are called up yonder I'll be there.'

"It was K.E. put out the Octopus Kit for Massage Parlors, Barber Shops and Turkish Baths, with which you can administer a high colonic, an unethical massage, a shampoo, whilst cutting the client's toenails and removing his blackheads. And the M.D.'s Can Do Kit for busy practitioners will take out your appendix, tuck in a hernia, pull a wisdom tooth, ectomize your piles and circumcise you. Well, K.E. is such an atomic salesman if he runs out of Octopus Kits he is subject, by sheer charge, to sell an M.D. Can

Do to a barber shop and some citizen wakes up with his piles cut out . . .

"'Jesus, Homer, what kinda creep joint you running here? I been gang fucked.'

"'Well, landsake, Si, I was just aiming to administer our complimentary high colonic free and gratis on Thanksgiving Day. K.E. musta sold me the wrong kit again . . . '"

MALE HUSTLER: "What a boy hasta put up with in this business. Gawd! The propositions I get you wouldn't believe it . . . They wanta play Latah, they wanta merge with my protoplasm, they want a replica cutting, they wanta suck my orgones, they wanta take over my past experience and leave old memories that disgust me . . .

"I am fucking this citizen so I think, 'A straight John at last'; but he comes to a climax and turns himself into some kinda awful crab . . . I told him, 'Jack, I don't hafta stand still for such a routine like this . . . You can take that business to Walgreen's.' Some people got no class to them. Another horrible old character just sits there and telepathizes and creams in his dry goods. So nasty."

The bum boys fall back in utter confusion to the brink of the Soviet network where Cossacks hang partisans to the wild wail of bagpipes and the boys march up Fifth Avenue to be met by Jimmy Walkover with the keys to The Kingdom and no strings attached carry them loose in your pocket . . .

Why so pale and wan, fair bugger? Smell of dead leeches in a rusty tin can latch onto that live wound, suck out the body and blood and bones of Jeeeeesus, leave him paralyzed from the waist down.

Yield up thy forms, boy, to thy sugar daddy got the exam three years early and know all the answer books fix the World Series.

Slunk traffickers tail a pregnant cow to her labor. The farmer declares a *couvade*, rolls screaming in bullshit. The veterinarian wrestles with a cow skeleton. The traffickers machine-gun each other, dodging through the machinery and silos, storage bins, haylofts and mangers of a vast red barn. The calf is born. The forces of death melt in morning. Farm boy kneels reverently—his throat pulses in the rising sun.

Junkies sitting on the courthouse steps, waiting on The Man. Red Necks in black Stetsons and faded Levis tie a Nigra boy to an old iron lamppost and cover him with burning gasoline ... The junkies rush over and draw the flesh smoke deep into their aching lungs ... They really got relief ...

THE COUNTY CLERK: "So there I was sitting in front of Jed's store over in Cunt Lick my peter standing up straight as a jack pine under my Levis just a-pulsin' in the sun ... Weell, old Doc Scranton walks by, a good old boy too, there's not a finer man in this valley than Doc Scranton. He's got a prolapsed asshole and when he wants to get screwed he'll pass you his ass on three feet of in-tes-tine ... If he's a mind to it he can drop out a piece of gut reaches from his office clear over to Roy's Beer Place, and it go feelin' around lookin' for a peter, just a-feelin' around like a blind worm ... So old Doc Scranton sees my peter and he stops like a pointin' dog and he says to me, 'Luke, I can take your pulse from here.'"

Brubeck and Young Seward fight with hog castrators through barns and cages and yipping kennels ... whinnying horses bare great yellow teeth, cows bellow, dogs howl, copulating cats scream like babies, a pen of huge hogs, spines bristling, give a great Bronx cheer. Brubeck the Unsteady has fallen to the sword of Young Seward, clutches at blue intestines spurting from an eight-inch gash. Young Seward cuts off Brubeck's cock and holds it pulsing in the smoky rose sunrise ...

Brubeck screams ... subway brakes spit ozone ...

"Stand back, folks ... Stand back."

"They say somebody pushed him."

"He was weaving around unsteady like he couldn't see good."

"Too much smoke in the eyes, I guess."

Mary the Lesbian Governess has slipped to the pub floor on a bloody Kotex ... A three-hundred-pound fag tramples her to death with pathic whinnies ...

He sings in hideous falsetto:

He is trampling out the vintage where the grapes of wrath are stored,
He has loosed the fateful lightning of his terrible swift sword.

He pulls a gilded wooden sword and chops the air. His corset flies off and whistles into the dart board.

The old bullfighter's sword buckles on bone and whistles into the heart of the *espontáneo*, pins his unconsummate valor to the stands.

"So this elegant faggot comes to New York from Cunt Lick, Texas, and he is the most piss elegant fag of them all. He is taken up by old women of the type batten on young fags, toothless old predators too weak and too slow to run down other prey. Old moth-eaten tigress shit sure turn into a fag eater ... So this citizen, being an arty and crafty fag, begins making costume jewelry and jewelry sets. Every rich old gash in Greater New York wants he should do her sets, and he is making money, 21, El Morocco, Stork, but no time for sex, and all the time worrying about his rep ... He begins playing the horses, supposed to be something manly about gambling God knows why, and he figures it will build him up to be seen at the track. Not many fags play the horses, and those that play lose more than the others, they are lousy gamblers plunge in a losing streak and hedge when they win ... which being the pattern of their lives ... Now every child knows there is one law of gambling: winning and losing come in streaks. Plunge when you win, fold when you lose. (I once knew a fag dip into the till—not the whole two thousand at once on the nose, win or Sing Sing. Not our Gertie ... Oh no a deuce at a time ...)

"So he loses and loses and lose some more. One day he is about to put a rock in a set when the obvious occur ... 'Of course, I'll replace it later.' Famous last words. So all that winter, one after the other, the diamonds, emeralds, pearls, rubies and star sapphires of the *haut monde* go in hock and replaced by queer replicas ...

"So the opening night of the Met this old hag appear as she thinks resplendent in her diamond tiara. So this other old whore approach and say, 'Oh, Miggles, you're so smart ... to leave the real ones at home ... I mean we're simply mad to go around tempting fate.'

"'You're mistaken, my dear. These *are* real.'

"'Oh but Miggles dahling, they're *not* ... I mean ask your jeweler ... Well just ask *anybody*. Haaaaaa.'

"So a Sabbath is hastily called. (Lucy Bradshinkel, look to thy emeralds.) All these old witches examining their rocks like a citizen find leprosy on himself.

"'My chicken blood ruby!'

"'My black oopalls!' Old bitch marry so many times so many gooks and spics she don't know her accent from her ass ...

"'My stah sahphire!' shriek a *poule de luxe*. 'Oh it's all so awful!'

"'I mean they are strictly from Woolworth's ...'

"'There's only one thing to do. I'm going to call the police,' says a strong-minded, outspoken old thing; and she clump across the floor on her low heels and calls the fuzz.

"Well, the faggot draws a deuce; and in the box he meets this cat who is some species of cheap hustler, and love sets in or at least a facsimile thereof convince the parties inna first and second parts. As continuity would have it, they are sprung at the same time more

or less and take up residence in a flat on the Lower East Side . . .
And cook in and both are working legit modest jobs . . . So Brad
and Jim know happiness for the first time.

"Enter the powers of evil . . . Lucy Bradshinkel has come to
say all is forgiven. She has faith in Brad and wants to set him up
in a studio. Of course, he will have to move to the East Sixties
. . . 'This place is impossible, dahling; and your *friend* . . . ' And a
safe mob wants Jim back to drive a car. This is a step up, you
dig? Offer from citizens hardly see him before.

"Will Jim go back to crime? Will Brad succumb to the blan-
dishments of an aging vampire, a ravening Maw? . . . Needless to
say, the forces of evil are routed, and exit with ominous snarls
and mutterings.

"'The boss isn't going to like this.'

"'I don't know why I ever wasted my time with you, you cheap,
vulgar little fairy.'

"The boys stand at the tenement window, their arms around
each other, looking at the Brooklyn Bridge. A warm spring wind
ruffles Jim's black curls and the fine hennaed hair of Brad.

"'Well, Brad, what's for supper?'

"'You just go in the other room and wait.' Playfully he shoos
Jim out of the kitchen, and puts on his apron.

"Dinner is Lucy Bradshinkel's cunt *saignant* cooked in Kotex
papillon. The boys eat happily looking into each other's eyes.
Blood runs down their chins."

Let the dawn blue as a flame cross the city . . . The backyards are
clean of fruit, and the ash pits give up their hooded dead . . .

"Could you show me the way to Tipperary, lady?"

Over the hills and far away to Blue Grass . . . Across the bone
meal of lawn to the frozen pond where suspended goldfish wait
for the spring Squaw Man.

The screaming skull rolls up the back stairs to bite off the cock of erring husband taking dour advantage of his wife's earache to do that which is inconvenient. The young landlubber dons a southwester, beats his wife to death in the shower . . .

BENWAY: "Don't take it so hard, kid . . . *Jedermann macht eine kleine Dummheit.*" (Everyone makes a little dumbness.)

SCHAFER: "I tell you I can't escape a feeling . . . well, of *evil* about this."

BENWAY: "Balderdash, my boy . . . We're scientists . . . Pure scientists. Disinterested research and damned be him who cries 'Hold, *too much!*' Such people are no better than party poops."

SCHAFER: "Yes, yes, of course . . . and yet . . . I can't get that stench out of my lungs . . ."

BENWAY (irritably): "None of us can . . . Never smelled anything remotely like it . . . Where was I? Oh yes, what would be result of administering curare plus iron lung during acute mania? Possibly the subject, unable to discharge his tensions in motor activity, would succumb on the spot like a jungle rat. Interesting cause of death, what?"

Schafer is not listening. "You know," he says impulsively, "I think I'll go back to plain old-fashioned surgery. The human body is scandalously inefficient. Instead of a mouth and an anus to get out of order why not have one all-purpose hole to eat *and* eliminate? We could seal up nose and mouth, fill in the stomach, make an air hole direct into the lungs where it should have been in the first place . . ."

BENWAY: "Why not one all-purpose blob? Did I ever tell you about the man who taught his asshole to talk? His whole abdomen would move up and down you dig farting out the words. It was unlike anything I ever heard.

"This ass talk had a sort of gut frequency. It hit you right down there like you gotta go. You know when the old colon gives you the elbow and it feels sorta cold inside, and you know all you have to do is turn loose? Well this talking hit you right down there, a bubbly, thick stagnant sound, a sound you could *smell*.

"This man worked for a carnival you dig, and to start with it was like a novelty ventriloquist act. Real funny, too, at first. He had a number he called 'The Better 'Ole' that was a scream, I tell you. I forget most of it but it was clever. Like, 'Oh I say, are you still down there, old thing?'

"'Nah! I had to go relieve myself.'

"After a while the ass started talking on its own. He would go in without anything prepared and his ass would ad-lib and toss the gags back at him every time.

"Then it developed sort of teeth-like little raspy incurving hooks and started eating. He thought this was cute at first and built an act around it, but the asshole would eat its way through his pants and start talking on the street, shouting out it wanted equal rights. It would get drunk, too, and have crying jags nobody loved it and it wanted to be kissed same as any other mouth. Finally it talked all the time day and night, you could hear him for blocks screaming at it to shut up, and beating it with his fist, and sticking candles up it, but nothing did any good and the asshole said to him: 'It's you who will shut up in the end. Not me. Because we don't need you around here any more. I can talk and eat *and* shit.'

"After that he began waking up in the morning with a transparent jelly like a tadpole's tail all over his mouth. This jelly was what the scientists call un-D.T., Undifferentiated Tissue, which can grow into any kind of flesh on the human body. He would tear it off his mouth and the pieces would stick to his hands like burning gasoline jelly and grow there, grow anywhere on him a glob of it fell. So finally his mouth sealed over, and the whole head would have amputated spontaneous—(did you know there is a condition occurs in parts of Africa and only among Negroes where the little toe amputates spontaneously?)—except for the *eyes*, you dig. That's one thing the asshole *couldn't* do was see. It needed the eyes. But nerve connections were blocked and infiltrated and atrophied so the brain couldn't give orders any more. It was trapped in the skull, sealed off. For a while you could see the silent, helpless suffering of the brain behind the eyes, then finally the brain must have died, because the eyes *went out*, and there was no more feeling in them than a crab's eye on the end of a stalk.

"That's the sex that passes the censor, squeezes through between bureaus, because there's always a space *between*, in popular songs and Grade B movies, giving away the basic American rottenness, spurting out like breaking boils, throwing out globs of that un-D.T. to fall anywhere and grow into some degenerate cancerous life-form, reproducing a hideous random image. Some would be entirely made of penis-like erectile tissue, others viscera barely covered over with skin, clusters of three and four eyes together, crisscross of mouth and assholes, human parts shaken around and poured out any way they fell.

"The end result of complete cellular representation is cancer. Democracy is cancerous, and bureaus are its cancer. A bureau takes root anywhere in the state, turns malignant like the Narcotic Bureau, and grows and grows, always reproducing more of its own kind, until it chokes the host if not controlled or excised. Bureaus cannot live without a host, being true parasitic organisms. (A cooperative on the other hand *can* live without the state. That is the road to follow. The building up of independent units to meet needs of the people who participate in the functioning of the unit. A bureau operates on opposite principle of *inventing needs* to justify its existence.) Bureaucracy is wrong as a cancer, a turning away from the human evolutionary direction of infinite potentials and differentiation and independent spontaneous action to the complete parasitism of a virus.

"(It is thought that the virus is a degeneration from more complex life-form. It may at one time have been capable of independent life. Now has fallen to the borderline between living and dead matter. It can exhibit living qualities only in a host, by using the life of another—the renunciation of life itself, a *falling* towards inorganic, inflexible machine, towards dead matter.)

"Bureaus die when the structure of the state collapses. They are as helpless and unfit for independent existences as a displaced tapeworm, or a virus that has killed the host.

"In Timbuktu I once saw an Arab boy who could play a flute with his ass, and the fairies told me he was really an individual in bed. He could play a tune up and down the organ hitting the most erogenously sensitive spots, which are different on everyone, of course. Every lover had his special theme song which was perfect for him and rose to his climax. The boy was a great artist when it came to improvising new combines and special climaxes, some of them notes in the unknown, tie-ups of seeming discords that would suddenly break through each other and crash together with a stunning, hot sweet impact."

"Fats" Terminal has organized a purple-assed baboon stick from motorcycles.

The Huntsmen have gathered for the Hunt Breakfast in The Swarm Bar, a hang-out for elegant pansies. The Huntsmen strut about with imbecile narcissism in black leather jackets and studded belts, flexing their muscles for the fags to feel. They all wear enormous falsie baskets. Every now and then one of them throws a fag to the floor and pisses on him.

They are drinking Victory Punch, compounded of paregoric, Spanish Fly, heavy black rum, Napoleon brandy and canned heat. The punch is served from a great, hollow, gold baboon, crouched in snarling terror, snapping at a spear in his side. You twist the baboon's balls and punch runs out his cock. From time to time hot hors-d'oeuvres pop out the baboon's ass with a loud farting noise. When this happens the Huntsmen roar with bestial laughter, and the fags shriek and twitch.

Master of the Hunt is Captain Everhard, who was drummed out of the Queen's 69th for palming a jockstrap in a game of strip poker. Motorcycles careening, jumping, overturning. Spitting, shrieking, shitting baboons fighting hand to hand with the Huntsmen. Riderless cycles scrabbling about in the dust like crippled insects, attacking baboon and Huntsman . . .

The Party Leader rides in triumph through yipping crowds. A dignified old man shits at sight of him and tries to sacrifice himself under the wheels of the car.

Party Leader: "Don't sacrifice your old dried-up person under the wheels of my brand new Buick Roadmaster Convertible with white-walled tires, hydraulic windows and all the trimmings. It's a chip Arab trick—look to thy accent, Ivan—save it for fertilizer . . . We refer you to the conservation department to consummate your swell purpose . . ."

The washing boards are down, and the sheets are sent to the Laundromat lose those guilty stains—Emmanuel prophesies a Second Coming . . .

There's a boy across the river with an ass like a peach; alas I was no swimmer and lost my Clementine.

The junky sits with needle poised to the message of blood, and the con man palpates the Mark with fingers of rotten ectoplasm . . .

Fadeout.

Dr. Berger's Mental Health Hour.

Technician: "Now listen, I'll say it again, and I'll say it slow. 'Yes.'" He nods. "And make with the smile . . . The *smile*." He shows his false teeth in hideous parody of a toothpaste ad. "'We like apple pie, and we like each other. It's just as simple as that'—

and make it sound *simple*, country simple ... Look bovine, whyncha? You want the Switchboard again? Or the pail?"

Subject (Cured Criminal Psychopath): "No! ... No! ... What's this bovine?"

Technician: "Look like a cow."

Subject—with cow's head: "Moooo Moooo."

Technician (starting back): "Too much!! No! Just look square, you dig, like a nice popcorn John ... "

Subject: "A mark?"

Technician: "Well, not exactly a mark. Not enough larceny in this citizen. He is after light concussion ... You know the type. Telepathic sender and receiver excised. The Serviceman Look ... Action, camera."

Subject: "Yes, we like apple pie." His stomach rumbles loud and long. Streamers of saliva hang off his chin ...

Dr. Berger looks up from some notes. He look like Jewish owl with black glasses, the light hurt his eyes: "I think he is an unsuitable subject ... See he reports to Disposal."

Technician: "Well, we could cut that rumble out of the sound track, stick a drain in his mouth and ... "

Dr. Berger: "No ... He's *unsuitable*." He looks at the subject with distaste as if he commit some terrible *faux pas* like look for crabs in Mrs. Worldly's drawing room.

Technician (resigned and exasperated): "Bring in the cured swish."

The cured homosexual is brought in ... He walks through invisible contours of hot metal. He sits in front of the camera and starts arranging his body in a countrified sprawl. Muscles move into place like autonomous parts of a severed insect. Blank stupidity blurs and softens his face ...

"Yes," he nods and smiles, "we like apple pie and we like each other. It's just as simple as that." He nods and smiles and nods and smiles and—

"Cut! . . ." screams the Technician. The cured homosexual is led out nodding and smiling.

"Play it back."

The Artistic Adviser shakes his head: "It lacks something. To be specific, it lacks health."

Berger (leaps to his feet): "Preposterous! It's health incarnate! . . ."

Artistic Adviser (primly): "Well if you have anything to enlighten me on this subject I'll be very glad to hear it, *Doctor* Berger . . . If you with your brilliant mind can carry the project alone, I don't know why you *need* an Art Advisor at *all*." He exits with hand on hip singing softly: "I'll be around when you're gone."

Technician: "Send in the cured writer . . . He's got *what*? Buddhism? . . . Oh, he can't talk. Say so at first, whyncha?" He turns to Berger: "The writer can't talk . . . Overliberated, you might say. Of course we can dub him . . ."

Berger (sharply): "No, that wouldn't do at all . . . Send in someone else."

Technician: "Those two was my white-haired boys. I put in a hundred hours overtime on those kids for which I am not yet compensate . . ."

Berger: "Apply triplicate . . . Form 6090."

Technician: "You telling me how to apply already? Now look, Doc, you say something once: 'To speak of a healthy homosexual it's like how can a citizen be perfectly healthy with terminal cirrhosis.' Remember?"

Berger: "Oh yes. Very well put, of course," he snarls viciously. "I don't pretend to be a *writer*." He spits the word out with such ugly hate that the Technician reels back appalled . . .

Technician (aside): "I can't bear the smell of him. Like old rotten replica cultures . . . Like the farts of a man-eating plant . . . Like Schafer's hurumph—" (parodies academic manner) "—Strange Serpent . . . What I'm getting at, Doc, is how can you expect a body to be healthy with its brains washed out? . . . Or put it another way. Can a subject be healthy *in absentia* by proxy already?"

BERGER (leaps up): "I got the health! . . . All the health! Enough health for the whole world, the whole fuckin world!! I cure everybody!"

The Technician looks at him sourly. He mixes a bicarbonate of soda and drinks it and belches into his hand. "Twenty years I've been a martyr to dyspepsia."

Lovable Lu your brainwashed poppa say: "I'm strictly for fish, and I luuuuuve it . . . Confidentially, girls, I use Steely Dan's Yokohama, wouldn't you? Danny Boy never lets you down. Besides it's more hygienic that way and avoids all kinda awful contacts leave a man paralyzed from the waist down. Women have poison juices . . ."

"So I told him, I said: '*Doctor* Berger, don't think you can pass your tired old brainwashed belles on me. I'm the oldest faggot in the Upper Baboon's Asshole . . .'"

Switch envelopes in clip clap joint where fraudulent girls put the B on you in favor of the House 666 and there is no health in them clap broads rotten to the apple corer of my unconsummate cock. Who shot Cock Robin? . . . The sparrow falls to my trustful Webley, and a drop of blood gathers at his beak . . .

Lord Jim has turned bright yellow in the woe withered moon of morning like white smoke against the blue stuff, and shirts whip in a cold spring wind on limestone cliffs across the river, Mary, and the dawn is broken in two pieces like Dillinger on the lamster way to the Biograph. Smell of neon and atrophied gangsters, and the criminal manqué nerves himself to crack a pay toilet sniffing ammonia in a bucket . . . "A caper," he says. "I'll pull this capon I mean caper."

PARTY LEADER (mixing another scotch): "The next riot goes off like a football play. We have imported a thousand bone fed, blue ribbon Latahs from Indochina . . . All we need is one riot leader for the whole unit." His eyes sweep the table.

LIEUTENANT: "But, chief, can't we get them started and they imitate each other like a chained reaction?"

The Diseuse undulate through the Market: "What's a Latah do when he's alone?"

P.L.: "That's a technical point. We'll have to consult Benway. Personally, I think someone should follow through on the whole operation."

"I do not know," he said for lack of the requisite points and ratings to secure the appointment.

"They have no feelings," said Doctor Benway, slashing his patient to shreds. "Just reflexes . . . I urge distraction."

"The age of consent is when they learn to talk."

"May all your troubles be little ones as one child molester say to the other."

"It's really ominous, my dear, when they start trying on your clothes and give you those doppelgänger kicks . . ."

Frantic queen trying to claw sport jacket off departing boy.

"My two hundred dollar cashmere jacket," she screeches . . .

"So he has an affair with this Latah, he wants to dominate someone complete the silly old thing . . . The Latah imitates all his expressions and mannerisms and simply sucks all the persona right out of him like a sinister ventriloquist's dummy . . . 'You've taught me everything you are . . . I need a new amigo.' And poor Bubu can't answer for himself, having no self left."

JUNKY: "So there we are in this no-horse town strictly from cough syrup."

PROFESSOR: "Coprophilia . . . gentlemen . . . might be termed the hurumph . . . redundant vice . . ."

"Twenty years an artist in the blue movies and I never sink so low as fake an orgasm."

"No good junky cunt hang up her unborn child ... Women are no good, kid."

"I mean this dead level conscious sex ... Might as well take your old clothes to the Laundromat ..."

"And right in the heat of passion he says, 'Do you have an extra shoe tree?'"

"She tell me how forty Arabs drag her into a mosque and rape her presumably in sequence ... Though they're bad to push— 'all right, end of the line, Ali.' Really, my pets, most distasteful routine I ever listen to. I was after being raped myself by a pride of rampant bores."

A group of sour Nationalists sits in front of the Sargasso sneering at the queens and jabbering in Arabic ... Clem and Jody sweep in dressed like The Capitalist in a Communist mural.

CLEM: "We have come to feed on your backwardness."

JODY: "In the words of the Immortal Bard, to batten on these Moors."

NATIONALIST: "Swine! Filth! Sons of dogs! Don't you realize my people are hungry?"

CLEM: "That's the way I like to see them."

The Nationalist drops dead, poisoned by hate ... Doctor Benway rushes up: "Stand back everybody, give me air." He takes a blood sample. "Well, that's all I can do. When you gotta go you gotta go."

The traveling queer Christmas tree burns bright on the rubbish heaps of home where boys jack off in the school toilet— how many young spasms on that old oaken seat worn smooth as gold ...

Sleep long in the valley of the Red River where cobwebs hang black windows and boy bones ...

Two Negro fags shriek at each other:

FAG 1: "Shut up, you cheap granuloma gash ... You known as Loathsome Lu in the trade."

Diseuse: "The girl with the innaresting groin."

Fag 2: "Meow. Meow." He slips on leopard skin and iron claws . . .

Fag 1: "Oh oh. A Society Woman." He flees screaming through the Market, pursued by the grunting, growling transvestite . . .

Clem trips a spastic cripple and takes his crutches . . . He does a hideous parody twitching and drooling . . .

Riot noises in the distance—a thousand hysterical Pomeranians. Shop shutters slam like guillotines. Drinks and trays hang in the air as the patrons are whisked inside by the suction of panic.

Chorus of Fags: "We'll all be raped. I know it, I know it." They rush into a drugstore and buy a case of K.Y.

Party Leader (holding up his hand dramatically): "The voice of the People."

Pearson the Money Changeling comes a-cropping the short grass seized by the extortionate commandant of Karma, hiding in a vacant lot with the garter snakes, to be sniffed out by the scrutable dog . . .

The Market is empty except for an old drunkard of indeterminate nationality passed out with his head in a pissoir. The rioters erupt into the Market yipping and screaming "Death to the French!" and tear the drunkard to pieces.

Salvador Hassan (squirming at a keyhole): "Just look at those expressions, the whole beautiful protoplasmic being *all exactly alike*." He dances the Liquefactionist Jig.

Whimpering queen falls to the floor in an orgasm. "Oh God it's too exciting. Like a million hot throbbing cocks."

Benway: "Like to run a blood test on those boys."

A portentously inconspicuous man, grey beard and grey face and shabby brown djellaba, sings in slight unplaceable accent without opening his lips: "Oh you dolls, you great big beautiful dolls."

Squads of police with thin lips, big noses and cold grey eyes move into the Market from every entrance street. They club and kick the rioters with cold, methodical brutality.

The rioters have been carted away in trucks. The shutters go up and the citizens of Interzone step out into the square littered with teeth and sandals and slippery with blood.

The sea chest of the dead man is in the Embassy, and the vice consul breaks the news to mother.

There is no ... Morning ... Daybreak ... *n'existe plus* ... If I knew I'd be glad to tell you. Either way is a bad move to the East Wing ... He is gone through an invisible door ... Not here ... You can look any place ... No good ... *No bueno* ... Hustling myself ... C'lom Fliday.

(Note: Old time, veteran Schmeckers—faces beaten by grey junk weather—will remember ... In 1920s a lot of Chinese pushers around found The West so unreliable, dishonest and wrong, they all packed in, so when an Occidental junky came to score, they say:

"No glot ... C'lom Fliday ...")

*islam
incorporated
and the parties
of interzone*

I was working for an outfit known as Islam Inc., financed by A.J., the notorious Merchant of Sex, who scandalized international society when he appeared at the Duc de Ventre's ball as a walking penis covered by a huge condom emblazoned with the A.J. motto: "They Shall Not Pass."

"Rather bad taste, old boy," said the duke.

To which A.J. replied: "Up yours with Interzone K.Y." The

reference is to the K.Y. scandal which was still in a larval state at that time. A.J.'s repartee often refers to future events. He is a master of the delayed squelch.

Salvador Hassan O'Leary, the After Birth Tycoon, is also involved. That is, one of his subsidiary companies has made unspecified contributions, and one of his subsidiary personalities is attached to the organization in an advisory capacity without in any way committing himself to, or associating himself with, the policies, actions or objectives of Islam Inc. Mention should also be made of Clem and Jody, the Ergot Brothers, who decimated the Republic of Hassan with poison wheat, Autopsy Ahmed, and Hepatitis Hal, the fruit and vegetable broker.

A rout of Mullahs and Muftis and Muezzins and Caids and Glaouis and Sheiks and Sultans and Holy Men and representatives of every conceivable Arab party make up the rank and file and attend the actual meetings from which the higher-ups prudently abstain. Though the delegates are carefully searched at the door, these gatherings invariably culminate in riots. Speakers are often doused with gasoline and burned to death, or some uncouth desert Sheik opens up on his opponents with a machine gun he had concealed in the belly of a pet sheep. Nationalist martyrs with grenades up the ass mingle with the assembled conferents and suddenly explode, occasioning heavy casualties ... And there was the occasion when President Ra threw the British Prime Minister to the ground and forcibly sodomized him, the spectacle being televised to the entire Arab World. Wild yips of joy were heard in Stockholm. Interzone has an ordinance forbidding a meeting of Islam Inc. within five miles of the city limits.

A.J.—he is actually of obscure Near East extraction—had at one time come on like an English gentleman. His English accent waned with the British Empire, and after World War II he became an American by Act of Congress. A.J. is an agent like me, but for whom or for what no one has ever been able to discover. It is rumored that he represents a trust of giant insects from another galaxy ... I believe he is on the Factualist side (which I also represent); of course he could be a Liquefaction Agent (the Liquefaction program involves the eventual merging of everyone into One Man by a process of protoplasmic absorption). You can never be sure of anyone in the industry.

A.J.'s cover story? An international playboy and harmless practical joker. It was A.J. who put the piranha fish in Lady Sutton-Smith's swimming pool, and dosed the punch with a mixture of *yagé*, hashish and yohimbine during a Fourth of July reception at the U.S. Embassy, precipitating an orgy. Ten prominent citizens—American, of course—subsequently died of shame. Dying of shame is an accomplishment peculiar to Kwakiutl Indians and Americans—others simply say "*Zut alors*" or "*Son cosas de la vida*" or "Allah fucked me, the All Powerful ..."

And when the Cincinnati Anti-Fluoride Society met to toast their victory in pure spring water, all their teeth dropped out on the spot.

"And I say unto you, brothers and sisters of the Anti-Fluoride movement, we have this day struck such a blow for purity as will never call a retreat ... Out, I say, with the filthy foreign fluorides! We will sweep this fair land sweet and clean as a young boy's tensed flank ... I will now lead you in our theme song, 'The Old Oaken Bucket.'"

A well head is lighted by fluorescent lights that play over it in hideous jukebox colors. The Anti-Fluorides file past the well singing as each dips up a drink from the oaken bucket ...

> The old oaken bucket, the gold oaken bucket
> The glublthulunnubbeth ...

A.J. had tampered with the water, inserting a South American vine that turns the gums to mush.

(I hear about this vine from an old German prospector who is dying of uremia in Pasto, Colombia. Supposed to grow in the Putumayo area. Never located any. Didn't try very hard ... The same citizen tells me about a bug like a big grasshopper known as the Xiucutl: "Such a powerful aphrodisiac if one flies on you and you can't get a woman right away you will die. I have seen the Indians running around pulling themselves off from the contact with this animal." Unfortunately I never score for a Xiucutl ...)

On opening night of the New York Metropolitan, A.J., protected by bug repellent, released a swarm of Xiucutls.

Mrs. Vanderbligh swatting at a Xiucutl: "Oh! ... Oh! ... OOOOOOOOOOOH!!!" Screams, breaking glass, ripping cloth. A rising crescendo of grunts and squeals and moans and whimpers and gasps ... Reek of semen and cunts and sweat and the musty odor of penetrated rectums ... Diamonds and fur pieces, evening dresses, orchids, suits and underwear litter the floor covered by a writhing, frenzied, heaving mass of naked bodies.

A.J. once reserved a table a year in advance *Chez Robert*, where a huge, icy gourmet broods over the greatest cuisine in the world. So baneful and derogatory is his gaze that many a client, under that withering blast, has rolled on the floor and pissed all over himself in convulsive attempts to ingratiate.

So A.J. arrives with six Bolivian Indians who chew coca leaves between courses. And when Robert, in all his gourmet majesty, bears down on the table, A.J. looks up and yells: "Hey, Boy! Bring me some ketchup."

(Alternative: A.J. whips out a bottle of ketchup and douses the haute cuisine.)

Thirty gourmets stop chewing at once. You could have heard a *soufflé* drop. As for Robert, he lets out a bellow of rage like a wounded elephant, runs to the kitchen and arms himself with a meat cleaver ... The Sommelier snarls hideously, his face turning a strange iridescent purple . . . He breaks off a bottle of Brut Champagne . . . '26 . . . Pierre, the Head Waiter, snatches up a boning knife. All three chase A.J. through the restaurant with mangled inhuman screams of rage . . . Tables overturn, vintage wines and matchless food crash to the floor . . . Cries of "Lynch him!" ring through the air. An elderly gourmet with the insane bloodshot eyes of a mandrill is fashioning a hangman's knot with a red velvet curtain cord . . . Seeing himself cornered and in imminent danger of dismemberment at least, A.J. plays his trump card . . . He throws back his head and lets out a hog call—and a hundred famished hogs he had stationed nearby rush into the restaurant, slopping the haute cuisine. Like a great tree Robert falls to the floor in a stroke where he is eaten by the hogs: "Poor bastards don't know enough to appreciate him," says A.J.

Robert's brother Paul emerges from retirement in a local nut house and takes over the restaurant to dispense something he calls the "Transcendental Cuisine" . . . Imperceptibly the quality of the food declines until he is serving literal garbage, the clients being too intimidated by the reputation of *Chez Robert* to protest.

SAMPLE MENU:

The Clear Camel Piss Soup with boiled Earth Worms

———

The Filet of Sun-Ripened Sting Ray
basted with Eau de Cologne and garnished with nettles

———

The After-Birth Suprême de Boeuf
cooked in drained crank case oil,
served with a piquant sauce of rotten egg yolks
and crushed bed bugs

———

The Limburger Cheese sugar cured in diabetic urine,
doused in Canned Heat Flamboyant . . .

So the clients are quietly dying of botulism . . . Then A.J. returns with an entourage of Arab refugees from the Middle East. He takes one mouthful and screams:

"Garbage God damn it! Cook this wise citizen in his own swill!"

And so the legend of A.J. the laughable, lovable eccentric grew and grew . . . Fadeout to Venice . . . Gondoliers singing and pathic cries swell up from San Marco and Harry's.

Charming old Venetian anecdote about this bridge, it seems some Venetian sailors take a trip around the world and all turn into fruits they fuck the cabin boy already, so when they get back to Venice it is necessary women walk over this bridge with their lungs hanging out to arouse the desires of these dubious citizens. So get a battalion of shock troops up to San Marco on the double.

"Girls, this is O.A.O., Operation All Out. If your tits won't stop them, bring up your cunts and confound these faggots."

"Oh Gertie it's true. It's all true. They've got a horrid gash instead of a thrilling thing."

"I can't face it."

"Enough to turn a body to stone."

Paul spoke wiser than he knew—being a really evil old shit—when he talk about men lying with men doing that which is inconvenient. Inconvenient is the word. So who want to trip over a cock on the way to a cunt, and when a citizen get the yen to hump a gash, some evil stranger rush in and do that which is inconvenient to his ass.

A.J. rushes across San Marco slashing at pigeons with a cutlass: "Bastards! Sons of bitches!" he screams . . . He staggers aboard his barge, a monstrous construction in gilt and pink and blue with sails of purple velvet. He is dressed in a preposterous naval uniform covered with braid and ribbons and medals, dirty and torn, the coat buttoned in the wrong holes . . . A.J. walks to a huge reproduction of a Greek urn topped by a gold statue of a boy with an erection. He twists the boy's balls and a jet of champagne spurts into his mouth. He wipes his mouth and looks around.

"Where are my Nubians, God damn it?" he yells.

His secretary looks up from a comic book: "Juicing . . . Chasing cunt."

"Goldbricking cocksuckers. Where's a man without his Nubians?"

"Take a gondola whyncha?"

"A gondola?" A.J. screams. "I put out for this cocksucker I should ride in a gondola already? Reef the mainsail and ship the oars, Mr. Hyslop . . . I'm gonna make with the auxiliary."

Mr. Hyslop shrugs resignedly. With one finger he begins punching a switchboard . . . The sails drop, the oars draw into the hull.

"And turn on the perfume whyncha? The canal stinks up a breeze."

"Gardenia? Sandalwood?"

"Naw. Ambrosia."

Mr. Hyslop presses another button and a thick cloud of perfume settles over the barge.

A.J. is seized with a fit of coughing . . . "Make with the fans!" he yells. "I'm suffocatin'!"

Mr. Hyslop is coughing into a handkerchief. He presses a button. Fans whir and thin out the ambrosia.

A.J. installs himself at the rudder on a raised dais. "Contact!" The barge begins to vibrate. "*Avanti*, God damn it!" A.J. yells and the barge takes off across the canal at a tremendous speed, overturning gondolas full of tourists, missing the *motoscafi* by inches, veering from one side of the canal to the other (the wake washes over the sidewalks drenching passersby), shattering a fleet of moored gondolas, and finally piles up against a pier, spins out into the middle of the canal . . . A column of water spurts six feet in the air from a hole in the hull.

"Man the pumps, Mr. Hyslop. She's shipping water."

The barge gives a sudden lurch throwing A.J. into the canal.

"Abandon ship, God damn it! Every man for himself!"

Fadeout to Mambo music.

The inauguration of Escuela Amigo, a school for delinquent boys of Latin American origin, endowed by A.J.—faculty, boys, and press attending. A.J. staggers out onto a platform draped with American flags.

"In the immortal words of Father Flanagan there is no such thing as a bad boy ... Where's the statuary, God damn it?"

TECHNICIAN: "You want it now?"

A.J.: "What you think I'm doing here Furthucrisakes? I should unveil the son of a bitch *in absentia*?"

TECHNICIAN: "All right ... All *right*. Coming right up."

The statue is towed out by a Graham Hymie tractor and placed in front of the platform. A.J. presses a button. Turbines start under the platform, rising to a deafening whine. Wind blows the red velvet drapes off the statue. They tangle around the Faculty members in the front row ... Clouds of dust and debris whip through the spectators. The sirens slowly subside. The Faculty disengages itself from the drapes ... Everyone is looking at the statue in breathless silence.

FATHER GONZALEZ: "Mother of God!"

THE MAN FROM *TIME:* "I don't *believe* it."

DAILY NEWS: "It's nothing but fruity."

Chorus of whistles from the boys.

A monumental creation in shiny pink stone stands revealed as the dust settles. A naked boy is bending over a sleeping comrade with evident intention to waken him with a flute. One hand is holding the flute, the other reaching for a piece of cloth draped over the sleeper's middle. The cloth bulges suggestively. Both boys wear a flower behind the ear, identical expressions, dreamy and brutal, depraved and innocent. This creation tops a lime-stone pyramid on which is inscribed in letters of porcelain mosaic—pink and blue and gold—the school motto: *"With it and for it."*

A.J. lurches forward and breaks a champagne bottle across the boy's taut buttocks.

"And remember, boys, that's where champagne comes from."

Manhattan Serenade.

A.J. and entourage start into New York night club. A.J. is leading a purple-assed baboon on a gold chain. A.J. is dressed in checked linen plus fours with a cashmere jacket.

MANAGER: *"Wait* a minute. Wait a *minute.* What's that?"

A.J.: "It's an Illyrian poodle. Choicest beast a man can latch onto. It'll raise the tone of your trap."

MANAGER: "I suspect it to be a purple-assed baboon and it stands outside."

STOOGE: "Don't you know who this is? It's A.J., last of the big time spenders."

MANAGER: "Leave him take his purple-assed bastard and big time spend some place else."

A.J. stops in front of another club and looks in. "Elegant fags and old cunts, God damn it! We come to the right place. *Avanti, ragazzi!*"

He drives a gold stake into the floor and pickets the baboon. He begins talking in elegant tones, his stooges filling in.

"Fantastic!"

"Monstrous!"

"Utter heaven!"

A.J. puts a long cigarette holder in his mouth. The holder is made of some obscenely flexible material. It swings and undulates as if endowed with loathsome reptilian life.

A.J.: "So there I was flat on my stomach at thirty thousand feet."

Several nearby fags raise their heads like animals scenting danger. A.J. leaps to his feet with an inarticulate snarl.

"You purple-assed cocksucker!" he screams. "I'll teach you to shit on the floor!" He pulls a whip from his umbrella and cuts the baboon across the ass. The baboon screams and tears loose the stake. He leaps on the next table and climbs up an old woman who dies of heart failure on the spot.

A.J.: "Sorry, lady. Discipline you know."

In a frenzy he whips the baboon from one end of the bar to the other. The baboon, screaming and snarling and shitting with terror, climbs over the clients, runs up and down on top of the bar, swings from drapes and chandeliers . . .

A.J.: "You'll straighten up and shit right or you won't be inna condition to shit one way or the other."

STOOGE: "You ought to be ashamed of yourself, upsettin' A.J. after all he's done for you."

A.J.: "Ingrates! Every one of them ingrates! Take it from an old queen."

Of course no one believes this cover story. A.J. claims to be an "independent," which is to say: "Mind your own business." There are no independents any more . . . The Zone swarms with every variety of dupe but there are no neutrals there. A neutral at A.J.'s level is of course unthinkable . . .

Hassan is a notorious Liquefactionist and suspect to be a secret Sender—"Shucks, boys," he says with a disarming grin, "I'm just a blooming old cancer and I gotta proliferate." He picks up a Texas accent associating with Dry Hole Dutton, the Dallas wildcatter, and he wears cowboy boots and ten-gallon hat at all times indoors and out . . . His eyes are invisible behind black glasses, his face smooth and blank as wax, above a well-cut suit made entirely from immature high-denomination bank notes. (Bank notes are in fact currency, but they must mature before they can be negotiated . . . Bank notes run as high as one million clams a note.)

"They keep hatching out all over me," he says shyly . . . "It's like, gee, I don't know how to say it. It's like I was a Mummy scorpion carrying those little baby notes around on my warm body and feeling them grow . . . Gosh I hope I don't bore you with all this."

Salvador, known as Sally to his friends—he always keeps a few "friends" around and pays them by the hour—got cured in the slunk business in World War II. (To get cured means to get rich. Expression used by Texas oil men.) The Pure Food and Drug Department have his picture in their files, a heavy-faced man with an embalmed look as if paraffin had been injected under the skin, which is smooth, shiny and poreless. One eye is dead grey color, round as a marble, with flaws and opaque spots. The other is black and shiny, an old undreaming insect eye. His eyes are normally invisible behind black glasses. He looks sinister and enigmatic—his gestures and mannerisms are not yet comprehensible—like the secret police of a larval state.

In moments of excitement Salvador is apt to lapse into broken English. His accent at such moments suggests an Italian origin. He reads and speaks Etruscan.

A squad of accountant investigators have made a life work of Sal's international dossier . . . His operations extend through the world in an inextricable, shifting web of subsidiaries, front companies, and aliases. He has held 23 passports and been deported 49 times—deportation proceedings pending in Cuba, Pakistan, Hong Kong and Yokohama.

Salvador Hassan O'Leary, alias The Shoe Store Kid, alias Wrong Way Marv, alias After Birth Leary, alias Slunky Pete, alias Placenta Juan, alias K.Y. Ahmed, alias El Chinche, alias El Culito, etc., etc. for fifteen solid pages of dossier, first tangled with the law in NYC where he was traveling with a character known to the Brooklyn police as Blubber Wilson, who hustled his goof ball money shaking down fetishists in shoe stores. Hassan was charged with third degree extortion and conspiracy to impersonate a police officer. He had learnt the shake man's Number One rule: D.T.— Ditch Tin—which corresponds to the pilot's K.F.S.—Keep Flying Speed . . . As The Vigilante puts it: "If you get a rumble, kid, ditch your piece of tin if you have to swallow it." So they didn't bust him with a queer badge. Hassan testified against Wilson, who drew Pen Indef (longest term possible under New York law for a misdemeanor conviction. Nominally an indefinite sentence, it means three years in Riker's Island). Hassan's case was nolle prossed. "I'd have drawn a nickel," Hassan said, "if I hadn't met a decent cop." Hassan met a decent cop every time he took a fall. His dossier contains three pages of monikers indicating his proclivity for cooperating with the law, "playing ball" the cops call it. Others call it something else: Abe the Fuzz Lover, Finky Marv, The Crooning Hebe, Ali the Stool, Wrongo Sal, The Wailing Spic, The Sheeny Soprano, The Bronx Opera House, The Copper's Djinn, The Answering Service, The Squeaking Syrian, The Cooing Cocksucker, The Musical Fruit, The Wrong Ass Hole, The Fairy Fink, Leary the Nark, The Lilting Leprechaun . . . Grassy Gert.

He opened a sex shop in Yokohama, pushed junk in Beirut, pimped in Panama. During World War II he shifted into high, took over a dairy in Holland and cut the butter with used axle grease, cornered the K.Y. market in North Africa, and finally hit the jackpot with slunks. He prospered and proliferated, flooding the world with cut medicines and cheap counterfeit goods of every variety. Adulterated shark repellent, cut antibiotics, condemned parachutes, stale antivenin, inactive serums and vaccines, leaking lifeboats.

Clem and Jody, two old-time vaudeville hoofers, cop out as Russian agents whose sole function is to represent the U.S. in an unpopular light. When arrested for sodomy in Indonesia, Clem said to the examining magistrate:

"'Tain't as if it was being queer. After all they's only Gooks."

They appeared in Liberia dressed in black Stetsons and red galluses:

"So I shoot that old nigger and he flop on his side one leg up in the air just a-kicking."

"Yeah, but you ever burn a nigger?"

They are always pacing round *bidonvilles* smoking huge cigars:

"Haveta get some bulldozers in here Jody. Clean out all this crap."

Morbid crowds follow them about hoping to witness some superlative American outrage.

"Thirty years in show business and I never handle such a routine like this. I gotta dispossess a *bidonville*, give myself a bang of H, piss on the Black Stone, make with the Prayer Call whilst dressed in my hog suit, cancel Lend-Lease and get fucked up the ass simultaneous . . . What am I an octopus already?" Clem complains.

They are conspiring to kidnap the Black Stone with a helicopter and substitute a hog pen, the hogs trained to give the Bronx cheer when the pilgrims show. "We try to train them squealing bastards to sing: 'Three cheers for the Red White and Blue,' but it can't be done . . ."

"We connect for that wheat with Ali Wong Chapultepec in Panama. He tells us it is a high grade of shit this Finnish skipper die inna local jump joint and leave this cargo to the madam . . . 'She was like a mother to me,' he says and those were his last words . . . So we buy it in good faith off the old gash. Laid ten pieces of H on her."

"Good H too. Good Aleppo H."

"Just enough milk sugar to keep her strength up."

"We should look a gift horse in the ass already?"

"Isn't it true that when you got to Hassan you gave a banquet for the Caid and served couscous made from the wheat?"

"We sure did. And you know, those citizens were so loaded on that marijuana they all wig inna middle of the banquet ... Me, I just had bread and milk ... ulcers you know."

"Likewise."

"So they all run around screaming they is on fire and the bulk of them die the following morning."

"And the rest the morning after that."

"What they expect already when they rot theirselves with Eastern vices?"

"Funny thing those citizens turn all black and their legs drop off."

"Horrible result of marijuana addiction."

"The very same thing occurred to me."

"So we deal directly with the old Sultan who is being a well-known Latah. After that everything is plain sailing you might say."

"But you wouldn't believe it, certain disgruntled elements chased us right down to our launch."

"Handicapped somewhat by lack of legs."

"And a condition in the head."

(Ergot is a fungus disease grows on bad wheat. During the Middle Ages Europe was periodically decimated by outbreaks of ergotism, which was called St. Anthony's Fire. Gangrene frequently supervenes, the legs turn black and drop off.)

They unload a shipment of condemned parachutes on the Ecuadoran Air Force. Maneuvers: boys plummet streaming 'chutes like broken condoms, splash young blood over potbellied generals ... shattering wake of sound as Clem and Jody disappear over the Andes in jet getaway ...

The exact objectives of Islam Inc. are obscure. Needless to say everyone involved has a different angle, and they all intend to cross each other up somewhere along the line.

A.J. is agitating for the destruction of Israel: "With all this feeling against the West a chap has a spot of bother scoring for the young Arab amenities ... The situation is little short of intolerable ... Israel constitutes a downright inconvenience." Typical A.J. cover story.

Clem and Jody give out they are interested in the destruction of Near East oil fields to boost the value of their Venezuelan holdings.

Clem writes a number to the tune of "Crawdad" (Big Bill Broonzy).

> *What you gonna do when the oil goes dry?*
> *Gonna sit right there and watch those Arabs die.*

Salvador emits a thick screen of international finance to cloak, at least from the rank and file, his Liquefactionist activities ... But over a few stiff *yagés* he lets his hair down among friends.

"Islam is jellied consommé already," he says, dancing the Liquefactionist Jig ... And then, unable to contain himself, he bursts into a hideous falsetto:

> *It's trembling on the brink*
> *One push and down it sink*
> *Hey, Maw, get ready my veil.*

"Well, these citizens have engaged the services of a Brooklyn Jew who passes himself off as the second coming of Mohammed ... In fact Doctor Benway delivered him by Caesarean section from a Holy Man in Mecca ...

"If Ahmed won't come out ... We'll go in and get him."

This shameless plant is accepted without question by the gullible Arabs.

"Nice folk, these Arabs ... Nice ignorant folk," Clem says.

So this phony gives out with daily Suras on the radio: "Now friends of the radio audience, this is Ahmed your friendly prophet ... Today I'd like to talk about the importance of being dainty and kissin' fresh at all times ... Friends, use Jody's chlorophyll tablets and be sure."

Now a word about the parties of Interzone ...

It will be immediately clear that the Liquefaction Party is, except for one man, entirely composed of dupes, it not being clear until the final absorption who is whose dupe ... The Lique-factionists are much given to every form of perversion, especially sadomasochistic practices ...

Liquefactionists in general know what the score is. The Senders, on the other hand, are notorious for their ignorance of the nature and terminal state of sending, for barbarous and self-righteous manners, and for rabid fear of any *fact*. It was only the interven-tion of the Factualists that prevented the Senders from putting Einstein in an institution and destroying his theory. It may be said that only a very few Senders know what they are doing and these top Senders are the most dangerous and evil men in the world ...

Techniques of Sending were crude at first. Fadeout to the Na-tional Electronic Conference in Chicago. The Conferents are put-ting on their overcoats ... The speaker talks in a flat shopgirl voice:

"In closing I want to sound a word of warning ... The logical extension of encephalographic research is biocontrol; that is, control of physical movement, mental processes, emotional re-actions and *apparent* sensory impressions by means of bioelec-tric signals injected into the nervous system of the subject."

"Louder and funnier!" The Conferents are trooping out in clouds of dust.

"Shortly after birth a surgeon could install connections in the brain. A miniature radio receiver could be plugged in and the subject controlled from State-controlled transmitters."

Dust settles through the windless air of a vast empty hall—smell of hot iron and steam; a radiator sings in the distance ... The Speaker shuffles his notes and blows dust off them ...

"The biocontrol apparatus is prototype of one-way telepathic control. The subject could be rendered susceptible to the transmitter by drugs or other processing without installing any apparatus. Ultimately the Senders will use telepathic transmitting exclusively ... Ever dig the Mayan codices? I figure it like this: the priests—about one percent of population—made with one-way telepathic broadcasts instructing the workers what to feel and when ... A telepathic sender has to send all the time. He can never receive, because if he receives that means someone else has feelings of his own could louse up his continuity. The Sender has to send all the time, but he can't ever recharge himself by contact. Sooner or later he's got no feelings to send. You can't have feelings alone. Not alone like the Sender is alone—and you dig there can only be one Sender at one place-time ... Finally the screen goes dead ... The Sender has turned into a huge centipede ... So the workers come in on the beam and burn the centipede and elect a new Sender by consensus of the general will ... The Mayans were limited by isolation ... Now one Sender could control the planet ... *You see control can never be a means to any practical end ... It can never be a means to anything but more control ... Like junk ...*"

The Divisionists occupy a midway position, could in fact be termed moderates ... They are called Divisionists because they literally divide. They cut off tiny bits of their flesh and grow exact replicas of themselves in embryo jelly. It seems probable, unless the process of division is halted, that eventually there will be only one replica of one sex on the planet: that is, one person in the world with millions of separate bodies ... Are these bodies actually independent, and could they in time develop varied characteristics? I doubt it. Replicas must periodically recharge with the Mother Cell. This is an article of faith with the Divisionists, who live in fear of a replica revolution ... Some Divisionists think that the process can be halted short of the eventual monopoly of one replica. They say: "Just let me plant a few more replicas all over so I won't be lonely when I travel ... And we must strictly control the division of Undesirables ..." Every replica but your own is eventually an "Undesirable." Of course if someone starts inundating an area with Identical Replicas, everyone knows what is going on. The other citizens are subject to declare a "Schluppit" (wholesale massacre of all identifiable replicas). To avoid extermination of their replicas, citizens dye, distort, and alter them with face and body molds. Only the most abandoned and shameless characters venture to manufacture I.R.s—Identical Replicas.

A cretinous albino Caid, product of a long line of recessive genes (tiny toothless mouth lined with black hairs, body of a huge crab, claws instead of arms, eyes projected on stalks), accumulated 20,000 I.R.s.

"As far as the eye can see, nothing but replicas," he says, crawling around on his terrace and speaking in strange insect chirps. "I don't have to skulk around like a nameless asshole growing replicas in my cesspool and sneaking them out disguised as plumbers and delivery men ... My replicas don't have their dazzling beauty marred by plastic surgery and barbarous dye and bleach processes. They stand forth naked in the sun for all to see, in their incandescent loveliness of body, face and soul. I have made them in my image and enjoined them to increase and multiply geometric for they shall inherit the earth."

A professional witch was called in to make Sheik Aracknid's replica cultures forever sterile ... As the witch was preparing to loose a blast of anti-orgones, Benway told him: "Don't knock yourself out. Friedrich's ataxia will clean out that replica nest. I studied neurology under Professor Fingerbottom in Vienna ...

and he knew every nerve in your body. Magnificent old thing . . . Came to a sticky end . . . His falling piles blew out the Duc de Ventre's Hispano Suiza and wrapped around the rear wheel. He was completely gutted, leaving an empty shell sitting there on the giraffe skin upholstery . . . Even the eyes and brain went, with a horrible schlupping sound. The Duc de Ventre says he will carry that ghastly *schlup* to his mausoleum."

Since there is no sure way to detect a disguised replica (though every Divisionist has some method he considers infallible) the Divisionists are hysterically paranoid. If some citizen ventures to express a liberal opinion, another citizen invariably snarls: "What are you? Some stinking nigger's bleached-out replica?"

The casualties in barroom fights are staggering. In fact the fear of Negro replicas—which may be blond and blue-eyed—has de-populated whole regions. The Divisionists are all latent or overt homosexuals. Evil old queens tell the young boys: "If you go with a woman your replicas won't grow." And citizens are forever put-ting the hex on someone else's replica cultures. Cries of: "Hex my culture will you, Biddy Blair!"—followed by sound effects of may-hem—continually ring through the quarter . . . The Divisionists are much given to the practice of black magic in general, and they have innumerable formulas of varying efficacy for destroying the Mother Cell, also known as the Protoplasm Daddy, by tor-turing or killing a captured replica . . . The authorities have fi-nally given up the attempt to control, among the Divisionists, the crimes of murder and unlicensed production of replicas. But they do stage pre-election raids and destroy vast replica cultures in the mountainous regions of the Zone where replica moon-shiners hole up.

Sex with a replica is strictly forbidden and almost universally practiced. There are queer bars where shameless citizens openly consort with their replicas. House detectives stick their heads into hotel rooms saying: "Have you got a replica in here?"

Bars subject to be inundated by low class replica lovers put up signs in ditto marks: " " "s Will Not Be Served Here . . .

It may be said that the average Divisionist lives in a continual crisis of fear and rage, unable to achieve either the self-righteous complacency of the Senders or the relaxed depravity of the Liquefactionists . . . However the parties are not in practice separate but blend in all combinations.

The Factualists are Anti-Liquefactionist, Anti-Divisionist, and above all Anti-Sender.

Bulletin of the Coordinate Factualist on the subject of replicas: "We must reject the facile solution of flooding the planet with 'desirable replicas.' It is highly doubtful if there are any desirable replicas, such creatures constituting an attempt to circumvent process and change. Even the most intelligent and genetically perfect replicas would in all probability constitute an unspeakable menace to life on this planet . . ."

T.B.—Tentative Bulletin—Liquefaction: "We must not reject or deny our protoplasmic core, striving at all times to maintain a maximum of flexibility without falling into the morass of liquefaction . . ."

Tentative and Incomplete Bulletin: "Emphatically we do not oppose telepathic research. In fact, telepathy properly used and understood could be the ultimate defense against any form of organized coercion or tyranny on the part of pressure groups or individual control addicts. We oppose, as we oppose atomic war, the use of such knowledge to control, coerce, debase, exploit or annihilate the individuality of another living creature. Telepathy is not, by its nature, a one-way process. To attempt to set up a one-way telepathic broadcast must be regarded as an unqualified evil . . ."

D.B.—Definitive Bulletin: "The Sender will be defined by negatives. A low pressure area, a sucking emptiness. He will be portentously anonymous, faceless, colorless. He will—probably—be born with smooth disks of skin instead of eyes. He always knows where he is going, like a virus knows. He doesn't need eyes."

"Couldn't there be more than one Sender?"

"Oh yes, many of them at first. But not for long. Some maudlin citizens will think they can send something edifying, not realizing that sending *is* evil. Scientists will say: 'Sending is like atomic power ... If properly harnessed.' At this point an anal technician mixes a bicarbonate of soda and pulls the switch that reduces the earth to cosmic dust. ('*Belch* ... They'll hear this fart on Jupiter.') ... Artists will confuse sending with creation. They will camp around screeching 'A new medium!' until their rating drops off ... Philosophers will bat around the ends and means hassle, not knowing that *sending can never be a means to anything but more sending, like junk*. Try using junk as a means to something else ... Some citizens with 'Coca-Cola and aspirin' control habits will be talking about the evil glamor of sending. But no one will talk about anything very long. The Sender, he don't like talking."

The Sender is not a human individual . . . It is The Human Virus.

(All viruses are deteriorated cells leading a parasitic existence . . . They have specific affinity for the Mother Cell; thus deteriorated liver cells seek the home place of hepatitis, etc. So every species has a Master Virus: Deteriorated Image of that species.)

The broken image of Man moves in minute by minute and cell by cell . . . Poverty, hatred, war, police-criminals, bureaucracy, insanity, all symptoms of The Human Virus.

The Human Virus can now be isolated and treated.

the
county
clerk

The County Clerk has his office in a huge red brick building known as the Old Court House. Civil cases are, in fact, tried there, the proceeding inexorably dragging out until the contestants die or abandon litigation. This is due to the vast number of records pertaining to absolutely everything, all filed in the wrong place so that no one but the County Clerk and his staff of assistants can find them, and he often spends years in the search. In fact, he is still looking for material relative to a damage suit that was settled out of court in 1910. Large sections of the Old Court House have fallen in ruins, and others are highly dangerous owing to frequent cave-ins. The County Clerk assigns the more dangerous missions to his assistants, many of whom have lost their lives in the service. In 1912 two hundred and seven assistants were trapped in a collapse of the North-by-North-East Wing.

When suit is brought against anyone in the Zone, his lawyers connive to have the case transferred to the Old Court House. Once this is done, the plaintiff has lost the case, so the only cases that actually go to trial in the Old Court House are those instigated by eccentrics and paranoids who want "a public hearing," which they rarely get since only the most desperate famine of news will bring a reporter to the Old Court House.

The Old Court House is located in the town of Pigeon Hole outside the urban zone. The inhabitants of this town and the surrounding area of swamps and heavy timber are people of such great stupidity and such barbarous practices that the Administration has seen fit to quarantine them in a reservation surrounded by a radioactive wall of iron bricks. In retaliation the citizens of Pigeon Hole plaster their town with signs: "*Urbanite Don't Let The Sun Set On You Here,*" an unnecessary injunction since nothing but urgent business would take any Urbanite to Pigeon Hole.

Lee's case is urgent. He has to file an immediate affidavit that he is suffering from bubonic plague to avoid eviction from the house he has occupied ten years without paying the rent. He exists in perpetual quarantine. So he packs his suitcase of affidavits and petitions and injunctions and certificates and takes a bus to the Frontier. The Urbanite customs inspector waves him through: "I hope you've got an atom bomb in that suitcase."

Lee swallows a handful of tranquilizing pills and steps into the Pigeon Hole customs shed. The inspectors spend three hours pawing through his papers, consulting dusty books of regulations and duties from which they read incomprehensible and ominous excerpts ending with: "And as such is subject to fine and penalty under act 666." They look at him significantly.

They go through his papers with a magnifying glass.

"Sometimes they slip dirty limericks between the lines."

"Maybe he figures to sell them for toilet paper. Is this crap for your own personal use?"

"Yes."

"He says yes."

"And how do we know that?"

"I gotta affidavit."

"Wise guy. Take off your clothes."

"Yeah. Maybe he got dirty tattoos."

They paw over his body probing his ass for contraband and examine it for evidence of sodomy. They dunk his hair and send the water out to be analyzed. "Maybe he's got dope in his hair."

Finally, they impound his suitcase; and he staggers out of the shed with a fifty-pound bale of documents.

A dozen or so Recordites sit on the Old Court House steps of rotten wood. They watch his approach with pale blue eyes, turning their heads slow on wrinkled necks (the wrinkles full of dust) to follow his body up the steps and through the door. Inside, dust hangs in the air like fog, sifting down from the ceiling, rising in clouds from the floor as he walks. He mounts a perilous staircase—condemned in 1929. Once his foot goes through, and the dry splinters tear into the flesh of his leg. The staircase ends in a painter's scaffold, attached with frayed rope and pulleys to a beam almost invisible in the dusty distance. He pulls himself up cautiously to a Ferris wheel cabin. His weight sets in motion hydraulic machinery (sound of running water). The wheel moves smooth and silent to stop by a rusty iron balcony, worn through here and there like an old shoe sole.

He walks down a long corridor lined with doors, most of them nailed or boarded shut. In one office, *Near East Exquisitries* on a green brass plaque, the Mugwump is catching termites with his long black tongue. The door of the County Clerk's office is open. The County Clerk sits inside gumming snuff, surrounded by six assistants. Lee stands in the doorway. The County Clerk goes on talking without looking up.

"I run into Ted Spigot the other day . . . a good old boy, too. Not a finer man in the Zone than Ted Spigot . . . Now it was a Friday I happen to remember because the Old Lady was down with the menstrual cramps and I went to Doc Parker's drugstore on Dalton Street, just opposite Ma Green's Ethical Massage Parlor, where Jed's old livery stable used to be . . . Now, Jed, I'll remember his second name directly, had a cast in the left eye and his wife came from some place out East, Algiers I believe it was, and after Jed died she married up again, and she married one of the Hoot boys, Clem Hoot if my memory serves, a good old boy too, now Hoot was around fifty-four fifty-five year old at the time . . . So I says to Doc Parker: 'My old lady is down bad with the menstrual cramps. Sell me two ounces of paregoric.'

"So Doc says, 'Well, Arch, you gotta sign the book. Name, address and date of purchase. It's the law.'

"So I asked Doc what the day was, and he said, 'Friday the 13th.'

"So I said, 'I guess I already had mine.'

"'Well,' Doc says, 'there was a feller in here this morning. City feller. Dressed kinda flashy. So he's got him a Rx for a mason jar of morphine . . . Kinda funny looking prescription writ out on toilet paper . . . And I told him straight out: "Mister, I suspect you to be a dope fiend."

" " "I got the ingrowing toe nails, Pop. I'm in agony,'" he says.

" " "Well," I says, "I gotta be careful. But so long as you got a legitimate condition and an Rx from a certified bona feedy M.D., I'm honored to serve you."

" " "That croaker's really certified," he say . . . Well, I guess one hand didn't know what the other was doing when I give him a jar of Saniflush by error . . . So I reckon he's had his too.'

" 'Just the thing to clean a man's blood.'

" 'You know, that very thing occurred to me. Should be a sight better than sulphur and molasses . . . Now, Arch, don't think I'm nosey; but a man don't have no secrets from God and his druggist I always say . . . Is you still humping the Old Grey Mare?'

" 'Why, Doc Parker . . . I'll have you know I'm a family man and an Elder in the First Denominational Non-sextarian Church and I ain't had a piece-a hoss ass since we was kids together.'

" 'Them was the days, Arch. Remember the time I got the goose grease mixed up with the mustard? Always was a one to grab the wrong jar, feller say. They could have heard you squealing over in Cunt Lick County, just a-squealing like a stoat with his stones cut off.'

" 'You're in the wrong hole, Doc. It was you took the mustard and me as had to wait till you cooled off.'

" 'Wistful thinking, Arch. I read about it one time inna magazine settin' in that green outhouse behind the station . . . Now what I meant awhile back, Arch, you didn't rightly understand me . . . I was referring to your wife as the Old Grey Mare . . . I mean she ain't what she used to be what with all them carbuncles and cataracts and chilblains and hemorrhoids and aftosa.'

" 'Yas, Doc, Liz is right sickly. Never was the same after her eleventh miscarriaging . . . There was something right strange about that. Doc Ferris he told me straight, he said: "Arch, 'tain't fitting you should see that critter." And he gives me a long look made my flesh crawl ... Well, you sure said it right, Doc. She ain't what she used to be. And your medicines don't seem to ease her none. In fact, she ain't been able to tell night from day since using them eye drops you sold her last month ... But, Doc, you oughta know I wouldn't be humping Liz, the old cow, meaning no disrespect to the mother of my dead monsters. Not when I got that sweet little ol' fifteen year old thing ... You know that yaller girl used to work in Marylou's Hair Straightening and Skin Bleach Parlor over in Nigga town.'

" 'Getting that dark chicken meat, Arch? Gettin' that coon pone?'

" 'Gettin' it steady, Doc. Gettin' it steady. Well, feller say duty is goosing me. Gotta get back to the old crank case.'

" 'I'll bet she needs a grease job worst way.'

" 'Doc, she sure is a dry hole ... Well, thanks for the paregoric.'

" 'And thanks for the trade, Arch ... He he he ... Say, Archy boy, some night when you get caught short with a rusty load drop around and have a drink of Yohimbiny with me.'

" 'I'll do that, Doc, I sure will. It'll be just like old times.'

"So I went on back to my place and heated up some water and mixed up some paregoric and cloves and cinnamon and sassyfrass and give it to Liz, and it eased her some I reckon. Leastwise she let up aggravatin' me ... Well, later on I went down to Doc Parker's again to get me a rubber ... and just as I was leaving I run into Roy Bane, a good ol' boy too. There's not a finer man in this Zone than Roy Bane ... So he said to me he says, 'Arch, you see that ol' nigger over there in that vacant lot? Well, sure as shit and taxes, he comes there every night just as regular you can set your watch by him. See him behind them nettles? Every night round about eight thirty he goes over into that lot yonder and pulls himself off with steel wool ... Preachin' nigger, they tell me.'

"So that's how I come to know the hour more or less on Friday the 13th and it couldn't have been more than twenty minutes half an hour after that, I'd took some Spanish Fly in Doc's store and it was jest beginning to work on me down by Grennel Bog on my way to Nigger town . . . Well the bog makes a bend, used to be a nigger shack there . . . They burned that ol' nigger over in Cunt Lick. Nigger had the aftosa and it left him stone blind . . . So this white girl down from Texarkana screeches out:

"'Roy, that ol' nigger is looking at me so nasty. Land's sake I feel just dirty all over.'

"'Now, Sweet Thing, don't you fret yourself. Me an' the boys will burn him.'

"'Do it slow, Honey Face. Do it slow. He's give me a sick headache.'

"So they burned the nigger and that ol' boy took his wife and went back up to Texarkana without paying for the gasoline and old Whispering Lou runs the service station couldn't talk about nothing else all fall: 'These city fellers come down here and burn a nigger and don't even settle up for the gasoline.'

"Well, Chester Hoot tore that nigger shack down and rebuilt it just back of his house up in Blood Valley. Covered up all the windows with black cloth, and what goes on in there ain't fittin' to speak of . . . Now Chester he's got some right strange ways . . . Well it was just where the nigger shack used to be, right across from the old Brooks place floods out every spring, only it wasn't the Brooks place then . . . belonged to a feller name of Scranton. Now that piece of land was surveyed back in 1919 . . . I reckon you know the man did the job too . . . Feller name of Hump Clarence used to witch out wells on the side . . . Good ol' boy too, not a finer man in this Zone than Hump Clarence . . . Well it was just around about in there I come on Ted Spigot a-screwin' a mud puppy."

Lee cleared his throat. The Clerk looked up over his glasses. "Now if you'll take care, young feller, till I finish what I'm a-saying, I'll tend to your business."

And he plunged into an anecdote about a nigra got the hydro-phobia from a cow:

"So my pappy says to me: 'Finish up your chores, son, and let's go see the mad nigger . . .' They had that nigger chained to the bed, and he was bawling like a cow . . . I soon got enough of that ol' nigger. Well, if you all will excuse me I got business in the Privy Council. He he he!"

Lee listened in horror. The County Clerk often spent weeks in the privy living on scorpions and Montgomery Ward catalogues. On several occasions his assistants had forced the door and carried him out in an advanced state of malnutrition. Lee decided to play his last card.

"Mr. Anker," he said, "I'm appealing to you as one Razor Back to another," and he pulled out his Razor Back card, a memento of his lush-rolling youth.

The Clerk looked at the card suspiciously: "You don't look like a bone feed mast-fed Razor Back to me . . . What you think about the Jeeeeews . . . ?"

"Well, Mr. Anker, you know yourself all a Jew wants to do is doodle a Christian girl . . . One of these days we'll cut the rest of it off."

"Well, you talk right sensible for a city feller . . . Find out what he wants and take care of him . . . He's a good ol' boy."

interzone

The only native in Interzone who is neither queer nor available is Andrew Keif's chauffeur, which is not affectation or perversity on Keif's part, but a useful pretext to break off relations with anyone he doesn't want to see: "You made a pass at Aracknid last night. I can't have you to the house again." People are always blacking out in the Zone, whether they drink or not, and no one can say for sure he didn't make a pass at Aracknid's unappetizing person.

Aracknid is a worthless chauffeur, barely able to drive. On one occasion he ran down a pregnant woman in from the mountains with a load of charcoal on her back, and she miscarried a bloody, dead baby in the street, and Keif got out and sat on the curb stirring the blood with a stick while the police questioned Aracknid and finally arrested the woman for a violation of the Sanitary Code.

Aracknid is a grimly unattractive young man with a long face of a strange, slate-blue color. He has a big nose and great yellow teeth like a horse. Anybody can find an attractive chauffeur, but only Andrew Keif could have found Aracknid; Keif the brilliant, decadent young novelist who lives in a remodeled pissoir in the red-light district of the Native Quarter.

The Zone is a single, vast building. The rooms are made of a plastic cement that bulges to accommodate people, but when too many crowd into one room there is a soft *plop* and someone squeezes through the wall right into the next house—the next bed that is, since the rooms are mostly bed where the business of the Zone is transacted. A hum of sex and commerce shakes the Zone like a vast hive:

"Two thirds of one percent. I won't budge from that figure; not even for my snookums."

"But where are the bills of lading, lover?"

"Not where you're looking, pet. That's too obvious."

"A bale of Levis with built-in falsie baskets. Made in Hollywood."

"Hollywood, Siam."

"Well, American *style*."

"What's the commission? . . . The commission . . . The Commission."

"Yes, nugget, a shipload of K.Y. made of genuine whale dreck in the South Atlantic at present quarantined by the Board of

Health in Tierra del Fuego. The commission, my dear! If we can pull this off we'll be in clover."

(Whale dreck is reject material that accumulates in the process of cutting up a whale and cooking it down. A horrible, fishy mess you can smell for miles. No one has found any use for it.)

Interzone Imports Unlimited, which consists of Marvie and Leif The Unlucky, had latched onto the K.Y. deal. In fact they specialize in pharmaceuticals and run a 24-hour Pro. station, six ways coverage fore and aft, as a side line.

(Six separate venereal diseases have been identified to date.)

They plunge into the deal. They perform unmentionable services for a spastic Greek shipping agent, and one entire shift of Customs inspectors. The two partners fall out and finally denounce each other in the Embassy, where they are referred to the We Don't Want To Hear About It Department and eased out a back door into a shit-strewn vacant lot, where vultures fight over fish heads. They flail at each other hysterically.

"You're trying to fuck me out of my commission!"

"*Your* commission! Who smelled out this good thing in the first place?"

"But I have the bill of lading."

"Monster! But the check will be made out in my name."

"Bawstard! You'll never see the bill of lading until my cut is deposited in escrow."

"Well, might as well kiss and make up. There's nothing mean or petty about me."

They shake hands without enthusiasm and peck each other on the cheek.

The deal drags on for months. They engage the services of an Expeditor. Finally Marvie emerges with a check for 42 Turkestani kurus drawn on an anonymous bank in South America, to clear through Amsterdam, a procedure that will take eleven months more or less.

Now he can relax in the cafés of The Plaza. He shows a photostatic copy of the check. He would never show the original of course, lest some envious citizen spit ink eradicator on the signature or otherwise mutilate the check.

Everyone asks him to buy drinks and celebrate, but he laughs jovially and says, "Fact is I can't afford to buy myself a drink. I already spent every kuru of it buying Penstrep for Ali's clap. He's down with it fore and aft again. I came near kicking the little bastard right through the wall into the next bed. But you all know what a sentimental old thing I am."

Marvie does buy himself a shot glass of beer, squeezing a blackened coin out of his fly onto the table. "Keep the change."

The waiter sweeps the coin into a dust pan, he spits on the table and walks away.

"Sorehead! He's envious of my check."

Marvie had been in Interzone since "the year before One" as he put it. He had been retired from some unspecified position in the State Dept. "for the good of the service." Obviously he had once been very good looking in a crew cut, college boy way, but his face had sagged and formed lumps under the chin like melting paraffin. He was getting heavy around the hips.

Leif The Unlucky was a tall, thin Norwegian with a patch over one eye, his face congealed in a permanent, ingratiating smirk. Behind him lay an epic saga of unsuccessful enterprises. He had failed at raising frogs, chinchilla, Siamese fighting fish, ramie and cultured pearls. He had attempted, variously and without success, to promote a Love-Bird Two-in-a-Coffin Cemetery, to corner the condom market during the rubber shortage, to run a mail order whore house, to issue penicillin as a patent medicine. He had followed disastrous betting systems in the casinos of Europe and the race tracks of the U.S.

His reverses in business were matched by the incredible mischances of his personal life. His front teeth had been stomped out by bestial American sailors in Brooklyn. Vultures had eaten out an eye when he drank a pint of paregoric and passed out in a Panama City park. He had been trapped between floors in an elevator for five days with an oil-burning junk habit and sustained an attack of D.T.s while stowing away in a foot locker. Then there was the time he collapsed with strangulated intestines, perforated ulcers and peritonitis in Cairo and the hospital was so crowded they bedded him in the latrine, and the Greek surgeon goofed and sewed up a live monkey in him, and he was gang-fucked by the Arab attendants, and one of the orderlies stole the penicillin substituting Saniflush; and the time he got clap in his ass and a self-righteous English doctor cured him with an enema of hot sulphuric acid; and the German practitioner of Technological Medicine who removed his appendix with a rusty can opener and a pair of tin snips (he considered the germ theory "a nonsense"). Flushed with success he then began snipping and cutting out everything in sight: "The human body is filled up vit unnecessitated parts. You can get by vit vone kidney. Vy have two? Yes dot is a kidney . . . The inside parts should not be so close in together crowded. They need Lebensraum like the Vaterland."

The Expeditor had not yet been paid, and Marvie was faced by the prospect of stalling him for eleven months until the check cleared. The Expeditor was said to have been born on the Ferry between the Zone and the Island. His profession was to expedite the delivery of merchandise. No one knew for sure whether his services were of any use or not, and to mention his name always precipitated an argument. Cases were cited to prove his miraculous efficiency and utter worthlessness.

The Island was a British Military and Naval station directly opposite the Zone. England holds the Island on yearly rent-free lease, and every year the Lease and Permit of Residence is formally renewed. The entire population turns out—attendance is compulsory—and gathers at the municipal dump. The President of the Island is required by custom to crawl across the garbage on his stomach and deliver the Permit of Residence and Renewal of the Lease, signed by every citizen of the Island, to The Resident Governor who stands resplendent in dress uniform. The Governor takes the permit and shoves it into his coat pocket:

"Well," he says with a tight smile, "so you've decided to let us stay another year have you? Very good of you. And everyone is happy about it? . . . Is there anyone who isn't happy about it?"

Soldiers in jeeps sweep mounted machine guns back and forth across the crowd with a slow, searching movement.

"Everybody happy. Well that's fine." He turns jovially to the prostrate President. "I'll keep your papers in case I get caught short. Haw haw haw." His loud, metallic laugh rings out across the dump, and the crowd laughs with him under the searching guns.

The forms of democracy are scrupulously enforced on the Island. There is a Senate and a Congress who carry on endless sessions discussing garbage disposal and outhouse inspection, the only two questions over which they have jurisdiction. For a brief period in the mid-nineteenth century, they had been allowed to control the Dept. of Baboon Maintenance but this privilege had been withdrawn owing to absenteeism in the Senate.

The purple-assed Tripoli baboons had been brought to the Island by pirates in the seventeenth century. There was a legend that when the baboons left the Island it would fall. To whom or in what way is not specified, and it is a capital offense to kill a baboon, though the noxious behavior of these animals harries the citizens almost beyond endurance. Occasionally someone goes berserk, kills several baboons and himself.

The post of President is always forced on some particularly noxious and unpopular citizen. To be elected President is the greatest misfortune and disgrace that can befall an Islander. The humiliations and ignominy are such that few Presidents live out their full term of office, usually dying of a broken spirit after a year or two. The Expeditor had once been President and served the full five years of his term. Subsequently he changed his name and underwent plastic surgery, to blot out, as far as possible, the memory of his disgrace.

"Yes of course . . . we'll pay you," Marvie was saying to the Expeditor. "But take it easy. It may be a little while yet . . ."

"Take it easy? A little while!"

"Listen . . ."

"Yes I know it all. The finance company is repossessing your wife's artificial kidney . . . They are evicting your grandmother from her iron lung."

"That's in rather bad taste, old boy . . ."

"Frankly I wish I had never involved myself in this uh matter. That bloody grease has too much carbolic in it. I was down to Customs one day last week. Stuck a broom handle into a drum of it, and the grease ate the end off straight away. Besides, the stink is enough to knock a man on his bloody ass. You should take a walk down by the port."

"I'll do no such thing!" Marvie screeched. (It is a mark of caste in the Zone never to touch or even go near what you are selling. To do so gives rise to suspicion of retailing, that is, of being a common peddler. A good part of the merchandise in the Zone is sold through street peddlers.) "Why do you tell me all this? It's too sordid! Let the retailers worry about it."

"Oh it's all very well for you chaps, you can scud out from under. But I have a reputation to maintain . . . There'll be a spot of bother about this."

"Do you suggest there is something *illegitimate* in this operation?"

"Not *illegitimate* exactly. But shoddy. Definitely shoddy."

"Oh go back to your Island before it falls! We knew you when you were peddling your purple ass in the Plaza pissoirs for five pesetas."

"And not many takers either," Leif put in. He pronounced it "eye-ther."

This reference to his Island origin was more than the Expeditor could stand ... He was drawing himself up, mobilizing his most frigid impersonation of an English aristocrat, preparing to deliver an icy, clipped "crusher," but instead, a whining, whimpering, kicked dog snarl broke from his mouth. His pre-surgery face emerged in an arc light of incandescent hate ... He began to spit curses in the hideous, strangled gutturals of the Island dialect. (The Islanders all profess ignorance of the dialect or flatly deny its existence. "We are Breetish," they say. "We don't got no bloody dealect.") Froth gathered at the corners of the Expeditor's mouth. He was spitting little balls of saliva like pieces of cotton. The stench of spiritual vileness hung in the air about him like a green cloud. Marvie and Leif fell back twittering in alarm.

'He's gone *mad*," Marvie gasped. "Let's get *out* of here."

Hand in hand they skip away into the mist that covers the Zone in the winter months like a cold Turkish Bath.

the examination

Carl Peterson found a postcard in his box requesting him to report for a ten o'clock appointment with Doctor Benway in the Ministry of Mental Hygiene and Prophylaxis ...

"What on earth could they want with me?" he thought irritably ... "A mistake most likely." But he knew they didn't make mistakes ... Certainly not mistakes of identity ...

It would not have occurred to Carl to disregard the appointment even though failure to appear entailed no penalty ... Freeland was a welfare state. If a citizen wanted anything from a load of bone meal to a sexual partner some department was ready to offer effective aid. The threat implicit in this enveloping benevolence stifled the concept of rebellion ...

Carl walked through the Town Hall Square ... Nickel nudes sixty feet high with brass genitals soaped themselves under gleaming showers ... The Town Hall cupola of glass brick and copper crashed into the sky.

Carl stared back at a homosexual American tourist who dropped his eyes and fumbled with the light filters of his Leica ...

Carl entered the steel enamel labyrinth of the Ministry, strode to the information desk ... and presented his card.

"Fifth floor ... Room twenty-six ..."

In room twenty-six a nurse looked at him with cold undersea eyes.

"Doctor Benway is expecting you," she said smiling. "Go right in."

"As if he had nothing to do but wait for me," thought Carl ...

The office was completely silent and filled with milky light. The doctor shook Carl's hand, keeping his eyes on the young man's chest ...

"I've seen this man before," Carl thought ... "But where?"

He sat down and crossed his legs. He glanced at an ashtray on the desk and lit a cigarette ... He turned to the doctor a steady inquiring gaze in which there was more than a touch of insolence.

The doctor seemed embarrassed ... He fidgeted and coughed ... and fumbled with papers ...

"Hurumph," he said finally ... "Your name is Carl Peterson I believe ..." His glasses slid down onto his nose in parody of the academic manner ... Carl nodded silently ... The doctor did not look at him but seemed nonetheless to register the acknowledgment ... He pushed his glasses back into place with one finger and opened a file on the white enameled desk.

"Mmmmmmmm. Carl Peterson." He repeated the name caressingly, pursed his lips and nodded several times. He spoke again abruptly: "You know of course that we are trying. We are all trying. Sometimes of course we don't succeed." His voice trailed off, thin and tenuous. He put a hand to his forehead. "To adjust the state—simply a tool—to the needs of each individual citizen." His voice boomed out so unexpectedly deep and loud that Carl started. "That is the only function of the state as we see it. Our knowledge . . . incomplete, of course . . ." He made a slight gesture of deprecation . . . "For example . . . *for example* . . . take the matter of uh *sexual deviation.*" The doctor rocked back and forth in his chair. His glasses slid down onto his nose. Carl felt suddenly uncomfortable.

"We regard it as a misfortune . . . a sickness . . . certainly nothing to be censured or uh sanctioned any more than, say . . . tuberculosis . . . Yes," he repeated firmly as if Carl had raised an objection . . . "Tuberculosis. On the other hand you can readily see that *any* illness imposes certain, should we say, *obligations,* certain *necessities* of a prophylactic nature on the authorities concerned with public health, such necessities to be imposed, needless to say, with a minimum of inconvenience and hardship to the unfortunate individual who has, through no fault of his own, become uh infected . . . That is to say, of course, the minimum hardship compatible with adequate protection of other individuals who are not so infected . . . We do not find obligatory vaccination for smallpox an unreasonable measure . . . Nor isolation for certain contagious diseases . . . I am sure you will agree that individuals infected with hurumph what the French call '*les maladies galantes*' heh heh heh should be compelled to undergo treatment if they do not report voluntarily." The doctor went on chuckling and rocking in his chair like a mechanical toy . . . Carl realized that he was expected to say something.

"That seems reasonable," he said.

The doctor stopped chuckling. He was suddenly motionless. "Now to get back to this uh matter of sexual deviation. Frankly we don't pretend to understand—at least not completely—why some men and women prefer the uh sexual company of their own sex. We do know that the uh phenomenon is common enough, and, under certain circumstances, a matter of uh concern to this department."

For the first time the doctor's eyes flickered across Carl's face. Eyes without a trace of warmth or hate or any emotion that Carl had ever experienced in himself or seen in another, at once cold and intense, predatory and impersonal. Carl suddenly felt trapped in this silent underwater cave of a room, cut off from all sources of warmth and certainty. His picture of himself sitting there—calm, alert with a trace of well-mannered contempt—went dim, as if vitality were draining out of him to mix with the milky grey medium of the room.

"Treatment of these disorders is, at the present time, hurumph symptomatic." The doctor suddenly threw himself back in his chair and burst into peals of metallic laughter. Carl watched him, appalled . . . "The man is insane," he thought. The doctor's face went blank as a gambler's. Carl felt an odd sensation in his stomach, like the sudden stopping of an elevator.

The doctor was studying the file in front of him. He spoke in a tone of slightly condescending amusement:

"Don't look so frightened, young man. Just a professional joke. To say treatment is symptomatic means there is none, except to make the patient feel as comfortable as possible. And that is precisely what we attempt to do in these cases." Once again Carl felt the impact of that cold interest on his face. "That is to say, reassurance when reassurance is necessary . . . and, of course, suitable outlets with other individuals of similar tendencies. No isolation is indicated . . . the condition is no more directly contagious than cancer . . . Cancer, my first love . . ." The doctor's voice receded. He seemed actually to have gone away through an invisible door, leaving his empty body sitting there at the desk.

Suddenly he spoke again in a crisp voice. "And so you may well wonder why we concern ourselves with the matter at all?" He flashed a smile bright and cold as snow in sunlight.

Carl shrugged: "That is not my business . . . what I am wondering is why you have asked me to come here and why you tell me all this . . . this . . ."

"Nonsense?"

Carl was annoyed to find himself blushing.

The doctor leaned back and placed the ends of his fingers together:

"The young," he said indulgently. "Always they are in a hurry. One day perhaps you will learn the meaning of patience. No, Carl . . . I may call you Carl? I am not evading your question. In cases of suspected tuberculosis we—that is, the appropriate department—may ask, even *request*, someone to appear for a fluoroscopic examination. This is routine, you understand. Most of such examinations turn up negative. So you have been asked to report here for, should I say, a psychic fluoroscope? I may add that after talking with you I feel *relatively* sure that the result will be, for practical purposes, negative . . ."

"But the whole thing is ridiculous. I have always interested myself only in girls. I have a steady girl now and we plan to marry."

"Yes Carl, I know. And that is why you are here. A blood test prior to marriage—this is reasonable, no?"

"Please, doctor, speak directly."

The doctor did not seem to hear. He drifted out of his chair and began walking around behind Carl, his voice languid and intermittent like music down a windy street.

"I may tell you in strictest confidence that there is definite evidence of a hereditary factor. Social pressure. Many homosexuals latent and overt do, unfortunately, marry. Such marriages often result in . . . Factor of infantile environment." The doctor's voice went on and on. He was talking about schizophrenia, cancer, hereditary dysfunction of the hypothalamus.

Carl dozed off. He was opening a green door. A horrible smell grabbed his lungs and he woke up with a shock. The doctor's voice was strangely flat and lifeless, a whispering junky voice:

"The Blomberg-Stanislouski semen flocculation test . . . a diagnostic tool . . . indicative, at least in a negative sense. In certain cases useful—taken as part of the whole picture . . . Perhaps under the uh *circumstances*." The doctor's voice shot up to a pathic scream. "The nurse will take your uh *specimen*."

"This way please . . ." The nurse opened the door into a bare white-walled cubicle. She handed him a jar.

"Use this please. Just yell when you're ready."

There was a jar of K.Y. on a glass shelf. Carl felt ashamed, as if his mother had laid out a handkerchief for him. Some coy little message stitched on, like: "If I was a cunt we could open a dry goods store."

Ignoring the K.Y., he ejaculated into the jar, a cold brutal fuck of the nurse, standing her up against a glass brick wall. "Old Glass Cunt," he sneered, and saw a cunt full of colored glass splinters under the Northern Lights.

He washed his penis and buttoned up his pants.

Something was watching his every thought and movement with cold, sneering hate, the shifting of his testes, the contractions of his rectum.

He was in a room filled with green light. There was a stained wood double bed, a black wardrobe with full-length mirror. Carl could not see his face. Someone was sitting in a black hotel chair. He was wearing a stiff-bosomed white shirt and a dirty paper tie. The face swollen, skull-less, eyes like burning pus.

"Something wrong?" said the nurse indifferently. She was holding a glass of water out to him. She watched him drink with aloof contempt. She turned and picked up the jar with obvious distaste. The nurse turned to him: "Are you waiting for something special?" she snapped.

Carl had never been spoken to like that in his adult life.

"Why no . . ."

"You can go then." She turned back to the jar. With a little exclamation of disgust she wiped a gob of semen off her hand.

Carl crossed the room and stood at the door.

"Do I have another appointment?"

She looked at him in disapproving surprise: "You'll be notified of course." She stood in the doorway of the cubicle and watched him walk through the outer office and open the door. He turned and attempted a jaunty wave. The nurse did not move or change her expression.

As he walked down the stairs the broken, false grin burned his face with shame.

A homosexual tourist looked at him and raised a knowing eyebrow.

"Something *wrong*?"

Carl ran into a park and found an empty bench beside a bronze faun with cymbals.

"Let your hair down, chicken. You'll feel better." The tourist was leaning over him, his camera swinging in Carl's face like a great dangling tit.

"Fuck off, you!"

Carl saw something ignoble and hideous reflected back in the queen's spayed-animal brown eyes.

"Oh! I wouldn't be calling any names if I were you, chicken. You're hooked too. I saw you coming out of The Institute."

'What do you mean by that?" Carl demanded.

"Oh nothing. Nothing at all."

"Well, Carl," the doctor began, smiling and keeping his eyes on a level with Carl's mouth. "I have some good news for you." He picked up a slip of blue paper off the desk and went through an elaborate pantomime of focusing his eyes on it. "Your uh test . . . the Robinson-Kleiberg flocculation test . . ."

"I thought it was a Blomberg-Stanislouski test."

The doctor tittered. "Oh dear no . . . You are getting ahead of me young man. You might have misunderstood. The Blomberg-Stanislouski, weeell . . . that's a different sort of test altogether. I *do hope* . . . not necessary . . ." He tittered again: "But as I was saying before I was so charmingly interrupted . . . by my hurumph learned young colleague. Your R.K. seems to be . . ."—he held the slip at arm's length—". . . completely uh negative. So perhaps we won't be troubling you any further. And so . . ." He folded the slip carefully into a file. He leafed through the file. Finally he stopped and frowned and pursed his lips. He closed the file and put his hand flat on it and leaned forward.

"Carl, when you were doing your military service . . . There must have been . . . in fact there *were* long periods when you found yourself deprived of the uh consolations and uh *facilities* of the fair sex. During these no doubt trying and difficult periods you had perhaps a pinup girl? Or more likely a pinup harem? Heh heh heh . . ."

Carl looked at the doctor with overt distaste.

"Yes, of course," he said. "We all did."

"And now, Carl, I would like to show you some pinup girls." He pulled an envelope out of a drawer. "And ask you to please pick out the one you would most like to uh make heh heh heh . . ." He suddenly leaned forward, fanning the photographs in front of Carl's face. "Pick a girl, any girl!"

Carl reached out with numb fingers and touched one of the photographs. The doctor put the photo back into the pack and shuffled and cut and he placed the pack on Carl's file and slapped it smartly. He spread the photos faceup in front of Carl.

"Is she there?"

Carl shook his head.

"Of course not. She is in here where she belongs. A woman's place, what???" He opened the file and held out the girl's photo attached to a Rorschach plate. "Is that her?"

Carl nodded silently.

"You have good taste, my boy. I may tell you in strictest confidence that some of these girls . . ."—with gambler fingers he shifts the photos in three-card-monte passes—"are really *boys*. In uh *drag* I believe is the word?"

His eyebrows shot up and down with incredible speed. Carl could not be sure he had seen anything unusual. The doctor's face opposite him was absolutely immobile and expressionless. Once again Carl experienced the floating sensation in his stomach and genitals of a sudden elevator stop.

"Yes, Carl, you seem to be running our little obstacle course with flying colors . . . I guess you think this is all pretty silly, don't you now . . . ???"

"Well, to tell the truth . . . Yes . . ."

"You are frank, Carl . . . This is good . . . And now . . . Carl . . ." He dragged the name out caressingly like a sweet-con dick about to offer you an Old Gold (just like a cop to smoke Old Golds somehow) and go into his act . . .

The con dick does a little dance step.

"Why don't you make The Man a proposition?" He jerks a head towards his glowering superego who is always referred to in the third person as "The Man" or "The Lieutenant."

"That's the way the Lieutenant is, you play fair with him and he'll play fair with you . . . We'd like to go light on you . . . If you could help us in some way."

His words open out into a desolate waste of cafeterias and street corners and lunch rooms. Junkies look the other way munching pound cake.

"The Fag is wrong."

The Fag slumps in a hotel chair knocked out on goof balls with his tongue lolling out. He gets up in a goof ball trance, hangs himself without altering his expression or pulling his tongue in.

The dick is diddling on a pad.

"Know Marty Steel?" Diddle.

"Yes."

"Can you score off him?" Diddle? Diddle?

"He's skeptical."

"But you can score." Diddle diddle. "You scored off him last week didn't you?" Diddle???

"Yes."

"Well you can score off him this week." Diddle ... Diddle ... Diddle ... "You can score off him today." No diddle.

"No! No! Not that!!"

"Now look are you going to cooperate"—three vicious diddles—"or does the ... does The Man cornhole you?" He raises a fey eyebrow.

"And so, Carl, you will please oblige to tell me how many times and under what circumstances you have uh indulged in homosexual acts???" His voice drifts away. "If you have never done so I shall be inclined to think of you as a somewhat atypical young man." The doctor raises a coy admonishing finger. "In any case ..." He tapped the file and flashed a hideous leer.

Carl noticed that the file was six inches thick. In fact it seemed to have thickened enormously since he entered the room.

"Well, when I was doing my military service ... These queers used to proposition me and sometimes ... when I was blank ..."

"Yes, of course, Carl," the doctor brayed heartily. "In your position I would have done the same I don't mind telling you heh heh heh ... Well, I guess we can uh *dismiss as irrelevant* these uh understandable means of replenishing the uh *exchequer*. And now, Carl, there were perhaps"—one finger tapped the file, which gave out a faint effluvium of moldy jockstraps and chlorine—"occasions. When no uh economic factors were involved."

A green flare exploded in Carl's brain. He saw Hans' lean brown body twisting towards him, quick breath on his shoulder. The flare went out. Some huge insect was squirming in his hand. His whole being jerked away in an electric spasm of revulsion.

Carl got to his feet shaking with rage.

"What are you writing there?" he demanded.

"Do you often doze off like that? in the middle of a conversation . . . ?"

"I wasn't asleep—that is . . ."

"You weren't?"

"It's just that the *whole thing* is unreal . . . I'm going now. I don't care. You can't force me to stay."

He was walking across the room towards the door. He had been walking a long time. A creeping numbness dragged his legs. The door seemed to recede.

"Where can you go, Carl?" The doctor's voice reached him from a great distance.

"Out . . . Away . . . Through the door . . ."

"The Green Door, Carl?"

The doctor's voice was barely audible. The whole room was exploding out into space.

have you
seen
pantopon
rose?

"Have you seen Pantopon Rose?" said the old junky . . . "Time to cosq," put on a black overcoat and made the square . . . Down Skid Row to Market Street museum shows all kinds masturbation and self-abuse. Young boys need it special . . .

The gangster in concrete rolls down the river channel . . . They cowboyed him in the steam room . . . Is this Cherry Ass Gio the Towel Boy or Mother Gillig, Old Auntie of Westminster Place?? Only dead fingers talk in Braille . . .

The Mississippi rolls great limestone boulders down the silent alley . . .

"Clutter the glind!" screamed the Captain of Moving Land . . .

Distant rumble of stomachs . . . Poisoned pigeons rain from the Northern Lights . . . The reservoirs are empty . . . Brass statues crash through the hungry squares and alleys of the gaping city . . .

Probing for a vein in the junk-sick morning . . .

Strictly from cough syrup . . .

A thousand junkies storm the crystal spine clinics, cook down the Grey Ladies . . .

In the limestone cave met a man with Medusa's head in a hat box and said, "Be careful," to the Customs Inspector . . . Freeze forever hand an inch from the false bottom . . .

Window dressers scream through the station, beat the cashiers with the fairy hype . . . (The Hype is a short change con . . . Also known as The Bill . .)

"Multiple fracture," said the big physician . . . "I'm very technical . . ."

Conspicuous consumption is rampant in the porticos slippery with Koch spit . . .

The centipede nuzzles the iron door rusted to thin black paper by the urine of a million fairies . . .

This is no rich mother load, but vitiate dust, second run cottons trace the bones of a fix . . .

coke
bugs

The Sailor's grey felt hat and black overcoat hung twisted in atrophied yen-wait. Morning sun outlined the Sailor in the orange-yellow flame of junk. He had a paper napkin under his coffee cup—mark of those who do a lot of sitting over coffee in the plazas, restaurants, terminals and waiting rooms of the world. A junky, even at the Sailor's level, runs on junk Time and when he makes his importunate irruption into the Time of others, like all petitioners, he must wait. (How many coffees in an hour?)

A boy came in and sat at the counter in broken lines of long, sick junk-wait. The Sailor shivered. His face fuzzed out of focus in a shuddering brown mist. His hands moved on the table, reading the boy's Braille. His eyes traced little dips and circles, following whorls of brown hair on the boy's neck in a slow, searching movement.

The boy stirred and scratched the back of his neck: "Something bit me, Joe. What kinda creep joint you run here?"

"Coke bugs, kid," Joe said, holding eggs up to the light. "I was traveling with Irene Kelly and her was a sporting woman. In Butte, state of Montany, her got the coke horrors and run through the hotel screaming Chinese coppers chase her with meat cleavers. I knew this cop in Chi sniff coke used to come in form of crystals, blue crystals. So her go nuts and start screaming the Federals is after him and run down this alley and stick his head in the garbage can. And I said, 'What you think you are doing? and her say, 'Get away or I shoot you! I got myself hid good!' When the roll is called up yonder we'll be there, right?"

Joe looked at the Sailor and spread his hands in the junky shrug.

The Sailor spoke in his feeling voice that reassembles in your head, spelling out the words with cold fingers: "Your connection is broken, kid."

The boy shied. His street-boy face, torn with black scars of junk, retained a wild, broken innocence; shy animals peering out through grey arabesques of terror.

"I don't dig you, Jack."

The Sailor leapt into sharp, junky focus. He turned back his coat lapel, showing a brass hypo needle covered with mold and verdigris.

"Retired for the good of the service ... Sit down and have a blueberry crumb pie on the expense account. Your monkey loves it ... Make his coat glossy."

The boy felt a touch on his arm across eight feet of morning lunch room. He was suddenly siphoned into the booth, landing with an inaudible *schlup*. He looked into the Sailor's eyes, a green universe stirred by cold black currents.

"You an agent, mister?"

"I prefer the word ... vector." His sounding laughter vibrated through the boy's substance.

"You holding, man? I got the bread ..."

"I don't want your money, Honey: I want your Time."

"I don't dig."

"You want fix? You want straight? You wanta, nooood?" The Sailor cradled something pink and vibrated out of focus.

"Yeah."

"We'll take the Independent. Got their own special heat, don't carry guns only saps. I recall, me and the Fag fell once in Queens Plaza. Stay away from Queens Plaza, son ... evil spot ... fuzz haunted. Too many levels. Heat flares out from the broom closet high on ammonia like burning lions ... fall on poor old lush worker, scare her veins right down to the bone. Her skin-pop a week or do that five-twenty-nine kick handed out free and gratis by NYC to jostling junkies ... So Fag, Beagle, Irish, Sailor beware! Look down, look down along that line before you travel there ..."

The subway sweeps by with a black blast of iron.

(Queens Plaza is a bad spot for lush workers ... Too many levels and lurking places for subway heat, and impossible to cover when you put the hand out ...)

(Five months and twenty-nine days: sentence given for "jostling," that is, touching a flop with obvious intent ... Innocent people may be convicted of murder but not of jostling.)

(Fag, Beagle, Irish, Sailor: old time junkies and lush workers of my acquaintance ... The old 103rd Street klatch ... Sailor and Irish hanged themselves in the Tombs ... The Beagle is dead of an overdose and the Fag went wrong ...)

*the
exterminator
does
a good job*

The Sailor touched the door gently, following patterns of painted oak in a slow twist, leaving faint, iridescent whorls of slime. His arm went through to the elbow. He pulled back an inside bolt and stood aside for the boy to enter.

Heavy, colorless smell of death filled the empty room.

"The trap hasn't been aired since the Exterminator fumigated for coke bugs," said the Sailor apologetically.

The boy's peeled senses darted about in frenzied exploration. Tenement flat, railroad flat vibrating with silent motion. Along one wall of the kitchen a metal trough—or was it metal, exactly?—ran into a sort of aquarium or tank half filled with translucent green fluid. Moldy objects, worn out in unknown service, littered the floor: a jockstrap designed to protect some delicate organ of flat, fan shape; multi-leveled trusses, supports and bandages; a large U-shaped yoke of porous pink stone; little lead tubes cut open at one end.

Currents of movement from the two bodies stirred stagnant odor pools; atrophied boy-smell of dusty locker rooms, swimming pool chlorine, dried semen. Other smells curled through pink convolutions, touching unknown doors.

The Sailor reached under the washstand and extracted a package in wrapping paper that shredded and fell from his fingers in yellow dust. He laid out dropper, needle and spoon on a table covered with dirty dishes. But no roach antennae felt for the crumbs of darkness.

"The Exterminator does a good job," said the Sailor. "Almost too good, sometimes."

He dipped into a square tin of yellow pyrethrum powder and pulled out a flat package covered in red and gold Chinese paper.

"Like a firecracker package," the boy thought. At fourteen lost two fingers . . . Fourth of July fireworks accident . . . later, in the hospital, first silent proprietary touch of junk.

"They go off here, kid." The Sailor put a hand to the back of his head. He camped obscenely as he opened the package, a complex arrangement of slots and overlays.

"Pure, one hundred percent H. Scarcely a man is now alive . . . and it's all yours."

"So what you want off me?"

"Time."

"I don't dig."

"I have something you want." His hand touched the package. He drifted away into the front room, his voice remote and blurred. "You have something I want . . . five minutes here . . . an hour someplace else . . . two . . . four . . . eight . . . Maybe I'm getting ahead of myself . . . Every day die a little . . . It takes up The Time . . ."

He moved back into the kitchen, his voice loud and clear: "Five years a piece. Nobody gives a better deal on the street." He put a finger on the dividing line below the boy's nose. "Right down the middle."

"Mister, I don't know what you're talking about."

"You will, baby . . . in time."

"O.K. So what do I do?"

"You accept?"

"Yeah, like . . ." He glanced at the package. "Whatever . . . I accept."

The boy felt a silent black *clunk* fall through his flesh. The Sailor put a hand to the boy's eyes and pulled out a pink scrotal egg with one closed, pulsing eye. Black fur boiled inside translucent flesh of the egg.

The Sailor caressed the egg with nakedly inhuman hands— black-pink, thick, fibrous, long white tendrils sprouting from abbreviated finger tips.

Death fear and Death weakness hit the boy, shutting off his breath, stopping his blood. He leaned against a wall that seemed to give slightly. He clicked back into junk focus.

The Sailor was cooking a shot. "When the roll is called up yonder we'll be there, right?" he said, feeling along the boy's vein, erasing goose pimples with a gentle old-woman finger. He slid the needle in. A red orchid bloomed at the bottom of the dropper. The Sailor pressed the bulb, watching the solution rush into the boy-vein, sucked by silent thirst of blood.

"Jesus!" said the boy. "I never been hit like that before!" He lit a cigarette and looked around the kitchen, twitching in sugar need. "Aren't you taking off?" he asked.

"With that milk sugar shit? Junk is a one-way street. No U-turn. You can't go back no more."

They call me the Exterminator. At one brief point of intersection I did exercise that function and witnessed the belly dance of roaches suffocating in yellow pyrethrum powder ("Hard to get now, lady . . . war on. Let you have a little . . . Two dollars.") Sluiced fat bedbugs from rose wall paper in shabby theatrical hotels on North Clark and poisoned the purposeful Rat, occasional eater of human babies. Wouldn't you?

My present assignment: Find the live ones and *exterminate*. Not the bodies but the "molds," you understand—but I forget that you cannot understand. We have all but a very few. But even one could upset our food tray. The danger, as always, comes from defecting agents: A.J., the Vigilante, the Black Armadillo (carrier of Chagas vectors, hasn't taken a bath since the Argentine epidemic of '35, remember?), and Lee and the Sailor and Benway. And I know some agent is out there in the darkness looking for me. Because all Agents defect and all Resisters sell out . . .

the
algebra
of need

"Fats" Terminal came from The City Pressure Tanks where open life jets spurt a million forms, immediately eaten, the eaters canceled by black time fuzz . . .

Few reach the Plaza, a point where The Tanks empty a tidal river, carrying forms of survival armed with defenses of poison slime, black flesh-rotting fungus, and green odors that sear the lungs and grab the stomach in twisted knots . . .

Because Fats' nerves were raw and peeled to feel the death spasms of a million cold kicks . . . Fats learned The Algebra of Need and survived . . .

One Friday Fats siphoned himself into The Plaza, a translucent-grey foetal monkey, suckers on his little soft, purple-grey hands, and a lamprey disk mouth of cold, grey gristle lined with hollow black erectile teeth, feeling for the scar patterns of junk . . .

And a rich man passed and stared at the monster and Fats rolled pissing and shitting in terror and ate his shit and the man was moved by this tribute to his potent gaze and clicked a coin out of his Friday cane (Friday is Moslem Sunday when the rich are supposed to distribute alms).

So Fats learned to serve The Black Meat and grew a fat aquarium of body . . .

And his blank periscope eyes swept the world's surface . . . In his wake of addicts translucent-grey monkeys flashed like fish spears to the junk Mark and hung there sucking and it all drained back into Fats so his substance grew and grew, filling plazas, restaurants and waiting rooms of the world with grey junk ooze.

Bulletins from Party Headquarters are spelled out in obscene charades by hebephrenics and Latahs and apes. Sollubis fart code, Negroes open and shut mouth to flash messages on gold teeth, Arab rioters send smoke signals by throwing great buttery eunuchs—they make the best smoke, hangs black and shit-solid in the air—onto gasoline fires in a rubbish heap, mosaic of melodies, sad Panpipes of humpbacked beggar, cold wind sweeps down from postcard of Chimborazo, flutes of Ramadan, piano music down a windy street, mutilated police calls, advertising leaflet synchronize with street fight spell SOS.

Two agents have identified themselves each to each by choice of sex practices foiling alien microphones, fuck atomic secrets back and forth in code so complex only two physicists in the world pretend to understand it and each categorically denies the other. Later the receiving agent will be hanged, convict of the guilty possession of a nervous system, and play back the message in orgasmal spasms transmitted from electrodes attached to the penis.

Breathing rhythm of old cardiac, bumps of a belly dancer, *put put put* of a motorboat across oily water.

The waiter lets fall a drop of martini on the Man in the Grey Flannel Suit, who lams for the 6:12 *Knowing That He Has Been Spotted.*

Junkies climb out the lavatory window of the chop suey joint as the El *Rumbles* past.

The Gimp, cowboyed in the Waldorf, *Gives Birth To A Litter Of Rats.*

(Cowboy: New York hood talk means kill the mother fucker wherever you find him. A rat is a rat is a rat is a rat. Is an informer.)

And even foolish virgins heed the English colonel who rides by brandishing a screaming *Peccary* on his lance.

The elegant fag patronizes his neighborhood pissoir to receive a bulletin from Dead Mother, lives on in synapses and will evoke the exciting Nanny Beater.

Boys jacking off in the school toilet know each other as agents from Galaxy X . . . adjourn to a second-run night spot where they sit shabby and portentous drinking wine vinegar and sucking lemons to confound the Tenor Sax (a hip Arab in blue glasses) suspect to be Enemy Sender.

Malarials of the world bundle in shivering protoplasm . . . Fear seals the turd message with a cuneiform account.

Giggling rioters copulate to the screams of a burning Nigra. Lonely librarians unite in soul kiss halitosis.

That grippy feeling, brother? Sore throat persistent and disquieting as the hot afternoon wind? Welcome to the International Syphilis Lodge—"Methodith Epithcopal God damn ith." (Phrase used to test for speech impairment typical of paresis)—or the first touch of chancre makes you a member in good standing.

The vibrating soundless hum of deep forest and orgone accumulators, the sudden silence of cities when the junky cops and even The Commuter buzzes clogged lines of cholesterol for contact. Signal flares of orgasm burst over the world. A tea head leaps up screaming "I got the fear!" and runs into Mexican night bringing down back brains of the world. The Executioner shits in terror at sight of the condemned man. The Torturer screams in the ear of his implacable victim. Knife fighters embrace in adrenaline. Cancer is at the door with a Singing Telegram . . .

hauser
and
o'brien

When they walked in on me that morning at 8 o'clock, I knew it was my last chance, my only chance. But they didn't know. How could they? Just a routine pick-up. But not quite routine.

Hauser had been eating breakfast when the Lieutenant called: "I want you and your partner to pick up a man named Lee, William Lee, on your way downtown. He's in the Hotel Lamprey. 103 just off B' way."

"Yeah I know where it is. I remember him too."

"Good. Room 606. Just pick him up. Don't take time to shake the place down. Except bring in all books, letters, manuscripts. *Anything* printed, typed or written. Ketch?"

"Ketch. But what's the angle ... Books ..."

"Just do it." The Lieutenant hung up.

Hauser and O'Brien. They had been on the City Narcotic Squad for 20 years. Old-timers like me. I been on the junk for 16 years. They weren't bad as laws go. At least O'Brien wasn't. O'Brien was the con man, and Hauser the tough guy. A vaudeville team. Hauser had a way of hitting you before he said anything, just to break the ice. Then O'Brien gives you an Old Gold—just like a cop to smoke Old Golds somehow—and starts putting down a cop con that was really bottled in bond. Not a bad guy, and I didn't want to do it. But it was my only chance.

I was just tying up for my morning shot when they walked in with a passkey. It was a special kind you can use even when the door is locked from the inside with a key in the lock. On the table in front of me was a packet of junk, spike, syringe—I got the habit of using a regular syringe in Mexico and never went back to using a dropper—alcohol, cotton and a glass of water.

"Well well," says O'Brien . . . "Long time no see eh?"

"Put on your coat, Lee," says Hauser. He had his gun out. He always has it out when he makes a pinch for the psychological effect and to forestall a rush for toilet, sink or window.

"Can I take a bang first, boys?" I asked . . . "There's plenty here for evidence . . ."

I was wondering how I could get to my suitcase if they said no. The case wasn't locked, but Hauser had the gun in his hand.

"He wants a shot," said Hauser.

"Now you know we can't do that, Bill," said O'Brien in his sweet con voice, dragging out the name with an oily, insinuating familiarity, brutal and obscene.

He meant, of course, "What can you do for us, Bill?" He looked at me and smiled. The smile stayed there too long, hideous and naked, the smile of an old painted pervert, gathering all the negative evil of O'Brien's ambiguous function.

"I might could set up Marty Steel for you," I said.

I knew they wanted Marty bad. He'd been pushing for five years, and they couldn't hang one on him. Marty was an old-timer, and very careful about who he served. He had to know a man and know him well before he would pick up his money. No one can say they ever did time because of me. My rep is perfect, but still Marty wouldn't serve me because he didn't know me long enough. That's how skeptical Marty was.

"Marty?" said O'Brien. "Can you score from him?"

"Sure I can."

They were suspicious. A man can't be a cop all his life without developing a special set of intuitions.

"O.K.," said Hauser finally. "But you'd better deliver, Lee."

"I'll deliver all right. Believe me I appreciate this."

I tied up for a shot, my hands trembling with eagerness, an archetype dope fiend.

"Just an old junky, boys, a harmless old shaking wreck of a

junky." That's the way I put it down. As I had hoped, Hauser looked away when I started probing for a vein. It's a wildly unpretty spectacle.

O'Brien was sitting on the arm of a chair smoking an Old Gold, looking out the window with that dreamy what I'll do when I get my pension look.

I hit a vein right away. A column of blood shot up into the syringe for an instant sharp and solid as a red cord. I pressed the plunger down with my thumb, feeling the junk pound through my veins to feed a million junk-hungry cells, to bring strength and alertness to every nerve and muscle. They were not watching me. I filled the syringe with alcohol.

Hauser was juggling his snub-nosed detective special, a Colt, and looking around the room. He could smell danger like an animal. With his left hand he pushed the closet door open and glanced inside. My stomach contracted. I thought, "If he looks in the suitcase now I'm done."

Hauser turned to me abruptly. "You through yet?" he snarled. "You'd better not try to shit us on Marty." The words came out so ugly he surprised and shocked himself.

I picked up the syringe full of alcohol, twisting the needle to make sure it was tight.

"Just two seconds," I said.

I squirted a thin jet of alcohol, whipping it across his eyes with a sideways shake of the syringe. He let out a bellow of pain. I could see him pawing at his eyes with the left hand like he was tearing off an invisible bandage as I dropped to the floor on one knee, reaching for my suitcase. I pushed the suitcase open, and my left hand closed over the gun butt—I am right-handed but I shoot with my left hand. I felt the concussion of Hauser's shot before I heard it. His slug slammed into the wall behind me. Shooting from the floor, I snapped two quick shots into Hauser's belly where his vest had pulled up showing an inch of white shirt. He grunted in a way

I could feel and doubled forward. Stiff with panic, O'Brien's hand was tearing at the gun in his shoulder holster. I clamped my other hand around my gun wrist to steady it for the long pull—this gun has the hammer filed off round so you can only use it double action—and shot him in the middle of his red forehead about two inches below the silver hairline. His hair had been grey the last time I saw him. That was about 15 years ago. My first arrest. His eyes went out. He fell off the chair onto his face. My hands were already reaching for what I needed, sweeping my notebooks into a briefcase with my works, junk, and a box of shells. I stuck the gun into my belt, and stepped out into the corridor putting on my coat.

I could hear the desk clerk and the bell boy pounding up the stairs. I took the self-service elevator down, walked through the empty lobby into the street.

It was a beautiful Indian summer day. I knew I didn't have much chance, but any chance is better than none, better than being a subject for experiments with ST (6) or whatever the initials are.

I had to stock up on junk fast. Along with airports, R.R. stations and bus terminals, they would cover all junk areas and connections. I took a taxi to Washington Square, got out and walked along 4th Street till I spotted Nick on a corner. You can always find the pusher. Your need conjures him up like a ghost.

"Listen, Nick," I said, "I'm leaving town. I want to pick up a piece of H. Can you make it right now?"

We were walking along 4th Street. Nick's voice seemed to drift into my consciousness from no particular place. An eerie, disembodied voice.

"Yes, I think I can make it. I'll have to make a run uptown."

"We can take a cab."

"O.K., but I can't take you in to the guy, you understand."

"I understand. Let's go."

We were in the cab heading North. Nick was talking in his flat, dead voice.

"Some funny stuff we're getting lately. It's not weak exactly . . .

I don't know ... It's different. Maybe they're putting some synthetic shit in it ... Dollies or something ..."

"What!!!? Already?"

"Huh? ... But this I'm taking you to now is O.K. In fact it's about the best deal around that I know of ... Stop here."

"Please make it fast," I said.

"It should be a matter of ten minutes unless he's out of stuff and has to make a run ... Better sit down over there and have a cup of coffee ... This is a hot neighborhood."

I sat down at a counter and ordered coffee, and pointed to a piece of Danish pastry under a plastic cover. I washed down the stale rubbery cake with coffee, praying that just this once, please God, let him make it now, and not come back to say the man is all out and has to make a run to East Orange or Greenpoint.

Well here he was back, standing behind me. I looked at him, afraid to ask. Funny, I thought, here I sit with perhaps one chance in a hundred to live out the next 24 hours—I had made up my mind not to surrender and spend the next three or four months in death's waiting room. And here I was worrying about a junk score. But I only had about five shots left, and without junk I would be immobilized ...

Nick nodded his head.

"Don't give it to me here," I said. "Let's take a cab."

We took a cab and started downtown. I held out my hand and copped the package, then I slipped a fifty-dollar bill into Nick's palm. He glanced at it and showed his gums in a toothless smile:

"Thanks a lot ... This will put me in the clear ..."

I sat back letting my mind work without pushing it. Push your mind too hard and it will fuck up like an overloaded switchboard, or turn on you with sabotage ... And I had no margin for error. Americans have a special horror of giving up control, of letting things happen in their own way without interference. They would like to jump down into their stomachs and digest the food and shovel the shit out.

Your mind will answer most questions if you learn to relax and wait for the answer. Like one of those thinking machines, you feed in your question, sit back, and wait . . .

I was looking for a name. My mind was sorting through names, discarding at once: F.L.—Fuzz Lover; B.W.—Born Wrong; N.C.B.C.— Nice Cat But Chicken . . . putting aside to reconsider, narrowing, sifting, feeling for the name, the answer.

"Sometimes, you know, he'll keep me waiting three hours. Sometimes I make it right away like this."

Nick had a deprecating little laugh that he used for punctuation. Sort of an apology for talking at all in the telepathizing world of the addict where only the quantity factor—How much $? How much junk?—requires verbal expression. He knew and I knew all about waiting. At all levels the drug trade operates without schedule. Nobody delivers on time except by accident. The addict runs on junk time. His body is his clock, and junk runs through it like an hourglass. Time has meaning for him only with reference to his need. Then he makes his abrupt intrusion into the time of others, and, like all Outsiders, all Petitioners, he must wait, unless he happens to mesh with non-junk time.

"What can I say to him? He knows I'll wait," Nick laughed.

I spent the night in the Ever Hard Baths—(homosexuality is the best all-around cover story an agent can use)—where a snarling Italian attendant creates such an unnerving atmosphere sweeping the dormitory with infrared see-in-the-dark field glasses.

("All right in the North East corner! I see you!"—switching on floodlights, sticking his head through trap doors in the floor and wall of the private rooms, that many a queen has been carried out in a straitjacket . . .)

I lay there in my open-top cubicle room looking at the ceiling . . . listened to the grunts and squeals and snarls in the nightmare half-light of random, broken lust . . .

"Fuck off you!"

"Put on two pairs of glasses and maybe you can see something!"

Walked out in the precise morning and bought a paper . . .
Nothing . . .

I called from a drugstore phone booth . . . and asked for
Narcotics:

"Lieutenant Gonzales . . . who's calling?"

"I want to speak to O'Brien."

A moment of static, dangling wires, broken connections . . .

"Nobody of that name in this department . . . Who are *you?*"

"Well let me speak to Hauser."

"Look, Mister, no O'Brien no Hauser in this bureau. Now what
do you want?"

"Look, this is important . . . I've got info on a big shipment of
H coming in . . . I want to talk to Hauser or O'Brien . . . I don't do
business with anybody else . . ."

"Hold on . . . I'll connect you with Alcibiades."

I began to wonder if there was an Anglo-Saxon name left in
the department . . .

"I want to speak to Hauser or O'Brien."

"How many times I have to tell you no Hauser no O'Brien in
this department . . . Now who is this calling?"

I hung up and took a taxi out of the area . . . In the cab I realized what had happened . . . I had been occluded from space-time
like an eel's ass occludes when he stops eating on the way to
Sargasso . . . Locked out . . . Never again would I have a Key, a
Point of Intersection . . . The Heat was off me from here on out
. . . relegated with Hauser and O'Brien to a landlocked junk past
where heroin is always twenty-eight dollars an ounce and you can
score for yen pox in the Chink laundry of Sioux Falls . . . Far side
of the world's mirror, moving into the past with Hauser and
O'Brien . . . clawing at a not-yet of Telepathic Bureaucracies, Time
Monopolies, Control Drugs, Heavy Fluid Addicts:

"I thought of that three hundred years ago."

"Your plan was unworkable then and useless now . . . Like da
Vinci's flying machine plans . . ."

Atrophied Preface

WOULDN'T YOU?

Why all this waste paper getting The People from one place to another? Perhaps to spare The Reader stress of sudden space shifts and keep him Gentle? And so a ticket is bought, a taxi called, a plane boarded. We are allowed a glimpse into the warm peach-lined cave as She (the airline hostess, of course) leans over us to murmur of chewing gum, Dramamine, even Nembutal.

"Talk paregoric, Sweet Thing, and I will hear."

I am not American Express . . . If one of my people is seen in New York walking around in citizen clothes and next sentence Timbuktu putting down lad talk on a gazelle-eyed youth, we may assume that he (the party non-resident of Timbuktu) transported himself there by the usual methods of communication . . .

Lee The Agent (a double-four-eight-sixteen) is taking the junk cure . . . space-time trip portentously familiar as junk meet corners to the addict . . . cures past and future shuttle pictures through his spectral substance vibrating in silent winds of accelerated Time . . . Pick a shot . . . Any shot . . .

Formal knuckle biting, floor rolling shots in a precinct cell . . .

"Feel like a shot of *heroin*, Bill?"

"Haw haw haw."

Tentative half impressions that dissolve in light . . . pockets of rotten ectoplasm swept out by an old junky coughing and spitting in the sick morning . . .

Old violet brown photos that curl and crack like mud in the sun: Panama City . . . Bill Gains putting down the paregoric con on a Chinese druggist.

"I've got these racing dogs . . . pedigree greyhounds . . . All sick with the dysentery . . . tropical climate . . . the shits . . . you *sabe* shit? . . . *My Whippets Are Dying!*" he screamed . . . His eyes lit up with blue fire . . . The flame went out . . . smell of burning metal . . . "Administer with an eye dropper . . . Wouldn't you? . . . Menstral cramps . . . my wife . . . Kotex . . . Aged mother . . . Piles . . . raw . . . bleeding . . ." He nodded out against the counter . . . The druggist took a toothpick out of his mouth and looked at the end of it and shook his head . . .

Gains and Lee burned down the Republic of Panama from David to Darien on paregoric . . . They flew apart with a schlupping sound . . . Junkies tend to run together into one body . . . You have to be careful especially in hot places . . . Gains back to Mexico City . . . Desperate skeleton grin of chronic junk lack glazed over with codeine and goof balls . . . cigarette holes in his bathrobe . . . coffee stains on the floor . . . smoky kerosene stove . . . rusty orange flame . . .

The Embassy would give no details other than place of burial in the American Cemetery . . .

And Lee back to sex and pain and time and *yagé*, bitter Soul Vine of the Amazon . . .

I recall once after an overdose of majoun (this is cannabis dried and finely powdered to consistency of green powdered sugar and mixed with some confection or other usually tasting like gritty plum pudding, but the choice of confection is arbitrary . . .). I am returning from The Lulu or Johnny or Little Boy's Room (stink of atrophied infancy and toilet training) look across the living room of that villa outside Tanger and suddenly don't know where I am. Perhaps I have opened the wrong door and at any moment The Man In Possession, The Owner Who Got There First will rush in and scream:

"What Are You Doing Here? Who Are You?"

And I don't know what I am doing there nor who I am. I decide to play it cool and maybe I will get the orientation before the Owner shows . . . So instead of yelling *"Where Am I?"* cool it and look around and you will find out approximately . . . You were not there for *The Beginning*. You will not be there for *The End* . . . Your knowledge of what is going on can only be superficial and relative . . . What do I know of this yellow blighted young junky face subsisting on raw opium? I tried to tell him: "Some morning you will wake up with your liver in your lap" and how to process raw opium so it is not plain poison. But his eyes glaze over and he don't want to know. Junkies are like that most of them they don't want to know . . . and you can't tell them anything . . . A smoker doesn't want to know anything but smoke . . . And a heroin junky same way . . . Strictly the spike and any other route is Farina . . .

So I guess he is still sitting there in his 1920 Spanish villa outside Tanger eating that raw opium full of shit and stones and straw . . . the whole lot for fear he might lose something . . .

There is only one thing a writer can write about: *what is in front of his senses at the moment of writing* . . . I am a recording instrument . . . I do not presume to impose "story" "plot" "continuity" . . . Insofar as I succeed in *Direct* recording of certain areas of psychic process I may have limited function . . . I am not an entertainer . . .

"Possession" they call it . . . Sometimes an entity jumps in the body—outlines waver in yellow orange jelly—and hands move to disembowel the passing whore or strangle the nabor child in hope of alleviating a chronic housing shortage. As if I was usually there but subject to goof now and again . . . *Wrong! I am never here* . . . Never that is *fully* in possession, but somehow in a position to forestall ill-advised moves . . . Patrolling is, in fact, my principal occupation . . . No matter how tight Security, I am always somewhere *Outside* giving orders and *Inside* this straitjacket of jelly that gives and stretches but always reforms ahead of every movement, thought, impulse, stamped with the seal of alien inspection . . .

Writers talk about the sweet-sick smell of death whereas any junky can tell you that death has no smell . . . at the same time a smell that shuts off breath and stops blood . . . colorless no-smell of death . . . no one can breathe and smell it through pink convolutions and black blood filters of flesh . . . the death smell is unmistakably a smell and complete absence of smell . . . smell absence hits the nose first because all organic life has smell . . . stopping of smell is felt like darkness to the eyes, silence to the ears, stress and weightlessness to the balance and location sense . . .

You always smell it and give it out for others to smell during junk withdrawal . . . A kicking junky can make a whole apartment unlivable with his death smell . . . but a good airing will stink the place up again so a body can breathe . . . You also smell it during one of those oil burner habits that suddenly starts jumping geometric like a topping forest fire . . .

Cure is always: *Let Go! Jump!*

A friend of mine found himself naked in a Marrakech hotel room second floor . . . (He is after processing by a Texas mother who dressed him in girl's clothes as a child . . . Crude but effective against infant protoplasm . . .) The other occupants are Arabs, three Arabs . . . knives in hand . . . watching him . . . glint of metal and points of light in dark eyes . . . pieces of murder falling slow as opal chips through glycerine . . . Slower animal reactions allow him a full second to decide: Straight through the window and down into the crowded street like a falling star his wake of glass glittering in the sun . . . sustained a broken ankle and a chipped shoulder . . . clad in a diaphanous pink curtain, with a curtain-rod staff, hobbled away to the Commissariat de Police . . .

Sooner or later The Vigilante, The Rube, Lee The Agent, A.J., Clem and Jody The Ergot Twins, Hassan O'Leary the After Birth Tycoon, The Sailor, The Exterminator, Andrew Keif, "Fats" Terminal, Doc Benway, "Fingers" Schafer are subject to say the same thing in the same words, to occupy, at that intersection point, the same position in space-time. Using a common vocal apparatus complete with all metabolic appliances—that is, to be the same person—a most inaccurate way of expressing *Recognition:* The junky naked in sunlight . . .

The writer sees himself reading to the mirror as always . . . He must check now and again to reassure himself that The Crime Of Separate Action has not, is not, cannot occur . . .

Anyone who has ever looked into a mirror knows what this crime is and what it means in terms of lost control when the reflection no longer obeys . . . Too late to dial *P o l i c e* . . .

I personally wish to terminate my services as of now in that I cannot continue to sell the raw materials of death . . . Yours, sir, is a hopeless case and a noisome one . . .

"Defense is meaningless in the present state of our knowledge," said The Defense looking up from an electron microscope . . .

Take your business to Walgreen's

We are not responsible

Steal anything in sight

I don't know how to return it to the white reader

You can write or yell or croon about it . . . paint about it . . . act about it . . . shit it out in mobiles . . . *So long as you don't go and do it* . . .

Senators leap up and bray for the Death Penalty with inflexible authority of virus yen . . . Death for dope fiends, death for sex queens (I mean fiends), death for the psychopath who offends the cowed and graceless flesh with broken animal innocence of lithe movement . . .

The black wind sock of death undulates over the land, feeling, smelling for the crime of separate life, movers of the fear-frozen flesh shivering under a vast probability curve . . .

Population blocks disappear in a checker game of genocide . . . Any number can play . . .

The Liberal Press and The Press Not So Liberal and The Press Reactionary scream approval: "Above all the myth of other-level experience must be eradicated . . ." And speak darkly of certain harsh realities . . . cows with the aftosa . . . prophylaxis . . .

Power groups of the world frantically cut lines of connection . . . The Planet drifts to random insect doom . . .

Thermodynamics has won at a crawl . . . Orgone balked at the post . . . Christ bled . . . Time ran out . . .

You can cut into *Naked Lunch* at any intersection point . . . I have written many prefaces. They atrophy and amputate spontaneous like the little toe amputates in a West African disease confined to the Negro race and the passing blonde shows her brass ankle as a manicured toe bounces across the club terrace, retrieved and laid at her feet by her Afghan hound . . .

Naked Lunch is a blueprint, a How-To Book . . . Black insect lusts open into vast other-planet landscapes . . . Abstract concepts, bare as algebra, narrow down to a black turd or a pair of aging *cojones* . . .

How-To extend levels of experience by opening the door at the end of a long hall . . . Doors that only open in *Silence* . . . *Naked Lunch* demands Silence from The Reader. Otherwise he is taking his own pulse . . .

Robert Christie knew The Answering Service . . . Kill the old cunts . . . keep pubic hairs in his locket . . . wouldn't you?

Robert Christie, mass strangler of women—sounds like a daisy chain—hanged in 1953.

Jack The Ripper, Literal Swordsman of the 1890s and never caught with his pants down ... wrote a letter to The Press:

"Next time I'll send along an ear just for jolly ... Wouldn't you?"

"Oh be careful! There they go again!" said the old queen as his string broke spilling his balls over the floor ... "Stop them will you, James, you worthless old shit! Don't just stand there and let the Master's balls roll into the coal-bin!"

Dilaudid deliver poor me (Dilaudid is souped-up dehydrate morphine).

The sheriff in black vest types out a death warrant: "Gotta make it legal and exempt narcotic ..."

Violation Public Health Law 334 ... Procuring an orgasm by the use of fraud ...

Johnny on all fours and Mary sucking him and running her fingers down the thigh backs and light over the outfields of the ball park ...

Over the broken chair and out through the tool-house window whitewash whipping in a cold spring wind on a limestone cliff over the river ... piece of moon smoke hangs in china blue sky ... out on a long line of jissom across the dusty floor ...

Motel ... Motel ... Motel ... broken neon arabesque ... loneliness moans across the continent like fog horns over still oily water of tidal rivers ...

Ball squeezed dry lemon rinderpest rims the ass with a knife cut off a piece of hash for the water pipe—bubble bubble—indicate what used to be me ...

"The river is served, sir."

Dead leaves fill the fountain and geraniums run wild with mint, spill a vending machine route across the lawn ...

The aging playboy dons his 1920 autograph slicker, feeds his screaming wife down the garbage-disposal unit ... Hair, shit and blood spurt out 1963 on the wall . . . "Yes sir, boys, the shit really hit the fan in '63," said the tiresome old prophet can bore the piss out of you in any space-time direction . . .

"Now I happen to remember because it was just two year before that a strain of human aftosa developed in a Bolivian lavatory got loose through the medium of a chinchilla coat fixed an income tax case in Kansas City . . . And a Liz claimed Immaculate Conception and give birth to a six-ounce spider monkey through the navel . . . They say the croaker was party to that caper had the monkey on his back all the time . . ."

I, William Seward, captain of this lushed up hash-head subway, will quell the Loch Ness monster with rotenone and cowboy the white whale. I will reduce Satan to Automatic Obedience, and sublimate subsidiary fiends. I will banish the candiru from your swimming pools.

I will issue a bull on Immaculate Birth Control . . .

"The oftener a thing happens the more uniquely wonderful it is," said the pretentious young Nordic on the trapeze studying his Masonic homework.

"The Jews don't believe in Christ, Clem . . . All they want to do is doodle a Christian girl . . ."

Adolescent angels sing on shithouse walls of the world.

"Come and jack off . . ." 1929.

"Gimpy push milk sugar shit . . ." Johnny Hung Lately 1952.

(Decayed corseted tenor sings "Danny Deever" in drag . . .)

Mules don't foal in this decent county and no hooded dead gibber in the ash pits . . . Violation Public Health Law 334.

So where is the statuary and the percentage? Who can say? I don't have The Word . . . Home in my douche bag . . . The King is loose with a flame thrower and the king killer, tortured in effigy of a thousand bums, slides down Skid Row to shit in the limestone ball court.

Young Dillinger walked straight out of the house and never looked back . . .

"Don't ever look back, kid . . . You turn into some old cow's salt lick."

Police bullet in the alley . . . Broken wings of Icarus, screams of a burning boy inhaled by the old junky . . . eyes empty as a vast plain . . . (vulture wings husk in the dry air).

The Crab, aged Dean Of Lush Workers, puts on his crustacean suit to prowl the graveyard shift . . . with steel claws pulls the gold teeth and crowns of any flop sleep with his mouth open . . . If the flop comes up on him The Crab rears back claws snapping to offer dubious battle on the plains of Queens.

The Boy Burglar, fucked in the long jail term, ousted from the cemetery for the nonpayment, comes gibbering into the queer bar with a moldy pawn ticket to pick up the back balls of Tent City where castrate salesmen sing the IBM song.

Crabs frolicked through his forest . . . wrestling with the angel hard-on all night, thrown in the homo fall of valor, take a back road to the rusty limestone cave.

Black Yen ejaculates over the salt marshes where nothing grows not even a mandrake . . .

Law of averages . . . A few chickens . . . Only way to live . . .

"Hello, Cash."

"You sure it's here?"

"Of course I'm sure . . . Go in with you."

Night train to Chi . . . Meet a girl in the hall and I see she is on and ask where is a score?

"Come in sonny."

I mean not a young chick but built . . .

"How about a fix first?"

"Ixnay, you wouldn't be inna condition."

Three times around . . . wake up shivering sick in warm spring wind through the window, water burns the eyes like acid . . .

She gets out of bed naked . . . Stash in the cobra lamp . . . Cooks up . . .

"Turn over . . . I'll give it to you in the ass."

She slides the needle in deep, pulls it out and massages the cheek . . .

She licks a drop of blood off her finger.

He rolls over with a hard-on dissolving in the grey ooze of junk.

In a vale of cocaine and innocence sad-eyed youths yodel for a lost Danny Boy . . .

We sniffed all night and made it four times . . . fingers down the blackboard . . . scrape the white bone. Home is the heroin home from the sea and the hustler home from The Bill . . .

The Pitchman stirs uneasily: "Take over here will you, kid? Gotta see a man about a monkey."

The Word is divided into units which be all in one piece and should be so taken, but the pieces can be had in any order being tied up back and forth in and out fore and aft like an innaresting sex arrangement. This book spill off the page in all directions, kaleidoscope of vistas, medley of tunes and street noises, farts and riot yips and the slamming steel shutters of commerce, screams of pain and pathos and screams plain pathic, copulating cats and outraged squawk of the displaced bullhead, prophetic mutterings of *brujo* in nutmeg trance, snapping necks and screaming mandrakes, sigh of orgasm, heroin silent as dawn in the thirsty cells, Radio Cairo screaming like a berserk tobacco auction, and flutes of Ramadan fanning the sick junky like a gentle lush worker in the grey subway dawn feeling with delicate fingers for the green folding crackle . . .

This is Revelation and Prophecy of what I can pick up without FM on my 1920 crystal set with antennae of jissom . . . Gentle reader, we see God through our assholes in the flash bulb of orgasm . . . Through these orifices transmute your body . . . The way OUT is the way IN . . .

Now I, William Seward, will unlock my word hoard ... My Viking heart fares over the great brown river where motors *put put* in jungle twilight and whole trees float with huge snakes in the branches and sad-eyed lemurs watch the shore, across the Missouri field (The Boy finds a pink arrowhead) out along distant train whistles, comes back to me hungry as a street boy don't know to peddle the ass God gave him ... Gentle Reader, The Word will leap on you with leopard man iron claws, it will cut off fingers and toes like an opportunist land crab, it will hang you and catch your jissom like a scrutable dog, it will coil round your thighs like a bushmaster and inject a shot glass of rancid ectoplasm ...

And why a *scrutable* dog?

The other day I am returning from the long lunch thread from mouth to ass all the days of our years, when I see an Arab boy have this little black and white dog know how to walk on his hind legs ... And a big yaller dog come on the boy for affection and the boy shove it away, and the yaller dog growl and snap at the little toddler, snarling if he had but human gift of tongues: "A crime against nature right there."

So I dub the yaller dog Scrutable ... And let me say in passing, and I am always passing like a sincere Spade, that the Inscrutable East need a heap of salt to get it down ... Your Reporter bang thirty grains of M a day and sit eight hours inscrutable as a turd.

"What are you *thinking*?" says the squirming American Tourist ...

To which I reply: "Morphine having depressed my hypothalamus, seat of libido and emotion, and since the front brain acts only at second hand with back-brain titillation, being a vicarious type citizen can only get his kicks from behind, I must report virtual absence of cerebral event. I am aware of your presence, but since it has for me no affective connotation, my affect having been disconnect by the junk man for the nonpayment, I am not innarested in your doings ... Go or come, shit or fuck yourself with a rasp or an asp—'tis well done and fitting for a queen—but The Dead and The Junky don't care . . ." They are *Inscrutable*.

"Which is the way down the aisle to the water closet?" I asked the blonde usherette.

"Right through here, sir . . . Room for one more inside."

"Have you seen Pantopon Rose?" said the old junky in the black overcoat.

The Texas sheriff has killed his complicit Vet, Brubeck The Unsteady, involved in horse heroin racket.

A horse down with the aftosa need a sight of heroin to ease his pain and maybe some of that heroin take off across the lonesome prairie and whinny in Washington Square . . . Junkies rush up yelling: "Heigh oOO Silver."

"But where is the *statuary*?" This archetype bit of pathos screeched out in tea-room cocktail lounge with bamboo decorations, Calle Juarez, México, D.F. . . . Lost back there with a meatball rape rap . . . a cunt claw your pants down and you up for rape that's statutory, brother . . .

Chicago calling . . . come in please . . . Chicago calling . . . come in please . . . What you think I got the rubber on for, galoshes in Puyo? A mighty wet place, reader . . .

"Take it off! Take it off!"

The old queen meets himself coming round the other way in burlesque of adolescence, gets the knee from his phantom of the Old Howard . . . down Skid Row to Market Street museum shows all kinds masturbation and self-abuse . . . young boys need it special . . .

They was ripe for the plucking forgot way back yonder in the cornhole . . . lost in little scraps of delight and burning scrolls . . .

Read the metastasis with blind fingers.

Fossil message of arthritis . . .

"Selling is more of a habit than using."

—Lola La Chata, México, D.F.

* * *

Sucking terror from needle scars, underwater scream mouthing numb nerve warnings of the yen to come, throbbing bite site of rabies . . .

"If God made anything better he kept it for himself," the Sailor used to say, his transmission slowed down with twenty goof balls.

(Pieces of murder fall slow as opal chips through glycerine.)

Watching you and humming over and over, "Johnny's So Long at the Fair."

Pushing in a small way to keep up our habit . . .

"And *use* that alcohol," I say slamming a spirit lamp down on the table. "You fucking can't-wait hungry junkies all the time black up my spoons with matches . . . That's all I need for Pen Indef, the heat rumbles a black spoon in the trap . . ."

"I thought you was quitting . . . Wouldn't feel right fucking up your cure."

"Takes a lot of guts to kick a habit, kid."

Looking for veins in the thawing flesh. Hourglass of junk spills its last black grains into the kidneys . . .

"Heavily infected area," he muttered, shifting the tie-up.

"Death was their Culture Hero," said my Old Lady looking up from the Mayan codices . . . "They got fire and speech and the corn seed from Death . . . Death turns into a maize seed."

The Ouab Days are upon us
      raw peeled winds of hate and mischance
        blew the shot.

"Get those fucking dirty pictures out of here," I told her.

The Old Time Schmecker supported himself on a chair back, juiced and goof-balled . . . a disgrace to his blood.

"What are you one of these goof-ball artists?"

Yellow smells of Skid Row sherry and occluding liver drifted out of his clothes when he made the junky gesture, throwing the hand out palm up to cop . . .

smell of chili houses and dank overcoats

and atrophied testicles . . .

He looked at me through the tentative, ectoplasmic flesh of cure . . . thirty pounds materialized in a month when you kick . . . soft pink putty that fades at the first silent touch of junk . . . I saw it happen . . . ten pounds lost in ten minutes . . . standing there with the syringe in one hand . . . holding his pants up with the other

sharp reek of diseased metal.

Walking in a rubbish heap to the sky . . . scattered gasoline fires . . . smoke hangs black and solid as excrement in the motionless air . . . smudging the white film of noon heat . . . D.L. walks beside me . . . a reflection of my toothless gums and hairless skull . . . flesh smeared over the rotting phosphorescent bones consumed by slow cold fires . . . He carries an open can of gasoline and the smell of gasoline envelops him . . . Coming over a hill of rusty iron we meet a group of Natives . . . flat two-dimension faces of scavenger fish . . .

"Throw the gasoline on them and light it . . ."

quick . . .

white flash . . . mangled insect screams . . .

I woke up with the taste of metal in my mouth back from the dead

trailing the colorless death smell

afterbirth of a withered grey monkey

phantom twinges of amputation . . .

"Taxi boys waiting for a pickup," Eduardo said and died of an overdose in Madrid . . .

Powder trains burn back through pink convolutions of tumescent flesh . . . set off flash bulbs of orgasm . . . pinpoint photos of arrested motion . . . smooth brown side twisted to light a cigarette . . .

He stood there in a 1920 straw hat somebody gave him . . . soft mendicant words falling like dead birds in the dark street . . .

"No . . . No more . . . *No más* . . ."

A heaving sea of air hammers in the purple brown dusk tainted with rotten metal smell of sewer gas . . . young worker faces vibrating out of focus in yellow halos of carbide lanterns . . . broken pipes exposed . . .

"They are rebuilding the City."

Lee nodded absently . . . "Yes . . . Always . . ."

Either way is a bad move to The East Wing . . .

If I knew I'd be glad to tell you . . .

"No good . . . *no bueno* . . . hustling myself . . ."

"No glot . . . C'lom Fliday"

Tangier, 1959.

ORIGINAL
INTRODUCTIONS
AND ADDITIONS
BY THE AUTHOR

DEPOSITION: TESTIMONY CONCERNING A SICKNESS

I awoke from The Sickness at the age of forty-five, calm and sane, and in reasonably good health except for a weakened liver and the look of borrowed flesh common to all who survive The Sickness. . . . Most survivors do not remember the delirium in detail. I apparently took detailed notes on sickness and delirium. I have no precise memory of writing the notes which have now been published under the title *Naked Lunch*. The title was suggested by Jack Kerouac. I did not understand what the title meant until my recent recovery. The title means exactly what the words say: NAKED Lunch—a frozen moment when everyone sees what is on the end of every fork.

The Sickness is drug addiction and I was an addict for fifteen years. When I say addict I mean an addict to junk (generic term for opium and/or derivatives including all synthetics from Demerol to Palfium). I have used junk in many forms: morphine, heroin, Dilaudid, Eukodal, Pantopon, Diocodid, Diosane, opium, Demerol, Dolophine, Palfium. I have smoked junk, eaten it, sniffed it, injected it in vein-skin-muscle, inserted it in rectal suppositories. The needle is not important. Whether you sniff it smoke it eat it or shove it up your ass the result is the same: addiction. When I speak of drug addiction I do not refer to keif, marijuana or any preparation of hashish, mescaline, *Banisteriopsis caapi*, LSD6, Sacred Mushrooms or any other drug of the hallucinogen group. . . . There is no evidence that the use of any hallucinogen results in physical dependence. The action of these drugs is physiologically opposite to the action of junk. A lamentable confusion between the two classes of drugs has arisen owing to the zeal of the U.S. and other narcotic departments.

I have seen the exact manner in which the junk virus operates through fifteen years of addiction. The pyramid of junk, one level eating the level below (it is no accident that junk higher-ups are always fat and the addict in the street is always thin) right up to the top or tops since there are many junk pyramids feeding on peoples of the world and all built on basic principles of monopoly:

1—Never give anything away for nothing.
2—Never give more than you have to give (always catch the buyer hungry and always make him wait).
3—Always take everything back if you possibly can.

The Pusher always gets it all back. The addict needs more and more junk to maintain a human form . . . buy off the Monkey.

Junk is the mold of monopoly and possession. The addict stands by while his junk legs carry him straight in on the junk beam to relapse. Junk is quantitative and accurately measurable. The more junk you use the less you have and the more you have the more you use. All the hallucinogen drugs are considered sacred by those who use them—there are Peyote Cults and Banisteriopsis Cults, Hashish Cults and Mushroom Cults—"the Sacred Mushrooms of Mexico enable a man to see God"—but no one ever suggested that junk is sacred. There are no opium cults. Opium is profane and quantitative like money. I have heard that there was once a beneficent non-habit-forming junk in India. It was called *soma* and is pictured as a beautiful blue tide. If *soma* ever existed the Pusher was there to bottle it and monopolize it and sell it and it turned into plain old-time JUNK.

Junk is the ideal product . . . the ultimate merchandise. No sales talk necessary. The client will crawl through a sewer and beg to buy. . . . The junk merchant does not sell his product to the consumer, he sells the consumer to his product. He does not improve and simplify his merchandise. He degrades and simplifies the client. He pays his staff in junk.

Junk yields a basic formula of "evil" virus: *The Algebra of Need.* The face of "evil" is always the face of total need. A dope fiend is a man in total need of dope. Beyond a certain frequency need knows absolutely no limit or control. In the words of total need: "*Wouldn't you?*" Yes you would. You would lie, cheat, inform on your friends, steal, do *anything* to satisfy total need. Because you would be in a state of total sickness, total possession, and not in a position to act in any other way. Dope fiends are sick people who cannot act other than they do. A rabid dog cannot choose but bite. Assuming a self-righteous position is nothing to the purpose unless your purpose be to keep the junk virus in operation. And junk is a big industry. I recall talking to an American who worked for the Aftosa Commission in Mexico. Six hundred a month plus expense account:

"How long will the epidemic last?" I inquired.

"As long as we can keep it going. . . . And yes . . . maybe the aftosa will break out in South America," he said dreamily.

If you wish to alter or annihilate a pyramid of numbers in a serial relation, you alter or remove the bottom number. If we wish to annihilate the junk pyramid, we must start with the bottom of the pyramid: *the Addict in the Street*, and stop tilting quixotically for the "higher-ups" so called, all of whom are immediately replaceable. *The addict in street who must have junk to live is the one irreplaceable factor in the junk equation.* When there are no more addicts to buy junk there will be no junk traffic. As long as junk need exists, someone will service it.

Addicts can be cured or quarantined—that is, allowed a morphine ration under minimal supervision like typhoid carriers. When this is done, junk pyramids of the world will collapse. So far as I know, England is the only country to apply this method to the junk problem. They have about five hundred quarantined addicts in the U.K. In another generation when the quarantined addicts die off and pain killers operating on a non-junk principle are discovered, the junk virus will be like smallpox, a closed chapter—a medical curiosity.

The vaccine that can relegate the junk virus to a landlocked past is in existence. This vaccine is the Apomorphine Treatment discovered by an English doctor whose name I must withhold pending his permission to use it and to quote from his book covering thirty years of apomorphine treatment of addicts and alcoholics. The compound apomorphine is formed by boiling morphine with hydrochloric acid. It was discovered years before it was used to treat addicts. For many years the only use for apomorphine, which has no narcotic or pain-killing properties, was as an emetic to induce vomiting in cases of poisoning. It acts directly on the vomiting center in the back brain.

I found this vaccine at the end of the junk line. I lived in one room in the Native Quarter of Tangier. I had not taken a bath in a year nor changed my clothes or removed them except to stick a needle every hour in the fibrous grey wooden flesh of terminal addiction. I never cleaned or dusted the room. Empty ampule boxes and garbage piled to the ceiling. Light and water long since turned off for non-payment. I did absolutely nothing. I could look at the end of my shoe for eight hours. I was only roused to action when the hourglass of junk ran out. If a friend came to visit—and they rarely did since who or what was left to visit—I sat there not caring that he had entered my field of vision—a grey screen always blanker and fainter—and not caring when he walked out of it. If he had died on the spot I would have sat there looking at my shoe waiting to go through his pockets. Wouldn't you? Because I never had enough junk—no one ever does. Thirty grains of morphine a day and it still was not enough. And long waits in front of the drugstore. Delay is a rule in the junk business. The Man is never on time. This is no accident. There are no accidents in the junk world. The addict is taught again and again exactly what will happen if he does not score for his junk ration. Get up that money or else. And suddenly my habit began to jump and jump. Forty, sixty grains a day. And it still was not enough. And I could not pay.

I stood there with my last check in my hand and realized that it was my last check. I took the next plane for London.

The doctor explained to me that apomorphine acts on the back brain to regulate the metabolism and normalize the blood stream in such a way that the enzyme system of addiction is destroyed over a period of four or five days. Once the back brain is regulated apomorphine can be discontinued and only used in case of relapse. (No one would take apomorphine for kicks. *Not one case of addiction to apomorphine has ever been recorded.*) I agreed to undergo treatment and entered a nursing home. For the first twenty-four hours I was literally insane and paranoid as many addicts are in severe withdrawal. This delirium was dispersed by twenty-four hours of intensive apomorphine treatment. The doctor showed me the chart. I had received minute amounts of morphine that could not possibly account for my lack of the more severe withdrawal symptoms such as leg and stomach cramps, fever and my own special symptom, The Cold Burn, like a vast hives covering the body and rubbed with menthol. Every addict has his own special symptom that cracks all control. There was a missing factor in the withdrawal equation—that factor could only be apomorphine.

I saw the apomorphine treatment really work. Eight days later I left the nursing home eating and sleeping normally. I remained completely off junk for two full years—a twelve-year record. I did relapse for some months as a result of pain and illness. Another apomorphine cure has kept me off junk through this writing.

The apomorphine cure is qualitatively different from other methods of cure. I have tried them all. Short reduction, slow reduction, cortisone, antihistamines, tranquilizers, sleeping cures, Tolserol, reserpine. None of these cures lasted beyond the first opportunity to relapse. I can say definitely that I was never *metabolically* cured until I took the apomorphine cure. The overwhelming relapse statistics from the Lexington Narcotic Hospital have led many doctors to say that addiction is not curable. They use a Dolophine reduction cure at Lexington and have never tried apomorphine so far as I know. In fact, this method of treatment has been largely neglected. No research has been done with variations of the apomorphine formula or with synthetics. No doubt substances fifty times stronger than apomorphine could be developed and the side effect of vomiting eliminated.

Apomorphine is a metabolic and psychic regulator that can be discontinued as soon as it has done its work. The world is deluged with tranquilizers and energizers but this unique regulator has not received attention. No research has been done by any of the large pharmaceutical companies. I suggest that research with variations of apomorphine and synthesis of it will open a new medical frontier extending far beyond the problem of addiction.

The smallpox vaccine was opposed by a vociferous lunatic group of anti-vaccinationists. No doubt a scream of protest will go up from interested or unbalanced individuals as the junk virus is shot out from under them. Junk is big business; there are always cranks and operators. They must not be allowed to interfere with the essential work of inoculation treatment and quarantine. *The junk virus is public health problem number one of the world today.*

Since *Naked Lunch* treats this health problem, it is necessarily brutal, obscene and disgusting. Sickness is often repulsive details not for weak stomachs.

Certain passages in the book that have been called pornographic were written as a tract against Capital Punishment in the manner of Jonathan Swift's *Modest Proposal.* These sections are intended to reveal capital punishment as the obscene, barbaric and disgusting anachronism that it is. As always the lunch is naked. If civilized countries want to return to Druid Hanging Rites in the Sacred Grove or to drink blood with the Aztecs and feed their Gods with blood of human sacrifice, let them see what they actually eat and drink. Let them see what is on the end of that long newspaper spoon.

I have almost completed a sequel to *Naked Lunch.* A mathematical extension of the Algebra of Need beyond the junk virus. Because there are many forms of addiction I think that they all obey basic laws. In the words of Heisenberg: "This may not be the best of all possible universes but it may well prove to be one of the simplest." If man can *see.*

—William S. Burroughs
1960

POST SCRIPT . . .
WOULDN'T YOU?

And speaking *Personally* and if a man speaks any other way we might as well start looking for his Protoplasm Daddy or Mother Cell . . . *I Don't Want To Hear Any More Tired Old Junk Talk And Junk Con.* . . . The same things said a million times and more and there is no point in saying anything because *NOTHING Ever Happens* in the junk world.

Only excuse for this tired death route is THE KICK when the junk circuit is cut off for the non-payment and the junk-skin dies of junk-lack and overdose of time and the Old Skin has forgotten the skin game simplifying a way under the junk cover the way skins will. . . . A condition of total exposure is precipitated when the Kicking Addict cannot choose but see smell and listen. . . . Watch out for the cars. . . .

It is clear that junk is a Round-the-World-Push-an-Opium-Pellet-with-Your-Nose Route. Strictly for Scarabs—stumble bum junk heap. And as such report to disposal. Tired of seeing it around.

Junkies always beef about *The Cold* as they call it, turning up their black coat collars and clutching their withered necks . . . pure junk con. A junky does not want to be warm, he wants to be Cool-Cooler-COLD. But he wants The Cold like he wants His Junk—NOT OUTSIDE where it does him no good but INSIDE so he can sit around with a spine like a frozen hydraulic jack . . . his metabolism approaching Absolute ZERO. TERMINAL addicts often go two months without a bowel move and the intestines make with sit-down-adhesions—Wouldn't you?—requiring the intervention of an apple corer or its surgical equivalent. . . . Such is life in The Old Ice House. Why move around and waste TIME?

Room for One More Inside, Sir.

Some entities are on thermodynamic kicks. They invented thermodynamics. . . . Wouldn't you?

And some of us are on Different Kicks and that's a thing out in the open the way I like to see what I eat and vice versa mutatis mutandis as the case may be. *Bill's Naked Lunch Room.* . . . Step right up. . . . Good for young and old, man and bestial. Nothing like a little snake oil to grease the wheels and get a show on the track Jack. Which side are you on? Fro-Zen Hydraulic? Or you want to take a look around with Honest Bill?

So that's the World Health Problem I was talking about back in The Article. The Prospect Before Us Friends of MINE. Do I hear muttering about a personal razor and some bush league short con artist who is known to have invented The Bill? Wouldn't you? The razor belonged to a man named Ockham and he was not a scar collector. Ludwig Wittgenstein *Tractatus Logico-Philosophicus:* "If a proposition is NOT NECESSARY it is MEANINGLESS and approaching MEANING ZERO."

"And what is More UNNECESSARY than junk if You Don't Need it?"

Answer: "Junkies, if you are not ON JUNK."

I tell you boys, I've heard some tired conversation but no other OCCUPATION GROUP can approximate that old thermodynamic junk Slow-DOWN. Now your heroin addict does not say hardly anything and that I can stand. But your Opium "Smoker" is more active since he still has a tent and a lamp . . . and maybe 7-9-10 lying up in there like hibernating reptiles keep the temperature up to Talking Level: How low the other junkies are whereas WE— WE have this tent and this lamp and this tent and this lamp and this tent and nice and warm in here nice and warm nice and IN HERE and nice and OUTSIDE IT'S COLD. . . . IT'S COLD OUT-SIDE where the dross eaters and the needle boys won't last two years not six months hardly won't last stumble bum around and there is no class in them. . . . But WE SIT HERE and never in-crease the DOSE . . . never—never increase the dose never ex-cept TONIGHT is a SPECIAL OCCASION with all the dross eaters and needle boys out there in the cold. . . . And we never eat it never never never eat it. . . . Excuse please while I take a trip to The Source Of Living Drops they all have in pocket and opium pellets shoved up the ass in a finger stall with the Family Jewels and the other shit.

Room for one more inside, Sir.

Well when that record starts around for the billionth light year and never the tape shall change us non-junkies take drastic ac-tion and the men separate out from the Junk boys.

Only way to protect yourself against this horrid peril is come over HERE and shack up with Charybdis. . . . Treat you right kid. . . . Candy and cigarettes.

I am after fifteen years in that tent. In and out in and out in and OUT. *Over* and *Out.* So listen to Old Uncle Bill Burroughs who invented the Burroughs Adding Machine Regulator Gimmick on the Hydraulic Jack Principle no matter how you jerk the handle result is always the same for given co-ordinates. Got my training early ... wouldn't you?

Paregoric Babies of the World Unite. We have nothing to lose but Our Pushers. And THEY are NOT NECESSARY.

Look down LOOK DOWN along that junk road before you travel there and get in with the Wrong Mob. . . .

A word to the wise guy.

—William S. Burroughs
1960

AFTERTHOUGHTS ON
A DEPOSITION

When I say I have no memory of writing *Naked Lunch*, this is of course an exaggeration, and it is to be kept in mind that there are various areas of memory. Junk is a pain killer, it also kills the pain and pleasure implicit in awareness. While the factual memory of an addict may be quite accurate and extensive, his emotional memory may be scanty and, in the case of heavy addiction, approaching affective zero.

When I say "the junk virus is public health problem number one of the world today," I refer not just to the actual ill effects of opiates upon the individual's health (which, in cases of controlled dosage, may be minimal), but also to the hysteria that drug use often occasions in populaces who are prepared by the media and narcotics officials for a hysterical reaction.

The junk problem, in its present form, began with the Harrison Narcotics Act of 1914 in the United States. Anti-drug hysteria is now worldwide, and it poses a deadly threat to personal freedoms and due-process protections of the law everywhere.

—*William S. Burroughs*
October 1991

LETTER FROM A MASTER ADDICT TO DANGEROUS DRUGS

August 3rd, 1956.

Venice.

DEAR DOCTOR,

Thanks for your letter. I enclose that article on the effects of various drugs I have used. I do not know if it is suitable for your publication. I have no objection to my name being used.

No difficulty with drinking. No desire to use any drug. General health excellent. Please give my regards to Mr. _____. I use his system of exercises daily with excellent results.

I have been thinking of writing a book on narcotic drugs if I could find a suitable collaborator to handle the technical end.

Yours,

WILLIAM BURROUGHS.

Reprinted from *The British Journal of Addiction*, Vol. 53, No. 2.

The use of opium and opium derivatives leads to a state that defines limits and describes "addiction." (The term is loosely used to indicate anything one is used to or wants. We speak of addiction to candy, coffee, tobacco, warm weather, television, detective stories, crossword puzzles.) So misapplied the term loses any useful precision of meaning. The use of morphine leads to a metabolic dependence on morphine. Morphine becomes a biologic need like water and the user may die if he is suddenly deprived of it. The diabetic will die without insulin, but he is not addicted to insulin. His need for insulin was not brought about by the use of insulin. He needs insulin to maintain a normal metabolism. The addict needs morphine to maintain a morphine metabolism, and so avoid the excruciatingly painful return to a normal metabolism.

I have used a number of "narcotic" drugs over a period of twenty years. Some of these drugs are addicting in the above sense. Most are not:

Opiates.—Over a period of twelve years I have used opium, smoked and taken orally (injection in the skin causes abscesses; injection in the vein is unpleasant and perhaps dangerous), heroin injected in skin, vein, muscle, sniffed (when no needle was available), morphine, Dilaudid, Pantopon, Eukodol, paracodeine, Dionine, codeine, Demerol, methadone. They are all habit forming in varying degrees. Nor does it make much difference how the drug is administered, smoked, sniffed, injected, taken orally, inserted in rectal suppositories, the end result will be the same: addiction. And a smoking habit is as difficult to break as an intravenous injection habit. The concept that injection habits are particularly injurious derives from an irrational fear of needles—("Injections poison the blood stream"—as though the blood stream were any less poisoned by substances absorbed from the stomach, the lungs or the mucous membrane). Demerol is probably less addicting than morphine. It is also less satisfying to the addict, and less effective as a pain killer. While a Demerol habit is easier to break than a morphine habit, Demerol is certainly more injurious to the health and specifically to the nervous system. I once used Demerol for three months and developed a number of distressing symptoms: trembling hands (with morphine my hands are always steady), progressive loss of coordination, muscular contractions, paranoid obsessions, fear of insanity. Finally I contracted an opportune intolerance for Demerol—no doubt a measure of self preservation—and switched to methadone. Immediately all my symptoms disappeared. I may add that Demerol is quite as constipating as morphine, that it exerts an even more depressing effect on the appetite and the sexual functions, does not, however, contract the pupils. I have given myself thousands of injections over a period of years with unsterilized, in fact dirty, needles and never sustained an infection until I used Demerol. Then I came down with a series of abscesses one of which had to be lanced and drained. In short Demerol seems to me a more dangerous drug than morphine. Methadone is completely satisfying to the addict, an excellent pain killer, at least as addicting as morphine.

I have taken morphine for acute pain. Any opiate that effectively relieves pain to an equal degree relieves withdrawal symptoms. The conclusion is obvious: Any opiate that relieves pain is habit forming, and the more effectively it relieves pain the more habit forming it is. The habit forming molecule and the pain killing molecule of morphine are probably identical, and the process by which morphine relieves pain is the same process that leads to tolerance and addiction. Non habit forming morphine appears to be a latter day Philosopher's Stone. On the other hand variations of apomorphine may prove extremely effective in controlling the withdrawal syndrome. But we should not expect this drug to be a pain killer as well.

The phenomena of morphine addiction are well known and there is no reason to go over them here. A few points, it seems to me, have received insufficient attention: The metabolic incompatibility between morphine and alcohol has been observed, but no one, so far as I know, has advanced an explanation. If a morphine addict drinks alcohol he experiences no agreeable or euphoric sensations. There is a feeling of slowly mounting discomfort, and the need for another injection. The alcohol seems to be short-circuited perhaps by the liver. I once attempted to drink in a state of incomplete recovery from an attack of jaundice (I was not using morphine at this time). The metabolic sensation was identical. In one case the liver was partly out of action from jaundice, in the other preoccupied, literally, by a morphine metabolism. In neither case could it metabolize alcohol. If an alcoholic becomes addicted to morphine, morphine invariably and completely displaces alcohol. I have known several alcoholics who began using morphine. They were able to tolerate large doses of morphine immediately (1 grain to a shot) without ill effects, and in a matter of days stopped taking alcohol. The reverse never occurs. The morphine addict can not tolerate alcohol when he is using morphine or suffering from morphine withdrawal. The ability to tolerate alcohol is a sure sign of disintoxication. In consequence alcohol can never be substituted for morphine directly. Of course a disintoxicated addict may start drinking and become an alcoholic.

During withdrawal the addict is acutely aware of his surroundings. Sense impressions are sharpened to the point of hallucination. Familiar objects seem to stir with a writhing furtive life. The addict is subject to a barrage of sensations external and visceral. He may experience flashes of beauty and nostalgia, but the overall impression is extremely painful. (Possibly his sensations are painful because their intensity. A pleasurable sensation may become intolerable after a certain intensity is reached.)

I have noticed two special reactions of early withdrawal: (1) Everything looks threatening; (2) mild paranoia. The doctors and nurses appear as monsters of evil. In the course of several cures, I have felt myself surrounded by dangerous lunatics. I talked with one of Dr. Dent's patients who had just undergone disintoxication for a pethidine habit. He reported an identical experience, told me that for 24 hours the nurses and the doctor "seemed brutal and repugnant." And everything looked blue. And I have talked with other addicts who experienced the same reactions. Now the psychological basis for paranoid notions during withdrawal is obvious. The specific similarity of these reactions indicates a common metabolic origin. The similarity between withdrawal phenomena and certain states of drug intoxication, is striking. Hashish, *Banisteriopsis caapi* (harmaline), peyote (mescaline) produce states of acute sensitivity, with hallucinatory viewpoint. Everything looks alive. Paranoid ideas are frequent. *Banisteriopsis caapi* intoxication specifically reproduces the state of withdrawal. Everything looks threatening. Paranoid ideas are marked, especially with overdose. After taking *Banisteriopsis caapi*, I was convinced that the Medicine Man and his apprentice were conspiring to murder me. It seems that metabolic states of the body can reproduce the effects of various drugs.

In the U.S.A. heroin addicts are receiving an involuntary reduction cure from the pushers who progressively dilute their wares with milk sugar and barbiturates. As a result many of the addicts who seek treatment are lightly addicted so they can be completely disintoxicated in a short time (7 to 8 days). They recover rapidly without medication. Meanwhile any tranquilizing, anti-allergic, or sedative drug will afford some relief, especially if injected. The addict feels better if he knows that some alien substance is coursing through his blood stream. Tolserol, Thorazine and related "tranquilizers," every variety of barbiturate, chloralhydrate and paraldehyde, anti-histamines, cortisone, reserpine, even shock (can lobotomy be far behind?) have all been used with results usually described as "encouraging." My own experience suggests that these results be accepted with some reserve. Of course, symptomatic treatment is indicated, and all these drugs (with possible exception of the drug most commonly used: barbiturates) have a place in the treatment of the withdrawal syndrome. But none of these drugs is in itself the answer to withdrawal. Withdrawal symptoms vary with individual metabolism and physical type. Pigeon chested, hay fever and asthma liable individuals suffer greatly from allergic symptoms during withdrawal: running nose, sneezing, smarting, watering eyes, difficulty in breathing. In such cases cortisone and anti-histamine drugs may afford definite relief. Vomiting could probably be controlled with anti-nausea drugs like Thorazine.

I have undergone ten "cures" in the course of which all these drugs were used. I have taken quick reductions, slow reductions, prolonged sleep, apomorphine, anti-histamines, a French system involving a worthless product known as "amorphine," everything but shock. (I would be interested to hear results of further experiments with shock treatment on somebody else.) The success of any treatment depends on the degree and duration of addiction, the stage of withdrawal (drugs which are effective in late or light withdrawal can be disastrous in the acute phase), individual symptoms, health, age, etc. A method of treatment might be completely ineffective at one time, but give excellent results at another. Or a treatment that does me no good may help someone else. I do not presume to pass any final judgments, only to report my own reactions to various drugs and methods of treatment.

Reduction Cures.—This is the commonest form of treatment, and no method yet discovered can entirely replace it in cases of severe addiction. The patient must have some morphine. If there is one rule that applies to all cases of addiction this is it. But the morphine should be withdrawn as quickly as possible. I have taken slow reduction cures and in every case the result was discouragement and eventual relapse. Imperceptible reduction is likely to be endless reduction. When the addict seeks cure, he has, in most cases, already experienced withdrawal symptoms many times. He expects an unpleasant ordeal and he is prepared to endure it. But if the pain of withdrawal is spread over two months instead of ten days he may not be able to endure it. It is not the intensity but the duration of pain that breaks the will to resist. If the addict habitually takes any quantity, however small, of any opiate to alleviate the weakness, insomnia, boredom, restlessness of late withdrawal, the withdrawal symptoms will be prolonged indefinitely and complete relapse is almost certain.

Prolonged Sleep.—The theory sounds good. You go to sleep and wake up cured. Industrial doses of chloral hydrate, barbiturates, Thorazine only produced a nightmare state of semi-consciousness. Withdrawal of sedation, after five days, occasioned a severe shock. Symptoms of acute morphine deprivation supervened. The end result was a combined syndrome of unparalleled horror. No cure I ever took was as painful as this allegedly painless method. The cycle of sleep and wakefulness is always deeply disturbed during withdrawal. To further disturb it with massive sedation seems contraindicated to say the least. Withdrawal of morphine is sufficiently traumatic without adding to it withdrawal of barbiturates. After two weeks in the hospital (five days sedation, ten days "rest") I was still so weak that I fainted when I tried to walk up a slight incline. I consider prolonged sleep the worst possible method of treating withdrawal.

Anti-histamines.—The use of anti-histamines is based on the allergic theory of withdrawal. Sudden withdrawal of morphine precipitates an overproduction of histamine with consequent allergic symptoms. (In shock resulting from traumatic injury with acute pain large quantities of histamine are released in the blood. In acute pain as in addiction toxic doses of morphine are readily tolerated. Rabbits, who have a high histamine content in the blood, are extremely resistant to morphine.) My own experience with anti-histamines has not been conclusive. I once took a cure in which only anti-histamines were used, and the results were good. But I was lightly addicted at that time, and had been without morphine for 72 hours when the cure started. I have frequently used anti-histamines since then for withdrawal symptoms with disappointing results. In fact they seem to increase my depression and irritability (I do not suffer from typical allergic symptoms).

Apomorphine.—Apomorphine is certainly the best method of treating withdrawal that I have experienced. It does not completely eliminate the withdrawal symptoms, but reduces them to an endurable level. The acute symptoms such as stomach and leg cramps, convulsive or manic states are completely controlled. In fact apomorphine treatment involves less discomfort than a reduction cure. Recovery is more rapid and more complete. I feel that I was never completely cured of the craving for morphine until I took apomorphine treatment. Perhaps the "psychological" craving for morphine that persists after a cure is not psychological at all, but metabolic. More potent variations of the apomorphine formula might prove qualitatively more effective in treating all forms of addiction.

Cortisone.—Cortisone seems to give some relief especially when injected intravenously.

Thorazine.—Provides some relief from withdrawal symptoms, but not much. Side effects of depression, disturbances of vision, indigestion offset dubious benefits.

Reserpine.—I never noticed any effect whatever from this drug except a slight depression.

Tolserol.—Negligible results.

Barbiturates.—It is common practice to prescribe barbiturates for the insomnia of withdrawal. Actually the use of barbiturates delays the return of normal sleep, prolongs the whole period of withdrawal, and may lead to relapse. (The addict is tempted to take a little codeine or paregoric with his Nembutal. Very small quantities of opiates, that would be quite innocuous for a normal person, immediately re-establish addiction in a cured addict.) My experience certainly confirms Dr. Dent's statement that barbiturates are contraindicated.

Chloralhydrate and paraldehyde.—Probably preferable to barbiturates if a sedative is necessary, but most addicts will vomit up paraldehyde at once. I have also tried, on my own initiative, the following drugs during withdrawal:

Alcohol.—Absolutely contraindicated at any stage of withdrawal. The use of alcohol invariably exacerbates the withdrawal symptoms and leads to relapse. Alcohol can only be tolerated after metabolism returns to normal. This usually takes one month in cases of severe addiction.

Benzedrine.—May relieve temporarily the depression of late withdrawal, disastrous during acute withdrawal, contraindicated at any stage because it produces a state of nervousness for which morphine is the physiological answer.

Cocaine.—The above goes double for cocaine.

Cannabis indica (marijuana).—In late or light withdrawal relieves depression and increases the appetite, in acute withdrawal an unmitigated disaster. (I once smoked marijuana during early withdrawal with nightmarish results.) Cannabis is a sensitizer. If you feel bad already it will make you feel worse. Contraindicated.

Peyote, *Banisteriopsis caapi.*—I have not ventured to experiment. The thought of Banisteriopsis intoxication superimposed on acute withdrawal makes the brain reel. I know of a man who substituted peyote during late withdrawal, claimed to lose all desire for morphine, ultimately died of peyote poisoning.

In cases of severe addiction, definite, physical, withdrawal symptoms persist for one month at least.

I have never seen or heard of a psychotic morphine addict, I mean anyone who showed psychotic symptoms while addicted to an opiate. In fact addicts are drearily sane. Perhaps there is a metabolic incompatibility between schizophrenia and opiate addiction. On the other hand the withdrawal of morphine often precipitates psychotic reactions—usually mild paranoia. Interesting that drugs and methods of treatment that give results in schizophrenia are also of some use in withdrawal: anti-histamines, tranquilizers, apomorphine, shock.

Sir Charles Sherrington defines pain as "the psychic adjunct of an imperative protective reflex."

The vegetative nervous system expands and contracts in response to visceral rhythms and external stimuli, expanding to stimuli which are experienced as pleasurable—sex, food, agreeable social contacts, etc.—contracting from pain, anxiety, fear, discomfort, boredom. Morphine alters the whole cycle of expansion and contraction, release and tension. The sexual function is deactivated, peristalsis inhibited, the pupils cease to react in response to light and darkness. The organism neither contracts from pain nor expands to normal sources of pleasure. It adjusts to a morphine cycle. The addict is immune to boredom. He can look at his shoe for hours or simply stay in bed. He needs no sexual outlet, no social contacts, no work, no diversion, no exercise, nothing but morphine. Morphine may relieve pain by imparting to the organism some of the qualities of a plant. (Pain could have no function for plants, which are, for the most part, stationary, incapable of protective reflexes.)

Scientists look for a non-habit forming morphine that will kill pain without giving pleasure, addicts want—or think they want—

euphoria without addiction. I do not see how the functions of morphine can be separated. I think that any effective pain killer will depress the sexual function, induce euphoria and cause addiction. The perfect pain killer would probably be immediately habit forming. (If anyone is interested to develop such a drug, dihydro-oxy-heroin might be a good place to start.)

The addict exists in a painless, sexless, timeless state. Transition back to the rhythms of animal life involves the withdrawal syndrome. I doubt if this transition can ever be made in comfort. Painless withdrawal can only be approached.

Cocaine.—Cocaine is the most exhilarating drug I have ever used. The euphoria centers in the head. Perhaps the drug activates pleasure connections directly in the brain. I suspect that an electric current in the right place would produce the same effect. The full exhilaration of cocaine can only be realized by an intravenous injection. The pleasurable effects do not last more than five or ten minutes. If the drug is injected in the skin, rapid elimination vitiates the effects. This goes doubly for sniffing.

It is standard practice for cocaine users to sit up all night shooting cocaine at one minute intervals, alternating with shots of heroin, or cocaine and heroin mixed in the same injection to form a "speed ball." (I have never known an habitual cocaine user who was not a morphine addict.)

The desire for cocaine can be intense. I have spent whole days walking from one drugstore to another to fill a cocaine prescription. You may want cocaine intensely, but you don't have any metabolic need for it. If you can't get cocaine you eat, you go to sleep and forget it. I have talked with people who used cocaine for years, then were suddenly cut off from their supply. None of them experienced any withdrawal symptoms. Indeed it is difficult to see how a front brain stimulant could be addicting. Addiction seems to be a monopoly of sedatives.

Continued use of cocaine leads to nervousness, depression, sometimes drug psychosis with paranoid hallucinations. The nervousness and depression resulting from cocaine use are not alleviated by more cocaine. They are effectively relieved by morphine. The use of cocaine by a morphine addict always leads to larger and more frequent injections of morphine.

Cannabis indica (hashish, marijuana).—The effects of this drug have been frequently and luridly described: disturbance of space-time perception, acute sensitivity to impressions, flight of ideas, laughing jags, silliness. Marijuana is a sensitizer, and the results are not always pleasant. It makes a bad situation worse. Depression becomes despair, anxiety panic. I have already mentioned my horrible experience with marijuana during acute morphine withdrawal. I once gave marijuana to a guest who was mildly anxious about something ("On bum kicks" as he put it). After smoking half a cigarette he suddenly leapt to his feet screaming "I got the fear!" and rushed out of the house.

An especially unnerving feature of marijuana intoxication is a disturbance of the affective orientation. You do not know whether you like something or not, whether a sensation is pleasant or unpleasant.

The use of marijuana varies greatly with the individual. Some smoke it constantly, some occasionally, not a few dislike it intensely. It seems to be especially unpopular with confirmed morphine addicts, many of whom take a puritanical view of marijuana smoking.

The ill effects of marijuana have been grossly exaggerated in the U.S. Our national drug is alcohol. We tend to regard the use of any other drug with special horror. Anyone given over to these alien vices deserves the complete ruin of his mind and body. People believe what they want to believe without regard for the facts. Marijuana is not habit forming. I have never seen evidence

of any ill effects from moderate use. Drug psychosis may result
from prolonged and excessive use.

Barbiturates.—The barbiturates are definitely addicting if taken
in large quantities over any period of time (about a gram a day
will cause addiction). Withdrawal syndrome is more dangerous
than morphine withdrawal, consisting of hallucinations with
epilepsy type convulsions. Addicts often injure themselves flopping about on concrete floors (concrete floors being a usual
corollary of abrupt withdrawal). Morphine addicts often take
barbiturates to potentiate inadequate morphine rations. Some
of them become barbiturate addicts as well.

   I once took two Nembutal capsules (one and a half grain each)
every night for four months and suffered no withdrawal symptoms. Barbiturate addiction is a question of quantity. It is probably not a metabolic addiction like morphine, but a mechanical
reaction from excessive front brain sedation.

   The barbiturate addict presents a shocking spectacle. He can
not coordinate, he staggers, falls off bar stools, goes to sleep in
the middle of a sentence, drops food out of his mouth. He is con-
fused, quarrelsome and stupid. And he almost always uses other
drugs, anything he can lay hands on: alcohol, benzedrine, opiates, marijuana. Barbiturate users are looked down on in addict
society: "Goof ball bums. They got no class to them." The next
step down is coal gas and milk, or sniffing ammonia in a bucket—
"The scrub woman's kick."

   It seems to me that barbiturates cause the worst possible form
of addiction, unsightly, deteriorating, difficult to treat.

Benzedrine.—This is a cerebral stimulant like cocaine. Large doses
cause prolonged sleeplessness with feelings of exhilaration. The
period of euphoria is followed by a horrible depression. The drug
tends to increase anxiety. It causes indigestion and loss of appetite.

I know of only one case where definite symptoms followed the withdrawal of benzedrine. This was a woman of my acquaintance who used incredible quantities of benzedrine for six months. During this period she developed a drug psychosis and was hospitalized for ten days. She continued the use of benzedrine, but was suddenly cut off. She suffered an asthma type seizure. She could not get her breath and turned blue. I gave her a dose of anti-histamine (Thephorin) which afforded immediate relief. The symptoms did not return.

Peyote (mescaline).—This is undoubtedly a stimulant. It dilates the pupils, keeps one awake. Peyote is extremely nauseating. Users experience difficulty keeping it down long enough to realize the effect, which is similar, in some respects, to marijuana. There is increased sensitivity to impression, especially to colors. Peyote intoxication causes a peculiar vegetable consciousness or identification with the plant. Everything looks like a peyote plant. It is easy to understand why the Indians believe there is a resident spirit in the peyote cactus.

Overdose of peyote may lead to respiratory paralysis and death. I know of one case. There is no reason to believe that peyote is addicting.

Banisteriopsis caapi (harmaline, banisterine, telepathine).—*Banisteriopsis caapi* is a fast growing vine. The active principle is apparently found throughout the wood of the fresh cut vine. The inner bark is considered most active, and the leaves are never used. It takes a considerable quantity of the vine to feel the full effects of the drug. About five pieces of vine each eight inches long are needed for one person. The vine is crushed and boiled for two or more hours with the leaves of a bush identified as *Palicourea fam. rubiaceae*.

Yagé or *ayahuasca* (the most commonly used Indian names for *Banisteriopsis caapi*) is a hallucinating narcotic that produces a profound derangement of the senses. In overdose it is a convulsant poison. The antidote is a barbiturate or other strong, anticonvulsant sedative. Anyone taking *yagé* for the first time should have a sedative ready in the event of an overdose.

The hallucinating properties of *yagé* have led to its use by Medicine Men to potentiate their powers. They also use it as a cure-all in the treatment of various illnesses. *Yagé* lowers the body temperature and consequently is of some use in the treatment of fever. It is a powerful antihelminthic, indicated for treatment of stomach or intestinal worms. *Yagé* induces a state of conscious anesthesia, and is used in rites where the initiates must undergo a painful ordeal like whipping with knotted vines, or exposure to the sting of ants.

So far as I could discover only the fresh cut vine is active. I found no way to dry, extract or preserve the active principle. No tinctures proved active. The dried vine is completely inert. The pharmacology of *yagé* requires laboratory research. Since the crude extract is such a powerful, hallucinating narcotic, perhaps even more spectacular results could be obtained with synthetic variations. Certainly the matter warrants further research.*

I did not observe any ill effects that could be attributed to the use of *yagé*. The Medicine Men who use it continuously in line of duty seem to enjoy normal health. Tolerance is soon acquired so that one can drink the extract without nausea or other ill effect.

Yagé is a unique narcotic. *Yagé* intoxication is in some respects similar to intoxication with hashish. In both instances there is a shift of viewpoint, an extension of consciousness beyond ordinary experience. But *yagé* produces a deeper derangement of the

---

*Since this was published I have discovered that the alkaloid of Banisteriopsis is closely related to LSD6, which has been used to produce experimental psychosis. I think they are up to LSD25 already.

senses with actual hallucinations. Blue flashes in front of the eyes is peculiar to *yagé* intoxication.

There is a wide range of attitude in regard to *yagé*. Many Indians and most White users seem to regard it simply as another intoxicant like liquor. In other groups it has ritual use and significance. Among the Jivaro young men take *yagé* to contact the spirits of their ancestors and get a briefing for their future life. It is used during initiations to anaesthetize the initiates for painful ordeals. All Medicine Men use it in their practice to foretell the future, locate lost or stolen objects, name the perpetrator of a crime, or diagnose and treat illness.

The alkaloid of *Banisteriopsis caapi* was isolated in 1923 by Fisher Cardenas. He called the alkaloid telepathine, alternately banisterine. Rumf showed that telepathine was identical with harmine, the alkaloid of *Peganum harmala.*

Banisteriopsis caapi is evidently not habit forming.

Nutmeg.—Convicts and sailors sometimes have recourse to nutmeg. About a tablespoon is swallowed with water. Results are vaguely similar to marijuana with side effects of headache and nausea. Death would probably supervene before addiction if such addiction is possible. I have only taken nutmeg once.

There are a number of narcotics of the nutmeg family in use among the Indians of South America. They are usually administered by sniffing a dried powder of the plant. The Medicine Men take these noxious substances and go into convulsive states. Their twitchings and mutterings are thought to have prophetic significance. A friend of mine was violently sick for three days after experimenting with a drug of the nutmeg family in South America.

Datura—scopolamine. Morphine addicts are frequently poisoned by taking morphine in combination with scopolamine.

I once obtained some ampoules, each of which contained one-sixth grain of morphine and one-hundreth grain of scopolamine. Thinking that one-hundreth grain was a negligible quantity, I took six ampoules in one injection. The result was a psychotic state lasting some hours during which I was opportunely restrained by my long suffering landlord. I remembered nothing the following day.

Drugs of the datura group are used by the Indians of South America and Mexico. Fatalities are said to be frequent.

Scopolamine has been used by the Russians as a confession drug with dubious results. The subject may be willing to reveal his secrets, but quite unable to remember them. Often cover story and secret information are inextricably garbled. I understand that mescaline has been very successful in extracting information from suspects.

Morphine addiction is a metabolic illness brought about by the use of morphine. In my opinion psychological treatment is not only useless it is contraindicated. Statistically the people who become addicted to morphine are those who have access to it: doctors, nurses, anyone in contact with black market sources. In Persia where opium is sold without control in opium shops, 70 percent of the adult population is addicted. So we should psychoanalyze several million Persians to find out what deep conflicts and anxieties have driven them to the use of opium? I think not. According to my experience most addicts are not neurotic and do not need psychotherapy. Apomorphine treatment and access to apomorphine in the event of relapse would certainly give a higher percentage of permanent cures than any program of "psychological rehabilitation."

BURROUGHS
TEXTS ANNEXED
BY THE EDITORS

EDITORS' NOTE

Naked Lunch evolved slowly and unpredictably over nine tumultuous years in the life of its author, William Seward Burroughs. The novel was not created according to a predetermined outline or plan, but accumulated through a decade of travel and turmoil on four continents and continually edited and reedited not only by its author but also by his close friends Allen Ginsberg and Jack Kerouac. It went through innumerable partial and "final" drafts, mostly in Tangier, Morocco, and took its final shape only when Maurice Girodias told Burroughs in June 1959 that he needed a finished text within two weeks, for publication by his English-language Olympia Press in Paris. Thus, by its very nature, *Naked Lunch* resists the idea of a fixed text, and our re-creation of the history of its composition and editing has required a careful review of many disparate typescripts in various archival collections, as well as the two first editions, in 1959 (Oympia Press) and 1962 (Grove Press)—the texts of which are quite different. To understand how *Naked Lunch* was written, we must look at the life of its author during the decade before the book was born.

Burroughs began his first serious book project—now known as *Junky*—in spring 1950 in Mexico City. While "Junk," as he called it, still had no proper ending (and a year before Allen Ginsberg found a publisher for it), Burroughs began work on his next project, "Queer," during 1950–52. Leaving this book also unfinished, he made a six-month excursion through South America in January–July 1953, constantly writing letters to Ginsberg and already thinking of them as fodder for his next project, "Yage." In summer 1953 Burroughs's first book, *Junkie*, was published by a New York paperback house, and that fall he joined Ginsberg in New York to work on their South American correspondence. His dreamed-of love affair with Ginsberg did not materialize, and in December he sailed to the Mediterranean and—after a short visit to Rome—settled in Tangier. From there he wrote often to Ginsberg, who encouraged him and acted as his long-distance editor and agent. Seizing on the lifeline of Ginsberg's interest and attention, Burroughs emphasized their shared literary project and poured out his best material into the letters. As he wrote on June 24, 1954: "Let's get on with this novel. Maybe the real novel is letters to you."

In late 1954, led on by Kerouac to believe that Allen wanted Bill to come live with him in San Francisco, Burroughs returned briefly to New York and then to his parents' home in Palm Beach, Florida, on a mission of reunion. But he never made it to California; Ginsberg rejected him via letter, and he retreated to Tangier, saving what face he could. On December 13, 1954, Burroughs mentions the title of his novel project in a letter to Ginsberg, apparently for the first time: "If there is any possibility of publishing *Naked Lunch* I have some notes on cocaine that belong in it, but in the *Junk* section." As editor Oliver Harris explains in a footnote in *The Letters of William Burroughs, 1945–1959:* "At this time, Burroughs conceived *Naked Lunch* (a title he credited to Kerouac) as a tripartite work consisting of 'Junk,' 'Queer,' and 'Yage.' His new work, much of which would eventually be published under that title, was therefore considered as separate from the collective trilogy."

Although the book's eventual title now existed, it was unstable, and the name of Burroughs's novel project went through several changes before finally being reestablished in the winter of 1958–59 as *Naked Lunch*. There are slightly differing accounts of exactly how this title first came about, but Burroughs always gave Kerouac credit for its coining. Kerouac wrote to Ginsberg on July 14, 1955, urging him to "send ALL of Naked Lunch titled NAKED LUNCH" to Malcolm Cowley, adding that he had told Cowley "all about how we got to Title—send it as ONE NOVEL, stop goofing with this 3 part business. It's ONE NOVEL, one big Vision . . . the Junkie part leads reader on to more complicated works of QUEER and YAGE ahead."

Years later, in a June 1960 letter, Kerouac reminded Ginsberg of the origins of the title: "Don't hear from Burroughs [lately] but was pleased he mentioned I named Naked Lunch (remember, it was you, reading the ms., mis-read 'naked lust' and I only noticed) (interesting little bit of litry history tho)—" The typescript that contained the phrase "naked lust" became *Queer*; the phrase does not appear in either of the two final texts of the novel (Paris and New York), nor in Burroughs's 1989 *Interzone* collection, which includes most of the "early routines" that he was writing during this time as well as the full-length text of "WORD," a key part of the evolving novel but later mostly abandoned. The 1960 letter seems to fix the invention of "Naked Lunch" as a collaboration of Kerouac and Ginsberg.

In October 1955, in a letter to Kerouac and Ginsberg, Burroughs improvised a "routine" on the naming process itself. In passing, he notes how the eels of the Atlantic Ocean gather each year near Bermuda in the Sargasso Sea to mate, and how their anuses seal up during the ocean crossing; then he takes off: "Say, that's better than *Ignorant Armies* ('Dover Beach' by Matthew Arnold) as a title for my Interzone novel: *Meet Me in Sargasso; I'll See You in Sargasso; The Sargasso Trail;* [. . .] *Ticket for Sargasso; Meet in Sargasso; On the Road to Sargasso;* [. . .] *Sargasso Yen; Sargasso Time; Sargasso Kicks; The Sargasso Blues;* [. . .] *Sargasso Junction; Change for Sargasso; Sargasso Transfer; Sargasso Detour* [. . .] May [yet] come up with *the* Sargasso title." It is amusing to imagine that the three main works of the Beat Generation might have been known as *On the Road, Howl,* and *Sargasso Junction.*

Harris's introduction to the 1945–1959 letters, and the letters themselves, make it clear that the content of the *Naked Lunch* project mutated from week to week and month to month, in the Tangier years—and that the flood of letters to Ginsberg would contain the germ of the final text. Burroughs struggled fitfully with the "form" of his novel, but as he was writing more and taking off in new directions every day, he was unable to master the chaos of handwritten and typed pages accumulating in his garden room in the Muniriya Hotel in Tangier. Another obstacle was the narcotics habit Burroughs had wrestled with since New York in the mid-1940s which, by spring 1956, had brought him to the nadir of his worst addiction yet. With money from his parents he went to London for the "apomorphine cure" in Dr. John Dent's clinic, and then on to Venice, where his friend Alan Ansen lived, to recuperate.

Burroughs was back in Tangier that fall, and he kept sending new "routines" and letters to Ginsberg in San Francisco, who was planning two long trips with his new lover, Peter Orlovsky: to Mexico and then to Tangier and Paris. Burroughs was eager to see Ginsberg again, and to renew their coediting relationship at first hand: he needed help with the sprawling book project that he usually referred to in his letters to Kerouac or Ginsberg as "the novel" or "the MS."—or simply "the work." When Ginsberg & Co. arrived to visit Jack Kerouac in Mexico City in November, Kerouac decided to join their excursion. He sailed to Morocco on February 15, 1957, and three weeks later Ginsberg and Orlovsky made their ocean crossing.

Kerouac wrote to his agent Sterling Lord in late March and mentioned that he was earning his meals by typing "Bill Burroughs' manuscript"; when he composed the second part of *Desolation Angels* four years later, describing this period he wrote that the work gave him "horrible nightmares." After telling Malcolm Cowley that Burroughs "has just written the most fantastic book since Genet's OUR LADY OF THE FLOWERS and it is called WORD HOARD," Kerouac left two weeks later for London and New York, leaving Ginsberg and Burroughs to carry on. Soon Alan Ansen arrived from Venice to join them. In the third week of May, 1957, Ginsberg wrote to Lucien Carr:

> Ansen arrived from Venice to help work on Bill's book, we type & edit vast amount of material in relays, and also farm out some typing too, quite a bit done—one whole section of 120 pages finished and another about equal size to be done this week, then the harder job of going thru his letters from 1953–1956 extrapolating and integrating material, autobiography, routines, & fragments of narrative. Quite a job—we work 6 hours a day or more, goof, drink, lunch, I cook big suppers, live in Jack's old veranda great room overlooking bay & Spain [. . .] Expect to begin travelling when mss is near completion, maybe work on final stages in Venice, & Paris in fall to peddle it to Olympia Press. It's quite a piece of writing—all Bill's energy & prose plus all our organization & cleanup & structure so it's continuous & readable, decipherable. Will start sending out sample pieces to magazines in a month or so.

The manuscript they created (and provisionally titled) in April–May 1957 survives: on the top page Ginsberg has written "INTERZONE INDEX" and a list of eleven chapters (which are counted at 175 pages); Ansen has written, below, "DEFINITIVE TABLE OF CONTENTS OF INTERZONE" and a slightly different list of twelve chapters, with an appendix. (A few years later Kerouac wrote "Property of Allen Ginsberg, 170 East 2nd, Apt. #16, NYC 9" in a large hand across the middle.)

That summer Burroughs decamped to Copenhagen, where his old friend Kells Elvins was living with his third wife, a Danish film actress. There he worked on the "Freeland" section of his book, writing to Ginsberg on August 28: "Only Scandinavia could have catalysed the Great Work. . . ." He told Ansen he had cut the section called "Word" down to thirty pages; by December it was down to twenty pages, and by April 1958 Burroughs told Lawrence Ferlinghetti, Ginsberg's publisher at City Lights Books in San Francisco, that he had "cooked down" that material to three pages and that "The whole last section entitled WORD [is] to be ignored."

In fall 1957, back in Tangier, Burroughs seems finally to have abandoned the three-part scheme, writing to Ginsberg in Paris on September 20: "As regards MS. I think any attempt at chronological arrangement extremely ill advised. To my way of thinking, Queer and [Yagé] Letters have no place in present work. [. . .] The gap between present work, that is, last year or so, and work before that is such that I do not consider the previous material as pertinent and trying to fit it in according to any scheme would only result in vitiating the work. At present I am working on Benway and Scandinavian angles, also developing a theory of morphine addiction."

On January 16, 1958, Burroughs joined Ginsberg at the "Beat Hotel" (at 9, rue Git-le-Coeur) in Paris, and for several weeks they retyped the manuscript, incorporating Burroughs's recent changes and adding new sections based upon his research at the French medical library on the rue Dragon. Now the book was substantially complete and, at Ginsberg's suggestion, Burroughs on April 18 sent the "Interzone" manuscript to Ferlinghetti at City Lights Books, suggesting that the title of the WORD section might be changed to "Have You Seen Pantapon Rose?" (Burroughs usually misspelled the proprietary drug name Pantopon in this way, which we have corrected for this edition.) Ferlinghetti did not much like the material, and in any case, City Lights had not yet published any novels, only poetry, so he rejected it.

Over the next eighteen months, generally as the result of Ginsberg's campaigning, portions of the manuscript began to appear in small literary magazines. Poet Robert Creeley, editor of *Black Mountain Review*, published "From: *Naked Lunch*, Book III: In Search of Yage" in the autumn 1957 issue (actually issued in the spring of 1958); this was the first published appearance of the novel material, and of its ultimate title. LeRoi Jones ran the chapter "Have You Seen Pantapon Rose?" in the third issue of *Yugen* magazine, in 1958. And University of Chicago graduate student Irving Rosenthal published excerpts in the spring and autumn 1958 issues of the university's literary magazine, *Chicago Review*, which he edited. The chapter called "The Rube," in the autumn 1958 issue, with a provocative closing line—To be continued—came to the hostile attention of a Chicago gossip columnist, and consequently the faculty review board of student publications blocked the typesetting of the winter 1958 issue, which was intended to feature Jack Kerouac, Edward Dahlberg, and Burroughs.

Rosenthal and his poetry editor, Paul Carroll, and four other student editors resigned in protest and started a new magazine, *Big Table*, to publish the suppressed writings. Several hundred copies from the first printing of 10,000 in March 1959 were impounded by the U.S. Post Office in Chicago on grounds of obscenity. The American Civil Liberties Union brought a federal case against the Post Office, and finally won in June 1960. Meanwhile, press coverage of the case came to the attention of Maurice Girodias at the Olympia Press in Paris. Although he had rejected the manuscript on two previous occasions (the first as early as 1956), Girodias in June 1959 sent his assistant Sinclair Beiles to see Burroughs in his rooms at the Beat Hotel, not far from Olympia Press's offices, to tell him that Girodias must have the manuscript within two weeks; he wanted to capitalize on the immediate publicity of the court case.

With the assistance of Brion Gysin and Beiles, the book was edited and typed on deadline. Writing a foreword in 1978 for a bibliography of his work, Burroughs remembered: "Much of what went into the book had been previously retyped by Alan Ansen and Allen Ginsberg in Tangier. The sections were sent along to the printer as fast as they were typed, and I had planned to decide the final order of chapters when the galley proofs came back. Sinclair took one look at the galleys and said: 'I think this order is the best.' By some magic the chapters had fallen into place, and the only change was to shift the 'Hauser and O'Brien' section from the beginning to the end. One month after Sinclair's visit, *Naked Lunch* was out on the stands, setting a record for prompt publication." Although Burroughs in his letters consistently mentioned the title simply as "Naked Lunch," the Olympia edition was titled on the cover *The Naked Lunch.*

While that edition was at press in late July, Burroughs wrote to Ginsberg: "I had exactly ten days to prepare the MS. for the printers. Pressure welded the whole book together into a real organic continuity which it never had before. The book will be out this week. Realize that in the last month I have edited the entire MS., corrected the galley-proofs, and the final proofs, and designed a cover, and the book is rolling off the presses right now." Five thousand copies were printed by the first days of August. Inevitably, with such a rushed editing job—typeset by compositors who did not read English well—a number of errors crept into the text. Burroughs corrected about fifty of these when the book was reprinted a few weeks later, but a large number remained, most of which were already present in the earlier drafts of the manuscript.

Girodias's press specialized in publishing books written in explicit, censor-defying language—whether literary, like Henry Miller's *Tropic of Cancer*, or strictly for the porno market, like "Marcus van Heller's" *Roman Orgy*—and he had a counterpart in New York: Barney Rosset, whose fledgling Grove Press in 1959 made D. H. Lawrence's *Lady Chatterley's Lover* a best-seller. After winning a censorship case over that banned book, Rosset went after the rights for *Tropic of Cancer* and Girodias convinced him to publish *Naked Lunch*. The Grove contract with Olympia Press for *Naked Lunch* was made in November 1959.

Irving Rosenthal, with Allen Ginsberg's assistance, would be Rosset's editor for the American edition. Since Ginsberg was familiar with the earlier, longer, "Interzone" version of *Naked Lunch* (and still held the manuscript that Ferlinghetti had returned to him), he wrote to Burroughs to ask if some of the material excised from the Olympia edition could be incorporated into the Grove edition. Burroughs thought that this was a good way to make the book longer, and agreed in principle, writing to Ginsberg on July 3, 1960: "Insertion of deleted material. Your suggestion seems an excellent solution. Set them up and I will check over." In the same letter Burroughs agreed to the inclusion of his long first-person letter to *The British Journal of Addiction*, "Letter from a Master Addict to Dangerous Drugs," which was published in that journal in January 1957 at the behest of its editor, Dr. John Dent, and most of which was broken up into numerous footnotes in the Olympia edition of *Naked Lunch*. In early 1960, Burroughs's article "Deposition: Testimony Concerning a Sickness" had appeared in Grove's literary magazine, *Evergreen Review*, and this, too, he agreed to include in the Grove edition.

Rosenthal still felt that the book was not long enough, and once more asked if Burroughs had any more material to add. Burroughs's reply to Ginsberg on July 20, 1960, was unequivocal, if confusing, after his agreement to the "Interzone" restorations: "The Olympia edition, aside from actual typographical errors, is the way the book was conceived and took form. That form cannot be altered without loss of life. Definitely I feel that no material should be added in the text." Rather than argue the merits of the hundreds of cuts and changes that Burroughs had made to the text for the Olympia edition, Ginsberg, Rosenthal, or Grove's editors, simply took the 1958 "Interzone" manuscript and rearranged it in the running order of the Olympia edition, adding the new sections from the Olympia edition and making a few obviously needed amendments to the 1958 text. Thus, curiously, the Grove edition finally published in 1962 is based on an earlier version of the text than was the Olympia edition, published in July 1959.

Rosset had 10,000 copies of the new edition printed and bound in 1961, but his next Grove book, *Tropic of Cancer*, published in April 1961, immediately plunged him into the defense of dozens of censorship trials and obliged him to sit on all those copies of *Naked Lunch* in a warehouse until the situation cleared up. In early 1962 Grove won a key anti-censorship case in Chicago, and in August, at the Edinburgh Writers' Conference organized in Scotland by British avant-garde publisher John Calder, Burroughs's novel made news again when it was defended (amidst heated controversy) by—among others—Norman Mailer, Alex Trocchi, and Mary McCarthy. Now Rosset decided to move. He ordered several thousand more copies of *Naked Lunch* printed and, after sidestepping the moralistic objections of his usual printer and binder that October, put the novel in American bookstores by late November. Within a month 8,000 copies were sold.

But the censors struck again. In January 1963 Boston police arrested a bookseller offering the novel, though the case did not come to trial until two years later. Meanwhile John Calder published his edition in London in November 1964, using Olympia's version of the title, *The Naked Lunch* (as it is known in England to this day). A scathing review in the *Times Literary Supplement* by John Willett sparked off a contentious debate in the Letters section of that periodical; Calder gathered these remarks into a text he called "The 'Ugh' Correspondence" and included it in future British editions. Translations appeared in Germany (1962) and France and Italy (1964).

In early 1965 the literary value of the Grove Press edition was defended in court by Mailer and Ginsberg and the poet John Ciardi, but the judge ruled it obscene and Rosset appealed that decision to the Massachusetts Supreme Court. Rosset also published an edited version of the trial testimony, "The Boston Trial of *Naked Lunch*," in *Evergreen Review* in June 1965. The high court's ruling on July 7, 1966, that the novel possessed "redeeming social value" and therefore was not obscene freed Rosset to republish the book—and marked the end of overt literary censorship in the United States.

Grove's next edition, in October 1966, included the *Evergreen Review* trial-testimony excerpts, added in a bid to ward off future prosecutions. By the spring of 1974, more than 200,000 copies of Grove's *Naked Lunch* had been sold, and the book had been translated in Japan (1965); Norway, Sweden, and Denmark (1967); Finland and Spain (1971); and Holland (1972). At this writing editions have also appeared in Portugal and Brazil, Croatia, China, Russia, and Israel. With more than a million copies sold worldwide, *Naked Lunch* has secured a permanent place in postwar American literature.

In the summer of 1998 James Grauerholz was reviewing the large Burroughs manuscript collection at Ohio State University Library, most of which was placed there ten years earlier when Burroughs made a sale-and-deposit arrangement with the Special Collections library. Almost as an afterthought, Grauerholz asked head librarian Geoffrey Smith for a look at any Burroughs papers Ohio State had acquired before 1988, and upon examining these he was astonished to realize that the minimally catalogued materials that the library acquired in the mid-1960s included a nearly complete set of the final 1959 typescript from which Olympia typeset *Naked Lunch*—which Burroughs had always maintained was lost by Maurice Girodias. That discovery led to the editing of this new, restored edition. After 1962 there were two perfunctory revisions of the Grove text (one by Grauerholz, one by Steven Lowe), intended to correct the more obvious typesetting and spelling errors; but the book had never received the thorough textual analysis required to provide a "definitive" text for future English- and foreign-language editions.

We began by comparing the Grove text with the Olympia edition to identify Burroughs's own post-1959 editing decisions. We compared these against the 1958 "Interzone" manuscript, which Barry Miles discovered in the early 1980s in the Allen Ginsberg Collection at Columbia University's Butler Library, cataloged only as an "enclosure" with Burroughs's cover letter to Ferlinghetti. We consulted many jumbled original *Naked Lunch* first-draft pages preserved in the Robert H. Jackson Collection in the Special Collections library at Arizona State University, where we benefited from the kind assistance of librarian Marilyn Wurzberger. Ohio State's Geoff Smith, and that institution's cataloger John M. Bennett, gave us generous and valuable help. We also compared all the portions of the book that had appeared in literary magazines prior to Grove's 1962 publication, and—when available—the relevant typescripts held by libraries whose collections include materials from those early magazines. Two or three private collections appear to contain some more material that remains, for now, inaccessible, and undoubtedly Burroughs did lose or destroy many other partial drafts. In any case our review of textual sources has been as comprehensive as possible.

Had we been working in the early 1960s the job would have been more straightforward. We might have corrected the numerous punctuation and spelling errors in the Olympia edition and reinstated only those words, phrases, and paragraphs that arguably added something to the text. Since then, however, the book as it stands since Rosenthal's 1960 reassembly has entered the canon (the Calder edition differs from the Grove only in the extraneous material surrounding the main text, and all foreign translations are taken from the Grove edition). We could not, in heedless pursuit of some idea of academic purity, remove portions of the text quoted in long-published scholarly texts, and no longtime reader would be pleased to find that his or her favorite passage had been cut. Above all, and sadly, we no longer have our old friend William here with us to act as the final arbiter of any changes to his masterpiece. But Burroughs himself relied upon the Grove text for years; he read from it at public readings, and made spoken-word recordings from it. Therefore the Grove edition guided us.

Miles once asked Burroughs if the repeated passages in the book were all intentional; Burroughs replied that they were there by mistake, caused by the rush to get the text to Girodias—these sections being for the most part edited subsequent to the "Interzone" manuscript, from scattered drafts. We took this as authority to remove several repeated paragraphs that were clearly in the wrong place, but left others that seem to work well in both places where they appear in the text.

We corrected scores of spelling errors—mostly proper names of tribes and drugs, and anthropological references—and standardized the use of paragraphs. James Grauerholz was Burroughs's editorial assistant for twenty-three years, and his experience in typing and editing Burroughs's texts and going over them with him during that time was invaluable in knowing how the author would have wanted a passage to read.

Allen Ginsberg's "Howl" may refer partly to Burroughs in these lines: "[. . .] and who therefore ran through the icy streets obsessed with a sudden flash of the alchemy of the use of the ellipsis catalog a variable measure and the vibrating plane." We restored Burroughs's use of ellipsis, a form he borrowed from Louis-Ferdinand Céline's *Journey to the End of Night* and *Death on the Installment Plan*. These novels were translated into English by John Marks in 1934 and 1938, respectively, during Burroughs's college years, and he is known to have read them. His typescripts employ a curious device of two periods—rather than one, for a full stop, or three, for an ellipsis—at the end of most sentences; we have treated these as standard ellipses.

In summer 1959 Burroughs changed the grammar of a number of passages from the "Interzone" manuscript for the Olympia edition, and these changes we have retained as being his final draft, even if the later "Interzone"-based Grove edition omitted those earlier corrections. These changes—of tense and number— will be the most noticeable differences in this new edition.

Far from being truly "naked," this book has, over the years, become encrusted with an accretion of articles, letters, court transcripts, and other documents. The Olympia edition had none of this. When Burroughs agreed to have "Deposition: Testimony Concerning a Sickness" included in the Grove edition, he specifically said he wanted it used as an <u>appendix</u>; we have moved it to the back of the book. Since 1966 the U.S. edition has usually included the Boston trial of *Naked Lunch*, but this no longer seems relevant to the book; we have excised it but it remains available to interested scholars. The U.K. edition was encumbered with the *TLS* "Ugh" correspondence, added after its first publication in 1964, but we have not included "Ugh" as that exchange is now of historical interest only.

With resort to the original typescript sections and fragments and, in particular, the long chapters uncovered at Ohio State University in 1998, we have however created a new "annex" of materials, which comprises: earlier, abandoned "outtakes"; text fragments lost between the last typescripts and the Olympia edition, perhaps accidentally; alternative versions of familiar passages; and a few contemporaneous writings by Burroughs that—while never meant as part of *Naked Lunch*—nevertheless are relevant and illuminating. All these texts are gathered here at the back of the book, and they are sequenced to follow, roughly, the order of the final-text passages to which they might have pertained. These first-draft typescripts bear many marginal notes, repetitions in an effort to find the right phrasing, strike-throughs and unclear attempts to indicate transpositions. There are often gaps in sense, which one feels sure the author would have corrected on a second pass—if he ever made one. We have silently corrected only repetitions and misspellings; all editorial interpolations, changes for sense, changes in word sequence and restorations of struck-out lines are indicated by square brackets.

Neither editor can approach this book disinterestedly; each of us was profoundly affected upon encountering it in the 1960s. Perhaps that lingering dream, that wish that it might not end with the last page, has in some way come true through our painstaking assembly of all the worthwhile unpublished *Naked Lunch* pages we could find. If so, there is also a certain sadness at reaching the textual outer limits of what Burroughs's novel can ever encompass. But as we read the original book again—for the umpteenth time—we are astonished by its deathless hilarity, insight, and prophecy. *Naked Lunch* still speaks to us in a voice unlike any other heard before, or since.

—Barry Miles and
James Grauerholz
January 2001

SOURCES

Burroughs, William S. *Interzone*. Ed. by James Grauerholz. New York: Viking Penguin, 1989.

——. *The Letters of William S. Burroughs, 1945–1959*. Ed. by Oliver Harris. New York: Viking Penguin, 1993.

Clay, Steven, and Rodney Phillips. *A Secret Location on the Lower East Side*. New York: New York Public Library and Granary Books, 1998.

Ginsberg, Allen. *Howl, Original Draft Facsimile*. Ed. by Barry Miles. New York: Harper & Row, 1986.

Goodman, Michael Barry. *Contempory Literary Censorship: A Case History of Burroughs' Naked Lunch*. Metuchen, N.J.: Scarecrow Press, 1981.

Kerouac, Jack. *Selected Letters, 1940–1956*. Ed. by Ann Charters. New York: Viking Penguin, 1995.

——. *Selected Letters, 1957–1969*. Ed. by Ann Charters. New York: Viking Penguin, 1999.

Maynard, Joe, and Barry Miles. *William S. Burroughs: A Bibliography, 1953–73*. Charlottesville: University Press of Virginia Bibliographical Society, 1978.

Miles, Barry. *The Beat Hotel: Ginsberg, Burroughs and Corso in Paris, 1957–1963*. New York: Grove Press, 2000.

——. *Ginsberg: A Biography*. New York: Simon & Schuster, 1989. Revised ed. London: Virgin Books, 2000.

——. *William Burroughs, El Hombre Invisible: A Portrait*. New York: Hyperion, 1993.

Morgan, Ted. *Literary Outlaw: The Life and Times of William S. Burroughs*. New York: Henry Holt and Co., 1988.

Letter to Irving Rosenthal [1960]

July 20, 1960 Present Time
Cargo American Express
London England

Dear Irving:

First a general statement of policy with regard to <u>Naked Lunch</u>. The Olympia edition aside from actual typographical errors is the way the book was conceived and took form. That form can not be altered without loss of life. <u>Definitely I feel that no material should be added to the text.</u> I am now writing a sequel to Naked Lunch called "MR BRADLY MR MARTIN" in which I will use any material from the manuscripts that Allen [Ginsberg] has which seem pertinent. But I repeat none of that material should be added to present text. Above all the present ending should not be altered. In fact there is little of the old material that I will use anywhere. It is understanding out of date.

Yes it is definitely my intention that the book should flow from beginning to end without spatial interruption or additional chapter headings. I think the marginal headings are definitely indicated. <u>THIS IS NOT A NOVEL.</u> And should not appear looking like one. What is the point of chapter headings that merely repeat from the text? In short I am definitely opposed to *any* additional chapter headings.

On the other hand I think including the DEPOSITION article from Evergreen and the Journal of Addiction article is an excellent idea. <u>IN APPENDIX.</u> Also the enclosed note on Cut Up method which is used in the Sequel and illustrated in THE EXTERMINATOR and in MINUTES TO GO both now out in the States. I go into the matter of word forms in the sequel. If illustrations are used (And I think excellent idea) they should be presented with drawings from Brion Gysin since my drawings were derived from his. Would suggest a selection of drawings from Gysin and myself to be inserted at close of text before Appendix. Please let me know if Grove is willing to use Brion's drawings and I will contact him. Certainly I could not use my drawings alone without acknowledging their derivation from Gysin.

18. (sic) Insha allah means "Allah Willing."

19. M.S. Morphine Sulphate. Hospital Jargon.

20. Veganin is codeine aspirin tablets sold at five and dime in England. Sold anywhere in Europe without prescription.

21. Trak is the name I have given to The Sex And Dream Utilities. Explained in Sequel now in preparation.

22. It is Codeineeta. Latin American Codeine tablet.

23. Sobera De La Flor.

24. A oud is a two stringed instrument like a guitar. Or mandolin. Nimun is other boy's name. So you never know.

25. No holes barred is correct.

26. <u>Fugue</u> state is period of amnesia. The man speaking cultivates errors of speech for his legend.

27. A reg is a desert.

28. Meet lack is meet lack. Lack of meet. A meet is a meet. Where you meet somebody.

29. Chimborazo is famous snow capped peak in Ecuador. One of the sights of the world.

30. A rat is a rat is a rat is a rat. Is an informer.

31. A Nanny Beater is a beater of Nannies. A Beater of Queers.

32. I do not have copy to hand. Context? *Flesh Corset. A.* [Allen Ginsberg's hand]

33. Context? *M.I. is initials of party leader.—A.G.* [Ginsberg]

34. A Sabbath is a meeting of witches.

35. A motoscafi is a boat on Venice canals to transport passengers from here to there.

36. "Cosq" means prepare to make the street.

38. Repeat is intentional.

39. "Clutter the glind" since it refers to a type of navigation not yet extant has no known meaning.

40. "A pink scrotal egg." reference scrotum.

41. An insect that conveys Chagas Disease.

42. It is a made up name for drug and it should be ST (6) because that is the way it was made up.

43. "Nabor" is sensible idea like "thru." But it makes no never mind.

44. Black Yen is correct.

45. A lamp in the form of a cobra. Atrocity common in the 1920s and often correlated with pseudo Spanish subdivision architecture.

46. Come, now Irving. "Oh Oh what can the matter be Johnny's so long at the fair??????" You have heard that tune a thousand times. We all have. No folk song just an old song around for a long time.

47. The book should end with "No glot Clom Fliday." Explanation in footnote.

48. The Ouab days were the five days left over at the year's end in Maya Calendar. All bad luck of the year was concentrated in the Ouab Days.

THE ENCLOSED EXPLANATION OF THE CUT UP METHOD SHOULD BE INSERTED AT THE END OF THE ARTICLE DEPOSITION AND FOLLOWED BY THE CUT UP OF THAT ARTICLE WHICH WAS PRINTED IN CONTRIBUTORS NOTES. REMEMBER THAT SOME OF THE ERRORS IN OLYMPIA EDITION ARE INTENTIONAL. I CORRECTED THE BOOK FOR SECOND PRINTING AND FOUND AS I REMEMBER NOT MORE THAN FIFTY ACTUAL ERRORS.

LOVE
    William Burroughs

THE DEATH OF MEL THE WAITER [UNDATED, HANDWRITTEN, CIRCA LATE 1953]

I remember how I happened to write this book. I had a friend—no not a friend, a customer, more like—Mel the waiter. Every time he took a bang—I used to service him in his room, you understand—sounds like sex—much of junk talk is ambiguously sexual—lived over on Jane Street in one of those dirty red brick rooming houses—by an odd coincidence I used to live in the same place when I was fuckin Anderson or vice versa—long prick of coincidence, feller say—

So I remember once Mel took a bang—as I turned around, there he was, blacking out, and the dropper hanging in his arm, full of blood—And I jerked the dropper out and slapped his face with a wet towel, that is, Ritchie slapped his face, I didn't know him that well—understand what I mean?—you gotta know a guy to slap his face with a wet towel, you know what I'm talkin about?

Well suppose I come in in the middle, say 1000 years from now—new kicks and a new set up—I could just sit and listen—This is if I <u>sabe</u>'d the talk—and I'd dig the set up or the word for it—for example there's always a word for fuzz—Reminds me of Fay White and her Sunday language about Phil—"Phil isn't here, he had to go downtown"—or "Phil was involved in something that took him to Lexington."

Well so I figure Mel was going to conk out one day—and in fact he did—

Came out of Lexington clean after taking the cure—This happen to a lotta good people. Not that Mel the waiter was ever any good for anything. Ritchie told me how a friend of his died in his arms in Chicago (in Ritchie's arms, of course). They were clean more or less. And scored for a junky on the South Side and the other bum's friend froze and his eyes rolled back.

That's what happens—I got an overdose once in Yonkers—and Jane said my eyes rolled right back and showed the white scleras at her across the kitchen table like cataracts. But fear not, thou Wedding Guest, this body fell not down—well, not that time—where—when? Texas? New Orleans? Mexico?

Anyhoo I was thinking of Stan Kenton's "Jump for Joe" which seems to expand and expand with black blurs of sound in a great empty barn-like room out into Space—

So I see Mel the waiter—somebody wrote me—no, I'd been in New York—that in the winter, Al flipped as visions spilled out on the subway floor (and said "For God's sake, Al, pick 'em up. We're in a public place, it's a reflection.") I mean, there is a point when you say "What's the matter with you, you flippin or something?" And suddenly you see he <u>has</u> flipped.

Like in Mexico when old Garver came over to my moldy 5th patio pad with the impurities of amateur heroin in his brain like spirochetes—and I sleeping there and not hearing about it—11 o'clock on a clear bright Mexican morning—

So there he is, standing by my bed, cadaverous in a black-blue overcoat—midnight-blue overcoat—and his eyes brighter than I ever saw them, gleaming in the dark, the shades drawn, you understand, I mean, I was sleeping—And he says, "You going to lay there on your bed with all these shipments coming in?" And I says "Why not? What else? This isn't any fuckin farm." And he got right in bed with me, overcoat, shoes and all. And I said "What's the matter with you. You crazy?" And I looked into his bright eyes and saw that he was.

Well it was the same with Al then in the subway—so it was <u>Al</u> told me about Mel, on the subway, you understand—It was <u>before</u> that we were in front of a drug store which maybe brought up the whole subject—<u>He</u> told me Mel the waiter died—Though he didn't remember the name until I put him in mind of it—Died of an overdose after taking the cure at Lexington.

So it was later—I think in New Orleans. I was high on weed and play this Stan Kenton and I see Mel the waiter on the bed turning blue—around the lips—No, it <u>wasn't</u> in New Orleans, because Al was there—or was he? He <u>couldn't</u> have been there. But I can <u>feel</u> him there.

Blue and the room opening out into space, and neon sign outside the window blinking red-purple light across Mel's face, on and off, off and on—and the dropper full of blood hanging in his arm like part of the sign and the neon.

So that's the end—The Long Fin—or something like that. But when I started to write I barely used that idea at all.

OUTTAKES: THE VIGILANTE

Going to see his model mistress on Jane Street . . . I knocked and said "It's me, Bill" and heard her turn the key . . .

She stood there looking at me, all the bones sticking out in her face, a little gold ring of iris around suffering black holes [of her pupils] . . . I nodded . . . and she got the works . . .

"Age before beauty," I said . . .

"It's my trap and my works."

"My bread, most of it, Baby . . . Lest you forget, lest you forget . . ." I filled the dropper and then tossed her my tie . . . "Go on . . . Tie up."

I felt along her arm and slid the needle in . . . blood flowered in the dropper like a red orchid . . . Then I pressed the bulb slow as she pulled the tie loose, watching the junk drain in, the young face take on the ageless forms of junk, the skin smooth, the lids droop . . . I looked at her without desire . . . She was no longer a woman . . .

Then it hit me, that sweet stuff seeps through your screaming flesh like water on parched land, lungs aching, legs twitching, acid tears searing your eyes . . . [Now] all gone [the trouble and the pain all gone away] at the magic touch of [The Substance] G.O.M.

[I crossed myself and fell on my knees and went through the junk sacrament while Joan danced the junky jig around the room . . .]

I got up and danced the junky jig.

Like I say she got on in Europe . . . Cocaine parties in the toilet of progressive schools in Switzerland, majoun orgies in Tanger, shifty, dirty connection by the canals of Copenhagen—nobody so dirty as a dirty Dane unless it's a dirty Swede—her first boyfriend died of an overdose in Oslo . . .

"He used to nod out on a quarter grain . . . Something with his metabolism, you know . . ."

I nodded . . . all the dead walking through the room, the Sailor hanging from a cell door, his tongue lolling out the way it would fall out when he was loaded on goof balls . . . "Some things I find myself doing I'll just pack in, is all," he said to me once . . . that was back in my bisex salad days . . . Mel the waiter, overdose after a cure, turning blue around the lips under the neon lights in a cheap hotel, flash on and off and the dropper hanging to his arm full of blood like a glass leech . . .

So many I hear their sighs and whimpers in junk kick and junk orgasm half hard rubbing along the smooth wooden edge of a precinct cell and a drunk snarled "What are you doing?"

[And I looked at him with metabolic hate, drawing myself away—]

"Leave me the fuck alone, will you?"

And he knocked me into a corner, blood running out my mouth and [I] wouldn't look at him . . . now he is shaking the bars and screaming "Let me out of here!" . . . I mean for the Jail House Pest Dept. . . . and an old red-haired junky came over and sat beside me with a handkerchief and a cup of water and

washed the blood off my face with gentle larcenous old woman
fingers . . .

And I gave them all [a] sleepy benediction . . . and snuggled
down into my junk and went on the nod . . .

About this time I meet this Italian tailor *cum* pusher I know
from Lexington and he gives me a good buy on H . . . At least it
was good at first but all the time shorter and shorter . . . "Short
Count Tony" we call him . . . "Order a suit off him hit you at
the knees."

But we fill in the short count with milk sugar and start pushing in a small way to feed the Chinaman, serving the young kid
junkies he know got landlocked when their man killed himself
with acid H in the vein, dried up the city on this klatch . . .

The Man wants to touch these wild kids . . .

Young faces in the blue alcohol flame, invaded, possessed by
The Substance . . .

"But what you care so long as you get it in the vein? Here I got
a cool shooting gallery for you kids and what consideration do I
get? So long as you get it in the vein that's all you care . . ."

The Pusher sits there eating the young blood, his face in the
blue flicker cruel and sated and sexless, Aztec Earth Mother,
Priest and Agent of Junk . . .

"Say, you're looking great, kid . . . Now do yourself a favor and
stay off . . . I been getting some really great shit lately . . . Remember that brown shit, kid, sorter yaller, like snuff? Cooks up brown
but clear . . ."

"No, I'm off and . . ."

"Sure you're off, kid . . . Now I live just here . . . Feel like a
little joy bang? I mean one bang never put anybody back on . . .
No need to get hooked at all if you know when to stop and where
. . . Right here, kid . . ."

* * *

Back to New York, face stained with malaria and hepatitis, junk is way up and cut to the bone and the fear flares out of every junky's eye flashing on and off like a lighthouse . . .

Get on that boat, junky, get out from under. The U.S.A. is burned down dust bowl, cattle and junkies low for relief as they nuzzle the dry opium pipes and empty caps . . .

All ashore who's going ashore . . . Hold back that clicking subway door . . .

The Old World . . .

The Zone: Easy to get in and hard way out . . . Junk sickness stands at the control box, the yammering boy need intercepts a queen's rush for the airport, the CID warrant waits in Gibraltar . . .

In the gathering grey twilight of junk . . . shooting every hour— looked at my shoe all day . . . grey pictures on a grey screen, fading slower and slower . . .

Your time is running out almost gone it was panic got me to the airport and on the plane with an eau de cologne bottle full of junk solution . . . fixed in the airport washroom at Paris, on to the grey [streets of London] . . .

Apomorphine puked up my monkey in bloody pieces into a basin carried out . . . flesh hangs on the bones the untenanted body, and then suddenly you are back inside moving and I walked through Hyde Park . . .

Venice . . . rich yellows and blue hashish in the streets like deep stone canyons, blue doors yellow lights . . . little bars where sad old Spanish drunks sniff pensively . . . *Tapas* and soccer scores on the wall . . .

Outtakes: The Rube

That's the way the ball bounces. I would usually go in first just to ask the doctor for a hospital address or anything just so I could

get a look at him and hear him talk . . . Then I planned the strat-
egy and I was seldom wrong . . . putting my finger unerringly on
the doctor's weak point. Was he a count? Carl was a baron . . . A
Marxist? The Rube had got on junk, was C.P. and so forth.

A few iconoclastic types I tackled myself. Doctors mostly sus-
tain themselves in a medium of false ideas, the word "doctor"
casting about them, so they think, a sort of magical aura. They
are all a set-up for some line of con . . .

When we reached Chicago . . . There is something about Chicago that paralyzes the spirit under a dead weight of a formalism dictated by hoodlums, a hierarchy of decorticated wops . . .
And everywhere the smell of atrophied gangsters, the dead
weight of those dear dead days hanging in the air like rancid
ectoplasm . . . You suffocate in the immediate past, still palpable,
quivering like an earthbound ghost, slipping around the corner in a junky's body stealing out of a night spot, the old time
jazz or just the soul of the Twenties disembodied will hit you in
Lincoln Park, or there on the Near North Side at Dearborn and
Halsted the feel of the Twenties will hit you. And the souls are
crushed in the weight of hoodlum formalism breaks everybody
down to the side-of-the-mouth sober order, the studied deadpan poise. Here the dream is suffocating, more real than the
real, the past actually, incredibly, invading the present. It's almost like you could reach out and have your youth over again,
so solid, nostalgia taking solid form and face . . . But the fraud
is immediately apparent. And the horror, the fear of stasis and
decay closes round your heart.

We move on west and south, stopping on red clay side roads
to fix at noon in Tennessee and Carl got out to piss and found a
little pink arrowhead . . .

And always cops . . . Smooth college trained State cops impersonal and polite with their grey eyes weighing you up and
the practiced patter that has no relation with the appraising eyes

looking at your clothes, your luggage, your car, weighing and sifting.

In Cuernavaca Joan met this pimpish trombone player and I could see them fitting right together like a broken coin . . . glad to be rid of her . . . on South . . .

Kicked my habit in Panama with PG . . . It's easier to kick in a warm place . . . sleeping naked and the whole town looks like [a] 1910 degraded leech on the canal, pimps and whores . . . No habit . . . on South . . .

And when I walked away from them I carried part of her inside half a man ambiguous broken . . .

Up a great brown tidal river to anchor at the Port City in water hyacinths and banana rafts . . . The Republic's one gunboat stranded in a mud flat, criss-crossed by sagging catwalks . . . A young solder shits through rust hole in the deck and pensively wipes his ass with the flag, watching the boats from distant lands . . .

The town is an intricate split bamboo structure in some places six stories high overhanging the street, [propped with beams and pillars and railroad sections to form arcades where the inhabitants can keep out of the warm rain that falls at ten-minute intervals . . .]

Ambiguous *marica* pimps—Negroes, Chinese, Indian—drift under street lamps eating purple ices, lean against outcroppings of limestone, talk in silent, catatonic gestures, frescoes of delicate depravity, flat, two-dimensional, Egyptian hieroglyphics . . . Plaintive boy-cries drift through the night . . . "Paco. Joselito. Enrique."

Stale patter of commerce: "*A ver* Luckies?" "Nice girl Meester . . ." "Panama hats?" "Squeezed-down heads?" (The best Panama hats are not made in Panama.)

A hideous soiled mouth blows smoke rings into the night . . . "Smoke Trak Cigarettes . . . They do the work . . ."

This is Trak country and the TRAK, the sinister sex utilities combine, can shut off the orgones for the non-payment ...

The jungle invades the city in great rank weed-grown parks where armadillos infected with the Earth-Eating Disease gambol through ruined kiosks, the stone Liberator, tired horse and tired rider ... [stone generals like frozen lunatics advocate liberty under the iguana's eye,] the candiru finds its silent purposeful way into swimming pools, an old Chinese, fine and yellow as an ivory chessman, sits on an anthropomorphic limestone seat, sipping paregoric ...

The smooth brown loin of the pimp swells and rots with lymphogranuloma, albinos blink in the sun, boys sit in long rows under the cool arcades reading comics—they do not move their legs as people walk by ...

There is something here you never see or find, in a silk stocking thrown over a rotten teak wood balcony, [up under the town's sizzling iron roofs where plants in tin cans grow on perilous balconies,] bureaucrat in a black suit and black glasses, the dull liver-sick hate congested in his eyes like toad poison ...

Smell of the tidal river and the mud flats, sewage and drying cocoa beans ...

Now the *Vagos Jugadores de Pelota* storm the stale streets of commerce leaping, back-kicking, and the Civil Guard discreetly turns away and drops his pants looking for crabs, in a vacant lot ...

For the ball players can sound a "Hey Rube" bring a million adolescents, breaking all the frontiers, through the miasmal river towns of Quevedo and Babahoya, [windy rubbly mountain plateaus, clouds of La Paz, and the mists of Bogotá and Lima and the cold] windy mountain plateaus ... [Windy, dusty mountain towns—thin air like death in the throat—cold mist of Lima that gets down inside you like junk-sick cold,] blighted leprosy area of Tolima, hardwood coastal forest, with cities of Wanted Men, [ghost towns of Esmereldas ...] a Negro pensively scratches his balls ...

End of the Road towns, Puyo and Mocoa, Puerto Limón and Pucallpa, under silent wings of the anopheles mosquito ...

There are sinister road houses in the jungle around the Port City stocked with whores, purposeful agents of disease. Dope peddlers lurk in the toilet with loaded needle dart out and shoot it into [a] tourist without waiting for his consent ... The doormen are cops, expert lush rollers like all cops of the area, can lift the generalissimo's wallet with a macho goose, and club a drunken sailor into the jungle mud ...

I was studying a small sign on a deserted building: "Down with Trak and the Sex Utilities ..."

Dark, greasy men plucked at my sleeve, flashing gold teeth in a little snarl.

"*Psst!*"

"*Seguridad.*"

They studied my papers over each other's shoulder, the ones behind leaping up with little plaintive cries ... Mosquitoes moved delicate and tenuous in the air ...

A group of detectives began chanting in unison: "*Comisaría! Comisaría! Comisaría!*"

The *comandante* emerged through a metal door, slapping at a small pistol impatiently ... The pistol shifted from one holster to another on little steel tracks ...

He was sitting in a garage under the street level, full of metal barriers and gates and lockers that swung smoothly on oiled hinges ... I noticed that he wore a pilot's uniform ... Tin planes rested on his shoulders like monster insects ... His face was a mechanic's face invaded by steel and oil ...

"We let the signs stand because we are a democracy ... But it is not good to stand and read them."

"You can say that again," said a snide Liberal journalist with narrow shoulders and bad teeth, standing by a file cabinet ... "You might get yourself on the Trak list ... As you may or may not know Trak has special police for crimes committed on Trak premises with extraterritorial rights through the world ... I've got it all right here ... Take years to write ..."

The *comandante* smiled and jerked his head towards the journalist ...

"*Mucho polito*," he said ...

He handed back my passport with a heel click ...

A boy named Joselito moved into my room, suffocating me in soccer scores ... We wore the same clothes and laid the same *novia* who was thin and sickly and always making magic with candles and religious pictures and drinking aromatic medicine in little plastic eye cups and never touched my penis during the sex act ...

Through the customs checks and police controls, through the pass and down in a blast of safe-conducts, warm wind in the face and three monkeys ran across the road, down into the sound of running water—everybody on the bus high, laughing and talking at once, swinging around the curves over a misty void, and the driver pointed out the white crosses with little brays of laughter and sipped *aguardiente* from a bottle proffered by a shy Indian cop.

"*Veinte y dos muertos.*"

"*Dos jóvenes quemados vivo.*"

"*Viva la sport!*" ejaculates an American queen, two cameras dangle on his great bosom, extension and light filters across his breast, seeking the young subject with a dead tinted eye ... He leans back into the seat and squeeze the light filters ...

Down into the End of the Road towns on the edge of *yagé* country ...

Up through the river towns, Babahoya, Quevedo, Puerto Limón, black Stetsons and the grey malaria faces color of dirty paper, muzzle-loading shotguns and vultures pecking in the streets ... down from the mountains to buy powder and shot and tonic and *aguardiente* (government monopoly, tastes like kerosene) ...

The sad-eyed student from the Capital talked apologies waiting for the bus to load its cargo of bananas and Coca-Cola ... "They have no instruction ... Nothing to do but drink in this place ... Much malaria ..." He warned me against the Río de Oro, one of the many sections in the coastal forest regions that is peopled entirely by wanted criminals in such force the civil guard is unable, unwilling and shit scared to set a flat foot in the area ...

[The criminals are self-righteous, the police furtive and seedy ...]

Came to the town of Quevedo, sullen violence in the mud streets, muttering grey phantoms of malaria walk the mud streets along the river ...

In my hotel room two straw pallets on wooden bunks ... [Copper lustre pitcher dry, dusty.] A scorpion crawls slowly up the split bamboo wall.

On one bunk was a young man who got up and introduced himself ... He was on his way to the coast to join the Air Force ... "*Yo soy un pobre muchacho pero tengo los sentimientos elevados ... Y soy hombre ...*"

He died testing a condemned parachute misconverted and reconverted by Trak, Inc.—a scandal involving a sinister Albanian Fixer known as Mr. IN who got his start as a Congressional lavatory attendant ... Boy blood spatters The Operator massive with his weight of centuries sit there and take his cut and never give anything back ... Got the big fix up his ass with heroin, diamonds and antibiotics ...

A whore half Negro and Chinese with high small breasts and white teeth stood in the door and asked for a cigarette ...

She steps in and takes off her pink slip and stands naked ... The boy drops his clothes and lies down naked on a pallet, chewing gum and waiting ...

OUTTAKES: BENWAY

Doctor Benway is interviewing a young doctor's application for Benway's special corps of trouble-shooting analysts:

"Your first case, on which you will have the opportunity of trying your mettle or perhaps the *Amok's* mettle heh heh heh will be an incipient Amok . . .

"Now of course you know in a general sort of way what an Amok is, and have probably collected a battery of misconceptions on the subject . . . In fact Western misconceptions as regards anything pertaining to the humph 'mysterious Orient' are quite as staggering in their magnificent disregard for facts as infantile theories on sex and birth—In fact I had one patient who at the age of twenty believed that there were no women, only castrated men, and that birth took place through the navel . . ."

APPLICANT: "Good sir, to the purpose."

BENWAY: "*Touché*, young man, *touché* . . . Oh yes, misconceptions . . . So let me give you a brief rundown: The classical Amok is a shy withdrawn person with deep suppression of aggressive impulses . . . with final results that can only be described as humph regrettable . . .

"Why do Amoks always use knives? Why not a gun or a flame thrower? Is their predilection for knives merely a result of their general backwardness—Amoks are not a phenomenon of eighteenth-century drawing rooms, over-civilized urban environments—or does it have a deeper root?

"But the most interesting and enigmatic point is, what finally activates the deeply repressed killing reflex? Curiously enough, we would expect that one day some writer, some bus driver, some store clerk would insult the wrong man and reap the humph whirlwind . . . But such is almost never the way it happens . . . No, what distinguishes Amok from an outbreak of simple bad temper implemented by natural recourse of a tool-using animal bent on mayhem at least, is that it has nothing to do with—"

Spilling out in ambiguous dancing and sudden electric outbursts of violence, a young man leapt to his feet—thrusting out a knife and spinning around, his knife vibrating with a sort of electric life scream ... *No me toca, maricas!* ... His eyes light up, flicker and go out ... he collapses and shits in his pants with fear and rushes out ... A patient old sodomist in violet tinted glasses and a gabardine suit follows ...

Theft and murder are epidemic and usually unpunished ... There are whole areas, etc ... People walk about with the shadow of paranoid madness in their eyes ... it's like the South if they didn't have the Nigra ...

The inhabitants of this area seem mostly of white stock ... They do not present the fascinating, highly colored repertoires of skin diseases found among the Mountain and Coastal Indians ...

Troy is this the face that launched a thousand ships and burnt the topless towers of Ilium Troy a paco plate him or God and taxes are in the Spanish toilet sign rooms to let and junk junk the opium don't want it any more goes good with coffee the lamb eat him up she ate the whole [Juimee] whole and now where are on the owl and came to Troy around the long bend of the dead river here in the vast delta country and the others who were [in] vast tree houses on the little islands here and there, swamps and springs and clear streams and every variety of fish and serpent. And came at last to the [lake] where on the delta shore islands are more and more frequent ... and now the sea itself and the lad is there gleaming into a quiet harbor and up onto the shore ... and pulled himself up on the coast ... he pointed to the—

—gave Carl a long grave look before he smiled. The city was laid out in a series of parks along canals and lagoons ... People nodded and waved to him casually ... He never [saw] an averted eye ... Sometimes he was ignored by someone, obviously thinking about something ...

Nor must you by psychic maneuvers prevent him from expressing his aggressive impulses ... this is always sensed and deeply resented by the patient.

Should I search him for knives at the door?

No, this would increase anxiety and bury the affect even deeper?

What's the matter, young man, does the job scare you?

Frankly, yes ...

This is good, fear is a thing out in the open and always healthy ... The best bullfighter of them all used to shake and vomit before a fight ... Just remember this paradox ... In our profession there is nothing to fear but Tense ... If you defend yourself you are lost ... The patient would not be Amok if you had done your job ... Your physical defense would fail in any case ... These things are not easy to describe ... But believe me, hate and aggression only gain strength from your resistance ... In short, we are surround by threatening phantoms which only [have] the strength that is body to attack us if we fear and succumb to anxiety and defend ourselves against them ...

Discussions as to which is the most dangerous type patient ... Benway says a Latah is more dangerous than an incipient Amok ... In fact he is an incipient Amok of the most insidious and treacherous type ... Don't ever press him too hard ...

OUTTAKES: THE BLACK MEAT

The Generalissimo unveiled his statue in person ... one of those pigeon shit bronze capers on a horse ... static self project, severed protoplasm rotting inside it and proliferating insect forms which would, under normal circumstances, have been contained within the bronze shell forever ... But some joker of an apprentice had made an ass hole in the Generalissimo—covered but not sealed under a bronze uniform—flashed away with a street boy smile and a police bullet and running from a broken jeweler's window flopped across summer asphalt, a stained Mercury fallen to a silver bullet.

Blast of trumpets and The Anthem—Everybody on his feet to witness this exhibit ...

"Like we all called together here to look at his ugly old ass hole," a young Falangist whispered to his lover ... The boys snickered and froze under the hard violet-tinted stare of a fat liversick major sitting by the massive Earth Goddess bulk of his wife her fat upper lip daubed with soft black fur ...

As the cloth and cellophane covers are removed by a system of pulleys synchronized with air currents, loud farting noises rumble out of the statue and the ground under it ...

"I'll break that Technician down to a cesspool cleaner's assistant!" snarls the socially ambitious young major in charge of ceremony protocol.

And then such a horrible stink drifted out like vaporized verdigris ... stink of atrophied semen, young testicles frozen in junk, American suburbs where the male soul rots on transplanted sod ... bureaucrat Spanish homes under cold eyes of mustachioed matriarchs ... black ice of polished armoires and gilded mirror frames ... massive and damp and heavy as the women who sit there (through a pale green bubble of ferns and rubber plants).

Bogotá streets of rain and death haunted by killer cops and dead students ... raw pealed winds of hate and mischance sweeping in from the green savanna past the great Earth Goddess in black stone ... And always in the streets and corridors and windows and doorways black dogs of Paul's blighted road to Damascus and on meandering through inquisitions and burnings—Paul never miss a burning—

"Yes," the sheriff said, pushing a wad of snuff into his cheek. "Nothing like a good *slow* Nigga Burnin' to quiet a town down for a piece . . . And folks go around all dreamy and peaceful looking and sorta sleepy like they just ate something real good and plenty of it . . ."

(Stacked up cordwood of Belsen.)

The American fairy turns on his broken insect male body and tears at it like a conger eel transfixed by a fish spear—(The diver is composing an article for *Ball*)—will turn and bite its body right through above the fish spear and swim away, broken, galvanized fairy gestures flat as figures cut out of tin, dying spermatozoa on the suburb sheets in the hungover Sunday dawn . . .

"Get him underground he stinks something awful," said the British Sergeant.

"The future is ours. Of course we will use bits and pieces of Paul's machine during the hurumph *transitional period* during which POLICE as such will still be necessary . . . A period more or less elastic of course."

Benway spreads his hands in a great sweeping gesture and his smile flashes out and slaps across ten billion faces . . . police with flesh of black metal and all on cycles . . .

"Out to smell out *real crime* you dig . . . The Texas mother dressing her son in little girl clothes . . . child hands slapped away from his own zones every thought and feeling stamped with the shit seal of alien inspection . . . (The crime in short of malignant interference . . .) You see we are 'right cats' . . . out for the real enemy, the squares, the phonies . . . the COPS.

"This is all baby patting of course, as you can see, but if the tranquilizing suppository fits"—Benway shrugged—"shove it on up there . . ."

"Room for one more inside sir."

Time to consolidate or hurumph *coalesce* . . . process takes time . . . We will have time and dirty hands to deal the cards like they are all stacked . . .

The Sailor went to the fair to buy a dozen Time eggs . . . Oh Oh what can the matter be???

Lee walked back the way he had come through streets twisted in a slow arthritis of masonry . . . Up the winding stairs warped by the late unsteady returns of a vehement drunkard so that now you stagger up those stairs drunk or sober.

They were searching his room when he walked in.

"Police, Johnny."

One of them flashed a badge which caught the dim light like a fish side in deep black water . . . It was hard to see how many were there ferreting through his papers and notebooks with fingers light and cold as spring wind.

Lee looked at the flat two-dimensional faces boiling with ravenous black fuzz. "Campers," he decided . . .

Campers are individuals who move into an empty office in a government building and start operating . . . Sometimes they have bought the right to operate from high sources and official incorporation is assured. Others are pure phony shoestring operators with floating offices in a lavatory, broom closet, dark room of the mugging department . . . in corners and corridors and patios of government buildings, tenuous bureaus . . .

Outtakes: Hospital

"Three miles from the town of Camembert . ,. . Advanced identification . . . The Medical Examiner . . . Daring daylight assault on the Lavatory Attendants' Syndicate . . . light contusions . . . denied complicity . . ."

"Inspector René Parbleu says the slaying is an adjustment of scores growing out of the lucrative toilet paper contraband . . . El Culito was suspect to have 'held back the wad' on his confederates . . . present crime was an attempt to 'equalize pressures' . . ."

OUTTAKES: A.J.'S ANNUAL PARTY

The old queer squirm on a limestone bench in Chapultepec (Indian adolescents walk by, arms around each other's necks and ribs), strain his dying flesh to occupy young buttocks and thighs, tight balls and spurting cocks. A boy turn, grin at him and yell "Hi, Pop," their boy innocence aching whip across his sagging buttocks and drooping loins. He scream, an enigmatic Sybil with dark glasses and a grey face. Piss blood warm on his withered thighs.

Mark and Johnny sit facing each other in a vibrating chair, Johnny impaled on Mark's cock.

"All set, Johnny?"

"Turn it on."

Mark flips the switch and the chair vibrate. Mark tilt his head, look up at Johnny, his face remote, eyes cool and mocking on Johnny's face. Johnny scream, whimper, face disintegrate as if melting from within . . . Mark's hands run down Johnny's sides, sketch a woman in the air. He put his head gently over Johnny's cock and makes a gesture of pulling it out. Johnny scream like a mandrake, black out as his sperm spurt, slump against Mark's body an angel on the nod. Mark pats Johnny's shoulder absently . . .

Mark and Mary whisper. They laugh looking at Johnny.

"Turn around, Johnny," Mark orders.

Johnny obey, and Mark secure his hands behind him with leather-covered manacles, copper chain.

"To match your hair, Johnny," he says, ruffling Johnny's hair with casual affection.

Johnny is half asleep. "What's the angle?"

Mark stands over him, hands on hips, smiling. "What do you think?"

Mary bends over Johnny, pushing the hair out of his eyes. "We're going to hang you, Johnny."

Johnny's body contract, force the breath from his lungs. Tongue stick out. Lips swell with blood and eyes darken. The contraction hold, squeezing his body in three long spasms, shit spurt six feet from his ass, a final agonized spasm throw a drop of blood to the corner of Johnny's beautiful mouth. Lick sperm and blood into his mouth and fall asleep. Mary covers him tenderly with a soft warm blanket. She kisses him on his closed eyes. At the door Mark and Mary look back at Johnny, laugh softly.

Morning. Johnny wakes up and try to stretch. Mark and Mary stand by the bed.

MARK: "Come on, Johnny. It's all ready and waiting for you."

He helps Johnny sit up and swing his legs over the bed.

Mary sits down beside Johnny and combs his hair. "You're going to be a good boy, aren't you, Johnny?"

Johnny gets an erection. "Are you really going to hang me?"

"Of course we are, darling. But don't worry. It won't hurt."

"Are you going to drop me?"

MARK: "No. That would knock you out, couldn't feel it. I'm going to break your neck like this."

He puts one hand on Johnny's chin, the other on the side of his head, moves his hands in opposite directions, clicks his tongue. He pulls Johnny to his feet with one hand under his chin. Johnny sticks his tongue out and lolls his head. Mary takes one of Johnny's arms, Mark the other. They march him to a door open with electric eye.

OUTTAKES: ISLAM INCORPORATED AND
THE PARTIES OF INTERZONE

Clem keeps an Arab and a Jewish boy. They dance into a café in a chorus line, raising 1920s straw hats and chanting:

"Clem's the man the people choose . . .

"He loves the Arabs"—goosing the Arab—"*and* the Jews"—feeling up the Jew . . .

"Well, I'm off to evict an Arab from his iron lung. The citizen is delinquent. It's my clear duty to Wall Street."

"So we hold the Black Rock, pending they give with its weight in diamonds. Otherwise we build a pissoir around it in downtown Tel Aviv . . ."

They have a tape recording entitled "Your Reporter Interviews the Ergot Brothers," which they play with or without encouragement.

OUTTAKES: THE EXAMINATION

"You have my pants in thrall."

"In the words of the immortal bard, farewell thou art too dear for my possessing."

Carl could not help turning around when he reached the door . . . The doctor was gone . . . Carl stared stupidly at the empty desk . . . then he plunged through the door and down the stairs in a panic.

A week later he received a notice to appear at the Ministry, exactly like the first notice . . . He decided to ignore it but was unable to do so . . .

"I will tell him something . . ." he muttered as he walked up to the reception desk . . .

"Doctor Benway? Oh yes, he has his office in Public Health now . . . Right across the square and turn to your left . . ."

The nurse in Benway's office was doing crossword puzzles. A workman was painting the ceiling.

"Oh yes," she said. "Go on in, he's probably expecting some-one . . ."

The workman seemed to be poised like a ballet dancer on top of his stepladder . . . He cast a flirtatious glance at Carl using a paintbrush like a fan . . .

"Don't mind him," said the nurse. "He's just waiting on the Operation . . . He'll be much happier the doctor says."

When Carl walked in the doctor looked at him with a total lack of recognition.

"Hello"—he glanced ostentatiously at the card—"Carl."

Carl stared incredulously at the face across the desk. The man looked back, a calm kindly face perhaps a bit professionally kind. He looked like a successful banker.

"Well Carl it seems that you are causing your employer a certain amount of concern." He was drowned out by hammer-ing. The doctor smiled good-humoredly and his voice suddenly boomed out. "Yes, we are undergoing certain uh repairs here. Too bad we don't all close our *psyches* for repairs now and then. Not that we are exactly closed here . . . Oh dear no . . . Just operating on a skeleton staff is all. Why, like as not they've got your file mixed up with someone else's. But a man has to do the best with what there is, right? So let me see what this is all about. You understand I have a lot of phrases I use at random like: 'You seem to be a cause of concern to those near and dear to you,' or 'We're worried about you Carl'"—with a detective con smile.

"And so Carl . . ." The doctor slid off the desk and lay on his stomach on the floor, chewing his straw. "And so Carl, the revenooers have caught up to you." He got up on all fours and sniffed at Carl's leg.

"Aromatic," he said. "Sour mash. I can smell them." He stood on his head. "And so Carl, will you submit to a blood test or do I haveta get a search warrant?"

"But what? Why?"

"Well, if you must know, we are looking for a certain protein enzyme, identified precisely as a protein enzyme by one Doctor Heath of New Orleans, a learned colleague, may he fall down and rot for snatching my enzyme right from under my very nose."

The doctor rushed into the chair screaming "Mammy!"

"A buzzing in the ears perhaps?"

A power saw screams offstage . . .

"Enzymes," says the doctor. "The new look will be the anti-enzyme look. That is the look that is not dominated by one enzyme . . . Meanwhile . . ." he shrugs, "there is work to do."

He knocks out a wall partition with a sledgehammer. The wall opens into a Mayan tomb. Carl walks away leaving the doctor.

"*Cherchez la enzyme*, or look after the enzymes and the lieutenants J.G. will look after themselves . . . He he he. A trade joke Carl . . . You see every, uh, disorder, no matter how rarefied or seemingly completely over in the precinct of my uh psychically minded humph colleagues who have seen fit to put up a 'Dogs and Benway Keep Out' sign . . . This is our Live One. Advanced cases of lymphogranuloma, rank stool pigeons and 'Benway Keep Out' signs . . . has its corresponding enzyme system and its characteristic odor, so that when the medicine man of a primitive tribe talks of smelling out the sickness, instead of a well-bred leer, we should emulate his example."

"Mother thinks so too," said the painter.

(Commissar sniffing at his subordinate . . . "Don't you ever wash your brains, Comrade? I smell impacted disaffection . . ."

"Not me, boss . . .")

"I have sometimes wondered if the same enzyme was not instrumental in homosexuality, schizophrenia and drug addiction . . . In each case a protective covering over the cells . . . But in the case of addiction the covering can be removed . . . Could the lifelong addiction to a cellular cover ever be disintoxicated?"

"How the fuck should I know," said Carl sullenly.

"Would not the shock of life, the beauty of the world, all those rich luuuvely sensations simply incinerate that cold ass hole? Nay, the miserable flayed thing would turn from the blast of beauty and crawl around scratching for its filthy skin across a vast rubbish heap . . ."

"Oh spit cotton, you frantic old character," said Carl.

"You will be interested . . ."—he fixes Carl with electric menace—"to hear my General Theory of Addiction in its entirety . . . Mother thinks so too . . . She wants to keep my balls preserved in alcohol for her hope chest . . . Isn't that cute . . . You'd love my mummy."

"I hope to avoid her acquaintance . . ."

"Don't count on that, Gertie . . . Mother gets around . . . So the new look will be a combined look, that is, not dominated by any one enzyme, the Criminal, the Pervert, the Self-Righteous Little Man, the Priest, the Untouchable, every race and condition and potentiality no matter how vile and horrible must merge . . . into new forms . . . Just as the disciplines of physics, literature, etc., cannot maintain separate existence in the light of the Facts of ESP etc. . . . This must come, gentlemen . . . meanwhile man must work."

He knocks down a wall with a sledgehammer.

Carl walked through, out past urns like vast penises and . . . Two strange misshapen little men crouch naked before the door . . . They get huge erections, their bodies swell into huge erect penises with vestigial arms and legs . . . They turn into urns by the door . . .

The ceremony when the boy is chosen [by] popular acclaim and stripped naked in the sacred grove, feeling already the eyes running over him, licking his whole being, fondled and licked and petted ... He goes to the tree, garlanded and covered with perfumes, shitting and pissing, stopping frequently to indulge in sodomy or other perversions with sneering sadistic youths, so that it takes a week to make the journey ... and in each rest house are all manner of appliances ... Everyone is in heat ... He hangs there quivering.

They crawl around in shit and piss and jissom finally like a custard pie routine and get drunken adolescents reel to their feet in the country club kitchen ... 1920 road house music drifts in through the open window.

"Let's go to East Beaugard and get laid ..."

A pimp steps out [and] leans in through the window ... "Visit the House of David, boys, and watch the girls eat shit ... Makes a man feel good all over ... Just tell the madame you're a friend of mine ..."

He drops a cuneiform cylinder of black shit into the boy's hip pocket, feeling his ass with his supple fingers that seem to send messages in some lost tongue of a vile people who [live] in a valley in the Andes ... Cut off by tower[ing] snow-covered cliffs and a great waterfall ... The inhabitants are blonde and blue-eyed ... etc. ... Sex is the only occupation ... It is unlawful to masturbate [or] have orgasm alone, they all live in one vast stone house ... Turkish bath underneath ... where people are always getting lost ... It is rumored the Thurling, a sort of malicious boy's spirit, will lure you to an underground river where huge aquatic centipedes lurk ... But sometimes a Thurling takes a like to you and that is the best kick a man can have ...

Shoots blood all over the altar, a bloodless white statue ... frozen erection covered with ice in the moonlight ... in winter sun, Northern lights ... The tribe gives a vast sigh as they all come at once ... this is the moment they fall to the ground in the little death ...

One humming "Let me be your little death until your big death come ..."

Of course everybody wants the honor of having a Thurling in the family . . . Mothers carefully raise their children for maximum vileness . . . So vicious and vile are the children of the Valley that every house is an armed camp . . . No father would dream of sleeping without bolting his steel doors and windows and setting the alarm . . . lest his progeny crawl in and eat his prick off in the night . . .

Later of course they will be weaned and further processed so that by the age of four they are quite broken and would not dare to think about anything but sex . . .

A boy's first hard-on is pounced upon with wild yips of joy and photographed from every angle . . . All the nabors rush in and offer congrats . . . The father passes out photos at the office . . . to the boys in back room of Loki's Ass Hole . . . Little girls are stimulated with vibrators by idiot toothless grandfathers . . . Everybody's room has a one-way mirror and everybody can watch anyone else at all times . . . to conceal yourself is traitorous . . . To turn down any proposition *in toto* is also severely punished by enforced abstinence . . . So that people are always pausing in the street to watch politely while someone masturbates with shit or performs some perverted act . . .

The sexes are absolutely equal and take part in all orgies on the same traction . . . There is the annual sex exhibit which goes on for three months of the year with plays, lectures, sex devices . . . street boys hawk aphrodisiacs and pictures and animated fucking dolls, clothes are of course designed for speedy, graceful disrobing . . .

What is most sought after is the precise admixture of depravity and innocence . . . "Would you believe it," exlaimed the proud mother as her son comes walking in across the field with a string of bullheads, playing his harmonica, "that he's a fart queen?"

The mother grasped Lucy Bradshinkel's hand impulsively and leered deep into her eyes. "You wonderful woman," she said simply.

Said a travelogue voice: "Stay tuned to the Flying Explorer, will reach you at this time every Wednesday—and any other time you stand still for it . . ."

In fact every citizen spent at least half his time naked, indulging in some sex act or play in plain sight of everyone else . . .

It was like living in a sort of jelly that cushioned every movement . . . suggestively feeling your balls with throbbing caresses, oozing up your ass . . .

Train to Canada ah that is Gibson Girl Elinor Glyn. Rush for seat of course like a refugee train those are reserved seats . . . pulled him down . . . so what now Joan talking about Neal's work can be placed Joan is dead long live the queen strip polka . . . strip poker . . . play it skit hell group we said it . . . so the game with him and one other . . . is it not so as to see it like . . .

If all enzyme have images like all junkies look alike that is because of the special addict enzyme . . . All schizos look alike . . . All queers look alike . . . and all criminals and all Lesbians . . . Lesbians all have that cold fish look . . . So these archetypes all have the corresponding enzyme system . . . Withdraw the enzyme, you starve out the archetype . . . The new look will blend all the archetypes into a spontaneous matrix . . .

The new look will not be dominated by any one enzyme, will be the uninvaded look not of innocence but of knowledge.

Correspondingly any innocent, that is, uninvaded, person can be addicted to any of the enzyme archetypes . . . Junk is always our prototype, it gives us the general formula of addiction . . . So now where from junk? Lesbians . . . An enzyme has blocked the female hormone . . . Male, we have an enzyme . . .

Schizos and homos around the mouth . . . Junkies and Lesbians in the eyes . . .

To return to Carl . . . shots of the enzyme don't be naive . . . Instead of a separate person reaction—which the child cannot have—we have an enzyme reaction of female enzyme and the male image becomes unconscious or locked in covered by the female enzyme, the homo enzyme . . .

So child wants the female enzyme like morphine as part of his cells . . . Once it becomes part of his cells a cover to his cells he no longer wants it, he is it . . . this can only occur with the softening up enzyme of schizo, etc., which is predominant in childhood, adolescence, withdrawal . . . the softening up enzyme as soon as he is hooked on the female enzyme he won't want a woman any more but a man and they will want the precise male image of their own that has been made unconscious so the *exact image that wanted the woman almost always brutal and sadistic*—weakness for brutal and criminal types his male image is brutal mine is innocent or partly so but there is another half not yet fully consciously realized of extreme brutality . . .

Similarly the Lesbian reacts to the male and in her attempts to incorporate loses her desire for the male and the male enzyme blocks the female hormones . . .

Return to morphine . . . suppose I needed a female shot every four hours to maintain the female image and if I didn't get it there was an attack by the simplified cells living in the female medium . . .

In short we simply expose him to intense female image in state of softening up that is without his cell receptors must penetrate the cell . . . a virus invades the cell with an enzyme . . . penetrates the cell wall . . . now so we hope to stand on the sidelines and take over   who are we   don't know yet . . .

OUTTAKES: COKE BUGS

[. . .] screaming and the *vecinos* rush in like Furies.

Stumbled over Eduardo in the bathroom and he said "I'm

killing myself with this stuff" and looked at me with sick conning mooch eyes.

"Son of a bitch."

Half bottle of Fundador too soon after the half-assed cure. Hungarian abortionist don't know his piles from a finger stall. Put leeches on my needle scars to suck out the poison. Shots of Demerol by candlelight—they had turned off the lights and water. Was Weston glad to get rid of his evil and downright insolvent roomer. Never take a tenant with a monkey. And Kiki went away. Like a cat, somebody gives him more food and one day he is gone. Through an invisible door. You can look anywhere. No good. *No bueno.* Hustling myself.

Suddenly I see the chick in sharp focus. She is hooked and sick, sniffing and all the bones stand out in her face. She catches my look and walks over and leans on the table and says:

"Could you help me?"

"Sit down. The Man is four hours late. You got the bread?"

"Yes. That is, I got three cents."

"Nothing less than a nickel. These are double papers he claims. Say, I know an old croaker write for you like a major. Can't talk to him myself. We had a beef last time."

"But look—"

"He can't actually *do* anything. Just a bit of fun and games, you know."

"Ugh."

"Every day die a little. It takes up the time."

The croaker lives way out on Long Island . . . I keep falling asleep on the train, light yen sleep, waking up for the stops. Change here.

Stay away from Queens Plaza son. Evil spot, fuzz-haunted by—

Get off here. Bar. Grocery store. Antennae of television suck the sky like greedy periscopes . . . The doctor lives on a dead-end subdivision street. Old 19th-century Spanish house with rusty iron balconies.

Outtakes: Hauser and O'Brien

I was sitting in Joe's Lunch Room drinking coffee with a napkin under the cup which is said to be the mark of someone who does a lot of sitting in cafeterias and lunch rooms . . . Waiting on the Man . . .

"What can we say?" Nick said to me once in his dead junky whisper . . . "They know we'll wait."

Yes, they know we'll wait . . . Street corner, cafeteria, park bench, sitting, standing, walking . . . All those who wait learn that time and space are one . . . How long-far to the end of the block and back? How many cups of coffee in an hour?

There was a chick at the counter giving me the eye and I delineated a vague good impression like something half seen from a train window . . . back into the screaming, shuddering sickness, everything so sharp and clear it hurts, suddenly smeared with grey smoke—the clock had jumped ahead the way time will after 4 P.M. even for a sick junky—And I don't want to know about her or anybody . . .

I had an oil burner . . . Quarter piece of H a day . . . I was working the hole with the Sailor, out on the hyp afternoons . . . You never could make the Sailor, his brown eyes lit up inside catching points of light like an opal, looking at something way out, face yellow and smoothed and blank over high cheekbones, and he would sing over and over through his shiny yellow teeth: "Oh, oh, what can the matter be? Johnny's So Long at the Fair . . ."

I understand how the Sailor went wrong . . . He could not feel anything for anybody else . . .

The Sailor is dead . . . Almost everyone I know is dead now . . . The Sailor hanging to a cell door his tongue out the way it would fall right out of his mouth when he was loaded on goof balls, [Kammerer] drifting along under the Hudson, jettisoned murder weapons cutting his flesh like meteors, and Jane sitting there at the counter . . . I hear about it later in Tanger . . .

Met German . . . In Joe's Lunch Room met . . .

All off the junk . . . Twenty pounds of borrowed flesh . . . and strap-on . . . Compound interest I said:

Lazarus go home . . .

"I see things different now," he said . . . "They can't bluff me with that repossession shit . . . Tools of my trade . . . It's the law . . ." He showed me his strap-on under the table . . .

Anybody can quit . . . You gotta make a deal, that's all . . .

Lazarus go home . . . You bring down the living with your crystal—

Met Nick by the chess game in Washington Square and he told me about busts and death and kicks . . . we couldn't talk with all the dead junkies around us . . .

Little Arnie drunk in Joe's, off the junk . . . Twenty pounds of borrowed flesh . . .

Lazarus go home . . . Pay the Man and go home . . .

OUTTAKES: ATROPHIED PREFACE

The Voices rush in like burning lions.

"I'll rip through you," said, trembling, the Man of Black Bones.

"So told Lieutenant LeBee whose auntie was drowned at sea," said a little squeegy voice.

"Cross crystal panes of horror to the tilted pond . . ."

"Time to retire . . . Get a Frisk . . . glittering worms of nostalgia's housecall where young lust flares over the hills of home and jissom floats like cobwebs in a cold spring wind . . ."

"Lovely brown leg. Oh Lordy me baby on the brass bed and bed bugs crawl under the blue light . . . Oh God . . ."

"All the day you do it . . . Do it right now . . ."

"Suck the night tit under the blue flame of Sterno . . . Orient pearls to the way they should go . . ."

"The winged horse and the mosaic of iron cut the sky to blue cake . . ."

"On crystal balconies pensive angels study pink fingernails . . . Gilt flakes fall through the sunlight . . ."

"Distant rumble of stomachs . . . Porcine fairies wave thick wallets . . . Bougainvillea covers the limestone steps . . . Poisoned pigeons rain from the Northern Lights, plop with burning wings into dry canal . . . The Reservoirs are empty . . . Blue stairs end spiral down suffocate . . . where brass statues crash through the hungry squares and alleys of the gaping city . . ."

"Iridescent hard-on . . . Rainbow in the falls . . ."

"Can't hear nothing."

"Two kids got relief."

"Never more the goose honks train whistle bunk mate . . . Man in Lower Ten (eye caked with mucus) . . . Watch the boy get a hard-on . . ."

"Not a mark on him . . . What killed his monkey?"

"Suicide God, take the back street junk route . . . Detours of the fairy canyon shine in the light of dawn . . . Buildings fall through dust to the plain of salt marshes . . . Are the boys over the last ridge and into the safe harbor of Cunt Lick where no wind is?"

"By the squared circle cut cock my mouth the cunt off and the rag on . . . Bring your own wife . . . Panama Flo the sex fiend beat the Grey Nurse for steak-sized chunks . . ."

(The Grey Nurse is most dangerous form of shark. Like all sharks they bite out steak-sized chunks.)

"Wouldn't you?"

"Libido is dammed by the Eager Beaver."

"Notice is served on toilet paper."

"Smell shock grabs the lungs with nausea."

"Fat queen, bursting out of dungarees, carry a string of bullheads to the tilted pond . . ."

"TILT . . ."

"Grey head bob up in the old swimming hole . . . The boys climb up each other, scream . . . 'EEEEK . . . a Man . . .'"

"He will be fetched down, this creature."

"A fairy!"

"Monstrous!"

"Fantastic!"

"Get her!"

"Slam the steel shutter of latency! . . ."

"Radius radius . . . it is enough."

"Doctorhood is being made with me."

Middle-aged Swede in yachting cap, naked tattooed torso, neutral blue eyes, gives a shot of heroin to the schizophrenic . . . (whiff of institution kitchens).

Grey ghosts of a million junkies bend close as the Substance drains into living flesh.

"Is this the fix that staunched a thousand shits and burst the scented drugstores of Lebanon?"

"In a vale of cocaine and innocence, ski hut across the mountain, sad-eyed youths yodel for a lost Danny Boy . . ."

"We sniffed all night and made it four times . . . Fingers down the blackboard, scrape the white bones . . . Home is the heroin, home from the sea."

"Probing for a vein in the junk sick morning wind vibrates the window."

"Coffee and stale Danish in Joe's . . ."

"'Hello, Cash . . .'"

"'You sure it's there?'

"'Of course I'm sure . . . Go in with you.'

"'For tonight?'"

"A no-horse town . . . Hit the local croaker for M.S., shoot it all up in two hours . . . Night train to Chi . . . Meet a girl in the hall and I see she is on and ask: 'Where is a score?'

"'Come in, sonny.'

"I mean not a young chick but built . . . 'How about a fix first?'

"'Ixnay, you wouldn't be inna condition.'

"Three times around . . . wake up shivering sick in warm spring wind through the window, water burning the eyes like acid.

"'Now.'

"She gets out of bed naked . . . Stash in the cobra lamp . . . Cooks up . . .

"'Turn over. I'll give it to you in the ass.'

"She slides the needle in deep, pulls out and massages the cheek . . . She licks a drop of blood off her finger . . .

"He rolls over with a hard-on dissolving in the grey substance of junk . . ."

[Icarus,] his parachute a broken condom. In a rubbish heap across the bay, his jet vaporizes bone and shit to the blue substance of sky . . .

"I don't even feel like a human . . . When the poltergeists come down from the attic and shit in the living room and outnumber the haunted ten to one and their merry pranks are no longer virginal and they turn vicious in adolescence like apes . . . Sometimes I just don't know . . ."

Under the hard-faced matron's bandage the cunt of Radiant Jade . . .
"You see dearie the shock when your neck breaks has like an

awful effect." She titters nervously . . . "You're already dead of course or at least unconscious or at least stunned . . . But . . . And . . . Uh . . . Well . . . You see . . . It's a MEDICAL FACT . . . All your female insides is subject to spurt out your cunt the way it turned the last doctor to stone and we sold the results to Paraguay, as a statue of Bolívar."

"I have come to ascertain death . . . Not to perform a hysterectomy," snapped the old auntie [croaker] crisply . . . munching a soggy crumpet with his grey teeth, [smell of institution kitchen follow him like dank cloud] . . .

"Oh God another Snafu . . . That Pierpoint isn't . . ."

He pulled irritably at the Lesbian's legs—She boiled her lover, she strapped her lover over a bidet and filled it with boiling lye . . .

"It was a *crime passionnel*," she rhapsodied. "Judge you shoulda heard those screams . . . It was tasty . . ."

"I was carried away on a great glad gutty river . . . Who of you has known the Full Suppository? [Constipated purveyors of tired farts . . .]"

Come in please???? Well you, that was the hole story and I guess I oughta know . . . Lady name of LU LU . . .

Woke up in a Turkish Bath under a Johannesburg *bidonville* . . . "Where am I, you black bastards?"

Don't be like that? How many did you kill? "More the merrier" said Robert Christie . . .

Wouldn't you?

"Gentlemen already the foul banners of bloody Kotex fly over our peaceful cocks . . . The hideous subspecies of WOMAN must be rooted out and destroyed with antiseptic flame throwers lest the terrible She virus survive and rise again to desecrate our *fantastic* Greek cities . . . But where is the rough trade, Myrtle?"

They got on motor scooters and they all died away in the Italian night . . . And the old Thing that sells black market cigarettes . . . Laughed and laughed and laughed . . .

"The universe is curved . . . They must come back . . . I read it through the glory hole in the Old Court House Johnny . . . Here they come now . . ."

The boys approach with a vast swelling pathic scream . . . they advance across a plain, trees wither as they pass . . .

"I'd give my falsies for a man, Mary!"

"Treason . . . Hang that mad bitch before she grows a nasty cunt . . ."

When I was on the junk I minded my junky business, and nobody saw me except pushers and subway fuzz . . . The Independent got their own special heat, and they don't carry iron, just saps . . . Once over in Queens Plaza—that's a bad station, too many levels—they nailed the Fag and me, so I bit the heat's hand—I had my teeth in those days—so I bit him and cut, and he keeps yelling after me: "Stop or I'll shoot" and I knew he didn't have with what to shoot, so I keep cutting . . .

The Fag won't talk to the heat. Just say I am a Times Square kid name of Joe something. So they knock out what teeth he's got left . . . "They was loose anyhoo," he tells me later . . . He always comes on like a fag you dig it is part of his act, and he does five twenty-nine for jostling . . . Like I say junkies is ghosts and only certain people subject to see them . . .

(Five months and twenty-nine days is the sentence customarily given for attempt to roll a lush in or about the subway. The charge is called "jostling.")

A Mexico City pusher name of Lupita—all the big pushers in Mexico are women—Aztec Earth Goddess need plenty blood. So Lupita say: "Selling is more of a habit than using" and she is really making with the untutored wisdom—illiterate bitch you dig . . . A non-using pusher has a contact habit, and that's one you can't kick . . . Agents get it too . . .

Like I say The Reader will frequently find the same thing said in the same words. This is not carelessness nor is it for The Infatuation With Sound Of Own Words Dept. . . . It indicates space-time juxtaposition . . . a folding in and back (the universe is curved, feller say) . . . point of intersection between levels of experience where parallel lines meet . . .

Like I say prefaces atrophy, drop off, grow again. At one point the preface was 150 pages long, constituting a menace to the entire enterprise . . . It was amputated to a bleeding stump of three pages and slowly grew back . . .

"I am the Egyptian" he said looking all flat and silly.

And I said "Really Bradford, don't be tiresome . . ."

In the attic of The Big Store on bolts of cloth we made it . . . Careful, don't spill . . .

Don't rat on the boys . . . The cellar is full of light and air . . . In two weeks the tadpoles hatch . . . Wonder what became of Otto's boy who played the violin . . .

Dead bird, quail in the slipper, money in the bank . . . Fossil cunts of pre-dated chicks bounce all around us in Queens Plaza . . .

Lay them in the crapper . . . Just shove it in, vibration does the rest . . . Black dust rains down over us cancer curse of switch . . . Cock under the nut shell . . . Step right up . . . now you see it now you don't . . .

"Multiple fracture" said the Big Physician . . . "I'm very technical."

Wooden steps up a vast slope . . . scattered stone huts . . .

Faces with the eerie innocence of old peoples, mosaic of juxtapositioned golden strains of Negro substance seep up from the unborn South . . .

The man in a green suit, old-type English cut with change pockets outside . . . will swindle the aging proprietess of a florist shop:

"Old flub gotta yen on for me."

They was ripe for the plucking forgot way back yonder in the cornhole scraps of delight and burning scrolls . . .

O death where is thy sting? The Man is never on time . . .

P.S.

Ideas,
interviews
& features ...

Biography

WILLIAM SEWARD BURROUGHS II was born on 5 February 1914 in St Louis, Missouri. He enjoyed a comfortable upbringing – although he was always at pains to stress that he wasn't 'rich'. After studying English literature and Mayan archaeology at Harvard in the 1930s, where he was notorious for keeping a ferret and a loaded gun in his room, he was rejected by both the Navy and the OSS (the forerunner of the CIA) on physical grounds. He spent the next twenty years as a drop-out, drawing a monthly allowance from his parents while working variously at an advertising firm, a detective agency and as a bug exterminator in Chicago – a job which he loved.

It was in New York City in 1943 that Burroughs first met a group of bright young firebrand students, poets and writers that included his future wife Joan Vollmer, the poet Allen Ginsberg and a young merchant sailor named Jack Kerouac. This 'libertine circle' constituted the intellectual seed of what would later become the Beat Movement, but Burroughs spent just as much time with an altogether darker circle of friends in the mid Forties, robbing drunks on the subway and experimenting with heroin, or 'junk'. Burroughs would remain an addict for much of the rest of his life.

After his wife's tragic death in 1951 (see 'Did You Know?'), Burroughs threw himself into his writing and began the wanderings that would characterize his life, whether it be searching the jungles of South America for fabled hallucinogens, ghosting through the backstreets of Tangiers in search of heroin, or experimenting with both art and writing in Paris and London.

Although he began writing in the 1930s, he had little success until the early 1950s when he wrote two confessional books: a novel based on his addiction entitled *Junky* (1953) and *Queer* (written in the 1950s but not published until 1985). However, he is perhaps most famous for *Naked Lunch*. First published by the daring and influential Olympia Press in France in 1959, it aroused great controversy on publication and was not available in the USA until 1962 and in the UK until 1963.

Fiercely anti-censorship, supportive of relaxed drug laws and wary of the ways in which our lives are controlled, Burroughs enjoyed great fame towards the end of his life, and became something of an icon for disaffected youth. Burroughs was no Allen Ginsberg, however, instead becoming a cultural godfather for more rebellious elements of the counterculture, from the Rolling Stones to Punk and on through to Kurt Cobain.

Burroughs's other important works include the famous 'cut-up' trilogy of *The Soft Machine*, *The Ticket That Exploded* and *Nova Express*, as well as his later, more conventionally readable masterpieces *Cities of the Red Night* and *The Place of Dead Roads*. In 1983 Burroughs was elected a Member of the American Academy and Institute of Arts and Letters and named a Commandeur de l'Ordre des Arts et Lettres in France in 1984. He died in 1997 of a heart attack, in Lawrence, Kansas. ∎

◀ in what he called his 'Van Gogh kick'. He was sent to a mental hospital where he was diagnosed as paranoid schizophrenic.

From 23 December 1969, Burroughs began to use his own system to date letters and manuscripts. Based loosely on the ancient Mayan calendar, the Dream Calendar comprised of eight 23-day months: Terre Haute, Marie Celeste, Bellevue, Seal Point, Harbor Beach, Niño Perdido, Sweet Meadows and Land's End. A ninth month, Wiener Wald, was added later. He used the baffling system for well over a year, making it very difficult to date manuscripts during this period. However, it must be said that, when writing to friends, Burroughs was kind enough to give the real date as well . . . ■

A Tale of Two Wives

AFTER GRADUATING FROM Harvard, Burroughs spent much of the 1930s travelling throughout Europe, visiting Vienna, Budapest and Dubrovnik. It was there that he met a German Jewish woman named Ilse Klapper, who had fled Hamburg to escape the Nazis. In 1937, Burroughs married Ilse simply to give her the papers she needed to flee to the safety of the United States. They divorced after the Second World War, and remained friends.

His second marriage forms a tragic counterbalance to this simple act of kindness. In 1951, Burroughs and his wife Joan were living in Mexico, where they had moved to escape what they saw as draconian US drug laws. What really happened on the night of 6 September that year will never be known, but the next day the *New York Daily News* carried the following headline: 'William Seward Burroughs, 37, first admitted, then denied today that he was playing William Tell when he killed his pretty young wife during a drinking party last night.'

As legend has it, Burroughs did indeed suggest 'our William Tell act', placing an object on Joan's head – variously reported to be an orange, a champagne glass or a whiskey glass – before killing her with a single shot to the temple. However, in an interview with the *Paris Review* in 1965, Burroughs asserted that he was merely checking a revolver that he was to sell to a friend when it went off. Other contemporary reports have him accidentally dropping the gun. Whatever the truth, he fled Mexico, and was found guilty of *imprudencia criminal* (criminal negligence) *in absentia.*

He may not have been tried for the shooting but according to biographer Ted Morgan, he entered 'a nightmare that he would live for the rest of his days'. Ostensibly, Joan's death was an accident, but Burroughs was haunted by the dreadful thought that, subconsciously, he had meant to kill her. In the introduction to the novel *Queer*, he wrote: 'I am forced to the appalling conclusion that I would never have become a writer but for Joan's death, and to a realization of the extent to which this event has motivated and formulated my writing ... The death of Joan brought me in contact with the invader, the Ugly Spirit, and manoeuvred me into a life-long struggle, in which I had no choice except to write my way out.' ■

❝ Ostensibly, Joan's death was an accident, but Burroughs was haunted by the dreadful thought that, subconsciously, he had meant to kill her. ❞

Obituary

IN 1981, WILLIAM BURROUGHS finally turned his back on the celebrity and hangers-on of New York and moved to Lawrence, Kansas. There he filled his house with guns, cats and magazines that reflected his interests, such as *Gun World*, *American Survival Guide* and *UFO Universe*. After a breakfast of boiled eggs and methodone, he continued to work on *The Place of Dead Roads*, but this period also shows a move towards experimental painting, placing cans of paint in front of a plywood panel and exploding them with blasts from a twelve-gauge shotgun.

Burroughs died of a heart attack on 1 August 1997. The last entry in his Journal, written on 30 July, reads simply: 'Love? What is it? The most natural painkiller there is. LOVE.'

The reaction to Burroughs's death acknowledged the lack of critical consensus on the merits of his career, while bowing to his undeniable fame and influence. The *New York Times* summed him up as 'a renegade writer who stunned readers and inspired adoring cultists', while *The Guardian* cannily observed that 'his surprising endurance was proof that if you last long enough, the establishment develops an affection for you'. J.G. Ballard praised him as 'a writer of enormous richness', while Norman Mailer hailed him as 'the only American writer who may conceivably be possessed by genius'. But the compliment which Burroughs treasured above all others was an austere remark of Samuel Beckett's: 'Well, he's a writer.' ∎

❛ He filled his house with guns, cats and magazines that reflected his interests, such as *Gun World*, *American Survival Guide* and *UFO Universe*. ❜

Critical Verdict

IN 1956, THE poet Allen Ginsberg dedicated his collection *Howl* to William Burroughs, 'the author of an endless novel which will drive everyone mad'. Ginsberg's assessment wasn't far off the mark. When *Naked Lunch* was finally made available to British reviewers, it polarized opinion utterly. The *Times Literary Supplement* ran a review under the simple headline 'Ugh. . .', which sparked a frenzied correspondence in the *TLS* over the next thirteen weeks, as literary heavyweights lined up to support or decry the book. Publisher Victor Gollancz branded the book 'bogus high-brow filth', while Dame Edith Sitwell sniffed, 'I do not wish to spend the rest of my life with my nose nailed to other people's lavatories. I prefer Chanel Number 5.' By contrast, the book's importance and originality were hailed by such luminaries as Michael Moorcock, Anthony Burgess and Norman Mailer, who playfully branded much contemporary fiction as immoral in its refusal to enter this 'terrible borderland of sex, sadism, obscenity [and] horror . . . That is why I salute Mr Burroughs's work, because he has gone further into it than any other western writer today.'

American reviewers were more consistent in their praise. The *New York Times* heralded Burroughs's 'special literary gift', proclaiming *Naked Lunch* to be 'not a novel but a booty brought back from a nightmare . . . [a] coldly implacable look at the dark side of our nature'. Joan Didion applauded the sheer freshness and energy of Burroughs's voice, 'hard, derisive, inventive, free, funny, ▶

‘ Burroughs's work continues to excite and disgust readers in equal measure to this day, but his place in the canon of twentieth-century literature is no longer in question. ’

Critical Verdict *(continued)*

◄ serious, poetic, indelibly American . . . the voice of a natural', while *Newsweek* proclaimed the book a masterpiece, if 'a totally insane and anarchic one'. The *New York Herald Tribune* was quicker to embrace the disjointed, restless inventiveness of the book: 'What matters, as in all abstract art, are the effects created, and Burroughs's effects are stunning . . . his talent is something more than notorious. It may well turn out to be important.'

Burroughs's work continues to excite and disgust readers in equal measure to this day, but his place in the canon of twentieth-century literature is no longer in question. Paul Bowles called him 'the greatest American humorist', while J. G. Ballard, who has frequently acknowledged the influence of Burroughs on his own fiction, called him quite simply 'the most important writer to emerge since the Second World War'. ■

Social Context

MOST OF THE unruly manuscript that became *Naked Lunch* was written during Burroughs's time living in Tangier in the mid 1950s. In the wake of the Second World War, Tangier became an 'international zone' ruled by eight different nations: a political and moral vacuum that afforded a shadowy haven for smugglers, addicts, sexual tourists – and writers. Burroughs had moved to Tangier primarily for its plentiful supply of drugs and boys, but it also had a growing reputation as a literary centre, the place where Paul Bowles had written *The Sheltering Sky* and entertained Truman Capote, Tennessee Williams and Gore Vidal. Known by the locals as 'el hombre invisible' for the way that he moved around the city unnoticed, it was here that he began writing letters to his friend and former lover Allen Ginsberg – letters filled with the short, virtuoso flights of imagination or 'routines' that would become *Naked Lunch*.

Ginsberg and Jack Kerouac both visited Tangier during this period, and even helped to type up Burroughs's tatty, handwritten manuscript before the group decamped to Paris, where they lived in the self-styled 'Beat Hotel' in the Latin quarter. But while *Naked Lunch* remained unpublished (despite the best efforts of Ginsberg, who acted as both Burroughs's editor and literary agent), this period finally saw the success that his old friends had been promising for some while. Allen Ginsberg's breakthrough prose-poem *Howl for Carl Solomon* was published in the USA in the autumn of 1956 and caused something of a stir, being embargoed and then tried for obscenity the following year. After a ▶

> 6 Most of the unruly manuscript that became *Naked Lunch* was written during Burroughs's time living in Tangier in the mid 1950s. 9

◀ rallying round of the literary community, *Howl* was cleared; the following day, Sputnik 1 went into orbit and within weeks, Jack Kerouac's restless, drink- and jazz-fuelled *On the Road* was finally published, six years after its composition.

This was only the start of a hugely important period for literature – and especially the question of censorship – as a rush of youthful subversion and originality flooded in to fill the post-war void. In 1958, the year that Nabokov's *Lolita* was first published, a section of *Naked Lunch* finally made its first appearance in print, in an inflammatory issue of the *Chicago Review* that led to the periodical's temporary closure. The following year, the small English-language Olympia Press in Paris took the plunge and, spurred on by the infamy and publicity surrounding the book's part in the closure of the *Chicago Review*, published the first complete edition of what was then called <u>The</u> *Naked Lunch*. This, of course, was around the time of the famous trial of D. H. Lawrence's *Lady Chatterley's Lover*, which, although first written in the 1920s, was not published in an unexpurgated edition until 1959 in the USA and 1960 in the UK. Olympia Press was used to pushing the envelope, however, specializing in a mixture of pornography and quality literature that would not have got past the censor in Britain or America, including translations of erotic work by Guillaume Apollinaire and Dominique Aury, as well as the works of Samuel Beckett and Henry Miller. Elsewhere in the world in 1959, a similar sweeping-away of the old order continued apace: the space race began to

❛ In 1958, a section of *Naked Lunch* finally made its first appearance in print, in an inflammatory issue of the *Chicago Review* that led to the periodical's temporary closure. ❜

accelerate, the Barbie doll was born, and Castro came to power in the Cuban revolution.

J. G. Ballard's first encounter with *Naked Lunch*, recounted in an interview with *Salon* magazine, must surely have been a common one at the turn of the 1960s: 'A friend of mine had come back from Paris where *Naked Lunch* had been published . . . This was the heyday of the naturalistic novel, dominated by people like C. P. Snow and Anthony Powell and so on, and I felt that maybe the novel had shot its bolt, that it was stagnating right across the board . . . Then I read this little book with a green cover, and I remember I read about four or five paragraphs and I quite involuntarily leapt from my chair and cheered out loud because I knew a great writer had appeared amidst us.'

It was not until 1962, as the Beatles released their first record and with JFK in the White House, that *The Naked Lunch* – now entitled simply *Naked Lunch* – finally found a publisher in the States. The following year, which saw the publication of Sylvia Plath's *The Bell Jar* and John Fowles's *The Collector*, London-based publisher John Calder took a leap of faith – with understandable nervousness – and released a British edition of Burroughs's writing, a mixture of *Naked Lunch* and other pieces entitled *Dead Fingers Talk*. Burroughs's corrosive satirical vision, born almost a decade earlier in the lawless Interzone of post-war Tangier, had finally reached a British audience at the birth of an altogether different future shaped by the Cuban missile crisis and the assassination of JFK. ■

> ‘ Fiercely anti-censorship, supportive of relaxed drug laws and wary of the ways in which our lives are controlled, Burroughs enjoyed great fame towards the end of his life. ’

Influences

IT HAS BEEN written that each of the major Beat writers made a decade their own. The 1950s belonged to the free-spirited Jack Kerouac, while Allen Ginsberg was the embodiment of 1960s free love. The late 1970s belonged to Burroughs. 'Up there with the Pope,' said punk poet and singer Patti Smith, and Burroughs became something of a talisman for the New York Punk movement.

Burroughs's impact on writing has been well documented, from the detached, disjointed, forensic writing of J. G. Ballard's *The Atrocity Exhibition* to the work of Will Self and Thomas Pynchon, but his influence extended into other media. He is widely credited with inventing the term 'heavy metal', while countless bands have taken their names from memorable phrases in his writing, such as Soft Machine and Steely Dan (named after a dildo that appears in *Naked Lunch*). In his later years, Burroughs collaborated on recordings with several artists, including Kurt Cobain and Tom Waits.

The influence of his famous 'cut-up' techniques also merits a mention. Burroughs and his great friend, the painter Brion Gysin, experimented with randomly slicing up newspapers, manuscripts and poems (and, later, tape recordings and films), putting the pieces together to create fresh, surprising juxtapositions. David Bowie used this technique to write the lyrics for his 1974 album *Diamond Dogs*, while director Nicolas Roeg looked to Burroughs's 1966 film *The Cut Ups* when making the cult classic *Performance* starring Mick Jagger. ∎

> 6 Burroughs is widely credited with inventing the term "heavy metal". 9

Adaptation

'It's impossible to make a movie out of Naked Lunch. *A literal translation just wouldn't work. It would cost $400 million to make and would be banned in every country of the world.'* David Cronenberg

DAVID CRONENBERG MAY have been daunted by the prospect of filming Burroughs's unfilmable novel, but *Naked Lunch* (1991) is nonetheless a fascinating insight into the striking similarity of the creative processes of both men. Cronenberg famously went on to make a hugely controversial film of Ballard's *Crash* in 1996, and just as J. G. Ballard cheered when he read *Naked Lunch* for the first time, there is a palpable excitement in Cronenberg's acknowledgement of the debt that he owes to Burroughs's fiction. 'There was an incredible recognition when I started to read Burroughs, like "My God, this is in me too!"'

Naked Lunch is not a faithful rendering of the book, but takes instead key moments from Burroughs's own life and mixes them with pungent images and scenes inspired by the novel's themes of paranoia, metamorphosis and addiction. The story follows Bill Lee, a bug exterminator-cum-writer who accidentally shoots his wife, and whose typewriter transforms into a cockroach. After his wife's death, he descends into the hallucinatory, alien-filled inferno that is Interzone ...

For more information on the making of *Naked Lunch*, check out Mark Kermode's excellent *Sight and Sound* interview with Cronenberg at:
http://www.davidcronenberg.de/snsint92.html

> ❛ It's impossible to make a movie out of *Naked Lunch*. A literal translation just wouldn't work. ❜

Have You Read?

Junky
Written largely during his time with Joan in Mexico City, Burroughs's first published book was agented by Allen Ginsberg and originally appeared pseudonymously as *Junkie: Confessions of an Unredeemed Drug Addict* by William Lee (his mother's maiden name). This warts-and-all account of the hunger of drug addiction has a rare power and immediacy.

'A fiendish parable of modern alienation . . . An existentialist text on a par with the work of Sartre and Camus' – Will Self

Queer
Burroughs's second novel recounts the hallucinatory life of William Lee, an American who journeys to Ecuador with his reluctant lover, Eugene Allerton, in search of the drug Yage. However, the book is just as important for its introduction, written in 1985, in which Burroughs directly addresses the psychological impact of shooting his wife, Joan Vollmer, in 1951 – a tragedy which both haunted Burroughs for the rest of his life, and provided a key impetus for his work.

The Soft Machine
A ferocious assault on hatred, hype, poverty, war and addiction, *The Soft Machine* and its sequels, *The Ticket That Exploded* and *Nova Express*, take Burroughs's cut-up experiments to the limits of intelligibility, but retain a rare power. Borrowing from all areas of popular culture, from films, comics, Westerns and science fiction, the cut-up trilogy is filled with startling images, but don't expect anything as

prosaic as a story. As Burroughs wrote in *The Job*, 'When people speak of clarity in writing they generally mean plot, continuity, beginning middle and end, adherence to a "logical" sequence. But things don't happen in logical sequence . . .'

'The greatest satirical writer since Jonathan Swift' – Jack Kerouac

The Job

'*This is the space age. Time to look beyond this rundown radioactive cop-rotten planet.*'

In this collection of interviews with the French literary journalist Daniel Odier, Burroughs gives full rein to his abrasive views on sex, censorship, misogyny, addiction and the merits of the apomorphine treatment which briefly helped him to kick his junk habit. The book bristles with fierce invectives against what he saw as the police state we live in – 'Learn your maze and stay on screen' – and how to combat these imposed methods of control. Throw in pieces on his involvement with L. Ron Hubbard's Church of Scientology and the use of drugs in the creative process, and *The Job* is a powerful, immediate portrait of the abrasive, often paranoid, razor-sharp intelligence behind the fiction.

Cities of the Red Night

A mordant satire of cultural aspirations, homosexual eroticism and political power. The first of the 'Red Night' trilogy – completed by *The Places of the Dead Roads* and his final ▶

❝ "The greatest satirical writer since Jonathan Swift" – Jack Kerouac. ❞

Have You Read? *(continued)*

◄ novel, *The Western Lands – Cities of the Red Night* is often cited as Burroughs's most approachable work, and certainly the most readable by conventional standards. An apocalyptic vision of a people afflicted by a radioactive virus and an evil empire of zealous mutants, it uses the genres of science fiction, the detective story and the pirate yarn to give it shape.

'Not only Burroughs's best work, but a logical and ripening extension of all of Burroughs's great work' – Ken Kesey

'*Cities of the Red Night* is Burroughs's masterpiece. In it, the world ends with a bang – and a barely perceived whimper, disguised by the wicked smile of one of the most dazzling magicians of our time' – *Los Angeles Time Book Review*

Word Virus: the William Burroughs Reader
A comprehensive introduction to the best of Burroughs's writing.

Last Words: The Final Journals of William S. Burroughs, ed. James Grauerholz
Just that: journals from Burroughs's final days in Lawrence, Kansas, surrounded by his beloved cats. ∎

> ❝ "A fiendish parable of modern alienation . . ." – Will Self ❞

Recommended Criticism and Biography

With William Burroughs: A Report from the Bunker, *Victor Bockris*
Burroughs's fame in the late 1970s was largely due to this collection of transcripts put together by writer Victor Bockris, who arranged a succession of dinner parties in New York from 1974–9 at which famous people would dine with Burroughs. These included Andy Warhol, Lou Reed, Joe Strummer, Susan Sontag, Christopher Isherwood, Tennessee Williams and Mick Jagger.

The Adding Machine: Selected Essays,
William Burroughs
A perfect book for people who know the man's work and would like to know more about what drove him as a writer.

Literary Outlaw: The Life and Times of William S. Burroughs, *Ted Morgan*
Considered by many to be the best biography of Burroughs. An excellent account of the writer's life, and the era that shaped his work.

The 'Priest' They Called Him: The Life and Legacy of William S. Burroughs,
Graham Caveney
A look at Burroughs's complete writings as well as his forays into film, rock music and painting.

El Hombre Invisible. William Burroughs: A Portrait, *Barry Miles*
Biography by a friend from Burroughs's ▶

Recommended Criticism and Biography *(continued)*

◄ days in London. Miles has also published biographies of Allen Ginsberg and Jack Kerouac.

This is the Beat Generation, *James Campbell*
An excellent overview of the Beat movement from its early incarnation as the 'libertine circle' in Chicago to the height of its fame in the early Sixties.

The Birth of the Beat Generation,
Steven Watson
Chronicles the complex relationships between Burroughs, Ginsberg, Kerouac and the figures who surrounded them. ∎

Find Out More

WEBSITES

**http://www.salon.com/sept97/wsb970902.
html**
Conducted a month after Burroughs's death,
this *Salon* interview with J. G. Ballard is a
fascinating account of Ballard's creative debt
to Burroughs, and an assessment of his
impact on twentieth-century literature.

**http://www.willself.org.uk/junky/junky.
php**
Will Self's perceptive essay on *Junky* can be
found on Self's official website, or as an
introduction to the Penguin edition of the
book itself.

**http://books.guardian.co.uk/departments/
generalfiction/story/0,6000,1214565,00.
html**
Marianne Faithfull's memories of Burroughs
and of her recent live performance of his
final story, *The Black Rider*.

http://www.hyperreal.org/wsb/
One of the better unofficial Burroughs fan
sites, which contains links to many others.

RECORDINGS

Some have said that it is impossible to truly
understand Burroughs until you have heard
that voice: what biographer Barry Miles calls
'the flat mid-west accent, dry as paper, the
clipped syllables of a 1920s newscaster
affecting a campy edge ... the voice of a
banker saying those outrageous things'. ▶

Find Out More *(continued)*

◀ You can hear that voice for yourself in a 1984 radio interview posted at **http://wiredforbooks.org/williamburroughs/**, where Burroughs talks about his drug addiction, his time in Tangier, and his memories of Jack Kerouac and Allen Ginsberg.

Alternatively, try to get hold of *The Best of William S. Burroughs* (Giorno Poetry Systems), a series of recordings culled from a variety of rare, unreleased and out-of-print sources. Also look for *The 'Priest' They Called Him*, a recording of Burroughs reading an alternative Christmas poem, against a backdrop of Kurt Cobain's guitars. ■